PRAISE FOR
A PANTHER CROSSES OVER

"Absolutely stunning. *A Panther Crosses Over* is either time travel or reincarnation, a tactile trip of immense believability."
—Charlie Newton, award-winning author of
Traitor's Gate, *Privateers*, and *Canaryville*

"The author does an excellent job of staying true to historical detail while making his characters fully realized individuals who drive the plot to an emotionally satisfying conclusion. Foster deftly presents the conflict from an Indigenous perspective . . . a solid tale with a firm historical grounding that examines early American conflicts."
—*Kirkus Reviews*

"In *A Panther Crosses Over*, book one of his American Trilogy, Foster tells the epic story of a clash of civilizations in the vast Northwest Territory bounded to the north by the Great Lakes. Decades of war and shifting alliances of tribes, confederations, and empires culminate in the historic Battle of Tippecanoe in 1811. By then, Tecumseh, the great Shawnee warrior and statesman, has assembled a coalition of Native tribes to drive white settlers from the territory once and for all. William Henry Harrison, governor of the Indiana Territory, has other ideas.

Foster has written a work of fiction that brings the history to life and enriches and fills in the gaps with the novelist's art and insight. The tale he tells is Homeric, not just in the savage grandeur of the subject and the complex nobility of the heroes but in the poetry of the smallest details and the hidden mysteries of the hearts and minds of its great cast of (real) characters."

—Chris Flannery, host of *The American Story* podcast, senior fellow at the Claremont Institute

"Foster is a brilliant writer of historical fiction, covering times and places less well known than many others. *A Panther Crosses Over* is the latest and first of a trilogy that will cover a unique period of American historical life not so fully reported, involving characters we come to find fascinating and love . . . I was so deeply involved from the first pages that I stayed up all weekend to consume this wonderful tale of the Midwest's founding."

—Jay Weston, film producer of the Academy Award–nominated *Lady Sings the Blues* and Billy Wilder's final comedy, *Buddy Buddy*

A PANTHER
CROSSES OVER

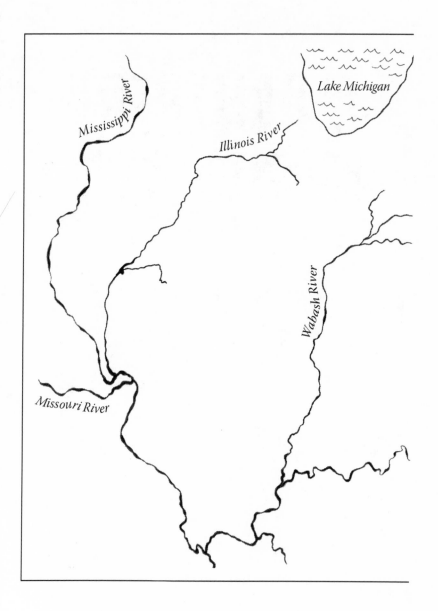

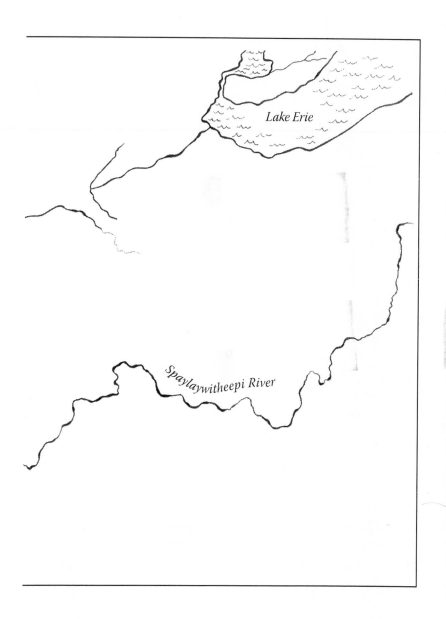

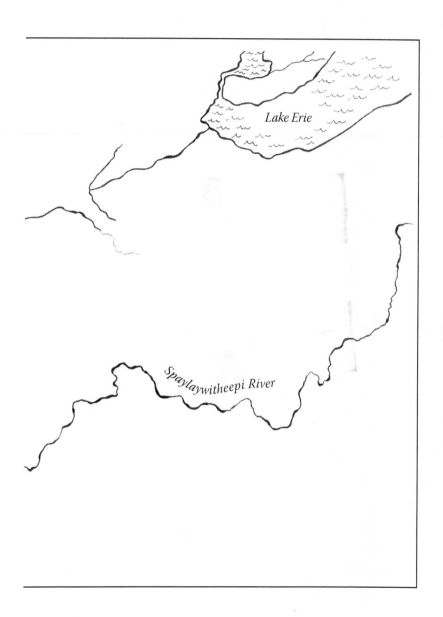

A PANTHER CROSSES OVER

~ The ~
AMERICAN TRILOGY
BOOK 1

A NOVEL

SAM FOSTER

Agave
Americana
Books

Published by Agave Americana Books, Redondo Beach, CA
samfosterbooks.com

Cover design: Paul Barrett and Rachel Marek
Cover image credits: © Rita Asia Chow (illustration)
and © W. Phokin/Shutterstock (texture)
Map design: Rita Asia Chow, Magdelena Lee

ISBN (hardcover): 978-1-7372601-2-7
ISBN (paperback): 978-1-7372601-0-3
ISBN (ebook): 978-1-7372601-1-0

Library of Congress Control Number: 2021916577

This work is dedicated to Allan W. Eckert. He was a historian who could make original letters, diaries, and documents sing a story. He was also the man who first introduced me to the piece of history that is the story of the Northwest Territory and the clash of civilizations that have not been so personified each by its own champion since Hector and Achilles.

PART I

"The indigenous population is that people which so totally obliterated their predecessors as to leave no anthropological evidence of their existence."

—Unknown

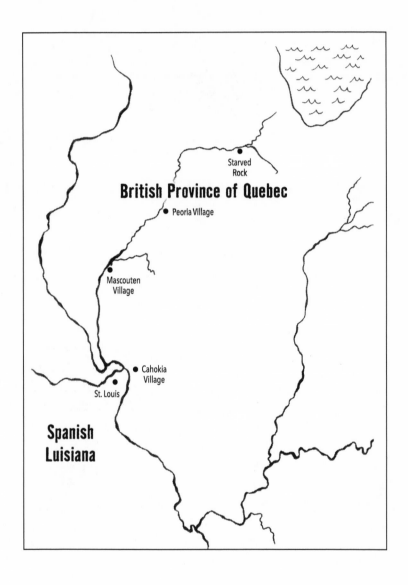

CHAPTER 1

JULY 27, 1769

British Province of Quebec

Salvation stood within sight.

The lightning-struck elm had been massive, and now, even destroyed, its solid black trunk extended twenty feet into the air in the center of the small meadow cleared by the fire. Nubs of the limbs made possible an ascent to the fire-burned opening he knew would be at the top. Not every man could climb it, but Pini could. Even they would not find him there. But he needed to lead them away first. And he needed to lead them away without making it obvious he wanted to be followed. Then he would circle back and hide in the safety of Mother Elm's hollowed core.

Pini chose a green, leafy branch to sweep his track. He expected them to see the knife cut where he took it. He was tired and they knew it, so they might expect such a mistake. He used a rawhide thong cut from his breeches to tie the branch to the back of his belt and made certain that it dragged the ground behind his heels. Then he raced across the small meadow, allowing the branch to cover his tracks. It did, but not well enough. Even if his footprints were not seen, the sweeping pattern of the branch would be too regular. They would know and follow. He was, at best, four hours ahead of the Ottawa. He'd have to find a way to lose them, backtrack to the meadow, and get up the elm before they arrived. He'd lost them before, though, and he could do it again.

Once through the meadow, he turned off the animal track he'd been following and headed downhill. Without the track, his trailing branch caught on bushes and slowed him, but he needed to keep up the deception awhile longer to maintain the fiction that he was doing more than leading them away. They would follow, but slowly. Pini knew they would see a periodic leaf turned over, moist side up, or a snapped twig tugged off by the small branch he pulled. Pini continued downhill. He needed water, a stream, in which to hide his tracks. He did not know the country well this far east of the Mississippi, but a stream would be found if he just kept downhill.

In less than a quarter hour, Pini came to the bottom of the hill and there it was—a stream not three feet wide but flowing smoothly. He untied the branch from his belt and threw it. Had he wanted to make certain it was not seen, he'd have carried it into the stream until some clump of brush appeared in which he could hide it. But he no longer cared. Once they got here, they would know he was running. And run Pini did. Right down the stream. He made no attempt to hide the mud his tracks kicked up in the water. They would know he was in the stream. What they would not know was where he got out. He would see to that.

What Pini needed was a rock outcropping coming straight up from the stream. He could climb rock and risk disturbing nothing. And it had to be on the east side of the stream so the one trace of his exit, water marks, would evaporate in the afternoon sun. In less than ten minutes of tramping downstream it came to him. He could not have asked for more. The granite outcropping did not come up from the stream but extended out above it. The shelf hung at least six feet above the water, too high for most men to jump up and grab. Most men didn't have the strength to pull themselves up and over such a height, but Pini did. However, he did not pull himself up—at least not at this moment. He continued downstream for another ten minutes and then stirred up a large cloud of mud from the bottom and let the trace of it drift on down in the water. Only then did he race back upstream to the rock. A high leap and a strong pull and he was over the shelf. It was solid granite. Not a pebble was disturbed to show any trace of his passage.

For the first half mile he was very cautious of his trail. He did not disturb a blade of grass or a leaf, and he did not walk on any open dirt to leave a footprint. After that, Pini loped easily through the broken forest for an hour until he was again close to the small meadow created by the burning of Mother Elm. Even in death, she was his salvation. She would shelter him from those damn Ottawa and their allies.

When he was within half a mile of the meadow, he became very cautious again. He did not want to take the risk that they might be such poor trackers as to miss the sign he'd left them. If they were, they would start to sweep the entire area, looking for his track. He couldn't risk them finding this track and running right up behind him. He wanted to reach the meadow at the exact spot he'd exited, and he did.

There was no sign of them. Not a single track. They had not come yet but would soon. He had to hurry now and hide before they arrived. Hurry, but make no mistake. Pini could do that. From here he would leave no footprint, no broken twig or disturbed leaf, nothing to show he had been here. As an extra precaution, he located a fallen branch to again sweep any track he might leave. He would walk backward, and on his toes, once he got to the meadow so if he did leave a track, it would be mistaken for his earlier track in leaving. He would sweep gently now. Even the tracks of his sweeping could not show this time. It took a quarter hour to reach the elm. Now he needed to climb with ease and certainty. Mother Elm had burned long enough ago that there was very little loose bark or ash left, but he could not risk knocking any of it off to show sign of his climb. He studied Mother Elm and what footholds she offered that would not break off and leave debris at her feet. Once Pini had planned his climb he made it swiftly, easily, and with grace but without a single mark on Mother Elm or at her feet.

Upon reaching her top, Pini eased up and over into the burned hole of Mother Elm's core. The opening at the top was wide, but not as deep as he'd hoped. It was tight. He would have to point his toes down and wiggle his hips in deep to ensure concealment. It took effort to push in that far, and he had to put his arms at his sides rather than over his head to ensure they didn't show out the top. Now all he had to do was wait. They would be here soon. For the first time in the weeks they had been chasing him, he might now come to know how many there were. They would stop here to study the ground and then follow his poorly concealed trail. Then a longer wait until escape.

It was midafternoon. Pini would stay here the remainder of the afternoon and evening and well into the dark of night. Then he could be out and gone. Tonight's quarter moon would give just enough light for him to find his way to the Wabash River, but not enough light for the Ottawa to track him even if they came back. By morning he'd have covered the ground to the river. There he'd find a log to float downriver far enough they would never know where he got out. Then he could cross the country back to the Mississippi and work his way upstream to Cahokia. From there he could easily make it back to his Peoria. Pini would be saved.

* * * *

The first voice Pini heard spoke with the accent of a Potawatomi.

"He's not going around the meadow. He's dragging a cut branch across his trail. How stupid does that young Illini think we are?"

"He doesn't. We've almost had him twice this week. He knows we're good," barked the guttural response, a tone Pini recognized as Ottawa. He knew this would be their leader. He had an urge to raise his head to get a look at the man, but Mother Elm held him so tight he feared he'd make a noise in pulling himself up the few fingers needed to look.

"Then why take the risk of cutting a branch?" the younger first voice asked.

A new voice, Kickapoo by the accent, responded, "He's tired. We've run him hard. He hasn't had much food for weeks and still runs faster than we. We'll have him soon."

The thought of food made Pini's stomach growl loud enough he feared for a moment his pursuers would hear.

"Remember, don't kill him. We'll take him back and kill him slowly for the amusement of all," commanded the Ottawa.

And then another voice, also Potawatomi, on the other side of the meadow. "I've found his track. He's running due east."

They left hurriedly, the group of at least the Ottawa he'd assumed to be their leader—it was after all an Ottawa he'd killed that brought them here—and one Kickapoo and two Potawatomi. Pini listened closely with some concern they'd find his back trail. He could be trapped here if they did. But within fifteen minutes all sound was gone. He wished he'd been able to get a better count. He'd heard four voices. If there were more, they had not spoken. But they were gone. He could rest here now.

* * * *

Voices woke him. His eyes opened wide with fear instantly. *Why are they back?* The sounds came straight toward him. His heart pounded and he felt the urgent need to urinate, a sensation he had not felt since his first battle with the Winnebago in his twelfth summer. *Why did I hide here? Was it a mistake? Is Mother Elm a death trap? Should I have kept running?*

But the voices were not excited. They were the same voices but tired. And they came slowly. And when they entered the meadow they stopped. *What are they doing?* The sky was darkening above him. He could not do more than look up, and there he could see a first star of evening.

"Where could he have gone? Once he got into that creek there was no sign of him getting out. We scoured all of it from his entry until the water cleared. Like magic he was gone."

"Our young warrior is very good. We heard that about him, remember? That he's the best of his generation. Great skills but no sense."

And now a new voice. This one a Potawatomi as well. "Our warrior of great skills eluded us today. But we are many. He is one. We will find him."

"Uhh," came the guttural Ottawa voice again. "For now, we rest. Chatonis, gather wood enough for warmth through the night. Spotka, there were deer sign just downhill. Slip down to the stream and see if you can get us fresh meat for dinner. I'm tired of pemmican."

"Yes, Opawana," came the response of one of the Potawatomi.

So, I will spend the night with you, Mother Elm. Your breast presses me very hard but your protection is sure. I will not leave you until the morning, it seems. But uncomfortable as he was, Pini smiled. He was safe and what a story to tell around the campfires. *Pini, greatest warrior of his generation. Killed the Ottawa of such importance that his tribe sought to kill me, chased me for weeks, and the many of them were unable to catch the one lone, great warrior, Pini. My fame to extend beyond the Illini Confederation.*

Fatigue and hunger again took Pini to fitful sleep, but this time with those heroic thoughts filling his dreams.

* * * *

The smell of cooking venison awoke him this time. His mouth watered and his stomach growled. He still had some jerky left, but he'd have to free his arms and force himself high enough to pull it from the pouch on his belt. In his sleep, she seemed to have gripped him even tighter. The effort to pull his arms free would be too great. It was a risk he would not take, even in the dark. One sound, one slip, and they would light Mother Elm on fire again and force him down. Hunger he could stand until breakfast. They would be gone with the light.

"It was a hard shot downhill and almost in the dark. Good hunting, Spotka."

A muted grunt was the only response.

And then the Ottawa leader, Opawana, spoke. "In the morning we leave our pursuit and go back."

"No!" was the response of a chorus of what sounded like close to a dozen voices.

"Be still! It was my uncle who was killed. I command here." There was silence and then he spoke again. "We have spent weeks acting as though we are hunting a lone wolf. But we are not. Oh, he runs alone and he outruns us. But he is fed by his pack. If Pini did not have the support, the food, the eyes and ears of the other Illini, we'd have had him long ago. So, we will eliminate his pack and make him into a lone wolf. Then he will be ours."

"How?" asked a Potawatomi voice.

"You all have wanted the Illini land for a long time. Is that not true?"

There was a general muttering of agreement.

"Then we Ottawa will give it to you. Tomorrow we head back to the main body. And when we are all together, we head for the Illini village at Mascouten Bay and eliminate it. After that, the Peoria and all of the other Illini septs. We eliminate all of his pack. Then the lone wolf will be easy to hunt."

There was a gentle murmuring. Spotka spoke into it. "It is a good land." And then almost as an afterthought he added, "Will Otussa agree with your plan?"

The answer came as a growl from Opawana's throat. "Otussa grieves for his father. But he listens to me. He will do as I . . . suggest."

There was no response of any sort. Pini could hear nothing below. He assumed it was stunned silence at the audacity of the Ottawa plan. Audacious as it was, the Ottawa had defied the British until their French allies abandoned them. Perhaps they could do it. He would have to run even harder now. His return was urgent. He must get to his people quickly. The Illini must prepare for the coming assault of the combined force of the Ottawa and all their rapacious neighbors.

* * * *

The snap of a branch in the campfire awoke him before the sun. He was confused. Thirst, hunger, exertion, and lack of sleep had addled his wits. The smell of the fire warming breakfast brought him back. The enemy would eat the remains of the deer, and he would remain hungry. He tried to yawn quietly to bring awakening air into his lungs, but his chest seemed unable to expand against the hardness of Mother Elm.

But his enemies would be gone soon and Pini could pull himself from her grip, climb down, and run. Run hard. He would be the salvation of his people. Not just the greatest warrior of his generation but the greatest Illini warrior ever.

His people saved by his wit and courage to stay in the enemy's midst and the skill to remain undetected by them. He had to wait just one more hour.

His pursuers left early, swiftly, and almost silently. Now he could go back to action. Pini pulled his arm up from alongside his body—or at least he tried to. The evening mist might have lubricated the trunk, for he seemed to have slid deeper into Mother Elm during the night. Or maybe his arms had swollen. He could not even roll his shoulders now. But he had to. He must. He tried to push up with his feet to lift himself enough to create space to raise his shoulders and then his arms. But his toes were pointed down and his feet wedged in too tight to raise his toes and push. His ankles were wedged too tight to allow any lift at all. He tried wiggling but such motion as he could get seemed to just settle him deeper. He stopped and exhaled for a moment.

Calm, Pini.

He took a deep breath and thought.

My fingers have some room between my thighs and the tree.

He straightened his fingers until he could dig nails on both hands into the softened wood of Mother Elm's old burned core and pushed. He rolled his head back, looked to the sky, and pushed hard. Harder.

Push, Pini. You can do this.

And then he screamed as the nail on his right middle finger bent backward and came off.

But his body didn't move at all.

The pain subsided and he pushed again against his ankles, with his bloodied fingers, and even with the back of his head hard against Mother Elm. He pushed until he was wet with sweat. Still, he did not move. He remained wedged tight.

The sun was on his head now, high overhead and hot. Sweat dripped off his brow and ran down his nose and onto his upper lip. It was salty but wet and he licked all he could get. Pini had not eaten since breakfast yesterday and had not drunk since he left the stream. His efforts were wearing on even his great strength. He would rest and shepherd his strength. His next efforts would move him.

The sun was gone from his head now. When he lifted his eyes, they were in shade. Now would be the moment of his release. He rolled his shoulders as high as he could get them; he put all the force of his legs on his wedged ankles; he pushed his fingers into her soft core and his head back against her tight canal. Now would be the moment of her release, of his rebirth. He pushed with all his strength, until he could push no more. But he did not budge. Mother Elm would not release him.

It was cool when he awoke. He felt weak and tired. But he was not resigned. He could go another day or day and a half without water. Perhaps in that time it would rain and lubricate his passage. Or perhaps he would shrink a little, just a little, and be able to move up. Up just enough to raise his elbows and move his hands up and across his chest. If he could free his hands, he could reach the lips of her opening and pull himself out. But for now, a prayer.

He said it aloud so she could hear him clearly. "Mother Elm, you have protected me. You have sheltered my life from my enemies. But now, Mother, it is time to free me, to give me back the life you have saved. Give it back, Mother, not just for me but for all of your people. Each moment you wait gives our enemies time to gather. I am their salvation, Mother. Free me. You must." Perhaps if Mother Elm would not free him, Kitchesmanetoa would intervene and send rain to make it all smoother and free his way out of this passage. With that thought, he passed again into unconsciousness.

The caw of the raven awakened him. It was close, very close. He raised his head and looked up. There the black beast was, sitting in the morning sun, on the lip of the opening, looking down at him. Pini smiled. "You are Kitchesmanetoa's messenger come to deliver me?" The raven tilted his head at an angle of interested inspection. And then he struck, his beak ripping Pini's eye out of its socket.

Pini screamed and threw his head down. It was his only protection.

With a final caw the messenger bird flew away.

Pini was trapped, not to be delivered, not to have his life renewed. Pini, greatest warrior of his generation, would die. But he would die with a last thought. Not many men could live after death, but Pini could and would.

For as long as the Tamaroa and the Cahokia and the Peoria and the Kaskaskia and the Metchigamea and the Mascouten live, as long as the Illini Confederation exists I will be remembered and my praises sung. Pini, assassin of Pontiac.

CHAPTER 2

AUGUST 1, 1769

Near Mascouten Bay on the Illinois River

The buffalo herd showed no sense of threat. But then, they weren't afraid of much. The small pack of wolves off to one side gave mute evidence that a calf or a young bull weakened by a fight had fallen behind, but the wolves were not threat enough to prevent the herd from grazing. Had they smelled the horses, they might have paid more attention. But Quaqui and his young son, Paskepaho, were downwind and not yet seen.

"Father, it is time for me. May I take one?"

Quaqui did not respond for a moment. Yesterday, when they had first seen signs of the herd, he knew this was coming. Paskepaho was tall for his age, within two fingers of matching his father's height, and he was becoming muscular, his shoulders and arms starting to show the fullness of manhood. But his hips were still boyishly thin with no real strength in his legs. Stamina he had; he always led the other boys in distance races, but not great strength. Quaqui had brought Paskepaho on this hunt to hone his skills. One of the responsibilities of fatherhood. He'd known there was some risk in the hunt, but he'd thought, if it came, it would be from the aggression of an Ottawa war party. That fool Pini had brought it on when he killed Pontiac.

Why did he do it? Was the young fool just seeking glory? Did the British hire him to take vengeance on their tormentor? Was it Makatachinga that put him up to it? Wouldn't have been hard to suggest eternal glory to that young stud. If Makatachinga did that, he's the bigger fool.

The Ottawa had insisted on unfettered access to Illini land to hunt Pini. While they were not entirely polite about it, he'd not really had any choice. His Mascouten Bay village, the smallest of Illini settlements, could not have prevented two hundred warriors from doing whatever they wanted. Quaqui had met with Otussa, son of Pontiac, and told him that Pini wasn't from Mascouten Bay, didn't live there, hadn't been there for over a year, and was not there now. Then he'd invited the Ottawa to stay the night and feasted them. He'd done it to give them freedom to see for themselves the young assassin wasn't around. Better that than have to give in to their demand to search. The Ottawa party was large enough he'd not wanted it to come to a fight.

Quaqui knew it was possible it could get worse but didn't think it would. They would eventually catch Pini and kill him and that would be the end of it. The Ottawa were not traditional enemies of the Illini, so they would go home. But their allies the Potawatomi and Kickapoo were what worried him more. They had always coveted the Illini's fertile land.

Nevertheless, he was fairly certain that the hunt for Pini would occupy the search party for long enough to allow him to leave his village responsibilities and take up those of a father. Paskepaho needed to test his skills in a hunt to help him on his pathway to manhood and perhaps even leadership among the Illini. The buffalo herd on this side of the Mississippi was small and not often seen, but here it was. There was prairie and grass and so there were buffalo. He knew just what Paskepaho wanted. To take the risk. To prove his courage and his worth. He would have been disappointed in his son had he not wanted it. But he'd have preferred that it was part of a larger hunt, part of a larger party where he could keep a closer eye on his only son, to protect him. But the gods granted the gifts they granted instead of the gifts people wanted. It was not for him to stand between Paskepaho and this gift.

"There are just the two of us. We have no woman to do the work after and will have to do it ourselves."

Paskepaho smiled up at him. "Then we will take just one beast, but it is mine." It was not a request.

"All right, but make it a cow. I don't want to deal with that thick hide on a bull. And listen to me. You have heard the stories. Your horse will be frightened of the horns. As it, and you, should be," he added. "You know you must approach on the cow's left and shoot hard behind the last rib and into the heart. I will be on her right, trying to keep her running straight. So, she may want to hook into your horse. If she does, give way. Even if it's the last instant. If your horse goes down, we have no hunt. If you give way, you will lose a little ground but we will catch her again."

Paskepaho smiled up again but said nothing. He turned his head back to the herd and started to slowly trot his horse toward them.

He is young but even now he thinks. The first time I did this I started out at full gallop and almost exhausted my horse before we caught the herd. And then Quaqui trotted after.

Not until they were within a hundred yards of the herd did one of the buffalo look up. They hadn't smelled the horses and so grazed peacefully until the vibration of the earth caught their attention. At first only one looked and then more but none moved. When they were within fifty yards one bellowed and then the whole herd turned and started to trot away. Those in the front ran, but those in the rear were trapped by their own mass and could only trot until the way opened before them.

Paskepaho, relieved of the need for any stealth, let out a huge whoop and kicked his horse hard. He pulled an arrow from his quiver and notched it, his horse at full run. Ever a good horseman, he looked at ease with his knees tight to his horse's ribs, arrow notched to the bow held in his left hand, and his right slapping his horse on the rump. One cow in the rear had to take a moment to turn her calf to the running herd and fell a few steps behind at the start. Quaqui ran his horse up on Paskepaho's right and used his bow to point her out. Paskepaho nodded in understanding and with his knee moved his horse five feet to the left so they would come up on either side of her. Quaqui moved half a length ahead.

They caught the trailing cow at the full run, hearts pounding harder than their horses' hooves and a prayer to Kitchesmanetoa on Quaqui's lips that no prairie dog hole lay in Paskepaho's path. Quaqui shot by the trailing calf and caught the cow, his leg so close to her that it rubbed against her furry hide. He would hold her from turning back to the bawling calf. Paskepaho was down low on his horse's neck with the bow flexed at full length, arrow ready to fly. The cow looked left for the calf but kept her head low. Quaqui knew she would hook now and raise her horns as she came around. He yelled at Paskepaho to pull away. He did not respond. As the buffalo threw her horns toward Paskepaho's horse her flank opened a bit, making the shot easier. Paskepaho was within a foot of her rib, lying almost prone across the horse's neck with the weapon drawn so tight the arrowhead touched the fully flexed bow. At the instant the cow hooked, he released the arrow. His horse tried to jump away but took the end of the horn in his front shoulder. He went down and Paskepaho with him.

The cow, Paskepaho's arrow buried behind her rib up to the feather, took two steps, staggered to her knees, and slid forward in the prairie grass, her heart stopping before she did. Paskepaho flew over the top of his staggering mount and rolled headfirst into the ground. He tumbled heels over head and then head over heels, his momentum carrying him gracefully up onto his feet.

Quaqui slowed his horse to a walk and came up beside Paskepaho, took in his son's grin, as wide and white as a full moon rising. He allowed his expression to show none of the relief or pride he felt.

"See how bad your horse is hurt. I'll get the calf."

Quaqui walked his horse toward the exhausted and bawling calf, now standing twenty yards beyond them. As he approached, the calf stood staring up in confusion. Quaqui's arrow flew just below its chin and straight into its heart. The small beast dropped where it stood.

By the time he got back, Paskepaho was standing by his horse, running his hand down the right shoulder near the open wound. "He'll have trouble carrying weight while it heals, but the horn didn't reach the bone. We'll find out if he limps after he's healed."

Quaqui dismounted. "We'll have to stay here until we can skin and slaughter these two. And we'll have to dry the meat here. We should have brought one of the women. You take my mount and go back and load everything in camp onto the packhorses and bring it all here. I'll have to stay and start the work. If we both leave, the wolves will have these two before we get back." Quaqui pointed with his chin toward the two dead buffalo. "But be very watchful, my son. Particularly as you enter our camp. I don't want you to have to confront angry Ottawas and their friends on your own. If they have entered our camp, just back out and return quietly. Now come have a treat before you go."

The two walked together, each leading his horse toward the dead calf. Quaqui leaned to grab one of the calf's front legs and roll it so it was flat on its back and all four stiffening legs straight up. He then took out his knife and opened the abdominal cavity, careful to cut around the stomach, which he released from the intestine and throat with practiced cuts. When he pulled the stomach free, he lifted it to his mouth and sucked from the stump of the esophagus. White curdled milk slowly ran down his lips until it covered his chin. With a loud burp, he handed the stomach full of curdled cow's milk to his son, who drank deeply.

"Better even than fresh liver seasoned with drops of the beast's own bile. I'll have that ready for your supper when you return."

He then handed Paskepaho the reins of his horse and watched him spring upon its back, pleased to see the fall had not left his son damaged. The father looked up at the son. "Remember, be very cautious of Ottawa, especially as you enter our camp."

Paskepaho nodded and started to trot the horse away.

Quaqui stopped him with a word. "My son."

The boy turned to look.

"Well done." Both men let themselves smile.

* * * *

By the time Paskepaho returned, Quaqui had the hide off both of the carcasses and had butchered the calf. He was standing over the cow, stripped to nothing but a breechcloth, blood covering his arms and upper body. He had slit open the belly and removed the innards, which were lying in a pile next to the carcass. He stood next to his work and watched his son ride toward him with the two packhorses tied behind his mount, one loaded with the carcasses of the two deer they had killed yesterday and the other with supplies needed for the planned weeklong hunt.

As Paskepaho dismounted, his father handed him the promised buffalo liver, sprinkled with bile.

"Glad to see you've done most of the work for me, Father."

"Woman's work and there is plenty left. With only three good horses, we're going to have to dry this meat before we go. You go find some dead wood and build a drying frame back in those woods. I want it to have a sheltered canopy to break up the smoke. And make sure the wood is dry enough to make very little of it."

He pointed at the vultures slowly circling even in the lengthening rays of the setting sun. "I'm worried about those. There are too many for some small kill. Who knows what attention they may attract?"

"Father, I couldn't see them while I traveled through the woods. It wasn't until I broke onto the prairie that they appeared in the sky. The Ottawa will be traveling in the forest where they are not likely to see the vultures, aren't they?"

"Probably, but we cannot be too cautious. I'll be happy when we are back in the protection of our village. But for now, make supper of that liver over there." He nodded over his shoulder toward the carcass. "And go find a stream to water the horses. Then go into the woods and find a small open space that's covered above to make a little camp and put up drying frames. When you find a suitable place come back and tell me where you are. Meantime, I'll finish this work. Now go."

* * * *

A few days later, Quaqui and his son rode slowly down a wooded path, carrying their haul of dried meat. They were close enough to home now that each gully, creek, ridge, and even some of the larger trees were known symbols of place and memory. The trail sloped down the last hill toward the river, slowly growing wider and more heavily trod. They were anxious to get home and to revel in the glory of a small, but very successful, hunt and even more in Paskepaho's passage toward manhood. The kill of the cow would mark him as a coming warrior, a youngster to be watched and evaluated by all his elders. But Quaqui led them slowly. He had a sense of unease that suggested he move at a pace that let him absorb all the information the land made available. That they had seen no one from the village was not, in and of itself, concerning, but it would not have been unusual to hear a welcoming voice by now. There was an odd stillness in the forest. Oh, there were birds flying between the trees, but he'd seen no small mammals since they started down the hill. He rode slowly. And then his nose gave evidence. He would not have expected to smell smoke this far away from the village, but it was there just at the edge of consciousness. Soon he would smell it fully.

"What is it, Father?" Paskepaho asked as Quaqui stopped his horse.

Quaqui responded by holding his hand up in a sign for stillness. Ever the teacher to his son, he finally spoke. "Can you sense the smoke? Not smell it or see it but sense that it is here?"

Paskepaho looked up as though to penetrate the forest canopy and twisted his head to find the wind and put his nose to it. But the wind was behind them and carried nothing but the musk of the decay of last year's leaves on the forest floor. Finally, he shook his head. "No."

"I cannot smell it yet, but it is there. Let's lead the horses off the trail." And then Quaqui kneed his horse to the left off the trail, leading the loaded packhorse behind him. Paskepaho followed, riding what had been a packhorse and leading his limping and wounded horse. Within several hundred yards the smell of smoke came to them both.

For another fifteen minutes, they wandered through the forest in an erratic path but one that led ever closer to their village at Mascouten Bay. At the outskirts of the village, Quaqui dismounted and motioned Paskepaho to do the same. He tied his horse and packhorse to a small tree and pulled the bow and his quiver from the saddle. Paskepaho started to follow. His father shook his head "No" and then spoke very quietly, making his words form on the inhale in a way that they carried no distance. "Tie your wounded horse but hold yours ready to ride. Keep your bow close. I'll be back within half an hour."

Paskepaho started to protest but the look on his father's face was too stern to brook any disagreement. Quaqui slipped soundlessly into the dense forest.

The only motion was from the gentle wind fanning the embers of the dying flames. The wind carried ash and the smell of burning flesh. Every one of the two dozen bark *wegiwas* was burned down to ashes. Not even a dog moved furtively. Bodies littered the ground. At the edge of the village were the bodies of the warriors, mostly Illini. Through the smoke of the burned *wegiwas* he could see to the river. A few of the canoes appeared to be missing but most lay burned at the water's edge. Bodies of women, children, and a few warriors lay scattered in the paths between the *wegiwas*. Many more on the beach. Fear, revulsion, and anger rose in him, but he remained as he was, motionless on his belly at the forest edge, surveying the destroyed village between him and the bay. The horror of the slaughter before him framed in the beauty of the summer growth of cattails and other littoral plants flowering in the bay made his sadness even less bearable. But he lay as he was, just watching and looking. Looking for any sign of life, either Illini or Ottawa. After fifteen minutes of observation, he rose and walked to examine what was the end of life as he'd known it.

The first corpse was Singing Bird, the old woman who knew more than anyone in the village, perhaps the nation, about herbs and their uses. They hadn't bothered to shoot her. She had been too easy to catch. The back of her head was smashed, her brain open to the air. Someone had taken the time to place the blow low on the back of her head where it would kill her but not destroy her beautiful long silver scalp. That the killer had taken with his knife.

At least she was dead when he ripped it off her skull.

The first arrow he found was in the chest of Howls at the Moon. It was an Ottawa, clearly marked by the use of the feather of a red-winged blackbird. His hair was gone too. All their hair was gone. Well, all of those save Buffalo Fish's family. They had been trapped in their *wegiwa*. Their hair had all been burned too short to pull as they baked inside. Buffalo Fish's body, his belly and chest looking like a porcupine's back with arrows for spines, blocked the door. Some of the arrows carried the distinctive red feathers, but not all. There were Potawatomi and Kickapoo shafts as well. It seems it took many to bring the big man down.

Quaqui walked very slowly. He was in no hurry at all to get where he was going. It seemed clear that the Ottawa had rushed from the wood and that many warriors had fallen at the edge of the village, trying to keep the murderers away from the families. But once the perimeter collapsed and the Ottawa got into the village, the fighting became each man trying to protect his own and cover their retreat to the edge of the bay and the canoes. He would count later, but there seemed to be as many as 120 corpses here. Not many would have gotten away. Later he would also count the burnt dugout canoes and try to estimate how many got out of the bay and into the river. There was time for all that. Time. That was all he had now. Time.

He knew Hukuwia, so he knew what she would have done. She had always been so pretty, tall with long legs, such beautiful glistening hair, and such magnificent breasts. But she was fierce. He remembered her fury when she had caught him watching her bathe when they were courting. She had rushed out of the pond and chased him, stark naked, with a tree branch she'd picked up while in full stride. She'd hit him hard across the shoulders and tried to smash his face when he turned to protect himself. It was the first time they ever made love. Hukuwia was fierce, and sometimes he thought this was as much her village as his. Every woman listened to her, some because she was wise, some because they feared her, but most because she protected them all.

He knew she would have done so today. That was what she always did—protect them. Paskepaho was their only child. She had no other children of her own to protect. The entire village was hers to protect and she would have tried. He would not find her at home. She would be on the beach. She would have been with the warriors in the last boat. But there was no last boat. Only the first boats got off. She would not have been in one of those.

Then he saw her. Naked and bloody, there on the beach. She'd tried to fight, but they had not been fearful enough to kill her from a distance. They had thrown her down and cut off her dress. He could see a light, straight cut down her chest and belly where the knife had cut past the soft skin of her dress and into the softer skin of her body. Her beautiful hair was gone, and the top of her head a mass of red gore where they had pulled her scalp off. Her chest was a mass of clotted blood as well where they had cut off the breasts he had spent so many happy hours adoring. And they had done it while she was alive. He knew because they had killed her slowly— arrows in the belly.

He stood staring down, beyond pain. He was almost removed, a warrior reading signs from the dead. He was standing, staring, his face expressionless when Paskepaho walked up. Quaqui said nothing as Paskepaho turned back to the horse he had been leading. When he returned it was with the hide of

his buffalo. H...
with the hide tha...
   "Come, Father...
away from looking at th...

*

They could not build a pyre large ...
ies, so they built three—one at the east ...
at the west end, and one in the middle. ...
hides between two horses and used them to ...
from the spot of its falling to the spot from wh...
rise. Quaqui did most of this work. His heart was ...
he did it. These were his people, his friends, his life. He ...
have been here. Should have fallen with them. But now he ...
alive and alone. He could not face that, the sadness and anger ...
and utter sense that his life had no meaning any longer. But
he could not allow his son into this new world. Hard as the
unknown future might be, Paskepaho would find his own way.
There had to be a way for him. There must.

   He would have preferred to go. If there was one thing in life
left for him to do, it was to warn Makatachinga and the Peoria
that the Ottawa were coming for them. But he had to honor the
spirits of these, his people, and not leave them to the coyotes
and the crows. He would hope to come back later to collect and
bury the bones, as was their custom.

   He let Paskepaho stack the wood at the bottom of the
pyres. By the end of the second day the three large pyres were
each laid with logs crisscrossed on the bottom and two lay-
ers of bodies stacked on top. They were gruesome, but that
only mattered in this life. What mattered for the next was
that their spirits be set free. The fires would be huge and the
smoke would carry far, but the Ottawa were long gone. If they
had any remaining interest in his Mascouten Bay village, they

e covered the corpse that had been his mother,
t had been his glory.

We have much to do." His son pulled him

e end of any joy, forever.

* * *

enough to stack 120 bod-
end of the village, one
They slung buffalo
move each body
ich it would
old while
should
was

CHAPTER 3

AUGUST 9, 1769

Near Peoria Village

Opawana's face was hard in the light of the dying fire. His nose, thin as the blade of his tomahawk, ran straight down to his narrow lips, which he held in perpetual stillness. His face would have been cruel, save that his eyes were overly large, almost like those of a newborn fawn. And they gave his face the expression of gentleness that his demeanor otherwise belied. He wore his hair like Pontiac, shaved save for a two-finger-wide strip down the middle of his head. The lack of hair made his jug-handle ears almost comical, but woe to the man who laughed at them. Opawana had the shoulders and the power of a bear and a temperament to match, one that didn't invite teasing except perhaps from his closest friends.

None of those were sitting by this fire.

There were perhaps fifty small fires, such as the one warming him, spread over the large meadow. Half of them were warming other Ottawa. But Opawana had chosen not to stay with his brother Ottawa. Instead he stayed with his mixed-tribe scouting party. There were things he wanted to know that only they could tell him. Opawana raised his eyes from the mysteries dancing in the low fire and looked across it to Spotka, the oldest and wisest of the Potawatomi in his party and one he'd come to know and respect during almost a month together, first hunting Pini and then destroying the Illini village at Mascouten Bay.

"Spotka, we have eliminated the Mascouten sept of the Illini Confederation, and tomorrow we will do the same to the Peoria. We Ottawa do it to make a lone wolf of this Pini so we can have him and take revenge for his killing of our war chief."

Spotka looked up and held the eyes of Opawana with his own. He did not blink but held hard to those large brown eyes, and he did not smile. Despite their month of travel together, the two men did not know each other well enough to consider themselves friends. The Ottawa only wanted revenge, and that was more easily obtained if they came into Illini territory at the head of the same coalition that had been strong enough to take every British fort west of Fort Pitt save Detroit. The combined strength of the Ottawa, the Potawatomi, the Kickapoo, and the Winnebago had made it impossible for the Illini to prevent their pursuit of Pini.

Opawana now asked his question. "Why are you here?"

Spotka thought the question surprisingly direct and made his response a bit circumspect. "We were your allies against the British and their little colonial dogs. Pontiac was beloved to us as well. Had our French father not left us, we would have taken Detroit. The only white men here would have been the French, who honor us and treat us like men and don't wish to take our lands but just trade with their friends, the children of Kitchesmanetoa. That is why we are here."

Opawana smiled one of his rare smiles. But it was a sardonic one. One that made his thin lips disappear entirely and brought out the cruelty in his face. "You want nothing? Just the honor of helping the Ottawa exact our revenge?" He paused and stared back into the fire as though momentarily seeking answers there. He looked back up and continued. "You have been away much of the summer. Your corn has grown. But is there meat drying in front of your bark-house? Will your family not go hungry this winter if you do not hunt before the snows come?"

Opawana watched patiently as Spotka took what seemed overlong in formulating his response. When he did it came out very slowly, as though Spotka wanted to ensure each word was correct. "Opawana, I am an admirer of yours, and I know for you revenge is personal. He was not just your war chief but your uncle. I'm sure it has been difficult for you trying to hold us all together, because of course we all want to go home with our spoils. But we are still here, and tomorrow we strike again. Why do you question our love of your tribe and your uncle?"

Opawana was silent for a long while and when he spoke was very direct. "You want the land. Will you stay until it is yours?"

Again Opawana stayed silent and watched Spotka slowly formulate his response, almost as though buying time to think. Spotka took out his pipe, loaded the bowl, and with a splinter from the fire, lit it. When it was glowing, he offered it to Opawana in a gesture somewhat formal for a late night chat. Opawana took several puffs, studying Spotka the whole time, and passed it back. The two warriors sat in the light of the fire, passing the pipe between them until the ritual, and the pipe, were complete. Spotka took a last long draw on the pipe, knocked the few remaining ashes out onto the ground, exhaled long, and then spoke.

"The French, Opawana."

This drew a sharp look from Opawana's tomahawk blade of a face.

"They are the ones that made the Illini rich and with power over the rest of us," Spotka continued. "They gave the

Illini guns and steel. After that all the power shifted. If we, all the neighboring tribes, were to have those magical things, we had to get them from the Illini. If they wanted anything we had, they traded for it or merely took it. But then in my grandfather's time it all changed. Not only did the neighboring tribes become resentful but the mighty Iroquois as well. The Iroquois had the same relationship with first the Dutch and then the English as the Illini had with the French. And the Iroquois wanted to control all the trade of furs for the white man's goods from the tribes west of the low mountains. You know that. The Ottawa lived under the Iroquois thumb as we Potawatomi lived under that of the Illini."

Opawana allowed his hatchet face to nod solemn agreement. But he knew his expression reflected more anger and hatred than understanding. He let his silence encourage Spotka to continue.

"In my grandfather's time, the Iroquois sent seven hundred warriors to chastise the Illini. And they did. They destroyed an entire village, in exactly the same place as the one we just destroyed. But it was far bigger then. Since the coming of the Iroquois, we, the Illini's neighbors, have not had to be so respectful. In winters long ago there was not always enough game for all the mouths of our families. Times past we would listen to our babies cry. Now we just come to the Illini prairie to hunt buffalo. The Illini dare not object. Periodically, some of our young men will move west or south with their wives and build small villages that encroach on traditional Illini hunting grounds. Again, the Illini dare not object. But would we like more, perhaps all, of their land? Perhaps. If Kitchesmanetoa gives it to us, we will be happy to receive it."

Then Spotka was quiet. There were no flames left, just glowing coals, when he spoke again. "I have been candid with my brother Opawana. Now it is his turn. Why do you ask?"

Opawana did not look up. "I too like this land. It is a good land. Very good."

* * * *

It was still black when Opawana nudged them awake. He said the same to each. "It is time."

In less than ten minutes, all were up. Just as they had not eaten yesterday, there would be no eating this morning, nothing until after the battle. One might survive a gut-shot only if the bowel was empty. After, they would eat what they found in the village. Within moments each warrior had consolidated, into a small bundle, all he had carried on the trail but would not need to kill Illini. The youngest around each fire was assigned to carry the bundles to the horses. Then the young handlers of bedrolls and baggage, as well as a small cadre of older warriors, collected the horses and quietly walked them deeper into the woods. Most of the others squatted, their bare asses to the small warmth of the coals, and relieved themselves.

Otussa's plan had been made, transmitted, and understood by all. The Illini did not live in fortified villages, and unless they had been warned would not even have sentries out. They had been masters for so long they no longer thought of being assaulted. Even after being weakened by the Iroquois three generations ago, they continued to live in the fantasy of safety.

Otussa had issued one last order. "Pini, if he is found, is not to be killed. Neither is Makatachinga."

The war party divided into two groups of two hundred warriors each. The first group stayed quietly gathered here. They would enter the Peoria village from the south. The other half had to swing far enough around to the east to circle the village without being seen and be in the trees on the north side before first light. Neither group would attack until dawn. The northern group, led by Otussa, would attack first. The southern group, led by Opawana, would wait long enough after the attack started to ensure all the Illini warriors had moved to face the initial assault. Only once their backs were turned would the southern group attack. This was not to be about mere victory. This was about annihilation.

Moments after dawn, the northern assault was announced with a startling war cry. Almost instantly, an overwhelming chorus of similar cries followed. Opawana and Spotka lay quietly on the ground listening. Opawana raised his eyes, not to see the attack but to watch the younger men around him and make certain none bolted early. He saw one or two raise up on their knees as though to sprint forward and with a stern look and a small motion of his hand ordered them down. His eyes swept the village before him now that there was light to see. He could see *wegiwas* starting at the river and running fifty paces back. He had assigned half his warriors to special tasks. Fifty were to race to the canoes along the river and make certain none of the Peoria escaped in them. He preferred they kill anyone who came to the canoes, but if they were overwhelmed, Opawana had instructed they were to push the canoes into the river and hold on until support could arrive. The most important thing was to make certain not a man, woman, or child escaped.

Now he saw Illini warriors coming out of every house, many naked but all armed. And in each case, they turned north to run to the fight. He had seen enough. Opawana rose and two hundred warriors rose with him. He bellowed his war challenge and they all raced forward together. When they reached the *wegiwas*, he and one hundred of the warriors continued forward to pinch the Illini warriors between them and the northern force. Fifty more rushed to the canoes on the river's edge. The remaining fifty started setting fire to the *wegiwas*. He'd told his warriors to fire them and kill whoever rushed out. He knew many of his young men would want to rush into the huts, shoot or tomahawk any warrior they saw there, and then rape the younger women. But he had forbidden rape during the assault. Opawana had no moral objection to the rape of Illini women; he forbade his warriors only because a warrior was never so vulnerable as when he was on his belly and distracted. A ten-year-old with a cooking pot could kill or disable him. The rape and torture would come later.

As Opawana ran past the second row of huts and toward the third he saw his first adversary. The Illini was on his knee facing north, musket at his shoulder. Opawana stopped just long enough to throw his own musket to his shoulder and blow off the back of the Illini warrior's head. He dropped the musket, pulled out his scalping knife, and used his other hand to pull the bloody head up. Scalping was a practiced gesture, and it only took a moment to circumvent the skull with the point of his knife, step on the dead man's back, wrap the victim's hair around his hand, and yank hard until the entire scalp ripped away.

In the moment it took he saw Spotka rush by him to take the lead. Opawana stuffed the bloody scalp into his belt and faced back to the battle in time to see Spotka completing the same ritual on another fallen Illini warrior. In his concentration, Spotka did not see the Illini squaw, tomahawk raised, rushing at his back.

Opawana screamed, "SPOTKA! DOWN!"

As Spotka dropped, Opawana's tomahawk flew over Spotka's head and landed blade first in the squaw's chest, dropping her in her tracks. Opawana ran the three steps to his victim, yanked the bloody tomahawk free as she gave a dying rattle. When he ran forward again he could see Otussa's Ottawa coming toward him. There were only two ranks of Illini left between them. He screamed at his men and those from the north who might hear him, "No more muskets. Don't shoot our own."

It was over in less than ten minutes. He could hear cries and screams of women and children as they were tomahawked, raped, and tortured. He had to say this for the Illini: he never heard one cry for mercy. They were proud.

* * * *

Pini was not there, but Makatachinga was. They had managed to take him alive. He was now tied, naked, to a post set upright in the middle of the village. Even though his entire world was burning up around him, Makatachinga's eyes remained stoic.

Makatachinga was the principal chief of the Illini Confederation. But he belonged to the Ottawa now and before he died, they wanted to know one thing. Who was pulling the strings on that fool Pini? Whose tool was he? Who had given him the order to kill Pontiac? Not that it mattered now, but they wanted to know. They wanted confirmation.

Opawana looked to Otussa, who nodded to him. He would let the older Opawana handle this. Opawana pushed his way through the warriors surrounding the post holding Makatachinga. Aside from the blow with the flat of a tomahawk that had knocked him unconscious, he seemed unhurt.

Good. The stronger he is the more torment he'll be able to tolerate before he dies, Opawana thought.

As Opawana approached, Makatachinga looked right at him. He seemed not to be fearful, though surely he knew what was about to happen to him. Opawana respected that and thought he might have liked this man if the circumstances of their meeting had been different.

Opawana stopped no more than two feet from the bound man. "Did you tell him to do it?"

Makatachinga did not speak. He looked at Opawana with contempt.

"I will ask just once more. Did you tell him to do it?"

Neither Makatachinga's demeanor nor his expression changed.

Opawana turned his back to the bound man. Addressing his warriors, he said, "I want three of the Ottawa nation's best archers there." He pointed to a spot twenty yards from the post. He then stepped to one side and said quietly to the warriors behind the post, "I'd move if I were you." And then with a rare and genuine smile he added, "Unless you know none of those three will miss."

The warriors behind the post scrambled aside.

Opawana looked up the line at the archers. "Each of you put one arrow in him. But don't kill him. If you do, I'll personally cut your balls off."

Almost four hundred assembled warriors roared with laughter as each of the three archers notched an arrow.

Opawana looked at the three Ottawa archers and pointed to the one on the left, a man famously accurate with a bow. "His right shoulder."

Almost instantly the arrow flew and noiselessly pinned Makatachinga's right shoulder to the post. Makatachinga's head came up sharply and his lips inhaled loudly, but other than that he made not a sound.

Opawana pointed at the archer in the middle. "His other shoulder."

The arrow flew and struck just below the left collarbone. The reaction was identical but almost instantly a small trail of blood appeared out of the corner of Makatachinga's mouth.

Opawana pointed to the warrior on the right, a very young archer he did not know. "In his balls. And if you miss, miss high."

The young brave looked nervous and when his arrow flew it was high. It struck in the midst of Makatachinga's pubic hair. Makatachinga screamed for the first time.

Opawana walked slowly back to him. This time he had to use Makatachinga's thick black hair to pull his head upright and stare into the tormented eyes as he put one hand around the shaft of the arrow in Makatachinga's belly. "Do you want to tell me now, or would you like me to pull it out?" He twisted the arrow gently to demonstrate the pain he intended to inflict. "Was it the tribe's decision to assassinate Pontiac while he was here? Or was it the British, seeking revenge, who led your young fool, Pini?"

Makatachinga's eyes still showed no fear, but now it was hatred that they showed. "From his youth he sought glory. Fame was all he desired. He didn't care how or why."

"Where is he now?"

It was clear the pain was telling on Makatachinga but he smiled as he spoke, exercising great effort to control himself. "The entire might of the Ottawa nation isn't enough to catch a lone young Illini boy? Bad leadership, I'd guess."

Opawana continued to hold Makatachinga up by the hair. As he drew his scalping knife, he slowly lowered Makatachinga's head so the top was showing. He drove the point of the knife into the skull at the back of the head and in one clean motion pulled the point of the knife halfway around the skull to the front. Again, Makatachinga inhaled sharply but made no other sound. Opawana again drove the point into the back of the skull and cut around the other side. And then he wound the rich black hair around his hand and held Makatachinga's face up near his and pulled with all his strength. As the scalp came off, Makatachinga screamed again. Opawana staggered backward with the force.

Opawana's shriek of triumph, chorused by all the warriors around him, drowned the sound of Makatachinga's screams.

Opawana raised the scalp above his head, blood running down his arm. And he commanded, "Every man put an arrow in this fool who stole our Pontiac from us. Don't kill him. Make him last."

CHAPTER 4

AUGUST 11, 1769

Peoria Village

Makatachinga's body swayed. Hanging forward as his shoulders and head were, with feet and hands bound to the post, it was the heavy breeze that caused the motion. There was no hair, just a scabbed mass of clotted blood across the entire top of the head. There were dozens of arrow shafts sticking out from the body, each fletched with distinctive red and black feathers.

Not one arrow in the chest or head. The Ottawa made it last. And they didn't allow any of their allies to participate in their act of revenge. Or perhaps they chose not to.

Quaqui stepped behind the post holding up the limp body of his principal chief and with one swing of his tomahawk severed the bonds that fixed Makatachinga's hands to the post. As the body fell forward and struck the ground, the air was filled with the sound of snapping arrows. The impact also dislodged the maggots that had been feeding around his wounds, giving the appearance of a white halo atop the gruesome corpse.

"There are hundreds of dead here. We will free the soul of Makatachinga and such others as we have the time to burn, but we have only tonight. We must leave here with the dawn. We were late getting here, the Ottawa traveled fast. We can't be late again."

"To where, Father?"

"The place the Illini have gone for many generations when the forces against us have been too great. We will go to the old French fort on top of the rock. 'Le Rocher' the French called it. It is impregnable. If there are survivors from our village, they will be there, as will any of the Peoria who still live.

"All the Ottawa want is revenge. But their allies will want to pluck our lands from us. If the invaders have done this to the Tamaroa, Cahokia, Kaskaskia, and Metchigamea, there will be few of us to stop them. We must concentrate our forces and gather together until the Ottawa leave, then deal with the Potawatomi and Kickapoo. The only safe place to wait is Le Rocher."

"I'll start collecting weapons and any food I can find," Paskepaho said. "Others may need it."

"No, don't. There are no horses here and ours are loaded with as much as they can carry. Use one of them to drag logs here. To this spot. This is where we will release the souls of Makatachinga and the others we have time and love enough to collect. One fire and then we leave. We may have very little time."

* * * *

Le Rocher lunged straight up from the south shore of the Illinois River just below the place where it was joined by the Vermilion. Normally, it would be no more than a four-day ride along the river from the camp of the Peoria to Le Rocher. But

Paskepaho knew, without having to be told, that this would not be a normal ride. There were four hundred warriors in these woods who would kill them on sight. They needed to avoid not only being seen but also leaving a trail to be followed. They were never on the main path, and on those occasions they crossed it, they took great precaution to cover their tracks. They had plenty of food, and water was abundant. What they needed was caution and that they had in abundance as well. A week later, they were within two miles of sanctuary.

"I don't like the idea of separating." Quaqui's normally placid face showed concern.

"Father, we cannot simply ride up to Le Rocher and presume access is safe. We both know that."

"True. We cannot do that. We must scout the entrance before we approach with the horses."

"One of us must, Father. We cannot leave our hobbled horses alone to make noise that invites our enemy or to be taken as prey by wolves."

Quaqui looked ever more concerned but did not speak. His son was being forced to mature faster than he'd expected or liked. Perhaps not fast enough to stay alive. But there was no choice.

"Go, Father. I will be safe here. I will keep the horses safe as well. If the enemy is already in place, then we will have to abandon the horses and supplies and sneak in without them. Go. Discover if we can bring in the supplies and the horses."

"If we can bring in these supplies, I will come back with men enough to lead the horses in. If not, I will come back for just you." And then he added, "If the enemy comes, abandon the horses and supplies and come by stealth in the night. Swim up to the rock on the river side and I will lower a rope. It is too steep to climb unaided. I'll need to drop down a rope to you. Your signal will be the call of the great horned owl."

Paskepaho nodded. Quaqui slid noiselessly around a massive black walnut and was gone.

* * * *

When Quaqui reached Le Rocher, he learned that no more than eighty warriors as well as a like number of women and children were there. But eighty warriors might be enough to save the Illini from extinction, he thought. Eighty warriors could hold the acre-and-a-half flat top of Le Rocher from an army of every warrior between here and Fort Pitt if required. The sides were the height of twenty men and virtually straight up. The French had built a staircase, but the first thing the arriving Illini had done was destroy it. Now, the only way up was to climb the cliff or trudge up a path narrow enough that three men could not stand shoulder to shoulder at its widest place.

As soon as he made contact with the other Illini, he organized a group of riders to go back for Paskepaho. The boy was waiting just where he had said he would be. Quaqui felt another surge of pride at his boy's instincts.

All the warriors had arrived with weapons, though the hundreds of arrows Quaqui and Paskepaho had collected would be welcomed and useful. Some had brought food, too, but the stores Quaqui and Paskepaho had packed on their horses would enable them to last longer than the Ottawa would stay. As for water, rain pooled into pockets in the sandstone that was the top. The old fort had not been used for a generation. What was left was completely rotten, but rotten or not the structures would provide shelter from sun and rain and any storm of arrows or bullets the besiegers might randomly fire upward.

They would be ready when the Ottawa came. But before the Ottawa, came more Illini. They came in small groups—stragglers all. They were Cahokia and Tamaroa, the remaining septs of the Illini Confederation. It became clear that, to the Ottawa, this was not war. This was annihilation. These on top of Le Rocher were all that were left of the proud, prosperous, and once dominant nation.

Very few warriors came. None had run. The ones here were like Quaqui and Paskepaho, warriors who had been hunting when the attack came. Of the women there were a few who had run with their children, but most who survived had been out collecting roots, herbs, and berries when the Ottawa came. In the end there were about two hundred on top of the rock, one hundred of whom were armed warriors. It was enough to hold Le Rocher from any force, but not enough to fight Otussa, Opawana, and their Ottawa warriors and allies in direct combat. They would remain here well supplied with food and with water, available from the river below and from the sky above. The Ottawa would not stay. It was not the Indian way. The Illini would wait the enemy out. When they left, these remaining would start over.

Quaqui was the only village chief to reach Le Rocher. Even though his village was the smallest in the confederation, all knew he was in charge. The survival of the entire nation was upon him, and he would not let the Ottawa destroy it as they had his village. The orders he gave were clear. All day and night the perimeter of Le Rocher was to be guarded. There was a warrior armed with a musket every twenty yards around the top. They were to lie on their belly and not make a target of themselves for some sharp, or lucky, shooting Ottawa. Quaqui stationed himself and a team of ten warriors in the middle of the old fort. They, and he, would go immediately to the spot from which any sentry fired. But the largest portion of his force, twenty warriors, was stationed at the top of the path. Five on either side of the path were lying prone and armed with muskets. There were also twenty women who had experience with muskets. They were assigned to run to the shooters the instant the enemy came. These women were to do nothing but load for them so the warriors could shoot constantly rather than being forced to stop and reload. The other ten stationed at the top of the path were armed with bows and arrows. Quaqui knew if they were rushed, it had to be up the path. And he knew if it happened, it would be a rush with great force. The idea would be to get as much firepower as possible down that path in the minute or less it would take the Ottawa to run from the bottom. And any warrior could get off three or four arrows in the time it took to load and shoot one round from a musket. The shooters were all instructed to aim for the lead men. Any who fell would not only be out of the fight, they would also create an impediment to slow the rush.

The impediment would allow his Illini to kill more Ottawa. And that was all Quaqui wanted. To kill Ottawa. He had responsibilities to his people, and he would fulfill them as best as he was able. But all he really wanted was to kill. And wherever the fighting was thickest he would be there—killing.

CHAPTER 5

AUGUST 20, 1769

Outside Le Rocher

Opawana knew he must defer to his younger cousin, but he didn't like it. Otussa was wrong, and his poor judgment was going to get warriors killed.

The first thing the French did after they built the stockade they called Fort St. Louis, on top of the one-hundred-foot-tall rock, was clear the trees for over two hundred yards around the base to create an open field of fire. And the Illini had had the good sense to burn what brush had grown up since the French abandoned the place. Only one old white ash stood taller than Le Rocher. A skinny young warrior climbed all the way to the thin branches swaying in the sky. His report was, "At least one hundred Illini warriors on top guard against incursion up the path or along the perimeter. Warriors entering the burnt ground will be very easy targets."

There were only two ways up—climb the cliffs or rush up the path. Neither option was good. If they scaled the cliff, the warriors climbing would be unable to fight back and easily killed. Without the concealment unburned brush would have given, warriors below could not even provide covering fire.

Otussa elected direct assault under the cover of darkness. It would make his warriors harder targets, but darkness would also make it impossible to offer any covering fire. Opawana counseled for siege—wait them out. But Otussa wanted this done, just like the destruction of the villages, in one irresistible rush. But the rush would not be irresistible and Opawana knew it.

Still Otussa insisted on his plan. The Illinois River had, in millennia of floods, cut the soft sandstone away under the river side of Le Rocher, creating an overhang along the face. Between the overhang and the river there was a small beach created by the alluvial soil deposited with each spring flood. The Ottawa and most of their allies had traveled on foot. But a few allies, chiefly the Chippewa, had arrived in canoes. Those were pulled up along that shore and Otussa had some of the warriors with them camp under the overhang to prevent any escape from that direction. The remainder of Le Rocher was surrounded by warriors hiding back in the tree line. During the assault, their main job was to prevent escape. Annihilation was to be complete. No Illini would ever be able to brag of Pontiac's death.

Otussa would lead the bulk of his warriors in rushing the path. Even with the path's zigzag up the cliff, a warrior could run from the bottom to the top in less than a minute. It would be very risky for those in front, but the defenders at the top of the path could reload their muskets no more than two times during that run. In the dark they not only would fire inaccurately but could not find targets easily or quickly. They would get off only one or two shots before they were overwhelmed. Otussa would lose a few warriors but destroy the defenders in one rush. That was his plan.

Tonight, there would be a quarter moon. It would provide enough light for a running warrior to see the path as well as enough for his tomahawk to strike accurately once he reached the top. But it would not be enough for the defenders to see targets clearly or aim well at them. This would be the night.

"Every fire is to be built large. Even though we will not eat before the fight, we will go through all the motions of a normal camp. We want the rush to be a surprise. Every warrior covering the escape routes will place himself quietly. Those rushing to glory will arm themselves quietly. The Illini will have no hint we are coming until I scream the charge. We will be taking scalps in less than two minutes after my war cry."

Those were Otussa's orders. Opawana had argued forcefully in private, but it was Otussa who led this war party. Opawana would not dispute with him before the others, and Otussa would not give in to his cousin. He would have this his way.

CHAPTER 6

AUGUST 20, 1769

Le Rocher

The cry pierced the darkness of the night with force and fear. And it was followed by two hundred others. Quaqui catapulted his body to standing, rifle in hand, with one motion. His understanding instant, there was no terror in him, only hate and a knowing that now, for the first time since he had seen her lying mutilated on the beach, he would be able to kill and exact some small measure of revenge for Hukuwia. But before his own desire came the requirement that he must lead.

His command was loud above the cries of the enemy. "Loaders to the top of the path now."

Paskepaho was on his feet beside him.

"Make certain the sentries on the perimeter are not pulled away. Keep them there," Quaqui commanded his son.

And then he turned and ran to the sounds of battle. Screams of the Ottawa were now met by those of the defenders roaring back defiance at death charging up the path. At the wings, swords of flame were shooting out of the muskets and into the night. For a moment, shooters stopped firing to reload but almost instantly the women began to arrive and with more coming, each of them loading and handing a primed musket forward, the shooters spat almost constants balls of destruction into the charging enemy. In the middle were no gouts of flame, only the deadly *whoosh* of arrows flying downward. Below, Quaqui could see little but could make out a mass, even darker than the palely lit night sky, rushing up and rounding the last corner of the path and coming straight at his thin line of defense. Quaqui brought the musket to his shoulder and aimed low at the rushing darkness not twenty yards below him and then slowly squeezed the trigger with loving gentleness. He was rewarded with a loud scream of pain below and then the perception of the mass of darkness below him becoming distorted and cluttered.

"Hit that dark wall coming. All. Do it now. Just shoot into the mass. Make them fall into one another." Quaqui's voice was loud but steady.

Now that he'd been away from the firelight for a moment, his eyes adjusted to the dark and he could see shapes—bodies and arms. Bow strings and musket shots and screams creating a symphony of death. This was the first time since the Ottawa had come to Mascouten Bay seeking Pini that he was able to fight back. The rushing mass was still coming forward, but no longer at a run. It was coming slowly now. He heard another scream and saw one body sway over the edge and then fall off the path.

The Ottawa had gambled on the speed of their rush overwhelming the top and being able to engage the defenders closely in hand-to-hand combat. Now the five guns on either side of Quaqui were firing almost constantly. The loaders were not only there but functioning smoothly in the limited light. And his archers two and three deep in the middle of the path put out a steady stream of fletched death. The Ottawa were close enough to make distinct and complete outlines even against the dark shadow of the cliff's edge. And their fallen were deep enough that those coming behind were having to stumble over them. They were charging toward a wall of death and knew it now. Soon they would quit.

And then one silhouette of darkness leaped high over the fallen bodies and rushed with speed and power straight toward him. As Quaqui jumped one step forward on the path to meet the shadow, blood raged in his body and joy in his head at the gift he was being given. The gift of forgetfulness, even if for just one moment, of the pain that had seared his heart for days.

"Don't shoot him. He's mine!" Quaqui commanded.

Without breaking stride, the Ottawa swung the tomahawk he held above him at Quaqui's head. But the blade never reached its goal. With a simple and swift motion Quaqui brought up the barrel of his empty musket and landed the extended bore of it into the belly of the charging warrior. The force of his own charge brought the barrel through the skin of the Ottawa's stomach and stopped him with breath gone and able to do no more than stagger another step until he fell at his goal—there but helpless.

"Don't kill him. He's mine. I want him alive."

Quaqui motioned to one of the loading squaws.

"Tie him hand and foot. Tie him until the leather cuts into his flesh. Do not let him escape."

Then he turned back to the battle. But there was no battle left.

* * * *

As light came to them from the east, they saw the path littered with Ottawa bodies but none standing save those retreating back down even more rapidly than they had come up.

"Shooters and loaders, stay just where you are and cover those who are going down the path to kill. Archers down the path. Scalp all. If they are alive, scalp them before you cut their throats. Don't go past the bottom of the cliff. We are not enough to lose so much as one of you to some distant firing Ottawa musket."

Quaqui turned to see Paskepaho standing behind him. "Did the sentries stay in place?"

"I held them as you commanded. Several wanted to rush to the path top. Then one sentry fired at an Ottawa trying to scale the cliff. After that it was easy to hold the sentries in place."

"Take me to the one who fired the shot."

Paskepaho walked him to an aging warrior stationed along the water side of the cliff. "This is the one who fired at the climber?"

Quaqui looked on what was certainly the oldest warrior here. His hair was white as a fish's belly. He was thin with shoulders folding inward. But his eyes gleamed with wisdom and just a touch of battle lust, as though even now the thrill of gambling with his own mortality touched his soul.

Quaqui peered over the cliff's edge and saw no body.

"What did you see in the dark that caused you to shoot, Grandfather?"

"Perhaps no more than a memory, my chief."

"Then why fire, Grandfather? Surely time and battle have made you immune to buck fever."

The old man smiled a wry smile. "Your son, Paskepaho, is a forceful young man of skill and admired by the other young warriors you have put on the perimeter. But I could see they were anxious and wanted to run to the known fight. I knew an enemy here would keep them in place, even if it was just one from my memory."

Quaqui gave a short, sharp laugh, the first he'd allowed in a week. "The nation needs wisdom, Grandfather. I'm glad you are here."

After they completed their tour of the perimeter Quaqui led Paskepaho back to the path. The twenty warriors at the top had collected almost forty scalps. Several shook them defiantly at the tree line where they knew the Ottawa looked on in depressed and angry silence.

"Have we lost any?" Quaqui asked no one in particular. He was met with a roar.

"NONE!"

The cry was followed by general cheering.

Quaqui walked to the supine body of the Ottawa prisoner. He was awake now and rolled onto his back with his feet bound and his hands pulled behind him. The hole in his belly where the bore of Quaqui's musket had punctured him was bleeding, but he would not die of it.

He will live, but he will wish the blow had killed him. "Paskepaho, have him dragged to the old French flagpole in the middle of the compound and tie him to it."

Quaqui then looked at the oldest squaw among the loaders. "Mother, you know what to do. Make the circle of wood no closer than six feet from him and four or five feet tall. Then try to find six or eight thin sapling branches as much as twelve or fifteen feet long. Sharpen the ends and lay them under the brush and pointed toward the prisoner. Spread them evenly around the circle."

The woman's eyes had held Quaqui's, attentive but expressionless until he finished. Then she broke into a wide grin. "I know what to do and how to do it." And she departed to execute her task.

CHAPTER 7

AUGUST 21, 1769

Outside Le Rocher

Whether Otussa lived or died was a question to which only Kitchesmanetoa knew the answer. It would be revealed in time. The wound had been cleaned and stuffed with buzzard down to staunch the bleeding. The ball had entered just below the ribs and exited below them as well. It did not appear to have cut the gut, and even if it had, Otussa had fasted for two days before the assault. If the gut wasn't opened by the shot, or if opened was at least clean, then he would live. If not, he would die slowly and in agony. But what was clear was that he would lead this war party no more. That duty now fell to Opawana.

Otussa was awake, his head supported by the trunk of a large oak and his body shaded by its leaves. Opawana approached slowly. He wanted to observe Otussa's face and have a sense of both his strength and his mood before starting the conversation. He was aware that Otussa's eyes followed him closely, almost cautiously. Opawana squatted down beside him but said nothing.

Otussa spoke first. "You were right, cousin. They had planned well. Better than I had guessed. They do not fight like men who know they will die."

"Oh, perhaps they do. Perhaps they fight like men with nothing to live for save a small victory before they depart."

Otussa inhaled sharply and closed his eyes to guard against the pain that momentarily took him. "Perhaps, but they do fight. About that you were right. They were ready for one bold rush. The one who stepped forward to meet Raven's Cry was certainly ready."

"That was Quaqui," Opawana said. "He was the chief of the Mascouten Bay village. We met him when we searched it, but I did not see him when we destroyed his village. Now I understand why."

"Raven's Cry going down was the last thing I saw before the shot hammered me over the edge. Did he get down?"

"No, Raven's Cry did not come back. He penetrated their line and was gone. That was the last any saw of him." Opawana paused for a moment before speaking again. "You know you haven't the strength to lead now. It must be me."

"And what will you do?" Again, the pain registered across Otussa's eyes as he spoke.

"I will do what your father taught us to do. I will wait."

"Wait for what?" Otussa asked.

"Two things. First we must wait for you to have the strength to travel."

"It will be spring before I can ride," he responded.

"You don't have to ride home, Cousin. You know our old friends, the Chippewa, have joined us. Those marvelous birchbark canoes of theirs are on the beach below the rock. They will paddle you up the Des Plaines fork and drag you on a travois across the very short portage to the Chicago River. From there, we can paddle you all the way home. It will only be a matter of weeks before you have the strength for that."

"You said two things." Despite the shade of the oak, Otussa's forehead formed beads of sweat at his efforts to speak.

"That rock has been the salvation of their nation before," Opawana said. "This time it is their death. We will wait until they are forced to come to us."

"How long will you be able to hold our warriors here?"

Opawana said nothing for several minutes. "We lost forty warriors last night. That is almost one in ten. But we still have more than three times the strength of the Illini. They cannot stand against us in open combat. We know it; they know it.

"Winter comes. Before the wisdom of your father we would have left now. Warriors have women and children at home to bring in the corn and beans and squash, but the hunters are needed to bring in game to put up for winter meat. And after such a loss as this their hearts would be gone and they would go with them. That was our way. It has been our way since storytellers had stories to tell. But Pontiac showed us another way."

Opawana looked up into the light dancing between the leaves of the oak in thought of his uncle and what he had taught them all. *With him we took ten of the eleven British forts west of Pittsburgh. And we would have taken Detroit as well, had the French not left us. And how did he do it? He waited and starved the redcoats and their little brothers, the Americans. He taught us hunger can be our ally.*

Otussa's soft moan brought Opawana's attention back to the moment. He looked down at the sweat on his cousin's forehead and the determined grimace on his face.

"So how long can I hold them? That is not the question, Cousin. The question is how long can the memory of your father, the immortal Chief Pontiac, hold them here. And I am certain he can hold them long enough."

"Why are you so certain, Opawana?" The grimace still held Otussa's face but not his voice.

"Because we don't have to wait for them to starve. The Illini may have a winter's worth of food up there. It doesn't matter because what they do not have is water. And I will make certain it remains that way. They will come to die gloriously in battle or wither and die pitifully on that rock. But they will die. Now rest, Cousin. Your efforts will not be in vain. Your father will be avenged." Opawana pointed to the rock rising in the distance. "Not one Illini will get off that rock alive. That is my promise to you and the forty."

* * * *

Opawana found Spotka sitting beside glowing coals, all that remained of his dinner fire, smoking a pipe and watching the last of the day's sun fading from yellow to pink in the western sky behind the rock. Spotka looked up but did not speak until his companion had folded into the earth beside him.

"What happens now?" Spotka asked with the calmness of acceptance.

"We will do as Pontiac taught us, Spotka. We will wait."

"For how long?"

Opawana nodded his head toward the rock looming darker in the western sky. "We lost forty warriors last night, including Otussa."

"He is dead then? Or dying?"

"Oh, he may live. I don't believe the ball opened his bowel. But he does not have the strength to be part of whatever happens now. There will be no more suicide rushes up that path. Not while the Illini have strength. Once they have lost their strength, perhaps then."

"And how long will that be?"

"Spotka, you see what I see and you know this country better than I. But we both know that rock has no water."

"The top is not entirely smooth. There are dips and crevices where rain puddles."

"And how many rains are left in the summer? And how well does the sandstone of the rock hold their water?" Allowing himself a rare smile, Opawana answered his own question. "They will run out, and soon."

"There is always the river. They may lower buckets."

"A good thought, my friend. Thank you for it. I will ensure the Chippewa cut loose any bucket lowered on their side of the rock. A man lives no more than three or four days without water. It will be soon."

The two sat in silence for a few moments before Opawana spoke again. "When you come back, where will you settle?"

"I will go to Mascouten Bay," Spotka answered. "The swamp above it, created by the Sangamon River, is very rich in meat and fish. The land rises slowly to the east, so moving the village from water's edge to the safety of high ground will be easy when the spring floods come. There is forest also to the east and open grazing ground both to the south and across the river. Deer and buffalo will be plentiful. And the river flows easily across the wide shallow created by the swamp. Crossing will never be difficult. It is good land, very good I think."

"Who will join you?"

"There are many of our younger Potawatomi who will bring their women and follow. A few Kickapoo were eying the place as well. I think we will have a village soon enough. Small perhaps, but with the Illini gone, we will not need much strength to hold it."

"And would one Ottawa family be welcome as well?"

Spotka took a long last pull on his pipe and then opened his face to a seldom seen grin. "Opawana, I have come to know you as a fine man and one to whom I owe a debt that cannot be repaid. If the Ottawa is you, you are welcome to my village, my home, from now until the sunset of my life."

Opawana smiled at the answer. Peace and silence remained between them. Silence warmed with the understanding that they would be sharing many years of their lives.

The silence was interrupted by a vague sound carried on the edge of the west wind. Both men inclined their ears, facing westward. The light of a large fire crowned the top of the rock with a yellow glow. The sound came again. It was a scream carried on the wind. Not a cry of jubilation or of warning but of pain and terror. It was too far to hear clearly, but in the evening stillness it became steady and louder until it was clear to both men what they were hearing.

CHAPTER 8

AUGUST 24, 1769

Le Rocher

Raven's Cry stared defiantly at the assembled Illini, his eyes finally coming to rest on the unyielding face of the warrior who had vanquished him. Their glares each carried a message. *You may have bested me in combat, but you won't have the joy of seeing me yield here.* And the simple unspoken response, *we'll see.*

The hands of the vanquished Ottawa were bound behind him but his feet left free to move. He was constrained only by a length of leather thong tied around his neck and then loosely looped around the post buried in the ground. It gave him a lead of three feet from the pole and let him circle at will. The brush and dried wood surrounding him were stacked chest high, six feet from the pole. Save for guards at the perimeter of Le Rocher, every Illini stood watching. The old woman who had originally tied him looked toward Quaqui, who merely nodded his approval. She approached the stacked wood, a firebrand in her hand, and lit the bottom of the pile in several places. The old woman then stepped back, her face suffused in a radiant smile.

The naked Ottawa warrior showed his indifference, stoic and unmoving. But Quaqui knew it would not last. As the flames rose, Raven's Cry's skin took on a glow the color of the fire. He still showed no emotion but started to circle, as though trying to find a place where the burning wood hadn't caught. There was none. When the first blister appeared on his buttocks, he gave in to his pain and cried out. And as every part of him started to blister, his cries turned to screams. As the hair on his head began to smolder, his pubic hair burst into flame and the screams became full throated and nonstop.

The woman who had lit the flame knelt down close enough to the fire to get her hands on one of the long, thin, green branches she had cut and placed on the ground earlier. She raised the pole, and using it like a long spear, shoved the sharpened end into a large blister on the Ottawa's shoulder. The blister popped open and a piece of roasted meat two fingers square flew off his shoulder. The Ottawa fell to his knees momentarily and then rose again to run from the heat.

When the stacked brush collapsed into burning coals, two other women appeared with shovels and scooped coals from the bottom of the fire. They threw them on his feet. The coals bouncing off his legs and feet soon paved his entire pathway with red and glowing embers. The skin on his face was beginning to peel when he went to his knees and seemed unable to rise. One of the women used her shovel to clear a path through the glowing coals, scooped it full, and taking a step toward him, threw her shovel full of glowing embers on his head and shoulders. There were no shouts left in the warrior, who moaned and collapsed facedown to breathe no more.

* * * *

Quaqui had thought roasting the Ottawa would bring him relief from the images of Hukuwia and Makatachinga and all the rest. But it did not. It did nothing. He had no sympathy but neither had he any joy or relief. The only relief he'd had in the days they had been trapped here was during the battle. The joy of killing violently had cleared his mind. Killing slowly did nothing for it.

But now came a problem on which he must focus to save his people. They were low on water. Some of the men who managed to get here had carried water bags, but almost none of the women had. They had all been away when their villages were attacked, not thinking they would be out more than an hour or two gathering whatever it was they sought. So, they had been forced to rely on muddy water settled into the crevices, cracks, and a few pools here on top of Le Rocher. But now even that source was running very low. What they had not drunk was seeping into the sandstone. If a late summer squall did not come soon, they would run out entirely. And doing so meant death either from dehydration or by a suicidal charge down to the river. A few braves might make it but most would not. More importantly, none of the women or children would.

Quaqui looked at Paskepaho beside him. "Bring the old man." As the boy left to follow his father's instructions, Quaqui turned to watch a summer squall darken the southern sky.

In less than two minutes the ancient one was beside him. "You wish to speak with me?"

Quaqui stood watching the dark squall line roll across the horizon. "Will any come in time?"

"Perhaps. That is up to Kitchesmanetoa. I cannot say. But I can say that to rely on that would be to rely on hope. Hope is not a strategy, my chief."

"Tell me what options you see."

"I see only two. First and best, on the far north side of the rock the river runs underneath. We could drop leather buckets on ropes and pull water up from the river."

"And if that doesn't work, what is the other choice?" Quaqui asked.

"Our young men could rappel down that same north face and fill buckets and tie them to ropes to be pulled up. Then they would climb back up other ropes extended down to them. But the cost would likely be great."

Quaqui stared down into a face with skin as wrinkled as a dried leaf. The eyes looked back with the quiet of indifference. "The Chippewa have canoes beached on the river side. Do you think they would leave them unguarded?"

"No, my chief, they would not. They are guarded. They are heavily guarded. And that is why the choice will be so costly. Our young warriors may get down the cliff quietly and they may get the buckets filled and tied to the ropes quickly, but unless the guards sleep, they will be on them by then. Our warriors will be on ropes climbing back up and completely vulnerable. Their lives are the price we will pay for the water."

Quaqui's eyes were called back to the south by a clap of thunder. "Otussa, son of Pontiac, led the Ottawa that came to Mascouten Bay. He is a warrior tried, tested, and bloodied in the war between the French and the British. You're right. Leaving those canoes unguarded is not a mistake he would make. But we have no warriors to lose, Grandfather. Why should we not merely lower the buckets into the river from here and pull them back up full?"

"The guards below will cut the ropes. Then we'll have neither water nor buckets." The quiet indifference of his eyes had not changed.

Thunder rolled past them to the south, pulling Quaqui's eyes away. In a moment he turned back. "Then we must do it when our buckets and ropes are covered by darkness. See how many ropes you can find long enough to drop buckets down the cliff. And see that we have a bucket for each. If we don't have enough, have the women sew some. They'll have horse leather from the beasts I led in."

The old man nodded understanding but did not move.

"You have more you wish to say, Grandfather? Speak."

"It will be almost three weeks until the moon is dark. Tonight, we will have less than half a moon, but it may still be enough for the Chippewa to see and each night after will become brighter."

"We will send the buckets down tonight, just before dawn when men are most attentive to their own peace."

* * * *

The air coming up from the river was cool. The quarter moon was close to setting and gave little light. The light of starry heavens showing down from above also reflected back up from the river. But it did not give enough light to see into the darkness below. The sun had not yet given any light in the east but would very soon, and when it did, the forest would start to fill with sounds and motion, the first being the awkward calls of the young male turkeys as they did their graceless flop from the low branches onto the ground. The drive to find a mate, the drive to renew life, would force them down from their roost, even while the night-hunting coyotes were still about. Those forest noises would awaken the warriors below. Now was the time.

The old man had found or had made ten ropes long enough to drop the one hundred feet to the river. He had also had ten buckets sewn from the horse hide of the beasts Quaqui had brought in. Quaqui had thinned the watch on the front path to ten men. He'd also had all the guards on the periphery give up their muskets in favor of bows. All the muskets the Illini had were with men placed along the water-facing side of Le Rocher, ready to shoot aimlessly into the dark should any of the bucket lines get cut. Perhaps that would push back warriors below trying to cut other lines. They had to retrieve some water or today all of his people would start to weaken.

The portion of Le Rocher that actually hung over the river was no more than forty or fifty feet wide. The ten warriors stood close together and let the ropes down, hand over hand, slowly so the leather buckets were noiseless as they bounced off the side of the rock. As they entered the water, several made small splashing noises. Quaqui frowned but there was nothing to be done. He saw the lines go taut and start to pull downstream as the buckets filled. In moments it would be time to retrieve them.

"Ahhiii!" came a cry from below as one of the warriors holding a rope suddenly had his shoulders pulled forward as his line was jerked down by the unseen enemy below. The warrior did not lose his grip and pulled hard to retrieve the precious water.

"Fire," Quaqui directed his musketeers. And then, "All! Pull them back up now."

Just as he said it the young warrior who was being pulled forward suddenly fell backward on his ass, his line flying up loosely in the air.

Quaqui saw gouts of red flame pour down the cliff from his muskets. Targetless but hopefully intimidating enough to make the enemy crawl back under the cliff and stop reaching out to cut the ropes. In the silence of reloading he could hear the cries and shouting and splashing from the enemy reaching for his buckets. His warriors pulled hand over hand rapidly. There were a few shots back up at them from below, but the Illini, protected by the height and darkness, pulled with all their strength. Others continued to fire down at the Chippewa.

A shout of pain from below announced luck in the random fire into the dark.

And then it was over. Six of the ropes came up neatly cut. One bucket came back up slashed down the side and almost empty. The other three were retrieved but had spilled out half their contents as they hurriedly bounced up the cliff.

None of the Illini were hurt. They had wounded or killed at least one of their enemy. They had retrieved five or six gallons of precious water. But there was no elation. None. They all knew they had failed. There were two hundred parched souls and they had supplied no more than a cup for each.

Quaqui looked at his warriors and took one step back so they could all see his face. "You have done well. If there is a failure, it is mine. I will think through this and plan better for tomorrow. And this is enough to keep us for today. Have all line up in front of the three buckets. Paskepaho, find three small cups. Each will drink in the morning air a cup of this water and thank Kitchesmanetoa for the day."

* * * *

Quaqui, Paskepaho, and Grandfather, the present, the future, and the past of the Illini, all stood together, again watching as an afternoon squall passed them to the south.

"Kitchesmanetoa is unkind again today," the old man said.

"We are his. This land is his. He will not suffer the Ottawa or the Potawatomi or any other to possess it. We are the instrument of his control of this best of lands. We will remain so," Quaqui said.

"If it is to be so, Father, then it is also for us to obtain water," Paskepaho observed.

"Yes, the water is there"—Quaqui nodded to the north end of Le Rocher—"one hundred feet away. We must obtain it."

After long moments of concentration, the old man spoke. "Then are we to take our people to the water, or are we to bring the water to our people?"

"If we all go, it will be slaughter. We cannot face that force"—Quaqui made a sweeping gesture of all before him—"so we must bring the water up. It will be very expensive water, but we must have it. We will have to pay the price."

CHAPTER 9

AUGUST 25, 1769

Outside Le Rocher

Opawana indulged a small, but cruel, smile as he watched the squall sweep across the southern horizon. Again, today there would be no relief for his trapped enemy. He knew they would be weakening by the moment. There was some shade provided on top of Le Rocher by the decaying remains of Fort St. Louis but not enough to offer all shelter from the sun. The sun, on this perfectly pleasant late summer day, was his ally. Moment by moment, and with the constancy of time, it was sucking the energy, the very life, from his enemy. What children there were up there would be collapsing into their mother's arms, and the very same mothers would be waiting listlessly for death or salvation. Today might be the day the weakest would depart. If there were any old ones up there, they would be the first to go. Even the warriors, who would be given the last of the water—certainly if they had any sense it would go to the warriors—would have cracked lips and sleepy eyes. And they would have no choice. Tonight, they would come down for water. They had learned dropping buckets would not work, even in the dark. Tonight, they would come down. For them to come down the path would be suicide and they would know it. They would come off the cliff above the river, but this time they would bring down warriors to protect the buckets. *When they arrive we will be there. Waiting.*

Opawana turned his glance to the side and studied his companion's face. Spotka was studying the southern sky as well. His face was steady and calm and betrayed no sense of his emotions. "They will come down tonight, Spotka."

"Yes, they will come."

"Which way?"

Without hesitation, Spotka responded, "From the cliff. They will send warriors with the buckets this time."

"You don't think they will come down the path."

Spotka turned to level his eyes with those of the Ottawa and smiled. A satisfying smile. "The gods sometimes bring favors. We should be prepared to accept one should it be offered."

"Send fifty of your Potawatomi to be with the Chippewa. I will place the others before the path."

"They will need to use every bush and clump of grass to cover their advance across the open ground. Some of those Illini can shoot well in the moonlight."

"They can move as slowly as they wish. They will have time. All the time between full dark until just before dawn."

CHAPTER 10

AUGUST 25, 1769

Le Rocher

The heat of the day was beginning to cool, shadows starting to lengthen. Quaqui turned, slowly surveying Le Rocher and his people on it. He moved very slowly. The only thing making him move at all was responsibility. His responsibility not just to these people but to the proud history of the Illini. The burden was now his. His alone. It was becoming clear that his responsibility was shifting. When he first arrived, he thought Kitchesmanetoa had brought him here to save his people. But he no longer believed that. If they were to be saved, it was Kitchesmanetoa who must do it. He had done what there was to do and it was not enough. Without water they could not save themselves, and he could not save them from an implacable enemy who fought with a new set of eyes. Indians did not lay siege. Indians fought, preferably by ambush or with overwhelming odds, and then went home to hunt and prepare for winter. Who were these Ottawa who did not seem to care if their own women and children had a winter without meat? These Ottawa who just sat and stayed and waited. And waited. Without water he could not outwait them. And only Kitchesmanetoa could bring water.

But this new knowledge did not free him of responsibility. This land was Kitchesmanetoa's, and he was Kitchesmanetoa's agent. If he could not save these people, then it was for him to make certain Kitchesmanetoa's land did not go to the Ottawa and the Potawatomi and the Kickapoo. And for that he would need others. He would need the French. Yes, these tribes he faced had been allies of the French before the French lost all their land east of the Mississippi to the British. But the French had been friends of the Illini even longer. And the French were still in St. Louis. That made the Illini their closest allies. They would help if he could get word to them. That was the responsibility that drove him now.

As he turned, his eyes took in what remained of his people. The women and children lay in a stupor with flies buzzing around their faces and no more than a periodic wave of the hand to drive them away. His warriors, to whom he had given the last cups of water this morning, all lay at their assigned places but lay so still he knew half were asleep. Well, he would wake them.

"Paskepaho." He spoke the name to get the undivided attention of his son standing beside him. "Go to each of the warriors. Have one in three stay in place and bring all of the others to me. And make certain Grandfather comes as well."

In ten minutes they were there, over sixty warriors representing a tradition of more history than any sitting before him could remember. They were what was left. It was for him to make them understand. He stood facing them all, a tall, proud man in his prime. He brought himself to his full height so all who heard would know they were led by a man of prowess and dignity. As he swept each of them with his eyes they came to stillness, all of their concentration on him.

"We are here, my warriors. Here. At Le Rocher. None of us needs me to tell you how we got here, but we are the fortunate remaining few. We are the Illini. Kitchesmanetoa has asked a strange thing of us. I do not know why it is us he asks, but he does. We are here and it is asked of us. Commanded of us. He has brought us a formidable enemy who fights with overwhelming power and in a strange, new way. And he makes us watch as the life-giving water passes us by, day by day. He brings each of us to this test. A test not just of you but of your nation. And we are the ones he has chosen to represent him and our nation."

No one spoke, but Quaqui could see eyes looking from one to another and he could see postures become more erect. If he could instill purpose, this might just work. If it did not work, at least he could lead them to die for what they saw as a reason.

"You all know the great challenge we face. Kitchesmanetoa does not bring us the water we need for us, our women, our children, our nation to survive. But he brings far better than that. He brings us the ability to get it ourselves."

And then a warrior in the back shouted, "He makes us Illini." And then all sixty plus rose and their voices sang out together, "Illini!" Quaqui looked around Le Rocher. All eyes turned to them. Some perplexed, some smiling, but all awake.

It took him several minutes to calm them all down and then he addressed them again. This time he could sense every ear on Le Rocher tuned to his words. "Tonight, we will get water. We will have to fight for it. They will expect us. We will have to get down the path, fight our way to the river, fill as many buckets as we can, and fight our way back up."

Quaqui stopped speaking for a moment until every eye was again focused on him. "I know what most of you want is to rush down the path, killing all before you. And even if it brings your death, you are thinking that is better than hiding on top of Le Rocher, starving to death."

There were murmurs of agreement. He held up his hands to calm them.

"But while it is a warrior's joy to die gloriously that is not a warrior's purpose. His purpose is to protect the tribe." Quaqui swept his arm in an arc to take in everyone on Le Rocher. "His job is to protect his own. Women and children. And if all of us in this little circle die gloriously, what happens to them? They will all be killed. There are four times as many of our enemies as us. How many of your mothers and sisters will be raped? How many killed slowly? And if we die, they will have that for their destiny, or they will jump to a quick death below. Do you want to see these women"—he again made a motion to encompass all on Le Rocher—"throw your children to their death and then leap to follow them?"

The joyous and foolhardy enthusiasm of young warriors shown just moments ago quieted. He hoped it quieted to a steely resolve that they would need.

"No, my warriors. Battle is not your task. Your task is not to bring your death but their life. And to do that you must bring up water. Now listen closely, my sons and warriors, this will take all of us."

* * * *

The light of the moon was not so great as to shut out the glory of the stars overhead. Not even a cloud separated their beauty from the eyes of the two men who stood at the top of Le Rocher looking east at the campfires of the enemy.

"Grandfather, I will need you here, at the top of the path. The enemy is very wise in the ways of war. They have tested us here and found us too strong for their assault. But they also know we must come tonight for water. And they are wise enough to know that we will no longer trust our buckets with ropes."

"Yes. They know. And you and I know they will be waiting down there, on that little strip of land where the cliff overhangs the river. I don't think just the Chippewa will be there to greet you."

Quaqui was surprised. "Grandfather, did I say I was going down?"

"No, but you are."

"How do you know that?"

"My chief, you have been magnificent. You have given them hope. They will die with hope."

"You think we will not succeed?"

They stood in the cool beauty of the summer night for a long time before the old one responded.

"This afternoon when you spoke, why did you explain to the warriors what choices their women would have if they died?" When Quaqui did not respond, the old warrior asked another question. "Let me ask it another way. To whom were you speaking when you explained?"

A sadness that overwhelmed him rooted Quaqui to the cliff. Just a black outline against a black sky. Something lifeless. But the old one knew and did not speak. The blackness that was Quaqui exhaled slowly until all the air that was in him had come out.

"The women have prepared more buckets and more ropes. Twenty of us will go down to fall upon those who await us on the little spit of beach. Twenty buckets will come down beside us. Once one of our warriors falls on top of the first Chippewa or Potawatomi waiting for us, it will become full-fledged battle. Perhaps we will get a bucket or two filled and the twenty pullers above may get a few up, but none of the warriors will come back. The Ottawa know we are weakened and tired. And they also know that we will weaken our defense of this path in our efforts to bring up water. They will be waiting to see if we are weak enough for them to succeed where they failed a few nights ago."

Quaqui continued, pointing at the blackness below, "At this very moment, their warriors are crawling across that open meadow to be ready to charge up the path again. That is why you must be here: To ensure the young warriors do not abandon guardianship of the path and try to come help in the fight on the beach below. To make certain they do not rush down the path to a glorious death. To make certain they hold this path until the last of them falls."

For the only time since Quaqui had known him, the old man seemed puzzled. "If all who go down the cliff will die, why do you go? You are needed here. Remember what you told the warriors. Their deaths must have a purpose."

"Grandfather, we will all die here. All of us. But your death and mine will have purpose. Yours will be to ensure the Ottawa do not get up this path in the dark and take our women and children. They must have time to jump. To make their deaths quick and painless. And my job will be to see that the Ottawa and the Potawatomi do not hold Kitchesmanetoa's land. That they do not hold the land of the Illini."

"If we all die, Quaqui, how will you accomplish that?"

"One will get away. That will be Paskepaho. He must get to St. Louis and the French. He is my son. The last Illini chief. He can speak for us. He must ensure that the French do not let them stay. That our enemies do not thrive on the land Kitchesmanetoa has given to the Illini."

Now it was the old man who froze to stone against the night sky. "It is a terrible burden to impose on any man, much less one so young."

"Grandfather, it is not I who puts such a burden on Paskepaho's back. Kitchesmanetoa puts it there."

* * * *

"Father, I am pleased you included me among the nineteen to go down with you. I will not fail you or embarrass you. You know that or you'd not have selected me."

They stood looking down into the inky black below. The light of the not-yet-set moon created depth and shadow on their faces, but it was low enough that the trees stopped its light at the base of the cliff. There was darkness below. Quaqui had to look down slightly, just slightly, to peer into his son's eyes. He could see excitement and pride there and perhaps just a touch of fear. *But then Paskepaho is not a fool. Courage is not lack of fear. Lack of fear is madness. Courage is feeling fear and overcoming it.*

"Walk with me, my son." Quaqui turned and walked away without acknowledgment. When he had traveled twenty paces away from the group of warriors gathered at the edge of Le Rocher, he slowed and put his arm around the shoulders of the youth and walked a few paces more. He was as far away from others as the confines of Le Rocher's top would allow when he stopped and turned to face Paskepaho.

"What you are about to do is the hardest thing you will ever have to do. But it is required."

"I know, Father," the youth said solemnly.

"No, Paskepaho. No, you do not know." He looked into his son's now puzzled face. "You are not going down that cliff to fight."

"But, Father."

Quaqui cut him off before he could say more. "What you are doing, my son, is far more difficult than that. And what's more, you must do it alone." He could see Paskepaho's face become ever more puzzled. "You are leaving."

The face changed instantly to defiance. "I will not!" he said with a firmness that surprised and pleased his father.

Quaqui did not growl or command. He merely said, "It is required of you. Not by me but by the nation that is the Illini."

Paskepaho's face changed once more in the moonlight. The face was all of confusion.

"Listen to me, my son. We will all die here. No. Say nothing. Just listen. They will meet us at the bottom. They will know we are coming. They know we have no choice. If we do not get water by this time tomorrow, they will simply walk up the path and kill us all. They know that. They know we must come. And we may get a bucket or two of water up. But that is not why we go down."

"Then why?"

"We go down to get our messenger into one of those very fast Chippewa canoes. The messenger who will go to the French. The French who are ever our friends. Only the French can save Kitchesmanetoa's land from the Ottawa and the Potawatomi and their allies. And that messenger is you. You must speak for all the Illini. You must rip our land from the victorious fingers of your enemies."

There was a long stillness between them in the quiet silver light of the moon before Paskepaho spoke.

"Father, if we all die here, who will be left for the French to give the land to?"

"That I do not know, my son, but I know who they must take it from. Your job is to make certain that happens. That the Potawatomi and the Kickapoo and the Ottawa do not live here. Who does live here is for Kitchesmanetoa to decide.

"We go down now. Stay with me. We, you and I, will get past the beach to a canoe and get you off. You must get at least a musket shot away from the shore before daylight. Travel near the far bank in the shadow of the trees when possible."

"Where is St. Louis?"

"Once the Illinois joins the Mississippi, stay toward the right bank. You will know the Missouri when you cross it because it is as wide as the Mississippi and as muddy as the Mississippi is clean. As soon as you cross the mouth of the Missouri, St. Louis will be on the right bank. Once there, insist you have messages from the principal chief of the Illini and they will take you to the governor. Now come. It is time to go down."

He embraced his son. A long embrace. And then turned and strode erect and strong to the waiting warriors. The ropes of the descending warriors were each fixed to a rock or some still unrotted portion of the old fort. Each warrior had a musket strapped to his shoulder and close fighting weapons in his belt. Most preferred tomahawks but a few carried war clubs. All had scalping knives. Quaqui handed the rope adjacent to him to his son, looked at each of the others, and then slid over the side. Quaqui was astonished that all landed quietly on the small spit of land. He gave a hard tug on his own rope, the designated signal to those above, and almost instantly ten buckets slid down the cliff to their right. The two warriors closest to the buckets started filling them. The others turned to the left along the slip of beach to hold against any attack.

As they did, the night sky opened with a roar of flame and explosions as muskets fired almost in unison from their left. The first screams of his warriors were in pain, and four fell onto the sand. Instantly his other warriors screamed their war cries and rushed into the night down the small strip of beach. Paskepaho screamed with them and started to rush by.

Quaqui gripped his shoulder hard. "No. With me. Remember. You must."

Beside the screams and yells of grappling warriors, Quaqui moved his son out into the river until they were chest deep. On the beach behind them, flashes of light from fired muskets showed his remaining warriors, shoulder to shoulder, their rush met by a body of warriors whose mass extended deeper into the night than the fire from Illinois muskets penetrated. While it showed him the force waiting for them was overwhelming, it also illuminated their path. He could see the silhouettes of canoes just up the beach and no Chippewa warriors guarding them. He pulled his feet up from the bottom and with a gentle but powerful stroke pulled himself forward in the water.

Any noise they made swimming was covered by the screams of pain and triumph just twenty feet to their left. Heads low, they silently pulled past the violence of death just feet away. There was no longer musket fire to illuminate their path, but down against the water, the setting sliver of a moon gave light enough to see they were near the last of the canoes. Quaqui changed the direction of his strokes and pulled himself onto the beach, motioning Paskepaho to remain with his head above the water. Quaqui felt in the bottom of the last canoe to make certain there was a paddle. With jubilation his exploring fingers found the prize he sought. He immediately stood taller to drive power into his legs and pulled on the gunnel of the canoe to slide it off the beach and into the river. It cleared the beach to flotation just as it reached Paskepaho, who with the lithe strength of youth pulled himself over the gunnel and into the boat. Paskepaho unslung his musket and placed it in the bottom of the boat. Finding the paddle and picking it up, he kneeled in the rear of the birchbark canoe. Quaqui also unslung his musket and dropped it into the boat, along with his powder horn and shot bag. *The powder will be wet but tomorrow Paskepaho can dry it all and have two loaded weapons to use.* Quaqui gave one hard shove to push his son toward the current without even a word of goodbye. Then he pulled his tomahawk from his belt and stepped to the next canoe.

The last he saw was his son's strokes pulling the boat into the current and pointing it downstream. Paskepaho needed to be gone into the safety of the night quickly. Quaqui stepped to the next canoe and with one powerful blow of his tomahawk punctured the bottom of the craft. And then the next.

With each stroke he reduced the chance of pursuit overtaking the last hope of the Illini. And each stroke took him closer to the dying sounds of struggle up the beach. He could hear the victorious cries of the Chippewa as they slaughtered the last of his warriors. He was now close enough to strike the Chippewa in the rear, but it was the remaining two canoes he needed to strike. He had to get them both. With only a few minutes' start, Paskepaho would be overtaken before dawn by any four men paddling any of these canoes. His tomahawk swung past the shoulder of the closest warrior and smashed into the bottom of one of the two remaining canoes. Even in the near dark the warrior turned to the threat. Quaqui raised his tomahawk from the bottom of the boat and with a backhand motion smashed it into the jaw of a warrior, not a Chippewa but an Ottawa. *I was right. They knew we were coming.*

The Ottawa cried in pain as he fell, a warning to the two closest warriors, who turned instantly to stare into the glimmering light at the threat poised behind them. Quaqui knew he had to cripple that last canoe. Instead of facing his enemy he vaulted over the canoe he'd just struck to land in the middle of the remaining one. His back to his enemies, he swung the tomahawk into the bottom of the last canoe just as he felt an immense blow on his back. The blow caused him to stagger forward into the canoe, his thighs against the prow the only thing holding him upright. The last thing Quaqui felt was the overwhelming power and pain of another blow on his back and then the cool comfort of the water of his river as he fell into it.

CHAPTER 11

AUGUST 26, 1769

Illinois River

When Paskepaho reached midriver, he paused to look back. The sun was rising, and Le Rocher stood clear against the morning sky. On the wind, his ears still gave him the war cries of the enemy. His eyes showed him a scene more surreal than horrifying. It was the outlines of women and children along the edge of Le Rocher. As he watched, one of the outlines picked up a small child and held it with tenderness he could feel even from this distance. And then, like a fledgling hawk, she pushed out of the nest. But unlike the hawk she did not soar. She and her precious bundle held motionless in the sky for just a moment and then fell, accelerating as they descended until their flight disappeared into the earth. As Paskepaho watched in agony, unable to look away, the dance with death continued, as one after another, the silhouettes stepped off the cliff and into oblivion.

Paskepaho's eyes filled with tears, knowing he was watching more than individual deaths. He was watching the death of a nation. His nation. As he dropped his eyes from Le Rocher, the fracturing of light through his tears brought him a speck of red vivid on the water. He blinked back to focus and saw floating slowly toward him the shafts of two arrows fletched with black and red and held erect by the back of the corpse on which they floated. He did no more than drop his paddle into the water as a rudder to point the canoe toward the floating corpse and let it drift alongside.

Even before he pulled the hair of the floating thing up, he knew what he would see. The passive and oddly relaxed face of his father floated beside him. Paskepaho was now truly alone. All he loved was gone. He had nothing left. Just as the thought came into his mind, however, he knew it was not true.

I do have something left. I have duty. That is what I have. That is my fate. Duty to my father. Duty to the Illini. Duty to Kitchesmanetoa. And I will do it. I have nothing else.

He hoisted the corpse that was his father into the boat. His first duty would be to release the soul of this brave and valiant man who was his father. The last principal chief of the Illini. He would do it this evening when he was far enough away to build a fire unseen. Then he would go to St. Louis and do as he had been charged by this man who now lay dead at his feet. He would ensure that if the Illini could not have this land, then neither could their enemies. He would make this the land of the Illini, even if just in memory. He would do it if it took his entire life.

He turned one last time to look back at Le Rocher. And he saluted it. *Goodbye, Starved Rock. The last stand of the Illini nation.*

PART II

"When a white man kills an Indian in a fair fight it is called honorable, but when an Indian kills a white man in a fair fight it is called murder. When a white army battles Indians and wins it is called a great victory, but if they lose it is called a massacre and bigger armies are raised. If the Indian flees before the advance of such armies, when he tries to return, he finds that white men are living where he lived. If he tries to fight off such armies, he is killed and the land is taken anyway. When an Indian is killed it is a great loss which leaves a gap in our people and a sorrow in our heart; when a white is killed, three or four others step up to take his place and there is no end to it. The white man seeks to conquer nature, to bend it to his will and to use it wastefully until it is all gone and then he simply moves on, leaving the waste behind him and looking for new places to take. The whole race is a monster who is always hungry and what he eats is land."

—Chiksika, Shawnee warrior and
brother of Tecumseh

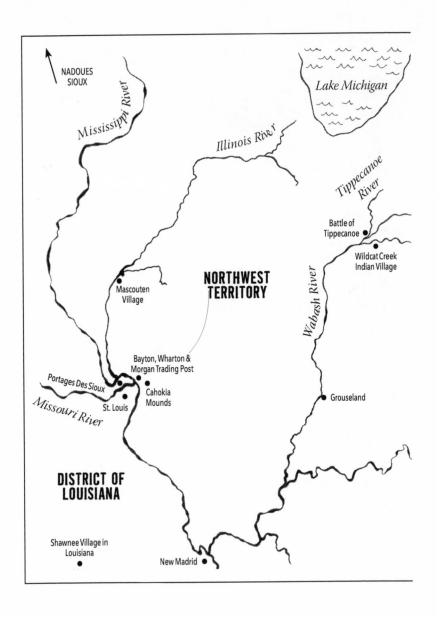

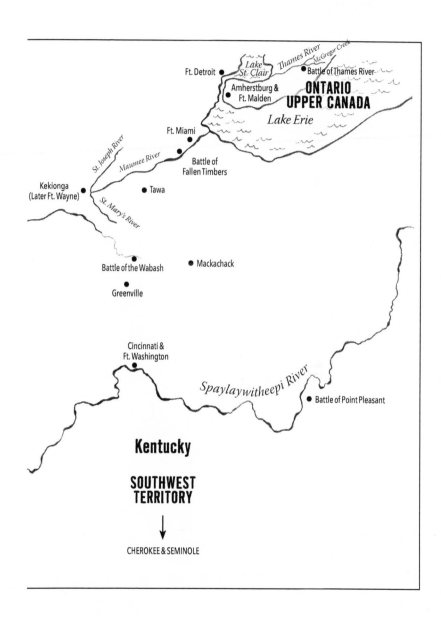

CHAPTER 12

OCTOBER 11, 1787

Northwest Territory near Mascouten Bay

Opawana sat motionless looking eastward to where the trail came out of the marsh surrounding Mascouten Bay. Even his horse seemed to sense the tension and did not so much as swat his luxurious chestnut tail at the buzzing flies. The motion of a single rider had attracted his attention long before he could make out who or what the rider was. By the time he could see the cloth bandana holding back long hair and the single feather distinctively in the front, rather than the rear, to mark him as Shawnee, fully nine other riders had come out of the head-high grass. Once he was certain of their number he turned to the young brave beside him and said, "Chaubenee, go back to the village and tell Spotka what we've seen coming. I'll wait here."

"Yes, Father," came the voice, oddly deep and full for one so young. He turned his horse sharply, causing Opawana to bark, "Slowly, Son. Slowly until you are out of sight. Only then put on speed." The order was given in his usual commanding way, but he offered a small smile to his son.

In many ways, Chaubenee was so clearly his mother's child. He had none of his father's distinctly Ottawa features—thin, hawklike face and nose, lithe body, and severe demeanor. The one facial feature he shared with his father was the eyes, over-large like a young fawn's. Other than that, he was all Seneca, his mother's tribe. Huge, powerful shoulders, thick waist and torso, full lips and nose, and boundless goodwill.

At five feet eight inches he was still three fingers shorter than his father, though at fully two hundred pounds he was already one of the strongest warriors in the village. Few, even those Opawana's age, would wrestle with young Chaubenee. But in what counted most, character, he was a copy of his father. Fearless in combat and counsel, Chaubenee moved through life as a force with which others must contend. At only fifteen, he had become an extraordinary young man.

Opawana watched Chaubenee go, then turned and watched the Shawnee grow larger as they came toward him. He did not think they were trouble. There was no conflict between the Potawatomi and Shawnee. *Unless this group is a small lead party for a much larger expedition, they are certainly not here to do damage. But they are all young warriors—no women, no children, and no older men. You can never be certain with a party of young warriors. I'll be happy if Spotka and a few warriors arrive before the Shawnee get within bowshot.*

But Opawana wasn't moving. He would show no fear or even concern and greet the Shawnee graciously as was expected.

As they came closer, he became even more assured of their peaceful intentions. They did not fan out in a way that would flank him. They stayed on the trail two abreast. The first two interested him. The leader was a man of about thirty years of age and clearly a warrior of authority. Opawana didn't even need to hear him speak to know that. His carriage was extremely erect, giving him the appearance of more height than Opawana guessed he would show standing on the ground.

But it was the rider beside him who held Opawana's attention. He was a younger, more muscular version of the lead warrior—Opawana guessed not more than eighteen years—with the same erect carriage and sense of self-confidence. It was the younger man's eyes, though, that intrigued Opawana. His eyes were already studying Opawana as Opawana studied him. Neither hostile nor fearful, just learning. Even at this distance, his eyes were almost hypnotic.

Opawana heard the riders coming behind him. They came with shouts that were louder than the hoofbeats of their running horses. When they were almost to him, he heard the hoofbeats of their horses slow and fan out wide across the prairie. Opawana glanced to his left and right. There were perhaps twenty Potawatomi on either side of him. Chaubenee came up on his right, and he knew without looking that Spotka would be on his left. The Shawnee neither quickened their pace nor in any other way changed their approach. When they were within the length of a horse, the leader stopped and motioned his followers to fan out on either side of him as well.

Only when that was done and the two lines of horsemen faced one another did the Shawnee speak.

"Greetings to the Potawatomi of Mascouten Bay from the Shawnee nation. I am Chiksika, son of Pucksinwah and ward of Chiungalla. This is my younger brother," he said, motioning to the young warrior with the expressive eyes, "Tecumseh."

It was Spotka who responded. "I am Spotka, chief of this small Potawatomi village. I knew of your father. He had a great name among all the tribes of the Great Lakes. He led us thirteen years ago at the Battle of Point Pleasant against Lord Dunmore. With great courage and skill."

Chiksika's lips gave away nothing of his thoughts, but his eyes gave a small flicker of appreciation of the reverence paid to his father. "I carried him from battle that day and stuffed buzzard down into his wound but to no avail. As is the custom of the Shawnee when our war chief dies, his children are adopted by our Second Civil Chief. That was Chiungalla, and Tecumseh and I are his wards."

"And what brings us the honor of your presence?" Spotka asked.

"We are not emissaries of our nation, Chief Spotka. We are merely here on a youthful journey."

"Then you are welcome to our village. Come with us. We'll take you to the *miskahmiqui*. Currently, we have no other visitors. There is room for all. This evening after you've rested, we will have a feast for the village. You can tell us more of your journey then."

Spotka wheeled his horse, as did Opawana, and they led their guests into the Potawatomi village at Mascouten Bay.

* * * *

The coals in the long pits glowed bright red and periodically snapped small shoots of flame as fat dripped from the roasting deer spitted above. The pits were lined with bubbling iron pots filled with corn and beans sizzling to completion. Several hundred men, women, and children sat in small groups along the edges of the pits, warmed against the cool breeze flowing off the river curving slowly around the village. A three-quarter moon lit the whole area with enough light that all could see from the first firepit to the last.

Opawana sat with Spotka and a group of village elders. He had invited Chiksika and his younger brother, Tecumseh, to join them. Each of the other Shawnee had been invited to one or another group of diners. Normally, each family would dine on their own, but tonight Spotka had ordered a village feast for the sole purpose of letting all hear the young Shawnee's story.

Spotka rose from the blanket on which he sat, stepped to the nearest pit, and banged loudly on one of the iron pots with the flat of his tomahawk. Slowly conversation died and when all was still, Spotka spoke.

"You all know we have been honored with a visit from ten fine young Shawnee warriors. The Shawnee have ever been our friends and allies. They have stood first in line as the Shemanese, the white soldiers with long knives that hang from their belt to their ankles, have come down the Spaylaywitheepi River from the other side of the mountains. In the beginning the Shemanese were British. Now, it appears, it is their younger brothers of the Thirteen Fires that come seeking our land."

There was a general grumbling. Spotka waited until he had silence to continue. "This group is led by Chiksika, eldest son of the well-remembered and admired war chief of the Shawnee, Pucksinwah, who led us, as well as the Miami, Delaware, Opawana's Ottawa, and his own Shawnee in the Battle of Point Pleasant against Lord Dunmore's invasion."

There were shouts of acclamation and again Spotka waited for silence. "This afternoon, he told me their visit was merely a 'youthful journey.' I said only after he had rested would I ask him to tell us of this 'youthful journey.' Chiksika and his party have rested and spent the evening drinking with us, and I think it is time, before we eat, for all of us to hear their story."

And with a nod to his guest, he said, "Chiksika, tell us all." And Spotka sat back down beside Opawana.

Chiksika rose with easy grace from his cross-legged position and when at full height took two steps backward until he was at the edge of the light and could face all two hundred villagers.

"Thank you, Spotka, and thank you, Potawatomi, for your grace and hospitality. You know by now that we are ten young warriors. I the oldest and my brother, Tecumseh, the youngest. We travel to meet all our neighbors, both those who are allies and those who are not, in the entire Great Lakes region and then south to the tribes of Tennessee and Alabama. We do it now because all of our lives we have had to stay close to home and be at war, or ready for war, with the Shemanese. We have not had the usual opportunities young men do to get to know those around us. But now we have a small window of time in which to do so, and we plan to use it.

"Let me explain why I say 'small window.' When I was five years old, long before the coming of the Thirteen Fires, in a time when we were asked to think of the King of England as our 'Great Father,' he proclaimed that none of his white subjects could cross the Appalachian Mountains, everything on this side of them being honored as Indian lands. Then only five years later, the British declared that we, all of us, were subjects of the Iroquois Confederacy."

There was general noise of objection and anger. Chiksika was content to wait for the noise to subside, knowing the etiquette that a speaker be allowed to speak.

"I don't say it is right, my brothers. I just say it is." He paused momentarily. "Within a moon of the British declaring our land belonged to the Iroquois, rather than to us, the Iroquois conveniently sold all of 'their land' west of the Appalachians to the British. We hear the price was ten thousand pounds sterling. A considerable sum.

"Before the year was out, Sir William Johnson himself, the King's agent to all his red subjects, came to the Shawnee and told us that all whites were forbidden from marking trees by cutting chips out of the bark—their way of showing personal ownership. Johnson said we had the right to kill any we caught doing it. The land was the King's and the King's only. No white individuals were allowed to own it.

"Less than five years later the leaders of the Thirteen Fires have sent parties to survey, that is, to measure and drive stakes in Mother Earth's heart, so she can be divided into small pieces and sold. Mother Earth made a slave to men!"

Again Chiksika waited for the roar of anguish to subside before he continued. "That is what his surveyors did all down the Spaylaywitheepi River, along both north and south shores, as they were ordered. And in the year of my father's death the King sent Lord Dunmore's army down the Spaylaywitheepi to invade our land for the sin of killing surveyors, which the King's agent, Sir William Johnson, had instructed us was our right.

"Within two years of the Battle of Point Pleasant, the Thirteen Fires rebelled from their Great Father, and a Virginian named George Rogers Clark formed an army of Kentuckians and captured most of the British forts south of the Great Lakes and east of the Mississippi River. The Virginia fire declared the land theirs and called it the Illinois County of Virginia. Shortly, the armies of the Thirteen Fires defeated the King's armies. The Virginia fire gave the lands conquered by Clark to the government of all the fires: America, as they now call themselves.

"But the Americans tell us not to worry. They say that just this year they have made a law they call the 'Northwest Territory Act,' which says no Indian lands may be taken without our consent. But at the same time the Shemanese have opened a 'land office' in Louisville, Kentucky, to accept the claims of whites for Indian land. This 'Northwest Territory Act' was said to have stopped the pressure from whites trying to steal our lands. But tell me, Brothers, do you think it will?"

There was a roar of "NOOO!" from two hundred voices.

"You are right. Of course, it will not. But we have some time to prepare before war starts again. And our way of preparing is to come to know all of our neighbors. To find out in what ways they are like the Shawnee and in what ways they are different. Perhaps we can learn from each other and maybe become stronger together.

"Before I sit down and let the women slice the deer and ladle up the corn and beans, let me say one more thing about why we have time."

Chiksika looked down at Spotka, a look of real affection on his face. "About one thing Spotka said, he is in error."

Opawana saw a startled look cross his chief's face as he held his breath in anticipation of what would come next.

"I am not my father's oldest son. I am the oldest born of his wife. But when I was fifteen my father captured a boy in Virginia. He was two years older than I and an odd white in many ways. When my father's party came on the boy, he was armed and had his ten-year-old brother with him. The armed Virginia boy knew he could kill one of the party. He also knew if he did, both he and his brother would be killed in retaliation. So, he made an offer. He would give up his gun and come with the Shawnee to whatever fate awaited him if Pucksinwah would let his brother go. It was agreed.

"All the way up the New River and down the Spaylaywitheepi, the white lad took whatever abuse was heaped upon him. He tried to learn our language, and once he had a few words, he made it clear he wanted to be adopted. He wanted to be Shawnee. My father liked him and thought he might do so. But when the war party got back to our village, the white boy had to do what all captives must do—run a gauntlet. Three hundred villagers lined up with switches, sticks, and in some cases, limbs, formed two lines about five feet apart, the lines ending at the pole in front of the *miskahmiqui*. If the captive got to the pole alive, my father agreed to adopt him. The white youth was very fast and quick and had strength and courage. He ran like a bat chasing mosquitoes. He took some blows—I know because I hit him with a raspberry vine than left nettles on his hip—but he dodged most. It looked like he would reach the post. When he was within twenty feet of his goal, a warrior armed with a small tree branch stepped into his running lane and swung full force at his head. The youth ducked the blow, wrenched the limb from the warrior's hand, knocked him down with it, and raced to the pole. We all cheered his courage wildly.

"My father adopted him. His name is Blue Jacket, and he is now one of our most revered warriors. I think someday he may replace our father as war chief of the Shawnee. After we heard about the new Northwest Territory Act, Blue Jacket went to Kentucky by himself to the home of one of our fiercest opponents. He risked immediate death in doing so. But he still has some skill with his native tongue. They worked out a prisoner swap. It was not easy and it did not go without problems, but the Shawnee returned all prisoners who had not been adopted and the whites returned all their captives, including my nephew Spemica Lawba. We will have peace for a while. I think perhaps two or three years.

"And so, for two or three years, my friends and I will have a youthful journey and hope to learn much that will help us in the battles to come. Much we hope to learn from the Potawatomi."

CHAPTER 13

OCTOBER 12, 1787

Mascouten Bay

Chaubenee rose in silence from the shadows, his bow string pulled taut, the arrow's fletching next to his ear. He released the arrow. It hit the doe just behind her shoulder. She sprang upright, took two steps, stumbled, and fell to rise no more. He'd seen Tecumseh rise and loose an arrow just as he did, his arrow striking between the third and fourth ribs of the young stag, which dropped like a stone with no motion but its falling. Within seconds he'd seen Tecumseh draw a second arrow, turn slightly toward the whitetail running straightaway from him, and shoot. His second arrow landed just below the raised tail. The beast staggered a step, righted itself, and stumbled on.

Tecumseh jumped up, dropping his bow and quiver as he cleared the brush behind which he'd been concealed. As he trotted across the meadow to follow the wounded doe, Chaubenee heard him shout. "Chaubenee, start cleaning the two we dropped. I'll go fetch the third. Her wound is mortal. She'll bleed out quickly."

* * * *

Around the fire that evening, as Chaubenee sat looking through the haze of the smoke, he received a rare smile from his father. Opawana's wide white teeth showed as he addressed his son. "You had a good hunt this morning. Two doe and a young buck and back before midmorning."

Chaubenee's face beamed the joy of receiving praise from his stern father. "He is a very good hunter, Father."

"You are not?" came a response wrapped in what was almost a snarl.

"Oh, you have taught me very well, Father. I killed the doe quickly and cleanly."

"Then why do you speak so of your hunting partner, Tecumseh?"

Chaubenee took a sip from his cup of whiskey, adjusted his back to a post of the *wegiwa* and responded slowly. "Last night at dinner, Tecumseh asked if I'd take him hunting in the morning so he could contribute to the larder. And of course, I agreed. It would give me a chance to get to know one of our Shawnee guests a bit. He was waiting in front of the *miskah-miqui* when I came to collect him just as grey appeared in the eastern sky. While we rode toward the marshland, Tecumseh said he'd like to learn the land and would be grateful if I'd let him lead. Simple politeness required a yes, and when we got to the trees around the eastern edge of the marsh we both dismounted and tied the horses.

"I, of course, knew the way to the meadow of most likely early morning grazing but deferred leadership as I'd promised. Tecumseh followed the tree line along the edge of the grass. When we passed a deer trail he studied it for a moment and then went on. When we came to a second, again he studied the bent blades but then oddly turned back the way we had come and quickly made his way back to the horses and then continued on along the tree line but in the opposite direction. This time when he came to a trail he got on his knees and studied it closely. Then he rose and began to follow that trail through the trees. It led to the meadow I would have selected based on prior knowledge. Tecumseh found it in no more than half an hour more than had I led us there directly.

"We arrived at the meadow as the sun was rising. I selected a well-hidden blind I knew was there. Tecumseh found his own not twenty yards from me and covered himself so thoroughly that even knowing he was there I could not see him. Nor did I hear one sound from his blind for three quarters of an hour.

"When the first doe appeared, we each knew to wait, as more of the harem and finally the buck would appear. The buck was young and his harem small. Just two does came into the meadow. He arrived shortly thereafter. When he did, we rose and fired simultaneously and each dropped ours—his the buck and mine one of the does—with instantly fatal shots. As the second doe fled, Tecumseh got off a wing shot at a running target and hit the white circle around her ass right in the middle. Knowing she would bleed out quickly from such a wound, he dropped his bow and quiver and trotted after her. He was back, with the doe draped over his shoulder, before I got the buck gutted and cleaned.

"A good, very good, hunter."

Opawana sat without motion or expression during Chaubenee's entire dissertation. When Chaubenee finished, his silence continued for a full minute.

"It appears from short observation that the sons of Pucksinwah do proud the memory of their father. Both are impressive. The older shows wisdom and has oratorical skills. He says Blue Jacket will replace his father. If he is a better leader than Chiksika, the Shawnee are indeed blessed with much talent among their young warriors. The younger is just that, young. That he shows skill with weapons and in hunting doesn't prove he will be a successful warrior, but it is a good start."

The father and son were silent, bathed in the warmth of the dying fire and the love of one another. Words would not enhance that warmth.

When Chaubenee spoke, it was to seek the wisdom of an elder whose intellect he revered. "Father, do you think Chiksika is right?"

"About what, Son?"

"Do you think the Americans will continue to come? Will we have to fight them?"

"Since I was a young man and a follower of Pontiac, I have fought the whites. They are many and they want two things we have—beaver and land. For almost ten years the British and their descendants, the Americans, busied one another with warfare. The Thirteen Fires are a young man who has overpowered his father. The father did strike many blows before losing, and it will take the son time to recover. And when he does recover, he will come in the strength and vigor of undefeated youth. I do not know that we can defeat them, but I know they will come. And I know I will fight to the death. I hope you will join me. Perhaps you will be victorious."

Again, the son sipped his whiskey, pondering the words he'd requested but now was not certain how to process.

"Father, be assured your fight is my fight and to the death. And for it I must prepare. Do you think joining the young Shawnee and using this peace to meet the tribes from the Great Lakes to the great water to the south will help me prepare?"

"Pontiac succeeded against the British not alone but in confederation with other tribes. No tribe can defeat the Shemanese alone." And then there was a long pause before

Opawana answered the question. "Yes, I think Chiksika is wise. He is your best preparation."

A smile spread across Chaubenee's broad face. "Then I have your permission to ask Chiksika if I may join them?"

Chaubenee thought his father's response would be instantaneous, but his father sat as stone in the smoke. When he spoke, his words were ominous. "Yes, you may ask. But beware Tecumseh."

"Why, Father?"

"He is flawed. He drinks too much."

* * * *

"If you're looking for Tecumseh he's inside the *miskahmiqui* sleeping it off. It seems that last night after dinner he had a brief romance with a jug of whiskey."

Chaubenee stared into the fresh, clean face of Chiksika. It wore a slightly bemused smile that relieved his normally sober countenance of some of its power. Chiksika was of modest height at a few fingers under six feet. His eyes were not hostile but cool, taking in much and giving away little. He wore his brown hair long and straight and, as was the Shawnee custom, crowned with a bright cloth bandana rolled some three fingers in width with a single eagle feather planted into the front of the bandana and sticking back over his head. His nose was regular and straight and his lips full, almost sensuous. Chaubenee paused for a moment before responding. It was the second time in twelve hours he'd heard reference to Tecumseh's fondness for drink, something he had not personally observed. It seemed incongruous with the skilled and disciplined young warrior whom he was coming to know and thus far, not only liked, but found entirely admirable.

"No, Chiksika, it is not Tecumseh I come seeking but his older brother. Is he available for a talk and perhaps a walk along the river?"

Chiksika smiled faintly at the formality of the request. "My time is yours, Chaubenee. Where shall we walk?"

Chaubenee turned without another word and walked toward the river, and when he arrived turned away from the Mascouten Bay and slough it protected and walked downriver along a well-beaten path. It was not until after they had passed through the village, with its canoes pulled up onto the beach, that Chaubenee spoke again. This time with an almost forced tone of congeniality. "I was much impressed with your address the night of your arrival. May I ask where you plan to go after you leave the Potawatomi?"

"Next we will go north first and west a bit to visit the Fox and the Sac. They have ever been friends of the Shawnee. We have fought common enemies on occasion. If we arrive before the snows, they will no doubt be sending war parties against their enemies, the Osage." He broke his comments for a moment, looked at Chaubenee walking beside him, and gave a small smile. "Perhaps an additional ten warriors will be welcome."

Chaubenee stopped entirely. As Chiksika stopped to continue conversation, Chaubenee turned and squared his shoulders to him and looking directly into Chiksika's face said, "Would eleven be even more welcome?"

Chiksika said nothing but stared into the large, expressive eyes. He could see nothing there but intentional control. "Why would you join us? Just to kill Osage?"

Chaubenee turned back to the path and continued walking. In the stillness, a wren could be heard making beautiful music that both warriors knew to be a battle cry warning all others away from his territory. Chaubenee allowed himself a smile when he spoke. "Combat is a natural thing to males of all species. Even now we hear the smallest of warriors calling out this challenge. And while all young warriors wish to test themselves and to earn scalps and renown, no, Chiksika, that is not the reason." He walked a few more paces and then stopped again. "You said war was coming with the whites; you said it would be several years but it would come; you said you were preparing by learning the land and even more by learning the peoples of the land. Is that not what you said, Chiksika?"

The elder warrior merely nodded his assent.

"My father," Chaubenee continued, "was with Pontiac from the beginning. And he knew that despite the Ottawa war chief's courage, wisdom, and skill, what made him win against the mighty British was his alliance with many of the tribes of the Great Lakes—Ottawa, Potawatomi, Miami, Chippewa, Mingo, Wyandot, Delaware, and yes, even the great Shawnee. My mother is a Seneca, one of the five tribes of the great Iroquois Confederacy. Before Pontiac's league, theirs was the strongest and most powerful Indian force."

Chiksika stopped abruptly and made a harsh, guffawing sound. And then he looked directly at his companion and spoke in hard tones. "Do you know who created the Iroquois? It was my great-grandfather, Opeththa." Chiksika looked down for a moment. When he looked back up he had regained control of himself. "My people, the Shawnee, are from the south. White men still attach our name to a river far, far south in the peninsula that extends into the southern sea. We have always been fierce and frequently wandering warriors and frequently called by others to assist." His tone was calm, soft, tutorial now. "Almost exactly one hundred years ago, your mother's people, the Seneca, were warring with the Miami. As was always the case then and often still is, it was over beaver and trade with the whites. The Seneca were strong, even alone, and the Miami feared they would be destroyed. Opeththa was chief of the Kispoko sept of the Shawnee, and that position is always the war chief of all Shawnee. The Miami sent Opeththa a wampum belt, offering his wandering warriors ownership of the Scioto River Valley if they would come defend it. They did, and so fiercely that it became the Seneca's turn to fear they would be destroyed. In desperation they went to their neighbors—the Mohawk, Oneida, Onondaga, and Cayuga—and asked for help. An alliance was formed, the Iroquois Confederacy. The Five Fires together were enough to hold back the Shawnee but not to defeat them. And for the last one hundred years an uneasy equality of power has held the Shawnee west of the mountains and the Iroquois to the east."

Chaubenee remained in rapt attention at Chiksika's recitation of the hundred-year history and then in silence let it wash over him. When he spoke again, he maintained the thread of his conversation.

"If it is true that there is power in unity of the Indians, perhaps that power will be enough to push the whites back over the mountains. I wish to be a part of that power."

Chiksika stared fixedly into Chaubenee's uniquely large eyes for long moments, neither man looking away. Both knew this was the moment the question would be answered.

When Chiksika spoke, it was with the softness of love and the firmness of authority. "Chaubenee, we the Shawnee are honored that a young warrior of your skills, thoughtfulness, and pedigree would wish to join us. But I will say no, at least for now. You are impressively mature for a warrior of your age, but you are young. What you do with the next years of your life will be critical. And where we go there will be great danger. While I know you are prepared, perhaps eager, to accept danger, I would feel a burden to the parents of a warrior so young. But next spring we will return. The next leg of our trip will be to the Spanish land the other side of the Mississippi and then to the south. If you still want to join us then, you will be received into our company with great joy."

CHAPTER 14

NOVEMBER 3, 1787

Northwest Territory near Mascouten Bay

Tecumseh hummed happily to himself, the sun flashing onto and off his face as he rode through the forest of oak and elm and hickory that bound the horse trail he and his traveling companions followed.

"Tecumseh, it's midmorning and you are half-drunk already. That stuff kills too many of us. I don't want my brother to be among them."

"Oh, Chiksika, worry not. I'm just having, as the Shemanese say, a hair of the dog that bit me."

"That dog bites you far too often, Little Brother."

"CHIKSIKA," came a loud shout from the front. "Wasegoboah comes and he's riding hard."

Both brothers turned their heads forward and Chiksika kicked his horse's ribs to move to the front of the group quickly. Wasegoboah was coming back toward the group, with dust flying under his horse's hooves.

He pulled his mount to a short, hard stop next to Chiksika. His thin lips were pulled up in a smile so broad they almost touched his high cheekbones. "Just over the hill! They are there! Dozens of them!" He panted from the exertion of his ride and his obvious excitement, his normally deep voice booming almost like a drum.

Tecumseh could see the concern all over his brother's face, despite Wasegoboah's joy. "Who is there?"

"Not who, what. What."

"Wasegoboah," Chiksika commanded, "talk straight."

"Buffalo, Chiksika! Buffalo!" And then he captured his breath and composure. "I've never seen them before, but it's them for certain—big, brown, and shaggy. Just over the rise in the open grass. They are there."

Tecumseh watched his brother's face open into a broad smile and with a small noise moved his horse forward, this time at a trot.

Moments later Tecumseh and his companions sat on their horses, fanned out across the hilltop, taking in a sight none had seen before. Wasegoboah had been correct. There were at least three dozen of the beasts quietly grazing in the open grassland extending to the horizon. The wind was behind the Shawnee so it was certain the beasts, not two hundred yards in front of them, knew they were there, but in their fearlessness they appeared not even to notice.

"If we take one of them, we'll have meat enough for all of us until we reach the Sac," Wasegoboah observed. "But how do we do it?"

"Perhaps we can circle around so we are downwind and stalk through the grass to within bowshot," one of the party offered.

"No, we have to get close enough to drive a lance between the ribs of a beast that large. We have to run one down," another responded.

"Do you suppose we can drive them over a creek bank or bluff?"

Tecumseh realized none of them really knew how to kill something that large. It was a hunt none had ever seen, much less participated in. He sat quietly on his horse, listening, and finally said, "I think with a knife. I think you open the throat. Might be exciting."

The comment brought peals of laughter. Tecumseh didn't respond and heads turned back to their conversation. And as they did, Tecumseh kneed his horse. It started at a trot toward the herd.

He was twenty yards down the slope when Chiksika shouted, "Tecumseh, where in the name of Moneto are you going?"

Tecumseh didn't respond but just continued to trot forward. When he was within one hundred yards of the herd, the closest of them looked up. Then others. They did nothing. Just looked. Tecumseh continued to trot slowly forward. When he was within fifty yards, the first turned and started to move away. Leisurely, the rest of the herd turned and joined in. By the time Tecumseh was within twenty yards he had his horse at a full gallop with the herd running before him.

Tecumseh guided his horse right next to the trailing buffalo, so close his horse was rubbing against the beast. His long scalping knife was in his teeth when he leaped onto the back of his prey. With one hand he held on to the long fur across the beast's massive hump, and with the other he pulled the knife from his teeth. He raised the arm, and reaching as far forward as he could, brought the blade down into the animal's neck. When he struck the creature, it stopped midstride and threw its massive shoulders contorting upward toward the blow. Tecumseh was hurled forward through space as though he were a frog leaping from the beast's back. The buffalo righted itself and staggered forward, trampling across Tecumseh's fallen body.

Tecumseh lay motionless, virtually senseless save for the terrible pain in his right leg. He could hear Chiksika's voice seeming from far away.

"Are you alive, Brother?"

He could only respond with a pain-filled moan. He was still conscious, but barely.

In his dreamlike fog, Tecumseh heard Chiksika's barked orders. "Wasegoboah, get back to the Potawatomi as fast as your horse can make the journey. We need their best healer. One who sets bones straight and fights infection. I want her here before dark."

The last thing he felt through his pain was the vibration of the ground as a horse thundered away.

* * * *

Tecumseh sat upright on a bed of twigs, his back propped against a wood frame in his *wegiwa*. Chaubenee, who had ridden through the winter's first ice storm to visit his fallen friend, looked down at his legs.

"Your healer did a fabulous job," Tecumseh said, his face beaming with joy. "They tell me I screamed when she pulled it straight, but I have no memory. When I woke, the leg was bound on all sides with straight sticks to hold it rigid, and the gouge of the buffalo's hoof was cleaned deeply and wrapped in leaves to stop any infection. I will walk again in the early spring, she tells me."

Chaubenee held his eyes for a moment. "Yes, you will live to hunt buffalo again, and hopefully in a more conventional manner."

The two chuckled together. When they spoke again it was Tecumseh who offered, "Perhaps yes, but there is one thing that will change."

"What is that?"

Tecumseh looked stern when he spoke. "I will never drink again."

"Never?"

"Never. I have learned a hard and very costly lesson, but I have learned it. There are many things the whites have brought us which have made our lives better." He looked around the room and pointed as he went. "Blankets, guns, gunpowder and shot, tomahawks and other metal tools, pots, books. It is a very long list of good things. Things without which we can no longer live. But the Shemanese whiskey brings only suffering. I will drink it no more, and insofar as it comes to me to influence others, they will not either." Tecumseh said this with such conviction that he almost believed it himself.

"Oh, my friend, you have used this time of rest wisely," Chaubenee replied. "I will hope to know you better and hear more as time goes on."

The flap to the *wegiwa* flew inward, escorted by a cold rush. Chiksika stepped through the opening, carrying a small basket. He stepped in and set the basket on the floor. Steam rose from it along with the smells of tea and soup. "Warmth and sustenance for both our guest and my patient," he said and handed each a mug of tea and another of soup. "May I join in the conversation?" Chiksika asked, even as he sat himself on a blanket and took two more mugs from the basket for himself. Both young men nodded assent.

For several minutes there was silence save for the sounds of drinking the warm soup. It was Chiksika who spoke first. "Chaubenee, you Potawatomi are incredibly kind and hospitable to your guests. You have feasted us in your village, and your healer has saved us from our own foolishness." With that he cast a judgmental look to his younger brother, who ignored it. "And now you bring us a method to prosperity."

Chaubenee indulged a small smile but said nothing. It was Tecumseh who responded. "What has he given us now?"

"Little Brother, Chaubenee came this morning with two packhorses. They are loaded with metal traps of various sizes."

Both brothers looked at Chaubenee, who seemed too embarrassed to speak. But the Shawnee did not speak. Finally, Chaubenee did. "We knew you were all capable warriors and would have no problem making a camp or feeding yourselves for half the year while Tecumseh's thighbone mended. But we didn't know if you'd brought powder and shot enough for a three-year journey, much less blankets and weapons to last the time. We also knew young men of energy would be bored. We suspected you'd trap to collect furs for trade next spring, but we had seen no traps so we assumed you'd use snares and deadfalls. Traditional, but not so efficient as Shemanese has taught us to be. Perhaps these gifts will help you along your path."

There was a long silence. Chiksika reached in one corner and pulled out a pipe and bag of tobacco. He stuffed the pipe bowl full and, stem fixed between his teeth, stepped into the open, only to return momentarily with his pipe smelling of its aromatic content. After sitting down and taking another puff, he passed it to Chaubenee. The three sat in silence passing around the pipe.

When they were done, Chiksika spoke words carefully considered during the smoking. "When the ground thaws I will return your traps. If at that time you wish to join us, you will be most welcome and considered a brother."

Chaubenee sat quietly composing himself. "It is time for me to go. I would prefer to be in the warmth of my own home when the night falls. And when we meet next, I will be packed and prepared to learn with you of the world I do not know."

Chaubenee rose to go, lifted the flap, and stepped out but stuck his head back instantly. He grinned mischievously, staring at Tecumseh. "I presume that new buffalo hide that covers you is from the beast that tried to kill you. Perhaps it is the first of many trophies I shall watch you win."

Tecumseh smiled broadly. Chiksika offered one last word as Chaubenee left the tent. "In the spring we will not go north. We go south to visit our mother." He rose and started to follow.

"Brother, stay with me for a moment longer. There is something I would like to say."

Chiksika let the *wegiwa* flap fall back in place, eased back onto the blanket beside his brother, and sat silently waiting for him to speak.

Tecumseh was silent for a moment, collecting his thoughts. He would try to say this just right. "Brother, dear older brother. Over the years you have taught me much and I have wanted to learn. I have not wanted to disappoint you. And in many ways, I think I have not. I have become competent in the arts of a Shawnee warrior. I have become proficient in all the tools of hunting and war. I believe I have not disappointed you in those ways.

"But in other ways I have failed you and myself entirely. I have tried to learn no more than that—to be a warrior. But my time here in thought has made me see that I have made a terrible error. I have failed to see that you have far more to teach me."

Chiksika did not move, but Tecumseh could see his eyebrows furrow with anticipation of what was to come.

"You, like our father, are more than a mere warrior. You are a leader of men, a leader of warriors and of our people. I have ignored all that you have tried to teach me about leadership. But I will no more. From this moment forward I will study all you have to teach."

He could see Chiksika slowly take in his words and process them. He did not smile but he rose and turned to leave, saying as he went, "Watch me, Tecumseh. Watch those things I do. Watch those things I do not do. Ponder why I do or do not do them. Then we will talk."

CHAPTER 15

MAY 15, 1788

Northwest Territory near Cahokia Mounds

The eleven young warriors rode single file and in complete silence. Even the birds and the beasts made no sound. It was as though every living thing was in awe of the men, or perhaps the gods, who had made these immense structures. For the last five miles they had traveled among them, at least one always within sight. And now they were in a lane between two of the most impressive mounds.

The one to the north was largest, perhaps as much as seven hundred yards long and at least one hundred feet tall. None had climbed any of the mounds save Chiksika, the only among them who had been here before. He told them the tops were completely flat. The sides of each sloped up at forty-five degree angles, their perfect symmetry interrupted only by a road wide enough for four men to ride abreast and angling laterally from bottom to top along one side of each of these mysterious and epic monuments. But monuments to what? Who the ancients were that built them, even legend did not say, nor how great the population of these ancients must have been to construct them. Nor why.

Tecumseh could not help but ponder their origin. If all seven thousand Shawnee, the entire population of the nation, attempted this and were free of defending or feeding themselves, they could not build even one in a lifetime. But here, near the edge of the Mississippi, there were dozens of them. And to what purpose? Did they live up there to avoid the spring floods along the river? Perhaps. Was each a temple to their gods? Who could know for sure?

What man could have conceived them? And whoever he was, he could not have built them alone. He would have had to convince thousands of people to join him in accomplishing his vision. Is it possible that anything a man can conceive he is also capable of accomplishing if he is just able to lead others to share both the vision and the work?

After they passed the last mound, the ground opened into prairie with spring grasses not yet up to the horse's knees. In the distance, a small structure was silhouetted against the skyline. Even from here it could be seen that it wasn't a log house but rather a structure made of hewed planks set not on the ground but raised on a stone foundation. The roof extended over the front wall and offered shade from a porch.

"That building is in no small part responsible for fate bringing me to travel with you," Chaubenee announced loud enough for all the company to hear.

His remark was astounding enough to cause Tecumseh to stop and turn toward him, as did all the others.

"What do you mean?" one asked.

"That trading post will be Baynton, Wharton & Morgan. It has been there since before I was born," Chaubenee stated.

"How can you know that? You've never been here." They stared at him with incredulity.

"I know," announced Chaubenee, "because this place is very important in Potawatomi history. It is here that Pini assassinated Pontiac." He smiled and reached forward to touch Chiksika's war club. "Like you, Chiksika, his favorite weapon was a war club.

"Pontiac and a few Ottawa warriors, including both his sons, visited the Illini after the war between the French and the British. Pini came to idolize Pontiac and attached himself to his company. Pontiac, like many of us"—Tecumseh saw Chaubenee's glance cast his way—"liked whiskey a bit too much. At this very post Pini offered to buy him a drink. As the rest of the party rode on, Pini offered Pontiac whiskey from a flask. And when Pontiac raised the flask and tilted his head, Pini caved in the back of his skull with the club."

"Why did he do it, Chaubenee?" Tecumseh asked. "I've never understood."

"Who does? But perhaps it is just this, we are talking about him. He's been dead almost twenty years, and we still mention his name. What other Illini warrior can any of us even name? Or perhaps he was a tool of his people. Perhaps their weakness and Pontiac's power caused them to fear just what came about, that they would lose their land, their heritage, to his power. They have been swept from history. Or perhaps Pini was a tool of the British. They certainly had cause to hate and fear Pontiac. And Baynton, Wharton & Morgan were, and are, British traders. Who is to say Pini's reason? No one truly knows.

"But for whatever reason he did it, Pontiac's sons avenged themselves on his entire nation. And when the Illini were gone, we moved onto their land. And here we are, companions because twenty years ago a turtle slid off a rock into a pond and made a ripple that swept all before it."

They turned again to continue toward the building that was their goal. As they approached, Chiksika beckoned Tecumseh to him. "They will not be used to Shawnee and perhaps unfamiliar with our tongue. Your English is better than anyone else's here—better than almost any Indian's anywhere—you will speak for us. But commit to nothing until I agree."

* * * *

The Englishman who stepped off the porch and toward them was tall, with a spare body and thin hair. His boots were polished and his tweed vest clean, matching his trousers.

"We don't see many Shawnee here, and you are most welcome. If you have English, it will be easier. If not, perhaps Kickapoo."

Tecumseh moved his horse half a length in front of the others and slid down slowly, his hands remaining on its withers. He took a stride forward, somewhat haltingly, making certain his balance was firm on his right leg before stepping fully onto it.

"My name is Tecumseh. And you're right, we are Shawnee save one Potawatomi"—he nodded toward Chaubenee—"We arrive with winter pelts to trade. Are you Mr. Baynton, Mr. Wharton, or Mr. Morgan?"

"My God, young man, your English is perfect. Wherever did you learn it?" He stepped forward and extended his hand, a smile on his thin face. "I'm Morgan. Forget the mister."

Tecumseh gave a very slight smile and stepped forward again, ensuring his right leg would support his weight. "Shawnee are the first Indians you whites meet coming down the Spaylaywitheepi. We've had much practice."

Morgan, well aware of the Shawnee's almost constant warfare with traffic from Fort Pitt down the Ohio River, was uncertain if the answer to his question displayed any threat. But trade was trade, and that was why he was here.

"You'll find water and shade for your horses around back. If you'd like to unpack the furs now and leave them on the porch, we can conduct business when you return."

* * * *

At their camp south of St. Louis, the fire roared and its colors twinkled on the Mississippi, mingling with those same colors cast on the water by the setting sun. Everything they owned was soaked from the drenching it got in crossing the river—everything, that is, except the lead casks of gunpowder for which they had traded the furs.

They were naked. All of their clothes were suspended on poles and quickly assembled racks to dry by the fire. Tecumseh was holding his war club at what he deemed the perfect distance from the fire.

"Tecumseh, how is it all the sons of Pucksinwah so revere their war clubs?" Chaubenee asked.

Tecumseh gave a warm smile as he slowly twisted the club before the fire. "Oh, Blue Jacket is quite fond of his musket and brace of pistols. But I love this best because it never has to be reloaded, and unlike a tomahawk or knife it doesn't have the unfortunate habit of remaining stuck in its victim. I like to move very fast in battle. And you're right. I do revere it. It was a gift from Chiksika, you know. From the buffalo that almost ended me. He insisted the tail be left on when it was skinned. It was he who cut the tail away from the hide, leaving the right amount of leather from the rump attached."

Tecumseh extended the head of the club toward Chaubenee, displaying the leather wrapped around a rock head larger than a fist, the lethal end of the club.

"Then he found the perfect round rock and wrapped the leather from the rump around it. He stitched the leather back around the rock, soaked the hide, and then allowed it to dry, shrinking so tight the rock could not be dislodged. The tail stiffened hard into a handle but left a flexible head, which strikes with crushing force." He extended the weapon to Chaubenee. "Here, try it."

Chaubenee accepted the club and swung it forcefully. The whip of the head made a small swishing noise as it passed through the air. "It's a bit too limber to be accurate, isn't it?"

"Yes, its one drawback is that when it gets wet it is a bit limber. But I will dry it slowly. Tomorrow the tail portion of the handle will be stiff again."

Tecumseh saw his brother standing naked by the river, pondering what, he could not tell. "Forgive me, Chaubenee, but I would talk to my brother for a moment."

He rose slowly and walked, still showing a tentativeness in his stride, to stand by Chiksika. Neither said a thing, seemingly entranced by the mystery of anything so powerful as that which flowed past them. Perhaps being naked made them feel vulnerable and magnified the power of the thing. Perhaps this river was awesome no matter the glory of the man.

Tecumseh reached to his neck and touched the one thing he still wore, his *opawaka*. It hung around his neck, suspended on a leather cord. The small leather bag attached to the cord was filled with little things evocative of the mysteries and powers that were the sum of his life. He never took it off. Touching it seemed to bring him back, away from the powers of things outside himself.

"Chiksika, I am glad the buffalo broke me so it took a full winter to heal." He said no more.

Chiksika continued to look at the water. "What has it given you that is so valuable you gladly gave up half a year's freedom for it?"

"It is not what it has given, Brother. It is what it has taken. It has taken away shame you would have felt for me had we gone to the Sac. It saved me from that."

Now Chiksika turned to look at him.

Tecumseh could see that, so far as the darkness would allow, his brother was trying to read the meaning of his face.

"What do you think you would have done to cause me shame among our friends?" he finally asked.

"I would not have fought the Osage. They, and perhaps you, would have felt me a coward."

There was a guffaw in the dark before Chiksika responded. "I know far better than that, Brother. But I do not know what your reason would have been."

"It is not the Osage who killed our father; it is not the Osage who steal our land; it is not the Osage who burn our homes. The Osage are not my enemy. It is Shemanese who are my enemy. They are your enemy, too. They are the enemy of every Indian. Pontiac was right. We can only win if we all fight them together. No Indian will be my enemy. Only Shemanese. They will be my enemy until they have been removed from Indian lands and to the other side of the mountains or until I die, whichever comes first."

The magical silence of the night was eventually broken by the croaking of a nearby bullfrog. It seemed to bring them back to life.

"Chiksika, when I was broken and told you I wanted to learn of leadership, the only wisdom you gave me was, 'Watch me, Tecumseh. Watch the things I do. Ponder why.' I have done that and one thing I observe is that you never ask any of us to do a thing that you yourself are not willing to do. Things that we see you do. As leader, are you not above that?"

"Tecumseh, as leader of this party I will one day be forced to ask you, or some other member of this party, to do a thing that will have danger to you, may get you killed," Chiksika told his brother. "And I will not always have time to explain why I am asking it. Courage, Tecumseh, is not found in lack of fear. Lack of fear is madness. Courage is recognizing your fear and then doing what is required despite it. Only a fool gladly rushes to danger. None of my friends are fools. So when I tell them to do something that must be done, I ask nothing of them I would not ask of myself. If they know that, only then will they instantly do as I ask."

Tecumseh saw the firelight reflected in his brother's eyes. They told him his words were true.

Chiksika finally gave a small, knowing smile. "You are doing as I ask so I will reward you. I will give you the most fundamental rule of leading men in combat. You must know three things. You must know your own strengths and you must know your enemies' weaknesses."

Again the long silence was only broken by the sounds of bullfrogs looking for mates and challenging rivals.

"Chiksika, you said a leader must know three things. You have only given two."

This time the older brother's smile was so big his teeth reflected the distant fire. "You do ponder. Good. Knowing those two things is useless unless the leader can find a way to pit his strength against his enemies' weakness."

* * * *

They had been following the trail that ran south along the river for two days. The bottom trail was too boggy from annual flooding for easy or comfortable riding, so they used the ancient trail that ran along the ridgeline west of the river. Normally, even in times of peace, a party of young warriors would consider a ridge trail too exposed for comfort, but this one was lined with oaks so massive as to cover their passage from all but the nearest observers. The farther south they rode, the more the limbs of trees were blanketed in a lovely, but somewhat eerie, long, grey and dull green moss. Spanish moss, Chiksika had told them it was called, and Spanish territory this was.

It was the Spaniards who had invited the Shawnee eight years ago and offered them a tract twenty-five miles square on the west side of the Mississippi just where the river stopped its eastward drift and turned back due south. Cape Girardeau it was called.

"My friend, Tecumseh, educate an ignorant Potawatomi." Chaubenee's goodwill beamed through in his self-deprecating humor. "Why have we crossed the mighty Mississippi to visit your mother and other Shawnee? Shawnee live north of the Spaylaywitheepi and between the Wabash and the Scioto, not in places where trees have beards."

"My friend wants a history lesson of the Shawnee, does he?" Tecumseh replied. "Well, we have time."

Tecumseh began. "Where to start? Since we have time, I suppose the beginning. Ten winters ago the Virginian, George Rogers Clark, led an expedition of Kentuckians into the portions of the British Province of Quebec south of the Great Lakes and destroyed British forts there. This is the same Clark who fought *with* the British five years earlier at the Battle of Point Pleasant—the battle where my father predicted his death and met it. The battle that was Chiksika's first.

"After Clark's victories over the English, many Shawnee began to doubt that we would ever hold the Americans back if they won their war with their British fathers. And it looked like they would win. For all our disregard of the British, we knew it was not they who wanted our land. The British wanted furs and would trade wonderful things to get them. But their American children wanted land—our land. And no matter how many we killed, and the Shawnee killed many, they kept coming.

"There are five septs of the Shawnee nation. Among them, the Thawegila harbored the gravest concern on this issue. A great counsel was held to decide whether to stay in our home of the last one hundred years or accept the Spanish offer of land well west of the Thirteen Fires. As has happened periodically in the history of the Shawnee, we could not agree. The Thawegila could not be convinced to stay. In the end their chief raised a wampum belt representing the five septs. He held it against the center log pole of the conference lodge and drove his tomahawk through the middle of the belt, releasing the beads to fall to the floor in separate pieces. We were no longer one. The Thawegila were going.

"But then, an even more unexpected thing happened. My ancestral sept is Kispoko, traditionally the most warlike of the five septs. The chief of the Kispoko is the war chief of the entire nation. My father had been such and led the Kispoko in peace and all the Shawnee in war. And the Kispoko, without my father's courage to lead them, decided to go, too. Chiksika, my older sister, and her unborn son and I had been adopted into the Chalahgawtha when our father died. The Chalahgawtha stayed, and we with them. Blue Jacket was married. He went to his wife's people—the Maykujay. My mother, Methotasa, went with the Kispoko, her adopted people. In all more than half the Shawnee moved behind the protective barrier of the great river."

Chaubenee rode silently for a few moments, then asked, "You said your mother went with her 'adopted' people. Why adopted?"

Tecumseh angled his horse close enough to Chaubenee's to put an arm around those big shoulders. "I must remember to choose my words with care, as you appear to listen to them. There is more. But I will tell it later."

On the fourth day, their trail turned west from the river. As they followed it, the terrain rolled ever more through the forest. But the soil got thinner and the trees smaller as they continued. Frequently the hills they passed over and around created lakes in the low spots between them. So, even though the dense forest became more of a broken forest with many open areas of grassland, it remained a beautiful ride. In midafternoon, the trail crested a low pass between two tall hills and as it did, one of the largest villages any of them had ever seen opened up below them. They stopped to let their eyes take in a village of over three hundred houses. Half of them were *wegiwas*, and quite a few, but not all the rest, were cabins.

"What are those strange pointed structures three or four times as tall as a man?" Chaubenee asked of no one in particular as he gestured toward the west side of the village before them.

"Those, my young friend, are the houses all the buffalo hunting tribes make and live in," Chiksika answered. Tecumseh recognized his brother's tone as one generally saved for instructing children. "They use buffalo hides. Wrap them around tall, thin, straight pines. They can be taken down and moved in an hour. Tribes who follow the buffalo, move often. They're called tepees. Besides being mobile, they're warmer than *wegiwas* in the winter. The insides can be heated. See the smoke coming out of the top?"

"It appears some of the Plains tribes have moved in with our Shawnee brothers," Wasegoboah observed.

They were still too far from the village to hear anything except the sharpest cries, but they could see the dust rise on the trail that led from the village as a party of a dozen horsemen raced toward them. They waited patiently to be received.

Their escort led them into the Kispoko village amid happy chatter of old friends catching up. Two riders had raced back before them to share the news of their arrival, and as they rode through the village, friends and acquaintances of almost a decade ago rushed to greet the entering Shawnee. None recognized Tecumseh, for he had been but a slip of a boy when they saw him last. None knew Chaubenee. All the others of their party were mobbed.

But good as the warmth of rekindled friendship was, the bad news came to them almost instantly.

"Your mother is not here. She left as soon as the weather warmed to go south to visit her family."

All conversation stopped and both Chiksika and Tecumseh instantly turned to face the speaker.

"But how? She is old and must be frail by now," Chiksika responded in disbelief.

The whole of it came out over dinner. Methotasa had had a very bad winter. She had been weak and not always in control of her mind. The village thought she would die before the winter ended. But she did not, and with the first warmth of spring her mind and her vigor returned. And she said she wanted to visit her family one last time. Not her children and Shawnee family. She wanted to go south to her Cherokee home one last time.

* * * *

Tecumseh and Chaubenee rode to the lake east of the village. Their companions had many old friends here. Friends to catch up with, to have a drink with, and with whom to fill in the stories of their lives during these eight years of separation. The lake was easy to find, the rising moon having given light to their trail. The brilliance still hung low in the eastern sky, painting a long, shimmering path leading across the lake before them.

"It almost makes you believe you could walk over, doesn't it?" Chaubenee asked.

Tecumseh said nothing but got down from his horse, pulled a pipe and tobacco from his pouch, squatted with his back to a rock, and stared at Chaubenee's magical path. He gathered such moss as was within arm's reach, added a few small, dry sticks on top, and used steel and flint to fire the dried moss. He stuffed the pipe and used one of the small twigs from the fire to light it, then took a very long draw on the pipe.

"That's just what we're doing, you know," Tecumseh said, small puffs of smoke evaporating into the darkness as he spoke.

"Walking across the lake?"

Tecumseh continued to exhale a long, slow stream of smoke. "This journey we are on follows a wavering, unpredictable, and mysterious path." He passed the pipe to Chaubenee, who pulled longingly at the stem.

Eventually Tecumseh continued, "But we do know where the path leads. It leads to our futures."

Chaubenee passed the pipe back, and Tecumseh said nothing as he again pulled sweet, aromatic peace into his lungs.

It was Chaubenee who spoke again. "Two days ago, you said you would tell me more of your mother 'later.' Is now 'later'?"

Tecumseh exhaled fully, passed the pipe back, and without looking at Chaubenee, told the story. "My mother was born Cherokee. You heard that when we arrived. When my father was twenty-one, he led a raiding party of young Shawnee warriors into Cherokee country. During the raid they attacked and took a small village. The Cherokee are great warriors and, in fact, will claim to be the best in the world. I don't think it is true, but you will soon hear them offer the claim." He looked at his friend with a smile that was visible in the moonlight. "The Cherokee fought hard, and when it was over, only three warriors were left alive, as well as fifteen-year-old Methotasa. My father was taken with her, and knowing what was coming next and wishing to protect her from it, took her several miles away, tied her to a tree, and slept there for the night. When they returned in the morning, all that was left of the three Cherokee was their charred remains.

"Pucksinwah wanted her, so they ended the raid and took loot and scalps they had collected, and along with the young maiden, headed home. Methotasa was adopted into the Shawnee and married my father. She had six children by him. Chiksika is the eldest. I also have a sister, Tecumapese, who is ten years older than me. And finally, my mother did something that no woman in the Shawnee nation had accomplished in four generations. She had triplets. All boys. That was three years after I was born, so they are about your age.

"My mother and father grew to love each other very much. I was six when my father was killed. One of the other warriors killed that day was Chaqui, my sister's husband. He never saw their son. I think it was too much for my mother. When I was young, Methotasa was full of life, love, and energy. But after her husband and son-in-law died, she died a little as well. Each year it showed more. By the time the Shawnee split, there was nothing left of her. Certainly nothing left to fight Shemanese. We all knew she had to come here, where it was quiet and safe, so she could be still until she died. I'm surprised she has lived this long. I doubt she has much time now.

"After our companions have seen all of their friends and family and the horses have rested, I'm sure Chiksika will say it is time to go."

* * * *

"The last word on her lips was 'Pucksinwah.'" The old woman's face was brown and wrinkled, but in the golden glow of the firelight it reflected a beauty that must have been unmistakable in her youth. "Odd, is it not, that the man who stole her from me thirty-five years ago is the one she loved to her last breath?"

Tecumseh and Chiksika hunkered by the hearth of the small cabin, warmed against the cool of the late spring evening. They had ridden here as rapidly as their party could travel, but they had still been too late. Neither spoke, having nothing to say and wanting to hear all their grandmother had to tell.

"At first we thought she was dead. We found the bodies of the others but not hers, so there was hope. Over the years, news came to us that the young warrior who led the raid had become war chief of our old enemies, the wandering Shawnee. And then we heard he had married a Cherokee captive and we thought it might be Methotasa. It will be easier to die knowing my baby found a good life and had two marvelous boys who now sit here before me."

Tecumseh looked up from the fire and into the old face filled not with hate for what was taken from her but joy at what she had been given. "Grandmother, it was not two; it was six." He could not help but smile when he said it.

The old woman's face rose and changed in such surprise that all the wrinkles momentarily disappeared. "Six? Tell me of the others."

Chiksika's stern face showed far more love and compassion than Tecumseh normally saw there. "Tecumseh and I have a sister, Tecumapese. She is two years younger than me and ten years older than Tecumseh. She is a widow and has a son, Spemica Lawba. He is fourteen now and truly a fine young man. In fact, he already has fame not only among the Shawnee but the Shemanese as well.

"Two years past Kentuckians under General Benjamin Logan brought a small and fast army north to wipe out Mackachack village, our home. When Logan struck, almost all our warriors were away. But our ancient and beloved chief, Moluntha, was there. Tecumapese screamed for her son and ran into the cane behind the village. Moluntha gave himself up, but one of the Kentuckians struck him from behind with a tomahawk. Spemica Lawba, seeing this, ran to defend the body from mutilation. At twelve, armed with only a scalping knife and tomahawk, he stood over the body, defending it with his life against a dozen soldiers. While the Kentuckians laughed and taunted him, Logan rode up, got off his horse, and without drawing a weapon approached Spemica Lawba, speaking gently. Logan told him Moluntha's body would be left safe from predation of animals or weather and for proper reverence and ceremony by the Shawnee. He also promised that Spemica Lawba would not be killed or tortured. Logan himself would see to his safety.

"Spemica Lawba believed the general and gave up his weapons. Not only did Logan look out for his safety but took him into his home and treated him as a son. We got him back only last year when our adopted and older brother, Blue Jacket, negotiated a peace with the Kentuckians that included a prisoner exchange."

The old lady's face beamed, the joy of being regaled at the glories of one of her progeny momentarily overcoming the loss of another. "What a courageous young man my great-grandson turns out to be." And then with an even broader smile, she said, "But it's not a surprise. After all, he is one-quarter Cherokee."

"Grandmother, there is even more to tell that will make you proud." Tecumseh continued, "Three years after I was born, Methotasa did something no Shawnee woman had done in four generations. She gave birth to triplets. All boys."

By now the old woman was all smiles. "That's because she's all Cherokee. We do extraordinary things, you know?" Slowly her face drained of its humor. The pain of loss did not return to her face, but wisdom and thoughtfulness did. "You two have suffered one of the most grievous pains any person, man or woman, can suffer. She who gave you life is gone. When it happens, a little of you dies as well. It is a small death but it is a death, and no one, especially a warrior, can accept the pain without lashing back at life. But warriors have a way to deal with the pain that women do not. You do not have to lash out at life; you may lash out at your enemies.

"There are eleven of you. We don't have as many Shemanese coming at us as the Spaylaywitheepi brings to you. But we have enough. And they want just what yours want—land. Our land. And the Cherokee, like the Shawnee, will not, do not, give in to theft of anything lightly. We fight to maintain that portion which Moneto gave us. It is the same fight as yours.

"Join us; join our young warriors for a while. Take out your pain on your enemies, not your friends. Let me take you to our war chief."

CHAPTER 16

SEPTEMBER 30, 1790

Washington District of North Carolina

Two dozen warriors stood hidden among a forest of beech trees with a few magnificent magnolias in full bloom. They stared down into a most pleasant valley with a stream, some ten or fifteen yards wide, splitting in half the grassland that made up the valley floor. The far rim of the valley was perhaps three miles distant as the crow flies. The bucolic perfection of the vista was marred only by a small village of ten log cabins situated between them and the creek.

Mukonse, the nominal leader of the war party, looked toward Chiksika and laid out the plan. "There is a drop of about three feet along this side of the stream right behind the cabins. A perfect place to hide a small party of warriors. You won't be able to cross the open meadow to use the cover of the bank until after dark. There will be just a sliver moon tonight so very little chance of your being seen doing it. Take half the party around to hide behind that bank. I will stay here with the other half. Before dark, the whites will bring their cattle into the pens by the cabins. Tomorrow at first light, or at least by sunrise, the men will come out to lead the cattle to graze. By then my half of the party will be in the trees next to the grass. When I judge the majority of Shemanese men are in the open, I will charge out with my men toward them. Only when they have all turned this way and given up the cover of their cabins do you rush in behind them."

Chiksika, who had learned from his father that the most important part of warfare was to outthink your enemy, nodded his agreement. "Mukonse, it is important that we learn to work together. You would agree?"

The Cherokee, his head covered in the traditional multi-colored cloth turban, nodded assent.

"Then," said Chiksika, "let us not split into Cherokee and Shawnee. You take six of mine and I'll take six of yours. We will learn from each other and about each other."

Mukonse pointed to six of his warriors and nodded toward Chiksika. "Go with him. He leads you."

Chiksika did the same and intentionally pointed to his younger brother. "Stay here. Learn from Mukonse and bring honor to the Shawnee."

Tecumseh said nothing but nodded acknowledgment.

As Chiksika turned to go, Mukonse gave one last instruction. "There are at least thirty armed men down there, perhaps forty. Surprise is critical as is the first salvo. Make certain you do not rush up from the creek bank until their backs are to you, and make your first shots count."

Chiksika made eye contact with each of the dozen men who would be with him, then turned and started off at a trot, making certain to pick a path that kept him hidden from the sight of his prey as he circled around the valley.

The Cherokee sat down in the grove, each picking a tree to rest against and taking a blanket and some jerky from his pouch. There would be no fire tonight.

* * * *

Tecumseh heard the shot explode and rose to his feet in the dark with one motion, war club in hand. Other shots fired intermittently around him. He struggled to separate shadow from figure in the thin moonlight.

Mukonse shouted a command, "Ambush! Scatter!"

Tecumseh's response was instantaneous, instinctive. "No, charge them! They are few." And then, without looking to see whether he was followed, Tecumseh screamed his war cry and rushed at an oncoming shadow. He saw the rifle butt coming and stepped under it, delivering a blow with his war club at the ribs of his opponent.

"To me," he yelled. "To me! We have them!"

As he drove steadily downhill, he heard other war cries coming up behind him. Another shadow stood in front of him. His club took the shadow in the head as he moved on.

And then it was over as quickly as it had started. There was no more firing. The Shemanese were gone, leaving only the sound of their running feet flying in fear into the safety of the night.

Tecumseh screamed at the top of his voice, "All back. Do not be trapped. Back now."

As Tecumseh walked back up the hill to the original campsite, grey light was beginning to show in the east. He stepped over the one whose skull he had crushed, shoved the point of his scalping knife into his forehead, and ran the tip skull deep around to the back. Then the same practiced motion on the other side, and he stood, one foot on his victim's back, wrapped his hand into the long hair, and yanked. With a deep popping sound, the scalp came loose.

He walked on up the hill, looking for his other victim. But he was not there. Perhaps the blow had not been as disabling as he had thought. With the frail dawn light filtered through the tree canopy, he could not yet see the markings to know how the man got away. He walked a few more steps into the grove where they had slept. All thirteen were there and looking at him in wonder. None said a word. They just stared. His wounded victim was also there, lying on the ground, his arms wrapped around his ribs and moaning.

Mukonse was the first to speak. "How did you know? How did you know they would run? When light is full we'll be able to read the sign, but I'm certain there were at least twenty Shemanese."

Tecumseh spoke slowly and almost gently. "Men, all men, fear the dark. That is especially true in a forest where their fears lengthen with the shadows. And I woke to one shot, not twenty. That told me that no matter how many there were, they were disorganized and working as individuals. Individuals, no matter how many, can always be beaten by a group acting together." He paused long. "We are a group acting together, aren't we, Mukonse?"

Tecumseh watched as they stripped his victim naked and tied him to a small tree. Every time they hit him in his crushed ribs, his scream was pure agony. Eventually, they tired of that. And then, one at a time, they stepped close to him and fired at him with their muskets. But the muskets were not loaded with a ball, only powder. And at five feet, the burning powder exploded from each musket hard enough to penetrate the skin and finish burning under it. Twice he fainted. The first time was when someone aimed at and hit his shriveled cock. The second time because he was past his ability to feel pain. He came to when one of them sliced the skin below his collarbone, grabbed hold of it, and yanked the skin off to the middle of his chest.

After two hours they were bored. Chiksika looked at Tecumseh, who had sat quietly with an impassive, even removed, look on his face the entire time. "He is yours, Tecumseh. We have left the scalp for you."

Tecumseh rose, pulled out his scalping knife, and walked toward the tree and the lump that had been a man hanging forward from it. When he reached him, he turned and faced the group, his passive expression now purple and contorted in rage. "You cowards," he shouted. "Is this a display of courage, my Shawnee and Cherokee brothers? To tie a man to a tree so that he is defenseless, so he cannot protect himself, and flay his body? He is our enemy and deserves to die, but he is a man and deserves the dignity Moneto gave to us all."

With that he whirled and as he did so, slashed his knife across the throat of the captive. Blood spurted forward from the severed artery, pumped three times, and then slowed to a steady flow.

Tecumseh turned to once more face the two dozen warriors frozen speechless for the second time today by the youngest Shawnee among them. His face was again a picture of serene calm. "Never again. Never will I go to war with any man who does not agree that killing is enough. The dignity of each of us"—and he panned them slowly—"requires that we recognize the humanity of even our enemies."

* * * *

Months later, the party of fifty warriors rode slowly to the crest of the hill where, in the shelter of the forest, they could once again look down on the village below. As Mukonse stopped, Chiksika and Tecumseh rode up beside him. As before, the cattle were spread out over the floor of the small valley but now with only dogs watching over them. The leaves of the trees had turned brilliant shades of red and orange. All of the women and children seemed to stay close to the cabins, the men not far away. The men, and a few of the women, carried muskets or had them resting nearby. Three more cabins were under construction.

"They are more cautious now," Tecumseh observed.

"The last time they didn't know we were along the creek. They never saw us. When the firing broke out up here"—Chiksika used the butt of his war club to point to the area around them—"it was still dark enough that we were able to slip away unseen. We can hide along the creek bank again. They will not know to expect it."

"It won't work this time," Tecumseh said.

Both men looked at him. "Why not?" Mukonse asked.

"You see how close they stay to the cabins? In the morning only a few men will take the cattle out. We can kill them easily, but the others will rush into their cabins and shoot at us through the windows and loopholes."

Chiksika smiled at his brother's wisdom. "Then we will have to fire the cabins to bring them out."

"Yes, but it will not be easy. This settlement is new. The logs in those cabins will still be green. It may take many fire arrows to get one of them lit."

Mukonse understood now. "If we have to get within arrow's range, it will make targets of us all."

"Yes, but we can be very difficult targets," Tecumseh responded. "They will be shooting through loopholes. It will be difficult to hit moving targets. If our archers ride right through the village and all take aim at just two cabins, we can get enough flaming arrows in them to make them burn. It will just take multiple waves."

Mukonse smiled. "Then tomorrow morning our warriors will meet the sun mounted. Let's come in from the east so the rising sun makes us harder to see. For now, let us get off this ridge and back where we can't be seen or ambushed again."

* * * *

As Tecumseh approached him, Chiksika sat with a pipe in one hand and a mug of whiskey in the other. His expression was sober in the extreme.

He rose saying, "Come, walk with me, Brother." And without waiting for a response, he set down the mug and walked into the forest. When they had walked far enough that no others were close enough to hear, Chiksika stopped and turned to face the trailing Tecumseh.

The moon was still low. Its beam, streaming below the tree branches, fully lit Chiksika's face. The face Tecumseh saw was calm and content—the most beautiful he had ever seen.

"My brother," Chiksika said, "you know the men in our family have sight. Our father had it. He knew the day of his death before it came." He paused and took a long pull on his pipe. The exhaled smoke drifted upward and cast small shadows on his face, adding a mystery to the peace that was so apparent. "I have it, too. Tomorrow, Tecumseh, when the sun is at its height and the trees cast no shadow, I will die."

Tecumseh inhaled sharply and started to speak.

Chiksika's expression did not change, but he held up his hand, palm out, in a gesture commanding silence. "I will be struck here." With the stem of his pipe he touched the flat at the top of his nose. "There is nothing to be done about this, Tecumseh. It will happen. It is not a thing from which I can run or from which I wish to run. My life has been rich, and I have done what I was supposed to do. Do you know what that was, Tecumseh?"

Tecumseh said nothing, just shook his head.

"When I carried our father from the field at Point Pleasant, he was conscious. His last words to me were, 'Raise Tecumseh well. He will be a chief of Shawnee. Make certain he is a good man.' And I have done so. You are a good man and already an extraordinary leader. You have asked to learn leadership from me, and I told you to watch and ponder. You have learned well. You are always the first to face danger. No man among us questions that you would do what you ask of them. And I have told you the three rules a successful commander must follow to win at war. And in such a short time you have not just learned them but developed an instinct for them. An instinct you have displayed these last months. I give you only one more rule of leadership. Some men are jealous of leaders. Beware them."

Chiksika's face changed slowly in the moonlight from one of serene peace to overwhelming love. "But about one thing our father was wrong. I have seen it. I know. You will never be a chief of the Shawnee. Instead, you will be a leader of Indians— all Indians. With you lies the Indians' hope of pushing the Shemanese back beyond the mountains."

* * * *

At the east end of the valley, a stream cut sharply downhill as it had done for millennia. In doing so, it had washed away the land before it, leaving nothing behind but a gap to the sky. When the sun burst through that gap just after dawn, exploding warmth and life into the valley before it, the Cherokee and Shawnee also burst through exploding fire and death.

Their screams penetrated the cool peace of the morning air with terror. Thirty warriors, hanging low behind their horses' withers and shooting flaming arrows from under the beasts' necks, raced down the valley and in a precisely orchestrated effort unleashed their fury onto the two easternmost cabins. Twenty other warriors, armed with muskets, raced up the sides of the valley, wide enough of the village to be out of musket range, hoping to catch those few leading the cows to pasture in the open. They caught two—a father and his son whose turn it was to do that risky early morning work. The man turned to fire back in a vain attempt to provide cover for his fleeing son. He missed and was run down by the lead warrior, who quickly dispatched him and chased after the fleeing boy. The rider's galloping horse was no more than ten paces behind the boy when he fired. The shot took the boy in the spine, throwing him forward to the ground with limbs spread eagle. The first two scalps of the day were collected.

The party shooting flames of destruction landed all thirty of their shots on one of the two chosen houses, turned their horses in a U, and raced back into the rising sun—their shield both in and out. Settlers ran to the two burning houses to throw blankets over the flaming arrows before they could combust the logs of the cabin. The Cherokee knew this would be the response and had shot their arrows high, some hitting the roofs. The twenty warriors armed with rifles dismounted and aimed their fire at those trying to extinguish the flames.

Both cabins became engulfed and had to be abandoned by their defenders. The Indians shooting from the flanks hit three more as they rushed back to cover. Those they managed to down were carried to safety by other whites. There was no knowing if they were dead or merely wounded.

The Indians lost nothing in the first rush—neither men nor horses. They had taken two scalps, shot three more, and burned two of the thirteen cabins. The warriors, safely out of range of their opponents, celebrated with shouts of joy.

"We will take losses next time," Tecumseh advised.

"How can you know that, my young warrior?" Mukonse asked an oddly morose Tecumseh.

"We have lost two advantages—surprise and the cover of sunlight shining into the eyes of those who would shoot back.

And the Shemanese have two great advantages over us. One, they are well hidden behind walls. Two, they know that if they lose, they die. If we lose, we just go home. And they know it."

Realizing the cabin timber was drier than they had thought, the allies changed their tactics slightly. In their second and third rushes they did not concentrate their fire so heavily. In those two rushes they managed to burn down at least four more cabins and saw at least five settlers hit. But the Shemanese fought back. Even through the loopholes they managed to hit horses. Several had gone down, spilling riders. All fallen riders had been collected save one. He was too stunned or hurt to grab an arm and swing up behind another rider or grab a horse's tail to be led out at a run faster than possible if unaided. He had lain on the ground too long. One settler, with courage to come from behind the walls, ran out, musket in hand, and using the stock as a club bashed in the fallen warrior's head. Then he drew a large knife and cut off the scalp, not cleanly or with a practiced motion, but he got it off. He then raised the bloody trophy and waved it defiantly at the retreating Indians.

* * * *

There was no longer need to hide in the woods, just to stay out of gunshot range. So, the war party moved up to just two hundred yards from the cabins.

"We lost only one warrior and five horses. We have three who will fight no more today, but they will live to fight again," Mukonse said. "We have only two scalps, but almost half the cabins are down and they have many wounded. I think one or two more rushes and this village of Shemanese will be vermin in our blanket no more."

Tecumseh's horse stood next to Chiksika. Chaubenee stood his horse on the other side of Chiksika. Without turning his head in either direction Tecumseh addressed all three. "Yes, one more rush, maybe two and they will be ours."

Chiksika touched his brother on the arm to get his attention. When Tecumseh turned to him, Chiksika pointed across the grass to a small, straight pine tree growing alone in the meadow. It cast no shadow.

Tecumseh looked at the ominous sign with intensity. A soft thumping noise caught his attention. Before he could move, the thump was followed by the sound of a shot fired in the distance. He turned to his brother, who still sat on his horse but with a half-inch hole starting to ooze blood right between his eyes.

Chiksika slumped over soundlessly. Only the quick strong arm of Chaubenee kept him from falling. Tecumseh jumped off his horse, grabbed his brother by the waist, and eased his burden to the ground. He laid him gently in the grass, rose back up on his horse, and stepped forward to face the line. "They are ours. One more rush. Now."

Not one warrior moved.

"Now!" Tecumseh screamed.

Even Chaubenee did not move.

Mukonse walked forward slowly until Tecumseh was looking directly into his eyes. Mukonse then put his hand on the young warrior's arm. "We will fight no more today, Tecumseh. Moneto did not take your brother to encourage us but to tell us the day is lost. Let us take his body and go home to mourn and honor his memory."

CHAPTER 17

OCTOBER 4, 1790

Cherokee Village, Southwest Territory

Tecumseh sat on the packed earthen floor of the cabin, watching the young Cherokee woman stir the bubbling cauldron inside the fireplace. Mukonse had offered her to tend to the care of the Shawnee warriors in the cabin, who were Tecumseh, Wasegoboah, Chaubenee, and until three days ago Chiksika. The other Shawnee in their party were in the adjoining cabin. The Cherokee had provided them a caretaker as well.

Without looking up or changing his vacant expression, Tecumseh asked, "Wasegoboah, do you remember the first raid Chiksika took me on?"

The older warrior raised his head, his low forehead pulled even lower with what looked like effort to make his brain recall. He spoke slowly, as was his habit, in his usually deep voice. "Oh, I remember, Tecumseh. You were eight years old. So that makes it what, fourteen years ago? It did not go well. We were taken in ambush and Chiksika was shot off his horse. You were but a boy and you ran."

"Yes," responded Tecumseh, "I ran. But you stood up for me to my brother and pointed out that I had come back." Tecumseh indulged a small smile and turned his head around to look at Wasegoboah sitting at the table. "Do you remember how we were armed?"

Again, Wasegoboah pulled his forehead into a thoughtful scowl and pondered for a long while. "Yes, I remember. There were only five of us. All carried scalping knives and tomahawks, save Chiksika. He always preferred that club of his to a tomahawk. I had a musket. I'd just gotten it in trade for two silver armbands. Chiksika had one as well. The others, including you, carried bows."

Tecumseh turned back to stare into the fire as though seeing a vision there. And still facing forward and addressing no one except the fire, and perhaps destiny, he said, "Fourteen years ago we did not all have muskets. Many still fought in the old way." Then, addressing the maiden before him, he asked, "How old are you? Maybe sixteen?"

She turned from the hearth to respond. "You are kind, Tecumseh. I am seventeen." And then, after a slow sigh, she added, her bright smile sweeping the room, "And not yet married."

"When you first remember, did all the Cherokee live in log cabins? Or were many still in *wegiwas*? Now even the guest houses are of logs?"

This time she looked only at Tecumseh. "My first memory is the inside of a *wegiwa*. I remember it was smoky and cold."

Tecumseh just nodded and lowered his eyes back to whatever vision it was he seemed to see in the flames. "They have changed us so."

He was silent for a moment but all in the cabin now stared at him, wondering where his mind was traveling. "Muskets, iron tomahawks, knives and traps and hoes, woven cloth blankets, log cabins with chimneys and doors, tables and chairs, iron pots, whiskey. Even machine-made beads." He paused for a very long time. "Will we ever be able to go back?"

The room was silent until Wasegoboah spoke. "Who would want to, Tecumseh? Why would anyone want to?"

"Then tell me"—Tecumseh still sat looking into the fire—"what will we do when we've driven them all out?"

There was long silence in the room. The maiden used an iron ladle to scoop the bubbling stew onto a metal plate with high sides and handed it to Tecumseh. She had set a pewter spoon into the plate as well. He stared at it for a minute and then looked up to acknowledge her grace.

And when he did, she answered his question. "We will create and craft our own."

"Really? From what?"

She smiled a child's gentle smile at him. "Tecumseh, we Indians are not stupid or slow. Perhaps Shemanese know things we do not and came to us with things we did not know, but we can adapt. Even now a Cherokee wise man, Sequoyah by name, is creating a Cherokee written language."

Chaubenee, who had sat in silence the whole time listening, finally spoke. "The maid speaks wisdom, Tecumseh. We will learn and adapt. But we will leave those things to the Sequoyah among us. It is for the likes of us, you and me, to drive the Shemanese out. The mountains run from the Great Lakes to the swamps of your ancient home. Let us leave the area east of them to Shemanese. We will keep the lands on this side."

Tecumseh rose with his plate in his hand and a smile on his face. "Shall we start tomorrow? Let us destroy that village and kill them all."

There was an exultant cheer as they all rose to accept their feast.

Tecumseh stood up from the table and excused himself from his fellows for an after-dinner stroll and a conversation with Mukonse. As he strolled through the village, many voices spoke regrets for the loss of his brother, but many more simply looked in awe at the young Shawnee who had, by his quick wits and force of will, turned an ambush into a victory. With the death of his older brother, he seemed now to have become the natural leader of the Shawnee. This was a man they would tell their grandchildren they knew and had ridden with.

The open and firelit doorway glowed welcome. Tecumseh stood and waited to be recognized.

"Tecumseh, my friend, come in. Let me offer you a place by the fire and a mug of whiskey," Mukonse said.

"I will be delighted for the former but pass on the whiskey," he responded. "But do pour one for yourself while we talk."

There was no ceremony to stand on, so both men sat in chairs before the hearth.

"Mukonse, you know I must have the village that took my brother."

Mukonse said nothing but merely grunted understanding.

"They are very weak now. Some will be rebuilding, but some will have given up and left. Those who remain will be concentrated in the few remaining cabins. If we go now, just one more assault and they will be ours. If we give them time to rebuild, they will be stronger both in their defense and in their minds."

"What do you propose?"

"I don't want any of our warriors killed. This is no suicide mission. I want two days to study the village and find how many are there, where they are located, and when most are outside. We will want to do as much by stealth as we can. Perhaps kill the few who go to bring the cattle in one evening, and then use the dark to fire the cabins."

"When do you propose to do this?" Mukonse asked.

"In four days it will be a quarter moon. Enough light to see them rushing out of the fired cabins and get good shots at them . . ."

"Particularly when backlit by the fires," Mukonse said.

Tecumseh nodded agreement. "Exactly, but not enough light to see a skillful and stealthy warrior creeping in through the grass. The dogs will give notice we're coming, but the warning won't do them much good.

"I propose to take my Shawnee in the morning. It will take two days to get there. If you arrive on the night of the fourth day, we will have had two days to scout and prepare. Can you arrive with ten warriors in four days?"

* * * *

Tecumseh and the other nine sat around the fire warming themselves. It had been a hard day's ride, but it would make tomorrow's ride to the Shemanese village an easy one. In the evening a chill had come into the air and the Shawnee felt far enough from any enemy that there was no risk of their fire being seen. But even with a fire and the canebrake to shelter them from the breeze, it was very cold. Tecumseh unrolled his buffalo robe and threw it around his shoulders. He did not participate in the chatter of his colleagues but enjoyed watching and listening.

And listen he did. Over the din of chatter, he heard the snap of a dried cane stalk behind him. The sound came from the direction of the creek they had crossed just before stopping to camp.

A clumsy deer? Or hog? Perhaps.

None of his warriors heard the sound. Tecumseh said nothing but now listened not to the conversation of his warriors but with intention to what was around them. Not ten minutes later he heard the sound again, this time in front of him.

He spoke softly, in a conversational tone, and speaking on the inhale so his voice did not carry, said, "My warriors, listen to me very closely but do not stop talking."

Wasegoboah studied him with eyes surrounded by a flat face and eyebrows pulled up into his wide forehead. "Now why would you ask that?"

Tecumseh fixed him with a stare of such intensity that Wasegoboah silenced himself.

Ever quick, Chaubenee spoke in a mirthful and loud tone, "Ah, Wasegoboah, ours is a wonderful leader, is he not? Pay heed."

The others stared momentarily and then one after another continued their conversations but each with one ear tuned to Tecumseh's corner of the fire. In the same flat but conversational tone, Tecumseh said, "We are surrounded and about to be rushed. Don't look, and don't pick up your weapons until I give the signal. Attempt to collect nothing. When I give the word, pick up whatever weapon you have at hand, turn, and rush into the cane and out of the light. Don't run together. Each his own direction. Work back around and cross the creek. Meet west of the trail twenty yards beyond the stream."

Tecumseh stood languidly and stretched his arms high. As he brought them down, he whipped the buffalo robe off his shoulders and threw it over the fire. All was instantly dark. He screamed, "Attack!"

They rose in the dark and screaming war cries, ran in all directions. Their cries were followed instantly by shots, sporadic and not concentrated. Now screams of confusion in English followed.

Even in the near dark Tecumseh could make out the bulky outline of Chaubenee as he ran directly into a Shemanese, bellowing as he bowled him over. The collision was followed almost instantly by a scream of pain. Charging behind Chaubenee, Tecumseh saw the bulky, dark shadow before him pull his scalping knife and strike down. There was no more noise.

Fifteen minutes later all gathered, feet and legs wet from the crossing, just where he'd told them to. None talked or offered verbal greetings. They were trained warriors and knew the Shemanese would be listening. Tecumseh touched each of them in turn until all nine were accounted for.

"What now?" one asked in the softest of whispers.

In the sliver moon, Tecumseh's smile was visible only to those directly before him. "I'd like my robe back."

No one chuckled, but he knew they all smiled. "I can hear them. They've rebuilt the fire and are gathered around. We'll be able to see them when we get close. They are rifling through our gear and will collect our horses. They have at least one wounded. The Shemanese will stay by the fire until they have tended him. Get close as you can, as quietly as you can, but stay out of the light. When I raise my war cry we rush together. If you have no weapon, rush anyway. You will get one soon enough."

Another fifteen minutes later, the wet, poorly armed Shawnee lay on their bellies three strides from the opening in the cane, watching eighteen settlers happily collecting trophies. Two more lay on the ground completely still.

Tecumseh sprang to his feet and screamed, "For Chiksika," and rushed, war club in hand, toward eighteen fully armed whites. He hit the first before the man had even managed to turn fully toward him. Before the enemy touched the ground, Tecumseh spun to his left and looking at the bore of a rising musket swatted it to the side with his left hand. He struck below the cheekbone of his opponent and heard the sound of a jawbone snapping. The air around him was filled with cries, those of battle all in Shawnee and those of fear and surprise in English.

All the Shemanese were running now, most already in the cane. Tecumseh's club caught the fibula of a leg extended to run. He heard it snap and the anguished scream of the man who could no longer run. Seeing no target before him, Tecumseh bent over and brought the club down on the forehead of his prey.

They were gone.

"Quickly, no celebration. All who can, grab a musket, load it, and fan out about fifty yards into the cane. I want no brave Shemanese coming back to shoot from the dark into the firelight."

Four warriors, including Wasegoboah, were off in an instant.

"Chaubenee, take two with you and go get our horses. They will not wander far." Tecumseh pointed to a bloodied warrior on his right. "Are you hurt?"

His response was a very broad smile. "The blood is not mine but his." The warrior pointed to a man with an open belly, writhing on the ground.

"Kill him and take your scalp. While you're at it, kill all the wounded. But don't take the scalps. Let the man who downed each take it when he returns." Tecumseh turned to the remaining warrior. Blood was running down his arm, which was opened at the shoulder. "Sit down by the fire and let me stop your bleeding and wrap that."

Tecumseh looked around the disheveled area of the fight until he found a Shawnee pack. He did not know whose it was, but he knew there would be buzzard down in it. Tecumseh squatted beside the man and studied the wound. He reached in the pack and pulled out a cloth shirt, which he cut down the back and into strips. He also found whiskey in the pack and wet the first strip, which he used to clean the wound. "This will sting," he said as he poured whiskey into the wound.

The warrior's eyes narrowed, but he did not move or make a sound.

Tecumseh packed buzzard down into the three-finger-wide gash, then soaked two long strips of cloth in the remaining whiskey and wound each tightly around the man's shoulder and upper arm. "You will fight tomorrow."

* * * *

The dogs barked furiously and ceaselessly. The moon was not yet up, and with nothing but starlight to see by, it was impossible to locate the beasts—presumably tied near the cabins. But it didn't really matter. Their attack did not assume surprise, and they had not counted on it. Still they crawled belly low. They didn't need to hide because it was too dark for any of the settlers to see them, much less aim accurately, but they knew once the dogs signaled their presence there would be random shots toward them. Chiksika had been killed by such a wild shot. Reason enough to stay low this time.

As Tecumseh directed, they approached the six remaining cabins in groups of three. One of the three carried a bow and quiver filled with arrows, the shafts of which were wrapped in tar-soaked rags. Each of the other two was armed with a musket. As soon as an archer put spark to the rags, they knew there would be musket shots from the cabins. The two armed with muskets were directed to provide cover. Not that they expected to hit anyone with nothing but a muzzle flash in the dark to aim at, but hopefully they could get close enough to keep the shooters in the cabins low and slow. And when the cabins caught fire, they would have plenty of targets, all backlit by the flames of destruction.

The first lit arrow was fired, arching high into the night and landing with a solid *thunk* on the roof of one of the cabins. The archer dropped immediately to the ground but not before the report of a musket sounded and the flash of the muzzle directly before him assured him that he had been the intended target. Then arrows started to fly from all around the cabins, each arching into the night sky, creating a wonderous vision of beauty and death. Muzzle flashes from each of the cabins created less artistic but equally deadly flames in the night.

As more and more spots of flame dotted the roofs of the cabins, the sliver of a moon rose in the east and created a silver backdrop for the yellow and red dotting the night sky. One roof had five or six flaming arrows stuck into it when the sound of a door banging open exploded toward them. They heard the sound of a body clambering up the side, and then one by one the flaming arrows started to go dark.

"Wait until there is only one left to approach. Aim on either side of it and low—he won't be standing. Soon as the flame flickers to his touch on the shaft, fire." Those had been Tecumseh's instructions.

The guns fired at almost the same instant. The shooters were rewarded with a grunt of pain and the sounds of a body flopping down off the roof.

By now the roofs of two of the cabins were fully engulfed. As Tecumseh watched, the door to one of them burst open, beaming a yellow glow into the night. Three black silhouettes raced past the exposing light and toward the corral in front of them. A dozen gouts of flame exploded into the night in their direction. The team of three warriors assigned to that cabin leaped up, abandoning the safety of the ground. One worked his way with caution toward the open door to see who else might be coming. The other two raced in pursuit of the three from the cabin, hoping to catch them before any or all could get a halter on a horse and race off. There would be no escape for the Shemanese this time.

* * * *

Four hours later, the sun again burst into the gap at the east end of the valley. This time it matched colors with the remaining fires that had been six cabins and displayed the smoke rising up from each. Bodies with hairless and bloody heads were scattered around the cabins in peaceful, if gruesome, poses. The war party had rounded up all the horses and was using them to take all they found—iron cookware and utensils, some blankets and linens that survived the fires, considerable furniture and tools, and, most prized, weapons, shot, powder, and whiskey.

Standing beside one of the smoldering cabins, Tecumseh could see the eleven survivors. The prisoners sat on the ground with their backs to the only structure not burning. It was a partially completed barn. There were five women, five white boys and girls who looked to be between four and eleven, and one smallish black boy of about ten years. All were dirty and most with the vacant and exhausted look of the shocked and defeated. Two Cherokee stood guard over them, jubilant with victory. As Tecumseh watched, a Cherokee warrior approached the group with a staggering step that suggested he'd been celebrating with a found jug of rum. He stopped motionless ten feet before the prisoners and examined them one at a time, looking slowly down the line, his head unmoving for a long while as he appeared to examine each. Tecumseh watched as only one held his eyes without fear. She was a woman of perhaps twenty-five with dirty blond hair that sweat plastered to her face. She wore a dirty gingham dress that suggested she'd thrown it on over her nightclothes before abandoning her burning home. She stared back at the warrior, the emotional force of her hate matching his of conquest.

He stepped slowly toward her, malevolence in every motion. As he approached her, she raised her eyes to maintain contact with his. When he stood over her, she spat upward toward him. The warrior yanked her upright with one hand

and with the other gripped the collar of her dress and ripped hard, the cloth coming loose from her shoulders to her waist. She screamed and kicked him. The warrior raised his hand, and his fingers curled into a fist.

Before he could strike, Tecumseh threw him to the ground from behind. The warrior, even in his drunken state, bounced to his feet, scalping knife in his hand.

Tecumseh did not move. He merely stared at the man. "I have said there will be no torture. None of our captives will be abused."

The drunken warrior rolled upward onto the ball of one foot and started to step forward. But something in the intensity of Tecumseh's eyes seemed to get through to his alcohol-addled brain. His own eyes seemed to register that to challenge Tecumseh now would surely invite death. He turned and walked off, muttering under his breath.

Tecumseh looked at the woman standing before him, naked to the waist but showing none of the fear that nakedness usually carried with it. As he unbuttoned his shirt her eyes hardened. When his shirt was open, Tecumseh pulled it off his shoulders and with his hand outstretched handed it to her. "Cover yourself and be calm." His English was without accent.

The woman did and sat back down, more stunned than relieved.

Tecumseh addressed the group. "I appear young to you, but I am in charge here. None of you will be harmed. There will be no torture; there will be no rape. When we get to the village, there will be decisions, some of which will involve you. You may be ransomed if that is possible and you so desire. You may be made a slave, but as long as you are with me, slavery will subject you only to work rather than cruelty. You may also be adopted."

He looked directly at the oldest white boy and smiled. "I know that might sound strange to you, but I have a brother who chose adoption." And then he looked at the two young girls. "My stepfather also has two adopted daughters. They taught me English." And then with a pleased, almost self-satisfied smile, he added, "They also taught me to read and write.

"I will ask you not to run. If you do, you will be chased and caught. I cannot assure you that such recapture will not be hard on you."

He looked to the side and saw Wasegoboah standing with no motion whatever. He pointed to the prisoners. "Wasegoboah, get them all on horses, slow horses. Have them ride double. I don't want them to run, but I don't want them to slow us."

* * * *

The village was in a festive, almost riotous, mood. Fires roared high. Food and goodwill were abundant. In addition to wiping out the small Shemanese village and collecting wealth in goods and prisoners, not one warrior had been killed.

Mukonse invited Tecumseh to sit with him during the feast. "My young Shawnee friend, the things your life holds before you are untold but will be amazing."

"Why do you say that, Mukonse?"

Mukonse cocked his head and put a whimsical look on his face. "Is that an excess of modesty, or do you tease me?"

Tecumseh's face took a very serious expression. "Neither."

Mukonse straightened his head and brought his face to composure. "Then I will say what you seem not to realize or admit to yourself. You have the three qualities leaders of war must have and one that even few leaders of nations have. You have courage. You can outthink and outwit your enemies. Know what they will do before they do it and what you need to do to turn it to your advantage. This is a skill not many warriors have. And you are a natural leader of men. And you have an ability few leaders of nations have. You have sight. Not only do you know what your enemies will do in war before they do it, but you seem to see what paths nations will walk.

"Do you know, Tecumseh, that your fame already extends far? While you were gone a party of Choctaw and Creek came through the village. One of the things they asked was to meet the young Shawnee who is said to be invincible. 'Invincible,' Tecumseh. That was their word."

At that moment a loud voice called out for Mukonse. Both looked up to see a half dozen Cherokee escorting a party of three Indians toward them. The Cherokee in front held the bridle of the leader's horse.

Tecumseh did not know the nation of the three. Neither their clothing nor trap gave him any clue. But their heads were wrapped exactly as his was, as most Shawnee were, with a bright bandana of cloth folded about three fingers wide and with a single feather coming from the front. But the feather this leader wore was of a bird unknown to him—white, perhaps ten fingers long, the tip of the feather oddly downy.

Mukonse's face lifted into a large smile as he rose to greet his guests, who dismounted before him.

The stranger spoke first. "Mukonse, my old friend, it is good to see you again. But I confess it is not you I have come to see. I believe the man I wish to see is this young Shawnee with you."

He then looked directly at Tecumseh. "Are you Tecumseh?"

The speaker was of medium height and thin, his muscles long and well defined. His eyes were the eyes of a hunter, set in very tight to his nose. The smile that had been broad, showing his perfect white teeth when he spoke to Mukonse, had transformed into something flat, almost hostile.

"Yes, I am Tecumseh, son of Pucksinwah." He stood very erect and spoke slowly and distinctly.

"Then you are also the great-grandson of the old enemy of my nation, Opeththa." He stared at Tecumseh, his expression unchanged.

Around them all conversation stopped.

Tecumseh looked directly into the stranger's eyes, trying to establish the danger there, but he did not speak.

"I am Osceola of the Seminole. When this was the home of the Shawnee, we warred often." And then a smile broke out on Osceola's face. "My grandfather told me the happiest day of his life was when it came to him that your great-grandfather, Opeththa, was taking the Shawnee north at the invitation of the Miami. Opeththa was a great warrior whose name still appears in Seminole legend. And now after four generations I hear that he has a young descendant who is already a legendary leader of men."

Tecumseh did not yet let his face warm. "Osceola, it pleases me that my nation and family are still remembered by their old enemies. But you and I are not enemies. No Indian is my enemy. My only enemy is Shemanese. I will hope that if my name is ever remembered by the Seminole, it will be as a faithful friend."

Mukonse stepped between the two men and put an arm on each of their shoulders. "Sit as friends and let the Cherokee be friend of both."

* * * *

Chaubenee and Tecumseh sat on the floor, passing a pipe back and forth.

"The tobacco is better here than at home," Chaubenee observed.

"Perhaps it will impart wisdom as well as peace," Tecumseh responded.

"What wisdom is it you seek, my friend?"

"A small thing." Tecumseh passed the pipe to his friend and opened his face into an ironic smile. "Just destiny. My destiny."

"Do you think that is perhaps too much to ask of tobacco, Tecumseh?"

"Then who shall I ask?"

"Only yourself, I think."

They sat silently for a long time. Tecumseh stared into the flames of the fireplace. Finally, he spoke. "Tell me what people say of me, Chaubenee."

"That is a much easier question. They say you are courageous in the extreme; they say you can outthink your enemy; they say you have never lost a warrior who followed you; they say you are already a great leader. They say you are invincible."

Again, there was long silence. When Tecumseh finally spoke it was with conviction. "Perhaps there is some truth in most of those things. But invincible?! Well, I have been so far. Before we go home, I'll need to discover that one way or the other."

* * * *

The Shawnee looked back down the trail they had just followed from the valley below. From the floor of the valley, where the trail started its rise toward them, they could see dust rising.

"They are coming to get their horses back," Chaubenee observed. "You surprised me, Tecumseh. Did you not know when we stole the horses just before dawn that we would have no more than an hour's head start?"

Tecumseh offered a smile that was almost mischievous. "I knew."

"Then why did we not take them early last night and have the whole of it to get away?"

"We have enough time." Then he added, looking deadly serious, "And I have other purposes." With that he looked at his faithful warriors. "Chaubenee and Wasegoboah, stay here with me. The rest of you drive the horses onward. There is no need to hide your trail or be secretive. Drive them hard and don't worry about tracks or dust." Tecumseh raised his hand to shelter his eyes as he looked into the lowering sun. "Wait for us after the sun sets. If we don't catch up by the time the moon rises, wait for us no longer. Head back to the Cherokee quickly. Take our horses as well. Now go!"

With puzzled expressions they each grabbed the lead on one of the seven horses they had managed to steal and headed toward the setting sun at a trot the horses could sustain for the remainder of the day.

Tecumseh pointed at a small coppice beside the road just behind them. "Come with me. We will hide there."

It took the eight white men following them over an hour to climb up from the valley. They had walked all day and were moving slowly now. But these were tough men used to long days and they showed no signs of quitting. Tecumseh knew what the Shemanese had known from the beginning. The Shawnee had taken their horses and were riding. The only chance the Shemanese had of catching them was to walk unceasingly into the night and catch the Shawnee after they had camped.

Again, he looked behind him at the setting sun. It was almost touching the horizon and would be by the time the Shemanese covered the one hundred yards that remained between them. He turned back to face Wasegoboah and Chaubenee, speaking softly, inhaling as he did. "These men are mine. They are mine alone."

A shocked Chaubenee opened his mouth to speak, but Tecumseh raised his hand palm up to stop him.

"Destiny calls me. I must do what I am called here to do. The discovery must be made." He then laid his musket down and took his club into his right hand and scalping knife into his left. "If I fall, you may kill them and recover my body. Otherwise they are mine."

He pressed flat against the tree and peered at the coming eight. They were walking two abreast up the trail and were no fewer than ten yards away. He turned behind and looked west. The sun lay on the horizon, making the shadows of the Shemanese long, flat, and behind them.

Tecumseh whirled from behind the tree, screaming with demonic volume as he raced the few steps that separated him from his enemies. He knew the cry would startle them and the sun momentarily blind them. The biggest man was in front and on his right. He carried a musket in his left hand, which proved to be a fatal mistake. He jerked his head up to the war cry, momentarily startled and blinded, motionless for less than a second. But he recovered and threw the musket from his left hand to his right, bringing it up to his shoulder. By then Tecumseh was on him. He slapped at the rifle as it came to the big man's shoulder and then swung a crushing blow with the club, striking the back of the man's skull.

As his enemy fell Tecumseh allowed his own body to spin with the force of the blow and came behind the man who had been walking beside him. He, too, was trying to spin toward Tecumseh but didn't make it in time to avoid the blow that struck his spine.

Tecumseh continued to spin, and as he turned he found another man's back. Tecumseh allowed the blade of his scalping knife to slash low, just above the man's knee, severing the hamstring. The Shemanese screamed and staggered forward, knocking another man down.

The next man stood his ground but could not get his musket up in the closed mass of bodies. Tecumseh dropped his club, letting it hang loose from the strap on his wrist, and grabbed the barrel of the musket. He shoved his scalping knife into the man's guts and left it there as he rushed past again, catching his war club by the handle. He raised it, but there was no enemy now before him.

The remaining men had fled into the shadows, terrified. Tecumseh stood staring at the four fallen men, two dead, one immobile from a severed hamstring and the other struggling to turn on what appeared to be a fractured spine. With a casual nonchalance Tecumseh dispatched each with a single stroke.

Wasegoboah and Chaubenee appeared as he was peeling off the fourth scalp. Chaubenee's beaming smile showed in the dying rays of the sun. "You are invincible."

Tecumseh's face did not show a victor's usual sense of triumph. "It is time to go home. I have work to do."

CHAPTER 18

DECEMBER 12, 1790

North Shore of Ohio River, Northwest Territory

"I've never crossed the Spaylaywitheepi this late in the year. For a few moments toward the end, my fingers were so stiff I feared I would lose hold of her tail." Chaubenee nodded toward the grey mare pushing up behind them to get closer to the warmth of the roaring fire.

Tecumseh's lips formed into a sympathetic if blue smile. "We are not so cold as you." He gestured around the fire at the other Shawnee. As he did, he placed a hand to his neck and stroked the *opawaka* hanging there. The faces of the other Shawnee warming at the fire all took on knowing grins as they laughed at Tecumseh's remark.

"Oh?" Chaubenee asked, grinning. "Do the Shawnee not feel the cold?"

"My dear Potawatomi friend, it is all in Shawnee training," Tecumseh explained. "During the winter of our twelfth year, each of us has to complete the same ritual. It is usually in the Moon of Bears Giving Birth but always when the rivers are frozen. During a ten-day period a boy must wake every morning at dawn and walk naked from his *wegiwa* to the river, chop a hole in the ice, jump in, and then walk back. It is so miserable that we sometimes lie in bed in fear of the coming day. And the tenth day is the worst. On that final day the boy must dive in, swim down, and collect a handful of river bottom, which he carries back to the *wegiwa* with him. Whatever is in the handful of bottom that attracts him he keeps and puts into his *opawaka*. It may be a pebble or an old crayfish shell. Anything. Mine was a small piece of quartz." Tecumseh again touched the bag at his throat. "As long as I have it, I will never be cold again."

Wasegoboah's bass voice floated across the fire. "At least not as cold as you were that morning."

At which all the Shawnee warriors laughed knowingly.

Tecumseh's face moved from mirth to sobriety. "Tomorrow morning we part, Chaubenee. The Shawnee back to Kekionga on the Scioto and you to Mascouten Bay. You return an adult warrior with glory and honor."

"Yes. And it will be a time of great change for me."

Tecumseh turned to look directly into his friend's face. "What change?"

"I will become a Potawatomi."

"You are a Potawatomi," Tecumseh replied quizzically.

Chaubenee's broad face opened into one of his usual smiles and his deep resonant voice explained, "No, I've lived with them my whole life, but I am an Ottawa. My father is an Ottawa, and so I am."

By now all around the fire were listening attentively. It was Wasegoboah who asked, "How will you change that? Why will you change that?"

"Do you remember Canoko?"

Wasegoboah's forehead furrowed as though in deep concentration. "No."

Tecumseh gave a short laugh. "You don't remember her because you have no eye for beauty, Wasegoboah. She was a young girl in her first flower. Very pretty, and Spotka's daughter as I recall."

"Oh, I have an eye for beauty, but I like my women all grown up and not little girls," Wasegoboah responded in his very deep, slow manner of speech.

"You're right on all counts, Tecumseh," Chaubenee responded. "She was in her first flower and she is Spotka's daughter. And she will be my wife."

"Married?" Wasegoboah shouted. "She's a child."

Chaubenee smiled. "We've been away three years, Wasegoboah. She will be a woman now. And it has been known since we, Canoko and I, were small children. Opawana's son will marry Spotka's daughter and become a Potawatomi." And then lowering his voice to almost a whisper, he added, "Some things are ordained."

When Chaubenee raised his head, his eyes again held their usual merry twinkle. "What of you, Tecumseh? What awaits you?"

Tecumseh collected his buffalo robe off the drying rack next to the fire, steam rising from it, and wrapped it around his shoulders. "So very much. I have five remaining siblings, as you know. Unless Blue Jacket is out with a war party or hunting, all will be in Kekionga. He will update me on all that has gone on these past three years. Even the little news that came to us while we were with the Cherokee says that much has changed.

"My sister Tecumapese's son, Spemica Lawba, was eleven when the whites captured him. I saw very little of him between the time Blue Jacket arranged the prisoner swap that returned him and our departure. He will be a young warrior now. The triplets will all be nineteen. I have a lot of catching up to do."

* * * *

The morning was bitter cold, long streams of breath showing from the horse's nostrils in the dark grey light of predawn. The ten had stopped their horses and sat at the fork in the trail. The path straight before them led along the north shore of the mighty Spaylaywitheepi. The smaller trail, breaking off to the left, headed north.

"This is where I must leave you." Chaubenee pointed down the black path, almost no light showing through the thick woods.

Tecumseh sat quietly looking down his path, which was beginning to become more visible in the burgeoning light of day. "Yes, this is where each of us must go face our separate destinies."

"Oh, Brother," Chaubenee replied, "I think our destinies, yours and mine, are entwined, woven together." And reaching out to put one huge paw on Tecumseh's shoulder he added, "I must go home and become a Potawatomi. And a man's first loyalty is to his tribe. But as long as we both live, unless my tribe calls me first, I will be there when you need me."

And with that, Chaubenee kicked his grey mare and plunged down the lightening path.

* * * *

For the last two hours of their ride up the Scioto River Valley, the nine remaining warriors had been escorted. At first it was just two scouts who, upon seeing them, had rushed to welcome them home and be the first to hear their stories. With each bend in the river, the size of their escort seemed to increase. By the time Kekionga, the principal village of the Shawnee, was within sight, it seemed every warrior in the Shawnee nation was in their train. As they rode down the main street of the village, past the large log structure that was the trading post still run by the British silversmith John Kinzie, women, children, and dogs joined the parade, shouting greetings and joy to the glorious returnees.

Tecumseh rode in the front, as had become the custom of the band this last winter. The news had reached them that Catahecassa had become principal chief while they were gone, so Tecumseh was prepared to see the tall, fat old man wrapped in a long blanket, standing before the door of the large log structure that was the center of the village. Tecumseh remembered the large man's narrow and hawkish face that was now staring unblinking at him as the company approached down the wide and straight lane. Catahecassa was flanked by a half dozen elders of the tribe. Tecumseh was pleased to see Blue Jacket among them. His face alone among the elders was willing to beam a broad and happy welcome. He was even more pleased to see Tecumapese standing near Blue Jacket.

The years had not changed her face or carriage. She had always been considered among the most beautiful of Shawnee women, tall and full-figured, with high cheekbones, straight nose, and grey, penetrating eyes, and at thirty-two she still was. Spemica Lawba was standing beside his mother, or at least Tecumseh presumed that was he. He was sixteen now and no longer a boy but glowing with the strength and power of young manhood. He had taken much more of his mother's face than that of his long dead father. She had blessed him with not only her high cheekbones and straight nose but also her steady grey eyes. Last in line were the triplets. Not identical, each had a separate face. The most distinctive among them was Tensk, a black cloth patch covering his left eye.

When Tecumseh was a horse's length before Catahecassa he stopped, and with a dignity matching Catahecassa's own, raised his right leg up and over his mount's withers and dropped gracefully to the ground. He strode the three paces to

Catahecassa slowly, maintaining eye contact with his nation's leader each step. When they were a pace apart, he stood looking but not speaking, leaving the old man the honor of greeting.

"You go away a boy and come back to us a leader of men." As he spoke Catahecassa raised his eyes over Tecumseh's head and scanned the eight remaining on their horses, taking in each set of eyes as though looking for consent or betrayal of that position. Catahecassa kept his eyes raised and turned his head to take in the entire party, addressing them rather than Tecumseh. "You are welcomed home. We mourn the loss of Chiksika, your original leader, but welcome each of you home with joy. Some of the glory of your exploits in the south has come to us. We look forward to hearing the tales from you." Then he raised his voice and his eyes even higher to address the assembled townsmen. "Tomorrow night we celebrate the return of our warriors with a feast. Let all the preparations begin." As the crowd roared assent, he turned and walked back through the open door.

Tecumseh was immediately surrounded by his family, who showered him with the warmth of their love, joy, and pride. Tecumapese, the first among them to hurl her arms around him, whispered, "You have many friends and admirers who want you. When you are done with them, come to the cabin. The fire is warm, and I will have food on and drink out when you arrive. We can talk then when your family can have you all to ourselves."

Tecumseh pushed her gently to arm's length to stare at the woman he admired most in all the world. "I will be there as soon as I can free myself. There is so much to tell. And I am hungry. But put out no whiskey for me. That I will not need."

Tecumapese looked at him curiously for a moment, then smiled again, turned, and pushed back through the crowd of admirers, each seeking their moment.

Spemica Lawba stepped past his departing mother to look eye to eye into his uncle's face. "Let me take your horse, Uncle. I'll rub him down and get some food and water into him as well." And without waiting for a response, he stepped past Tecumseh, took the horse by the halter, and led him away.

Blue Jacket was next to greet him. "You have brought honor to our father's house, Brother. Why am I not surprised you lead men to glory?" And then Blue Jacket threw his arms around his younger brother and picked him up into the air. "Welcome home. I have much to tell and discuss. Come to me in the morning and we will go for a long ride." And he turned on his heels and walked off.

The triplets stood behind—Sauwaseekau, Kumskaka, and Tensk. The first two stood almost shyly shoulder to shoulder. Tensk stood a half step behind, his face distorted into a frown.

"And what troubles you, Little Brother?" Tecumseh asked.

"You could have taken me along. I was sixteen and old enough. I know it was because my eye was stolen from me when Sauwaseekau's arrow missed his goose and took me instead."

Tecumseh threw back his head in a laugh, reached out, and tousled Tensk's hair, careful not to disturb the strap holding his patch in place. "Don't speak such silliness. Come, lead me to the cabin that is my home again."

When they reached the cabin, Tecumseh's horse was out of sight, but his pack animal and Wasegoboah's horse were tied outside the door. Stepping inside, he was immediately warmed by the fire and the odor of the venison steaks hanging there. Tecumapese and Wasegoboah stood before the fire, he with a mug of whiskey in his hand.

Tecumapese turned beaming to her brother. "Welcome to your home, Little Brother." And then after a pause, she said, "I suppose I can't call you that anymore. Wasegoboah has been telling me the stories of your leadership and courage. I knew it would be so."

Tecumseh returned the warmth of her smile and turned to Wasegoboah, changing his expression to one of bemused chastisement. "What tales do you tell of me, Wasegoboah?"

Wasegoboah raised to an almost self-righteously rigid posture and responded with his bull's voice. "Only small truths, Tecumseh." Silence filled the room and he added, "Spemica Lawba released your horse into the herd but forgot your pack animal. I just brought it home for you." He drained the rest of his cup, turned to the door, and left.

"Now sit," Tecumapese commanded as the door closed. "That steak will be done in minutes. I have enough to feed all the men of this family."

* * *

"How much have you heard of General Harmar's defeat?" Blue Jacket asked as the two horses trotted down the path along the river. The sun was just rising above the trees to beam directly on the water and pull wisps of fog up from its ice-laden surface.

"I heard enough to know you were a brilliant war chief," Tecumseh responded with obvious pride. "When we were little, I'd thought you would replace Father as war chief, but when the Kispoko went west I couldn't figure out how the structure would change."

"I don't know whether that's been decided," Blue Jacket responded flatly, without any sense of self-importance. "That I was raised a Kispoko, even though they have left, may have helped. Who knows who will follow me?"

"Tribal structure was perhaps part of the process. But the fact that you'd won so many victories and lost so few men had to be part of that decision," Tecumseh said with obvious pride. "And I hear it was the same with Harmar. Did he really come with fifteen hundred? Did you really stay before him until he tired so he failed one evening to put up breastworks around his camp?"

"All true more or less. The fifteen hundred included some wives and camp followers. And yes, he was coming to Kekionga and I did just let him keep coming, staying ever in front of him and harassing him with nothing more than scouts. They had to cut a road to bring their guns. Eventually they pushed too hard and set up camp exhausted without their usual security. We came to both flanks just before dawn. They ran quickly and we took many scalps before I called our warriors back. We killed something like two hundred that day."

They rode in silence for a moment before Blue Jacket spoke again. "Tecumseh, you just said when you were little you thought I'd replace Father as war chief. Did you never think I, the adopted white captive, was cheating Chiksika of that honor?"

Tecumseh was unprepared for any question of his loyalty to the man who had always been his eldest brother, and he stayed silent while he collected his thoughts and formed a response. When he did respond, it was simple. "You, Brother, are my father's eldest son and war chief of the Shawnee. As long as you are alive and I am Shawnee, I follow you."

Blue Jacket watched his eyes as he spoke but said no more. The sun was high enough to offer warmth against the chill of the winter morning. Blue Jacket stopped his horse to unwrap from his blanket, roll it, and tie it across the beast's haunches. "Tecumseh, I love this valley. It is the most beautiful place I have ever known. It was not my good fortune to be born Shawnee, but I always wanted to be. I was lucky to have Moneto grant my wish."

Staring out at the river, they could see ice along the bank. As the sun rose higher and the shade along the bank receded, ice twinkled in the light.

Eventually, Blue Jacket continued. "Perhaps that is why I am willing to fight so hard to maintain it. But I'm not certain I can." His voice reflected emotion that seemed to be the sound of his heart breaking within his chest.

"Tell me, Brother. Tell me all about the Shemanese." Tecumseh let his faith in Blue Jacket shine through. "And we will figure out how to defeat them."

Blue Jacket again started his horse down the well-worn path, the ice-constricted river on one side and dappled sunlight dancing among leafless branches on the other. "Shemanese are easy to kill. Sometimes as easy to kill as ants. But like ants they are unstoppable. They just keep coming. No matter how many we kill, more come down the Spaylaywitheepi, year after year, season after season. There are now so many Shemanese and their villages and towns in Kentucky that we will never get them out.

"The year after you left, in violation of every agreement we have had, Shemanese built a town on the north shore. Cincinnati, it is called. To protect it, they built a fort next to it. It is called Fort Washington after that great devourer of land and now president of the Thirteen Fires. The fact that the town is there was how Harmar's women came to be on this side of the river. It is also the place where he gathered his army of fifteen hundred. And we? We were less than three hundred with only our Miami friends and a few Potawatomi and less than fifty Ottawa."

Tecumseh interrupted. "If three hundred of ours defeat fifteen hundred of theirs, why do you fear?"

"The Indians are many nations. We each do as we will. But the Thirteen Fires fight as one. Whether a Shemanese family is from Virginia or Pennsylvania or New York or any other fire, if he lives in Kentucky, he fights for Kentucky. We are many nations and fight one at a time. As long as Indian nations fight Shemanese one at a time, they will defeat us one at a time."

The men turned and started back north up the river and rode in silence for a long while. It was not until they began to smell the smoke of Kekionga's morning cook fires that Blue Jacket spoke again. "There are two other things I must tell you if you have not already heard. First, Spemica Lawba has changed his name. He has begun calling himself Johnny Logan."

"Johnny Logan? Why?"

"You will remember the story of his heroic defense of the body of Chief Moluntha?"

Tecumseh nodded.

"Then you will remember that it was the general of the Shemanese army that attacked Moluntha's village who saved him from being killed and took him captive."

Again, Tecumseh nodded. "His name was Logan—General Benjamin Logan. And the other?"

"It is about the triplets. Well, two of the three."

"Which two and what of them?"

"Tensk and Sauwaseekau. Neither of them seems to have grown past the hunting accident all those years ago where Tensk lost his eye. Sauwaseekau appears to continue to feel guilt or at least mistrust himself with weapons. And Tensk cannot seem to get over his anger. Not just at his brother, but at the whole world."

CHAPTER 19

MAY 3, 1791

Kekionga, Northwest Territory

Tecumapese joined the women in the work of preparing the homecoming feast. The fire was blazing in the center of the village, directly in front of Catahecassa's lodge, which, as the largest structure in Kekionga, also served as the meeting house. She and the other women had stacked dead wood three feet high along a one-hundred-foot long pit and set it ablaze just at sunset. The flames now rose high enough into the night sky to outshine the full moon. It was the Crow Moon, so named because the corn had been planted and soon the fields would be littered with crows trying to consume the seed before it sprouted. She smiled, remembering her younger brothers and even her son hunting in those planted fields, with those black-feathered thieves as targets. They had all first learned the skills that would make them warriors in those fields. She remembered the proud look on Spemica Lawba's face when he brought home his first contribution to the family larder as crow stew at the age of six. Tonight, they would feast on meats brought in by hunters mature enough to bring in larger, and tastier, prey.

Tecumapese smiled, thinking about what came after the feasting and the drinking. Then would come dancing. The drums would call awake rhythms in their bodies that the cold and wet had suppressed. The drums would call them to move in ways of joyous expression. The men would be first. They would dance themselves to exhaustion. Women, the matrons, would follow. The mood, the renewal, the drink, the joy of being Moneto's chosen would inspire freedom in their spirits. The drums would inspire the same in their bodies.

But the finale was the greatest celebration of all. While the matrons danced, the marriageable women would quietly drift away from the fire and, drawn by either some predetermined plan or instinct—the men never knew which—would all converge at some point deep in the shadows. When the exhausted older women drew themselves back to their men and families and collapsed onto blankets and accepted an offered mug of whiskey and a shoulder or chest to lay their weary heads upon, the drums would start again. This time the beat would start in a stately manner—softly, like the gentle unfolding of warmth— and slowly rise in volume and tempo. Then they would appear. They would come in a line, led by one of the youngest, and slowly transform from figures of the shadows to flesh and blood women, healthy, strong women, proud women, women ready to take their places in the continuation of the Shawnee and offer themselves to warriors strong enough to accept them and courageous enough to admit that they were sometimes lonely.

Some years this ritual was danced only by maidens. But in times of strife, which was often with the Shawnee, women like Tecumapese would dance—widows, young, healthy, beautiful women who had more to give to the society than the care of their children, women who wished no more to be alone at night. Women such as these danced, and tonight she would be among them. Tecumapese smiled, knowing that in the dance, men did not dominate this ritual. Oh, the women would come first, using the light of the moon and dying embers to offer themselves, but the choice of partners was theirs. Hand signals, ones she'd not used in almost twenty years but remembered well, would give her control. The thought made her tingle in ways she had not in years. The hand signals would be sent in secret and hidden between the bodies of the dancing partners, not seen by any of the watching crowd and only felt by the couples. Through them the warrior made an offer. It was not an offer to marry but merely to commence flirtation, flirtation for the course of the dance. And with her hands she would tell him whether he could continue or not. If he got no affirming response, the warrior knew to spin to another partner. If his offer was accepted, he was allowed to become more daring, and again it was for her to accept or reject. At any time, partners could twirl away from each other and take up the dance with other seekers.

Only if, when the drums ended, she had her back to him and he had his hands firmly on her buttocks, would the couple race off into the night together with a public commitment made. Would she walk back to her family blanket and fall down giggling in an exhausted sweat, or would she race off into the night to become even more exhausted and sweaty? It all depended on who made the offer.

But that, she knew, was hours away. Between now and then there was much feasting and drinking and laughing, and perhaps some serious talking to be done.

* * * *

Tecumapese stooped, smoothing out the blankets for all her men and listening as Spemica Lawba and his two uncles stood talking and watching the fire roar. He was almost as tall as Tecumseh, but it was doubtful if, at sixteen, he still had enough growing years left to reach Blue Jacket's six feet one inch.

"Will you dance tonight, Nephew?" Blue Jacket asked, adopting a teasing tone older men used with youths who were, awkwardly, old enough to fight to the death with grown men but unable to muster any effective defense against young women.

"I will dance with the warriors," he responded in a flat tone that tried to conceal his understanding that he'd answered a different question than was asked.

Blue Jacket's teasing continued. "You know you can dance with them without any intention of marrying one. Many, perhaps most, of the men dancing with women will be there for the thrill of it. It is thrilling to be close enough to feel the brush of their skirt across your loins or to smell the sweet sweat of them."

"There is plenty of time for that, Uncle, but not yet." This time he smiled up at his uncle, a smile that accepted the teasing that had been clear in Blue Jacket's avuncular tone.

"Spemica Lawba." Tecumseh spoke the name with intention. "I have a question for you as well."

The younger man turned away from one uncle and toward the other.

"You say you will dance with the warriors. Will you fight with them as well?"

That the younger man was trying to keep any emotion from his expression was obvious to Tecumseh. It was equally obvious that he failed to do so.

His chin came up, his lips thinned, and the edges of his eyes pulled tightly back toward his ears. "Who will we fight with, Uncle?"

"Shemanese. He is the enemy of the Shawnee, and he comes again and soon."

"Uncle, not all whites are bad men. Many are kind and loving with knowledge and wisdom to share."

"Will Spemica Lawba fight or will Johnny Logan not?"

The fear disappeared from his face. The time for fear was
passed. The challenge was here. The challenge whose coming
he had dreaded. But now that it was here, its arrival was no
longer to be feared. "I will not fight General Logan's people. I
gave him my word."

This time it was Blue Jacket who spoke. "That was a thing
you should not have done."

Tecumseh stood looking at his nephew. The sadness on his
nephew's face was complete, but there was nothing to be done
about it. The choice had been Spemica Lawba's to make, and
he'd let Johnny Logan make it for him.

"Tecumseh, Blue Jacket, stop!" It was a firm command
thrown harshly in Tecumapese's normally gentle voice. "This
is a time of family and celebration. It is not a time for you two
to berate my son over his love of a man who spared his life."

CHAPTER 20

MAY 3, 1791

Kekionga, Northwest Territory

Tecumapese collected a large tray full of used dinnerware from the blankets and carried it away. The five brothers, who had danced with the warriors, sat exhausted together at the edge of the firepit, the slowly dying embers warming them against the cool of their evaporating sweat in the spring night air, each with the satisfied glow of exhaustion. They were surrounded by the giggles of the older women, who had just finished dancing and plopped themselves back down with children and husbands.

All seemed content except Tensk, who was never quite content and now just a little drunk. He propped himself up on one elbow, tilted his head toward the edge of the blanket, and expelled a huge belch.

"Brother, if you are going to throw up, do us all the kindness of doing so in the brush or a cornfield," Blue Jacket commanded.

Tensk rolled back to face them, a grotesque grin displaying all his teeth, gleaming yellow in the light of the fire. "I can hold my liquor." His voice slurred slightly. "Besides, I want to watch the rolling hips and swaying tits."

Blue Jacket reached across the blanket and smacked his brother across the side of the head with an open palm in a gesture that could have been taken as correction or teasing. "Enough, Tensk. Don't be vulgar." The words enabled Tensk to know the meaning of the blow. He spoke no more words and sat with a sullen look covering his face, shadows on one side and dark patch on the other reflecting the gloom of his spirit.

The drum released its first note, announcing the dance for couples. The dance that might end in new matings for the community. All conversation stopped. The drum sounded again, still softly. A second and then a third drum sounded with the same gentle sobriety. Silence for a moment and then the three drums sounded together. With each note struck, the tempo increased. And the volume with it. And then a girl appeared, stepping slowly with the music, almost not dancing, just swaying as she moved forward from darkness to light, her facial features still undefined, hidden in shadows at the edge of the light. Before her face was fully defined another body appeared behind her, slowly moving out of the dark. The rhythm seemed not to change as twenty women danced in line into the light at the edge of the fire. The first was no more than fourteen years old, with the ages of the other dancers increasing as each unfolded from the darkness.

As the last dancer came out of the darkness at the extreme edges of the fire, Tensk jerked upright. "It's Tecumapese!" He spoke with sober precision now.

All of the others sat up sharply and stared as their sister moved rhythmically into the light. They continued in rapt attention as the women danced their line along the length of the firepit until they finally turned to face the audience. The

tempo began to increase, each beat still distinct. Young warriors who would join began to stand up. The bravest of them
danced out into the firelight, coming around behind the wom-
en's line, selecting his chosen place behind one of the women.
When it appeared no more men would join, the tempo accel-
erated and the women turned to face the men behind them.
And at that instant one more man stood and moved quickly to
a station directly behind Tecumapese.

"Wasegoboah dances!" Tensk shouted.

The other brothers were too surprised to do anything but
stare.

As the tempo and volume increased, the dancers swayed
to the music and each other. Some couples would spin away
from one another, both always finding other partners within
easy reach. But Tecumapese and Wasegoboah did not spin
away. They stayed together in perfect harmony. As the tempo
increased, the bodies of the partners came closer together.
When the drums reached a crescendo that must have
exhausted the drummers but seemed only to excite the dancers, the partners turned so the backs of both were toward the
audience and they faced into the night. The signals being given
could not be seen.

And finally, all three drums came down on the same
booming note, followed instantly by complete silence, a silence
that seemed to hold dancers and watchers alike in frozen stillness. And then unfrozen, Tecumapese and Wasegoboah ran,
holding hands, from light into darkness.

It was Tecumseh who finally spoke. "Well, Brothers, it
looks like we are now six."

* * * *

Blue Jacket rose from the blanket, his look of amazement
replaced by a look of contentment. He stretched and looked

at his four brothers, all seeming lost in the same amazement that had struck him. "You triplets get yourselves to bed and try to keep Tensk out of trouble before you get him there. I'm going to bed myself." And he walked away. After two steps he stopped, looked back, and said, "Tecumseh, will you join me?" And without waiting he turned to walk again.

Tecumseh caught up with Blue Jacket and walked beside him, waiting for him to speak.

"The rains have passed, or most of them. The mud will dry and Harmar's replacement, General Arthur St. Clair, will be able to cut roads and drag his cannon. He will come soon. But we must know just when he comes. And we must know where he plans to strike and how many come with him. I have had great response from the tribes. Many will send warriors, but we need to give them time to collect, and not to be too early, lest they grow tired of waiting for St. Clair and go home."

Tecumseh had waited for this moment and was prepared. "Brother, I have pondered these things as well. The assembling of the tribes is up to you, and you seem pleased with the results so far. The other questions—when St. Clair comes, where he comes, and with how many he comes—are for me. I can find the answers."

Blue Jacket stared at him in the moonlight, his white face no longer white. God had given him the eyes and hair of a Shawnee. The sun had converted his white skin to a dark bronze. The bandana holding the eagle feather across his forehead covered the last of his whiteness. They conspired to make this man a Shawnee his own mother would take as such. The only thing not Shawnee in his face at this moment was the startle showing all over it. "How, Brother?"

Tecumseh could not help but indulge a small smile. "Will you give me fifty warriors with fast horses to have from now until the day we battle St. Clair?"

"Why?"

"It is about two hundred miles from here to Fort Washington. I will put a small camp of three warriors every twenty miles. The remaining twenty I will take with me to Fort Washington and spot them in the hills all around. Every day I will send a message with one rider. He goes fast because he only has to go twenty miles. Then the next rider takes the message. It will take less than a day for the message to get to you. Then you respond and it takes a day to get to me. Each horse and rider have two full days to rest between runs. And you will know what St. Clair is doing every day."

Blue Jacket just stared at Tecumseh and then let out a roar that caused several passersby to stop and stare. He wrapped his arms around his brother and threw him around with his feet flying in the air. "You will have your fifty within two days."

Tecumseh settled his feet on the ground and pulled his shirt down, as much to recover his dignity as to straighten it. "One more thing."

"Name it."

"Let Wasegoboah be among them."

CHAPTER 21

OCTOBER 22, 1791

Fort Washington adjacent to Cincinnati

Tecumseh, his hair tucked under a broad-brimmed hat, his pants legs tucked into boots, and his booming heart barely contained within his chest, strode with vigor through the front gate of Fort Washington. As always when he came here, he walked with purpose and with some piece of paper in his hand to look as though he were on a mission. Which he was. The first time he'd done this, his heartbeat was so loud he was certain that the guards would hear it. But he'd kept his face calm, given the guard a hand motion approximating a sloppy salute, and muttered "Scout" in heavily accented English. The guards let him pass without comment and now didn't even bother to examine him as he entered.

Through the spring and summer he'd been here a half dozen times, often being so brazen as to stop to read General Orders posted on the bulletin board outside St. Clair's headquarters. Now it was autumn. The leaves had changed, and the rains had come to turn the trails into mud baths. The breeze had changed from cool to cold as it whipped off the Spaylaywitheepi, and still St. Clair had not moved. But Tecumseh knew why. And with Tecumseh's knowing, Blue Jacket knew and the confederated tribes knew. And could plan.

Today would be the last time he'd have to take this risk. Today he was here to join all the other citizens of Cincinnati to cheer off St. Clair's forces as they marched out. And to count them accurately. There were seven hundred regulars, seven hundred Kentucky volunteers, and eight pieces of artillery being sent out to kill Shawnee. Trudging behind were an additional four hundred camp followers, consisting of wives, children, and prostitutes set out to make a killing of their own. Tecumseh followed the last of them out the gate and watched long enough to observe that they were taking the trail west toward Louisville.

Tecumseh knew that two miles away, Wasegoboah and a dozen others, wrapped in blankets and buffalo robes protecting themselves from the cold, waited for his return. When he finally arrived, everyone surrounded his horse. Tecumseh dismounted and addressed them all. "They have marched. But it appears they will not move directly up the Scioto. They are marching west, perhaps to go up the Little Miami. We must now change our plans in response. As soon as the other six return, we will all follow along their new route. Wasegoboah, come with me for a moment while I write a report."

As the others went to break camp and pack what few things besides bedrolls the scouting company carried, Tecumseh and Wasegoboah walked over to his pack and the stump he had used for a writing desk these last six months. Tecumseh removed a leather folio from the pack, sat on the stump cross-legged, and started to write.

"Adoption is sometimes a very good thing," Wasegoboah observed.

Tecumseh smiled up at him, understanding his meaning entirely. "It's been thirteen years since we adopted the McKinzie sisters."

"I was there the day they came to us. Little Moon was only eight and Little Sun eleven. Brave eleven-year-old she was, too. And well mannered. Looked right at Chiungalla, curtsied, and said, 'Hello, Sir. My name is Margaret McKinzie. I have entered my eleventh summer.'" Wasegoboah seemed lost in his reverie telling the story to one who already knew it.

"Little Sun proved to be a very good teacher." Tecumseh's face broke into a broad smile. "If we had to rely on Blue Jacket's English skills with his native tongue, this would all be gibberish."

"Who are you writing to?" asked Wasegoboah.

"I am telling Blue Jacket about the disposition of St. Clair's army and that they are heading west instead of north. I'm also telling him, and you, that we will follow. We will continue to send daily reports, but we'll have to swing the line of way stations so it constantly angles to the direction from which our scouts will ride. That may take constant change. As we move west, I'll leave it to you to keep those relays in the most efficient line possible and no more than twenty miles apart."

Wasegoboah merely nodded. Nothing more needed to be said. Tecumseh knew Wasegoboah understood what he required and would make certain he got it.

* * * *

They had followed St. Clair for a month as he wound his way north by northeast, up the Little Miami River. At the headwaters of the Little Miami, St. Clair turned back due north. It was a path that would intersect the Scioto at the place where it turned west. This course would require St. Clair to cross the Wabash before reaching the Scioto. That crossing would be near the beginning of the Wabash, where it was no more than a stream. It was now clear to Tecumseh that this would be St. Clair's course. He and his corps of scouts had watched every step of St. Clair's army. In order to drag their cannon along, they were forced to cut a road through each yard of the dense forest they traveled. As the fall rains got heavier so did the work St. Clair's men had to do. On some days of chopping trees, pulling stumps, and then rolling the limbers, hub deep in the mud, with mules and men straining to do so, they achieved no more than five miles of progress. But each night there was strength left to build a redoubt of some sort and put out scouts and flankers. They were cautious. And then, at the end of October, it happened. When it did, Tecumseh knew the Shemanese would be defeated.

"Wasegoboah, this news I carry myself." And he did, changing horses at every relay station but pushing himself on through exhaustion until he reached Kekionga.

As Tecumseh raced by the temporary structures put up in the harvested cornfields around the town, he saw them all. What an incredible job Blue Jacket had done. They were all there—Shawnee and Miami as expected. But also Wyandot, Delaware, Potawatomi, Kickapoo, Mingo, Wea, and Piankeshaw, as hoped for but uncertain, and Ottawa, Chippewa, Winnebago, Sac, Fox, and Seneca, not even hoped for. But they were all here, especially the Chippewa, hundreds of them. Virtually all the Indian tribes from north of the Spaylaywitheepi, east of the Mississippi, and west of the mountains. And a few British troops as well. He could see they brought no cannon, but some of the red-coated troops were here. Perhaps they would fight dressed as Indians rather than in red coats, but they would fight.

Tecumseh raced down the main street toward Catahecassa's council house. The Shawnee saw him coming. That it was Tecumseh himself and that he was racing down the lane must have told them his news was important, for he saw them all rushing along behind him. He also saw that other warriors who did not know him by sight had seen the Shawnee racing to follow the rider and so followed themselves. Within moments of pulling his horse to a stop at the council house door, three thousand warriors had gathered.

Blue Jacket, Catahecassa, and several elders greeted him. As Tecumseh caught his breath, Blue Jacket looked at him in great anticipation. Catahecassa's thin face was of stone with no expression of excitement, joy, or even appreciation showing.

When Tecumseh had spat out his report, Blue Jacket said, "Come, it is for you to deliver the news to our warriors." Blue Jacket stepped out the front door, reached over his head to grab the eave of the log roof, and pulled himself up, over, and back to a standing position in one smooth, athletic motion. He smiled down at Tecumseh and motioned him to follow.

When they stood side by side on the roof, three thousand warriors looked up at them in silent anticipation.

"Brothers," Blue Jacket roared over the crowd, "this is Tecumseh, whom many of you know and all know about. He is not only my brother but also the head of our scout corps. It is he who has given us daily information on St. Clair and his army for the last six months. Tecumseh brings this report himself because it is the final report we will need." And then with a nod to Tecumseh, he said, "Brother, tell all."

Tecumseh took a moment to start. He had never seen so many warriors in one place, and that every one of them was looking up at him gave him momentary pause. He started trying to match Blue Jacket's volume, but to maintain a tone of authority rather than screaming. "Brothers," he addressed them and paused again but only for a moment to ensure he had their undivided attention, "for six months now, my scouts and I have watched St. Clair's every move. He first said he would bring three thousand soldiers upon us. They never arrived.

He continued to expect more soldiers to arrive from over the mountains, but only seven hundred were sent. To supplement them he had to raise volunteers among the Kentucky farmers. Seven hundred of them also came to him. But he didn't have supplies enough to carry with them into their campaign. He waited the entire summer but the supplies never arrived. Always promised but never delivered. Not only have those supplies still not come but the rains have now imperiled his ability to bring his big guns. Perhaps he should have waited until spring, but St. Clair, for all his delay, is an impatient man. He committed to wipe out the Shawnee in 1791, and he will now try to do so."

The crowd erupted into a cacophony of objection and disbelief.

Tecumseh let them have their moment and then held up his hand, palm toward them, to request quiet. When he got it, he continued. "St. Clair left, expecting the supplies to arrive any day and left instruction they should follow and catch him when they arrived. He left Fort Washington with fourteen hundred soldiers plus four hundred women and children following. But he hasn't food to feed the camp followers. Their men try to hunt for them or share their own rations. Their trail has been wet and the work hard as they have had to cut a road to drag their supply wagons and the limbers for their eight cannons. St. Clair is a hard man, and on many days he drives them to exhaustion. Four days ago, four hundred of the Kentucky volunteers took off in the night. They took supplies with them."

The listening warriors laughed loudly at the weakness of those who came to fight them. Again, Tecumseh gave them time to quiet.

"But wait, it continues. St. Clair wants them back. He sent one hundred and forty of his regulars to retrieve them." And now Tecumseh raised his voice to provide them a mighty climax. "St. Clair now has less than nine hundred soldiers. Now is our moment, Brothers. Now! If we wait, his five hundred and forty men may come back and his supplies may catch up with him. We must strike now while St. Clair is at his weakest."

The audience was howling with excitement and rage.

Tecumseh called for silence one last time. "I have seen, Brothers. We will find him where the Wabash can be jumped by a horse."

Blue Jacket and Tecumseh dropped down from the roof and were mobbed by an audience wishing to be led to an orgy of destruction and death. The brothers let themselves be pulled away and to the encampment of the allied forces.

* * * *

A few days later, Tecumseh and Chaubenee rode side by side for the first time in almost a year.

"I told you I would be here when you called," the ebullient Potawatomi said.

"Yes, I knew you would," Tecumseh responded and then added with a huge smile of his own, "even though you are an old married man now."

"Hah! She can't keep me away. Besides, I lead these forty Potawatomi I bring."

"I have heard things, Chaubenee. You are only nineteen now, but I have heard that, when you married his daughter and became a Potawatomi, old Spotka stepped down and you have been named chief of the Mascouten Bay village. There is much expected of you now."

Chaubenee took on one of his few serious moments. "The main thing expected of me is to keep you alive. In our lives, the work will be yours. I just need to ensure fate doesn't change that on the bank of the Wabash."

* * * *

They intersected St. Clair exactly where Tecumseh had said they would, where the Wabash was narrow enough to be leaped by a horse. Of the three thousand confederated warriors, only the nine who had spent three years in Tennessee with him had knowledge of Tecumseh's "sight" until this moment. The others were in awe. They had arrived in this spot two days ago and hidden quietly and fasted the traditional time before battle, the time it took for the gut to clear and leave some hope of not dying a very painful death from sepsis if shot in the belly. Wasegoboah had reported at least twice a day. St. Clair's men were tired, wet, undernourished, and making straight for this Wabash. They would be here later this afternoon.

Blue Jacket and Catahecassa had agreed. Narrow as it was here, the Wabash still had to be crossed, and that would be an effort that would divide St. Clair's army. St. Clair with his men and machines would have to climb down the southern bank, cross the one-hundred-yard-wide mudflat with the stream-sized river's headwater in the middle, and then climb up the northern bank. If they crossed in the light, then the attack would be while half of St. Clair's army was on each side. But if St. Clair's army got here at dark and stayed on the south bank, the warriors would attack in the morning—in full light. Catahecassa had insisted that three thousand warriors shooting from all sides were bound to kill one another in anything less than full daylight. And even now at midday the sky was gloomy and overcast, with snow clouds hanging low. It would snow tonight for certain. They would remain three miles back from the river and wait for Wasegoboah's late afternoon report before closing the trap.

Before evening, Wasegoboah walked into camp and headed straight for Tecumseh. He knew he'd find him with Blue Jacket and Catahecassa.

"St. Clair's army is exhausted. In all of the days we have followed them, this is the first time they have failed to surround themselves with even the smallest breastwork. They have not even made a line of their wagons in order to provide some cover behind which to shoot." Wasegoboah's slow, almost pedantic voice could not hide the delight that also showed in his twinkling, if tired, eyes.

"Have they all stayed on the south side of the crossing?" Blue Jacket asked.

"St. Clair has sent two hundred fifty over as some sort of advance party. The others all stay on the south side. The wagons are in two lines about seventy feet apart, and the cannon in the open lane between."

Catahecassa and Blue Jacket gave one another small, self-satisfied smiles. Catahecassa spoke first. "Once it is full dark, Blue Jacket, you take your half of the warriors to the west side of their main camp and I will take mine to the east. If two hundred and fifty are isolated on this side of the river, we'll detach five hundred to surround them."

Catahecassa nodded and added, "Be certain every warrior understands, no matter what happens, no matter if some soldier takes a morning shit ten feet from him, no matter what, no noise is to be made, for any reason, until after it is full light. It will be for me to announce the assault with my war cry." Catahecassa turned his head slightly until he was facing directly at Tecumseh and repeated, "Me. It will be for me to call the attack."

Tecumseh's expression did not change while Catahecassa looked at him. When Catahecassa looked away, Tecumseh addressed himself to Blue Jacket. "We will need men to focus on those artillery pieces. I can use my fifty scouts plus the Potawatomi forty to kill all their crews and make certain they are neutralized."

Blue Jacket smiled a warm smile that he first pointed to Tecumseh and then toward Catahecassa. "That is a good idea. Keep your scouts and the Potawatomi with you and do it." Blue

Jacket added one comment: "It will snow tonight. I would suggest all our warriors wrap in robes or blankets. It will be long, cold hours on the ground before the battle begins."

* * * *

"AHHIAEEEEE!!" rang out from Catahecassa's large chest and two thousand five hundred musket balls poured into the killing ground between his warriors on the east and Blue Jacket's on the west.

Tecumseh could see the eight cannons in the middle of the open lane. Four stood side by side facing the river, and just behind them the other four faced in the opposite direction. There had been only one man standing next to them when Catahecassa's war cry started the battle. Tecumseh had aimed at him. His shot had spun the artilleryman around and dropped him to his knees, but he rose back up again, preparing the gun to fire. As Tecumseh reloaded, he saw the man heal over backward and stay down.

Chaubenee poked him in the ribs and said, "All this scouting hasn't improved your aim, has it?"

"But it hasn't hurt my speed. See if you can keep up." With that Tecumseh stood with his reloaded musket and started to run toward the guns. Before him was chaos. Some of the Shemanese officers had out their long knives and were trying to restore order. But the surprise and the terror were so complete that their men were simply standing like practice targets or cowering behind tents and under wagons.

Tecumseh's normal style would be to rush forward and never stop, to spin and move and kill with each step. But today that was the goal of others. His goal was to ensure those guns could not be loaded, aimed, or used. The Shawnee would learn to use them later.

He had broken his ninety men into four groups. He was with two of the groups on Blue Jacket's side of the battle. Wasegoboah had the other two on Catahecassa's side. All ninety were in the approximate middle of the line, where the guns were, but slightly separated, with one group focused on the guns pointing toward the Wabash and the other on the guns pointing south. Right now, the idea was to kill anyone who tried to use them. For that he and all his men could stay back fifty yards and on the ground shooting. At Catahecassa's war cry the guns had been over two hundred yards away and Tecumseh's men needed to get closer. He rushed forward to close the distance to a sure-kill range. He could see his men on both sides of the battle doing the same.

He could also see an older, fat Shemanese officer hobbling painfully along, screaming orders. And the orders he was screaming were for someone to get him a horse and for the artillerymen to get those cannons firing. Tecumseh knew it was St. Clair. The general got what he wanted. A younger officer raced his horse forward and offered the animal to St. Clair. The general raised his foot to the stirrup and started to hoist himself up, but St. Clair's foot gave way and he fell to the ground. Tecumseh could see no blood, but whatever was wrong with the general's foot was clearly painful. The young officer held the horse with one hand and helped his commander up with the other. This time when St. Clair tried to mount the young officer got his hands behind St. Clair's butt and pushed his commander into the saddle.

"Chaubenee," Tecumseh yelled over the din, "you loaded?"

"Yes!"

"Kill that horse."

Chaubenee did just as Tecumseh said. He shot St. Clair's horse right between the eyes. It collapsed with St. Clair still in the saddle but able to kick out his good foot and leap away before the beast collapsed on top of him.

As St. Clair struggled to rise, Tecumseh heard him scream, "Damn gout." But the old man was back on his feet, hobbling and again screaming for a horse and artillerymen.

Tecumseh looked up to see soldiers rushing to the cannon. His men were picking some off, but a Shemanese officer was leading the crew to load and aim the big guns. Tecumseh rolled on his side and reloaded. He came back to the prone position, took careful aim at the artillery officer, and lovingly stroked the trigger just as the cannon fired. When the smoke cleared, the artillery officer was down.

St. Clair was up on a remount. Now he trotted up and down the line, giving orders slowly but forcefully and forming small groups of terrified soldiers back into fighting units.

"Moneto is with that man." Chaubenee pointed to St. Clair. "He is the perfect target but musket balls seem to move around him."

"Moneto loves a brave warrior," Tecumseh responded.

Last night's pure, white snow was now covered with pools, streaks, and puddles of the vivid red of blood so fresh it had not had time to blacken. Some warriors took scalps as they killed, and the sight of bright-red heads on men lying on the snow only added to the macabre scene.

"I think it is time to rush those cannons. When you and I move, the others will join us," Tecumseh said as he sprinted toward the large brass guns. He reached them just as one crew was turning the loaded gun to shoot directly into Blue Jacket's assaulting force. Leaping, Tecumseh put one foot onto the barrel of the swiveling gun and hurtled into the crew behind it. His war club crushed the arm of a Shemanese who held it up as a shield protecting his skull. He screamed in pain. Tecumseh whirled as he dragged his scalping knife across the belly of a soldier raising a pistol toward his chest. He knew a third soldier was now behind him, but before he could turn a blow hurled the soldier into him. Tecumseh stumbled forward without falling and turned to see his attacker lying facedown on the snow, the back of his skull blown off.

There were four dozen of his scouts around him. Not one was hurt. The cannons were theirs.

Over the sound of the battle he heard St. Clair's voice bellow, "Form on me. We must retreat but we will do it in order."

Tecumseh looked to the sound of the voice. St. Clair was now mounted on a mule, but alive and leading his men.

Warriors rushed to collapse the flanks of St. Clair's retreating force. Many of the warriors had dropped their muskets and were using their preferred hand weapons. St. Clair had his much-reduced force in order and formed as they retreated down the trail without wagons, cannons, or women.

Catahecassa's voice boomed over the ground. "Leave them. We have killed enough."

* * * *

The heat and color of the fires were a stark contrast to the coldness of the grey skies and leafless, black trees. But it was the first warmth and the first food any of the three thousand had enjoyed in two days. A few warriors were still out on the battlefield, looking for friends and taking scalps, but most were eating, drinking, and nursing wounds.

"How many have we lost?" Catahecassa directed his question to Blue Jacket.

"Sixty-three total."

"And how many scalps did we take?"

"Eight hundred and thirty-two."

Catahecassa indulged a rare smile. "They will not be back for a long while."

Blue Jacket looked at Tecumseh. Neither was smiling.

CHAPTER 22

JULY 27, 1794

Fort Detroit, British Upper Canada

Colonel Richard England, commanding officer at His Majesty's Fort Detroit, was a vision of military power in his long red coat, white lace ruffled shirt, and long, black, highly polished boots, with a sword belt wrapped around his slim, athletic waist. Blue Jacket suspected that was exactly the image he intended to convey in this his first meeting with the leadership of his traditional allies, the Shawnee, in his long fight against what had become his traditional enemy, the Americans.

The colonel's old friend, the British Indian Agent for Upper Canada Alexander McKee, stood with him. Blue Jacket knew that McKee was, like himself, a turncoat American, and that McKee had been so disgusted by American colonial policy toward the Indians of the Ohio River drainage that in 1778 he defected to the British. McKee, who had been a friend to Pucksinwah, was fluent in Shawnee and married to a Shawnee. He could be trusted. It was he who had set up this meeting between the new commander and himself, Catahecassa, and Tecumseh.

For Blue Jacket and the Shawnee, this meeting was about one simple question: Could they count on British support against the latest American army being sent to crush them?

"General Anthony Wayne—his nom de guerre is 'Mad Anthony,' you know," Colonel England intoned in a high, almost squeaky voice, seemingly odd coming from a man so tall and well proportioned. England's face took on a distant look for a moment. "Yes, I know him. During the Revolution, we held this 'impregnable' little fort up on a cliff called Stony Point. I say impregnable cautiously because one night, almost moonless, Wayne and no more than two hundred of his men climbed that cliff. They carried muskets but they didn't fire them, you know. Just put bayonets on them and climbed. Took us by surprise. Also took almost five hundred of us prisoner." His words and self-deprecating smile let slip that he admired Wayne's audacity. "He is very good, you know. Perhaps the best the Americans have. But I'd heard he became a farmer in Georgia. Either he failed at that or duty has called him again." England's laugh came out as a giggle. "He is an odd combination of skills, you know. He prepares well and slowly, but when he attacks he is audacious. That's where the 'Mad Anthony' comes from, you know. When he comes, he will be well planned and prepared and then he will come in a rush."

"And when this madman attacks, where will the British be?" Blue Jacket asked in English, the words halting, belying the fact that he was speaking in his native tongue.

"Ever has King George, your Great Father, been a friend to the Shawnee." England paced slowly before the fireplace that was built into the wall behind his desk, his high nasal tone seeming to echo off the stone chimney and mantel. "And your Great Father continues to be, you know." England stopped pacing, looked directly at each of the three before he spoke again.

"I have been instructed to give you such aid as you need and I am able."

McKee spoke softly in Shawnee, translating England's words for the benefit of Catahecassa. When McKee finished, Catahecassa spoke directly to England, staring unblinking, his thin hatchet-like face immobile, as McKee translated. "We need supplies, guns, and ammunition, and we need your red-coated troops." It was the most direct statement Blue Jacket had ever heard Catahecassa make.

England said nothing for a full minute, watching smoke from the poorly drafting chimney play in the firelight. "You will have supplies, guns, and ammunition, but there are issues regarding our regular troops. Just eleven years ago your Great Father signed a treaty of peace with the Thirteen Fires. Sending our regular troops against their regular troops would be an act of war, and one I cannot commit without direct order. An order which, in the end, would have to come from the Great Father himself. But there are other things I can do."

After McKee translated, Blue Jacket addressed the Indian agent. "I talk with the Colonel in English." He then said, "You continue to translate, Alexander. Catahecassa can speak anytime if I've forgotten anything."

When McKee translated, Catahecassa said nothing.

"Colonel, what can you do for us?" Blue Jacket said.

England stared out the glass window from his office with its view onto Fort Detroit's parade ground. "Many things, Blue Jacket. Many things. You see those non-uniformed troops drilling on the parade ground?" He nodded toward the window. "They are not my troops but local militia. They fight just as well in war paint and feathers as they do in boots and flannel shirts." The colonel smiled, but the Shawnee faces remained impassive.

"And I can defend you," England added.

"How?" Blue Jacket asked.

"I cannot send troops to you, but you can come to me if you need me." England looked at them, but none spoke or gave a look of understanding so England continued. "The year you fought St. Clair, Sir John Graves Simcoe, the lieutenant governor of Upper Canada, built a fort at the falls on the Maumee, Fort Miami."

They all knew it and indicated so without speaking.

"If you are willing to let Wayne come to you and pick a place near there to fight him, I have been authorized to put extra troops and more guns at that fort. Not only can we support you from there, but if required you can come back under the cover of those guns. That is not sending our regulars to fight America's regulars, you see. That is simply offering protection to our friends."

It took half a minute for McKee to catch up in translation, but when he was done the scowl disappeared from Catahecassa's face.

* * * *

The three rode slowly south along the Maumee River, the summer day so lovely that even old Catahecassa seemed in good spirits. They had just passed the falls on the Maumee with Fort Miami still visible behind them. It was Catahecassa who spoke what was on all their minds. "If we are to accept the colonel's offer of protection, should it be required, we will have to pick a place near here to fight Wayne."

"It is an easy decision for me," Blue Jacket responded. "I would hope we don't have to fall back to the protection of British guns, but staying this far north makes it much easier for them to get us both supplies and the militia England promised. And while we hear Wayne is better than St. Clair or Harmar, we will probably be weaker."

"How?" asked Tecumseh.

"I think you know the answer, Brother. The western Potawatomi under your friend Chaubenee will stay with us, but I think their northern villages will not. And I fear the Chippewa are weary of war as well."

There was silence. Tecumseh held his face up to the sun, enjoying the warmth before he again addressed Blue Jacket. "In the last six years, you have destroyed both armies the Thirteen Fires have sent against us. You did not merely defeat them, you destroyed them. But it is as our brother Chiksika said, 'When one white is killed, three or four others step up to take his place.' I understand why they are weary, but we, and they, have one simple choice: fight and win, or cease to exist as a people. We must convince them."

Blue Jacket nodded his head in agreement. "And bringing the fight north makes it easier not only for the British to help but for the northern Potawatomi and the Chippewa to join." Then he stopped his horse entirely, and when Catahecassa did the same, Blue Jacket stared directly into the old man's close-set hunter's eyes. "So, yes, Catahecassa, my decision as war chief is easy. Fighting here has advantages. It increases our chance of winning. But that is just a military answer. Your decision is much harder. Will we, for the sake of that advantage, open every Shawnee village from the Spaylaywitheepi to here, including Kekionga, to Wayne's predations?"

Catahecassa turned his eyes away from Blue Jacket and nudged his horse forward. He did not speak but simply rode south across the grassland that spread out for the next three miles. They rode in silence, waiting for Catahecassa to wrestle with what may well have been the most consequential decision of his life. As they approached the place where the trail entered a small forest, they could see that many full-grown hardwoods had been thrown down, as though stepped on by giants from the sky.

Just before they entered the foreboding dark of the destroyed forest, Catahecassa stopped and turned to face both men. "Blue Jacket, you and your lieutenants prepare for war. I will start the work of moving all our villages and families north to Detroit or across the river into Canada. My heart and my mind tell me that if Wayne defeats us, the Shawnee are finished as a force to stop the Americans. If we do not win again, this land"—the old chief gestured with his arm swung in a wide circle—"will be American and the Shawnee will either become Americans or perish from the face of the earth. This last time I will fight and give you whatever you say you need to win. This last time." Then he turned again and entered the darkness.

It took them no more than ten minutes to ride through the forest before the land once again opened into prairie. Blue Jacket stopped and looked back. The others followed his gaze. "Wayne will come with cannon, and they will fire those deadly shells that open into dozens of musket balls. I think these fallen timbers will provide great concealment if not much cover for our warriors against such weapons. This is where I will fight Mad Anthony Wayne's army."

* * * *

A few weeks later, two thousand Indians lay hidden among the half-mile-wide section of fallen timbers. A mile in front of them, the flags of the Shemanese army waved proudly in the early morning breeze. They were coming. Blue Jacket stood with his long brass telescope, a gift of Richard England, propped across the trunk of one of the downed trees. He studied the disposition of the forty-six hundred soldiers he knew General Wayne commanded. His scouts had watched them for a month as they slowly and with great caution made their way up from Cincinnati. Wayne's army had always kept out scouts and flankers; each evening of the march they had constructed a strong redoubt around their encampment; when they stopped for more than a day's rest, they always constructed a fort of some kind. They had never given Blue Jacket an opportunity to surprise them, but he had learned the exact makeup of Wayne's army. He had twenty-two hundred regulars, sixteen hundred volunteers on foot, and eight hundred mounted Kentuckian volunteers in his force. He also had cannons.

Wayne would come today, and they knew it. Blue Jacket's army had fasted for the last two days, knowing when the enemy would arrive. What he now wanted to know was how Wayne would come at him. But he could see nothing in his telescope that gave a clue. Wayne's entire army stood spread out, regiment by regiment, across the grass in front of him. The guns were in the center and the cavalry was massed on Wayne's left, but none showed any signs of movement.

He handed the scope to Tecumseh. "Tell me what you see."

Tecumseh lay the telescope on the log in front of him and scanned Wayne's front. He started his scan on his right and saw eight hundred horsemen, but not one was mounted. Next were regiments of twenty-two hundred regulars lined up as though for a parade, but none at attention or even moving. They just seemed to be standing and talking. And then there he was. It had to be Wayne, a short and somewhat stubby man with a brilliant and beautiful uniform topped with an antique tricornered hat set so low that it almost covered his right eye.

Standing next to Wayne was a young, slim officer with a face so long and thin it made Catahecassa's look full. The nose was razor thin, its length accentuated by a forehead very high in one so young. The instant Tecumseh saw him, he shivered so hard he lost his grip on the telescope and dropped it.

"You all right?"

Before he answered Tecumseh reached to his throat and gripped his *opawaka*. He held it firmly for a moment while

Blue Jacket stared at him before he recovered the telescope. "I'm fine," he intoned very softly.

Pointing the telescope back to Wayne, Tecumseh got his second shock of the day. Standing next to the young lieutenant with the high forehead and the tomahawk-thin face stood his nephew, Spemica Lawba. He handed the glass back to Blue Jacket. "I do not believe they will come today."

"Why not?" Blue Jacket asked.

"Johnny Logan is with them. He will have told them our habit of fasting for two days before combat. I'm also guessing, shrewd as we hear Wayne is, he will hold us in place to let us starve—weaken a day or two."

* * * *

In the predawn hours of the next day, McKee brought aid to Blue Jacket and his army. On the grass behind the fallen timbers he had set up a dozen long tables, and on each were cauldrons of thin hot soup made mostly of beef broth as well as mugs of whiskey. "A gift from Colonel England," he said. "The soup is thin enough it won't foul your gut but will fill you and give you strength." And with a smile he added, "So will the whiskey."

The triplets—Tensk, Kumskaka, Sauwaseekau—had all come to Fallen Timbers and were with Tecumseh on Blue Jacket's right flank. In the stark black of predawn Blue Jacket had awakened all three and directed them. "The British have brought hot soup and whiskey and are passing it out. You'll find them through the trees behind us, about a quarter of a mile. McKee is right. We need strength. Wayne has tried to trick us into weakness. Broth will provide it without much risk. Go now but be back before the sky in the east is grey."

The three scrambled up from their places and scurried off in the dark.

Tecumseh shouted behind them, "Tensk, easy on the whiskey!"

Thirty minutes later Kumskaka and Sauwaseekau were back, awake and stronger.

"Where is your brother?" Blue Jacket, standing next to Tecumseh, demanded.

"He stayed for just one more whiskey," Kumskaka responded. He kept his head down, not willing to meet the look in either of his older brothers' eyes.

Tecumseh did not like it, but this was not the time for family discord. Tensk would be here either sober or drunk. They would deal with that problem then.

Blue Jacket had words of direction for the other two. "Wayne will come today. I think he will come as soon as there is enough light for his marksmen to see. And he will fire his cannons before that. When the cannonading starts, stay low and behind these trees. They will fire the shells that open into dozens of musket balls. The trees will offer cover for that. Only when it stops will his soldiers come. So as soon as the cannons stop, come to someplace where you can see his soldiers coming and can shoot them. Do you understand?"

Sauwaseekau looked boldly at his older brother. "Do not fear for us. We will make our names mentioned by the Shawnee today."

Blue Jacket was warmed by the boldness of the shyest and most reclusive of his brothers. "One last thing. You two fight together today. Never far apart. And do not—do not I repeat—stop to scalp your victims. You can get their hair later. To stop on a battlefield is to make an easy target of yourself. Move. Be a difficult target." With that he tousled the hair of each and went off to duties larger than his family.

The cannonade started at five thirty, but they were wrong. Wayne was not firing grapeshot. He was firing solid shot—iron balls six fingers in diameter. They did not spread out like grapeshot, but they did penetrate the fallen trees to turn cover into mere concealment. The trees offered Blue Jacket's warriors no protection. And it wasn't just the cannon balls that were lethal. As the trees were struck, the splinters that flew from the dead, dried trees became lances that penetrated flesh with ease.

The bombardment stopped by full light. As soon as it did, Wayne's mounted Kentuckians came whooping and screaming onto Blue Jacket's right—the flank he had directed Tecumseh to lead. Blue Jacket was certain that Tecumseh's warriors knew what to do. But he watched this first action closely just the same. Each of Tecumseh's warriors lay behind a log or stood behind a tree but all to the front, none deep in the woods. They did not rush out. They calmly took aim at a rider or horse coming toward them. Only when the target was within one hundred yards did they fire. The first blast was a bit too soon, the targets a bit too far, eyes not yet adjusted to the light, and fingers still stiff from the night's cold. Of the onrushing eight hundred, only a few riders were knocked off their horses and a few more horses went down. All the Indians had fired at once, and by the time they reloaded, the charging cavalry was less than fifty yards distant. More went down with the second blast, and the frightened horsemen seemed to rein in. The speed of the rush slowed almost to a stop, and horses, both with riders and without, started to mill in aimless circles.

A war cry was whooped, followed instantly by others, and the Indians rushed from cover to slaughter their directionless prey. Slowly the cavalry got sense of their dilemma and stopped milling and started running back the way they'd come, with five hundred Indians led by Tecumseh in terrible pursuit. All of the Indians on the right wing were racing onto the morning prairie with Tecumseh and the fastest warriors almost on the slowest of the horsemen.

And then Tecumseh seemed to see it. The woods that covered Wayne's left flank, his right, were alive with uniformed soldiers whose fire would cut them all down in the open. "GO BACK," he screamed loud enough to be heard over the racing hooves and hearts. "It is a trap." And he turned on his heels, screaming, and raced back to the cover of the fallen timber, pushing all his warriors before him.

Blue Jacket could see it was either the slowness of Wayne's soldiers to close the trap or the quickness of Tecumseh's thought that saved the Indians from disaster. They only lost five. All of them had either been wounded as Wayne's cavalry feigned retreat or twisted an ankle in the chase—injuries that made them too slow to return and so they did not. But there was no disaster. Only the fizzle of Wayne's first ploy of the day.

And now Wayne's strategy became his tactical might. His army came on—straight at Blue Jacket. Having no big guns to sweep the field, Blue Jacket's two thousand Indians used instead steady fire with their muskets to pick off the advancing infantry. The soldiers did not run forward as the Indians would have. They marched in formed regimental lines. As one soldier dropped, the man behind would step forward. And they kept coming all across Blue Jacket's front, the Indians in cover reducing their numbers as they did.

When the lead regiments got within thirty yards of the fallen timbers they finally dropped formation and started to run straight toward their opponents. They fired once and did not stop to reload. They had bayonets fixed and came straight in one screaming, charging mass. Two thousand Indians each got off one last shot and then switched to hand weapons. All along the front, the overwhelming mass of soldiers slowly pushed forward, the Indians in slow, steady retreat. Blue Jacket's warriors became more frantic as they neared the end of the wood. If they were pushed out of the cover of the fallen timbers, they would be open targets on the prairie.

With only one hundred yards of cover left, Blue Jacket sent runners to the leaders on his left and right. "Retreat now and swiftly! We will run under the guns of Fort Miami."

* * * *

Blue Jacket's move across the three miles of prairie took less than an hour. He was constantly last ensuring the covering fire of an orderly retreat. He could see Tecumseh moving slowly as well, his head moving constantly in search. Blue Jacket presumed it was a constant search for their brothers. Not once did he see any of the triplets. He'd not seen Tensk since he went for soup and whiskey and not seen Sauwaseekau or Kumskaka since the battle started. Blue Jacket arrived at Fort Miami to find almost one thousand warriors and some fifty Canadian militia dressed as Indian, milling before the closed gates. Blue Jacket saw Chaubenee pounding on the gate with the flat of his palm, demanding to be let in. He forced his way through the crowd and stood next to Chaubenee's wide shoulders.

"Will they not let you in?" Blue Jacket demanded of him.

Despite the chaos and conditions, Chaubenee could not help but smile. "Bastards have the bolt thrown and seem unwilling to open up."

"Hoist me up," Blue Jacket commanded. "I want to stand on your shoulders."

Chaubenee grabbed him around the waist and pressed him upward almost as though lifting a doll.

"Brothers," he screamed at the top of his lungs, perched precariously atop his big friend. "Be silent so I can talk to the British and get these gates open."

The men grew quiet, and Blue Jacket moved his feet around Chaubenee's huge shoulders to turn facing the fort. Chaubenee seemed indifferent to the load.

Blue Jacket looked straight up at the British redcoat staring down from the fighting platform above the gate. "Who is in charge here?"

In a rich brogue the redcoat responded, "Aye, t'would be Major William Campbell."

"Get him. Tell him I have orders from Colonel England."

The florid Irish face disappeared and Blue Jacket hopped down. Tecumseh had pushed through the crowd and was now standing beside him.

At that moment an aperture about six fingers square and at eye height opened in the gate. The face behind it showed nothing but narrow brown eyes and enough of a face to suggest the speaker was of unyielding temperament. The two men stood less than three feet apart but divided by eight fingers of log and a universe of society.

"Are you Major Campbell?"

"I am."

"I am Blue Jacket. I speak for the British allies who stand before you. Colonel England has offered us aid and promised us the protection of the fort should we need it. We do."

"I have no order to let you in."

"Colonel England committed to it."

"I have only one order from Colonel England in this regard. I am ordered to 'safeguard the integrity of the fort.' Allowing in one thousand warriors, being pursued by the army of a nation with which my country is not at war, will not, in my opinion, promote fulfillment of that order."

And then as an afterthought the Major added, "You may stand in the shelter of my guns if you wish. I will not fire on you. But neither will I fire on whatever force pursues you."

The aperture slid closed.

* * * *

Blue Jacket sat, face cradled in his palms, next to Tecumseh. Chaubenee huddled on the other side of a small fire, small enough that the flame would not give away their location. They were somber as were the other one hundred men in the grove.

"What will happen now?" Chaubenee asked without looking up.

"Wayne controls everything from the river to the Lakes. But we will fight." Tecumseh's face showed a determination that had not left him. "We must. We have no choice."

Blue Jacket raised his face from his hands and looked into his younger brother's eyes.

"Your eyes, Brother, are full of pain and sadness. We have won before and we will win again."

"Tecumseh, neither you nor I have that decision to make. And we both heard Catahecassa say this was his last fight."

Tecumseh's eyes glowed angry energy. "He is an old man and very tired. There is fight left in us."

Blue Jacket shook his head slowly. "He is an old man and tired who speaks for the Shawnee nation."

There was a muted shout on the far side off the grove and both looked up. In the dark they could see horsemen riding in at a pace that suggested both horses and riders were worn to exhaustion.

"That is Wasegoboah's mare." Blue Jacket, weary as he was, still rose in one fluid motion and walked toward the riders. "Come, Wasegoboah, we have meat and whiskey. Sit with us."

The exhausted leader slid off his horse and threw his arms around Blue Jacket, almost weeping. "I am so sorry about your brothers," he said.

Blue Jacket pulled back and straight up, startled. "What about them?"

"You don't know?"

"Know what?"

"Sauwaseekau and Kumskaka are dead."

"How?" Blue Jacket almost stammered.

"Bravely, facing their enemies. It was before the dawn, during the cannonading. They were sheltered together behind the same tree. A cannonball hit the trunk. It shattered in splinters. I don't think either felt a thing."

Blue Jacket turned, defeat showing in his posture for the first time, and shuffled back to his fire. "Sauwaseekau and Kumskaka are dead."

"And what of Tensk?" Chaubenee asked.

"I know nothing of him."

Tecumseh sat motionless, speechless and stunned, so Chaubenee took the lead. "Sit down, Blue Jacket, and join your brother in sorrow."

The war chief did and they all sat in silence. It was ten minutes before anyone spoke and then it was Tecumseh.

Looking at Blue Jacket, he asked, "Wayne had a young lieutenant with him. Man with a hatchet face and balding early. Do you know his name?"

"Yes, I do. It is Harrison. William Henry Harrison. Why do you ask?"

"Because he is a deadlier enemy than Wayne."

"How can you know that, Tecumseh?" Chaubenee asked.

Tecumseh looked up and with a small, sad smile on his face said, "Remember, my brother, I have sight."

There was a shuffling step at the edge of the fire and all three looked up. It was Tensk.

"Where have you been, Brother?" Blue Jacket asked.

"Drunk."

CHAPTER 23

NOVEMBER 10, 1794

Kekionga, Northwest Territory

Close to one hundred Shawnee chiefs crowded into the council room at Kekionga. Some were now chiefs in name only, as their villages had been destroyed by Wayne's army after the Battle of Fallen Timbers. All sat in silence watching the smoke from their long pipes mingle with the smoke from the fire as they were drawn up together toward the hole in the roof. All knew that, when the ritual was complete, Catahecassa would rise and address them.

As Catahecassa rose, Blue Jacket noticed that he had lost quite a bit of weight in the last months, and for the first time in memory their chief's body matched his overly thin face.

"My brothers," the old chief began, "this last year has been so difficult for the Shawnee that I begin to think the Thawegila and the Kispoko were correct. We should all have accepted the Spanish invitation to put the Mississippi between us and the Americans."

The assembly abandoned its customary silence before a speaker and broke into shouts of protest.

Catahecassa stood tall and impassive until they quieted. "Do not hear what I did not say. I did not say I will take any of my people west or go myself. I will not. I will die here."

Again, the assembly broke its traditional silence but this time with a less forceful and more agreeable noise.

"No," continued Catahecassa, "I will die here. That I will do. But what I will not do—what I will never do again—is fight the Shemanese."

And now there was silence. From some it was reverence for a heavy burden laid down. From others it was stunned disbelief.

Again, the rich voice, taught to project to a large audience, continued. "After much contemplation and consultation with many of you, two weeks ago I sent a message to Wayne in his new Greenville headquarters, to ask for peace between us. He has sent me his response and I have invited you here today to hear it.

"General Wayne makes three points in his response. First, he will offer no peace treaty now."

And again, there was a general rumble of discontent in the crowd.

Catahecassa quickly explained. "He will offer a truce, but there will be no formal treaty until next summer. During the Green Corn Moon, Wayne has invited us and all the tribes of the Great Lakes to a council to be held in Greenville. A formal treaty of eternal peace will be offered then. Between now and then, this truce he offers is dependent upon there being no violence between our young men and his soldiers or the white settlers. We in this room must see that happens."

As he said it, Catahecassa let his eyes drift to Blue Jacket and then fix on Tecumseh sitting beside him.

"And finally, Wayne has picked this spot, the marriage of the St. Joseph and the St. Marys Rivers to form the Maumee."

He paused long. "Our home . . ."

And he paused again before continuing, ". . . as the site of a major and permanent new fort to be named for him, Fort Wayne."

The silence was complete.

"Whether we stay or go will be told to us at the Council of Greenville. Between now and then we may stay."

* * *

"Blue Jacket, you are war chief," Tecumapese said as she prepared the evening meal. "What do you think of Catahecassa's pronouncement?"

Blue Jacket was sitting back in his chair, legs extended before him, both hands folded behind his head, almost dozing. But as always, when his sister asked a question, he had to pay attention. She was too smart and thought too well to be ignored. So, he straightened. "Tecumapese, he is the leader of us all. My burden is small beside his."

She straightened. Her skirts twirled as she turned. "What do you really think? Tell me."

Blue Jacket paused to consider his answer before speaking. "Our brother said it perfectly, 'When we kill one white man, three or four others rise to take his place.' No matter how many times we beat them they keep coming. When do we say, 'We are beaten, give us what you will. We will accept it'?"

Tecumseh stood and put the knuckles of both hands on the table and leaned forward, the fire flickering contorted patterns on his normally composed features. "Blue Jacket, you know the answer to that, I hope. I hope your answer is the same as mine. When we meet them in hell and not one day before."

Blue Jacket's face did not change. This was his brother, not some rival challenging his authority. "Perhaps, Brother, but have you thought about others besides the warriors? Death is easy for us. What about the widows and the old men and women and the babies. What is to become of them when you and I are dead?"

Tecumseh filled his pipe and then stepped beside Tecumapese to pull a splinter from the woodbox, light one end in the flame, and use it to light his pipe before throwing the splinter into the fire. He seated himself and took a very long pull. "What if we didn't have to die?"

Blue Jacket's face took on a smile of irony. "How do we do that? How do we fight without dying?"

"You are right, of course, some of us must die. But not so many."

Blue Jacket said nothing, knowing Tecumseh would tell more.

"When we have two thousand warriors fighting forty-six hundred soldiers, many die. When we have three thousand warriors fighting nine hundred soldiers, very few die. What if we had fifty thousand warriors to face them? How many would die?"

For the first time in the conversation Wasegoboah's bass voice projected out from the deep shadow of his corner of the room. "Where, young Tecumseh, will you get these fifty thousand warriors?"

Every eye in the room turned to him. Even the perpetually self-obsessed Tensk raised his face from his mug and seemed to lift his mind back into the room. The fire gave warmth and perhaps hope to the faces painted with skepticism.

Tecumseh, one who was preternaturally disposed to persuade, kept his head down and only let it rise to the firelight when all were looking. He looked into the blackness from which Wasegoboah's voice had come. "You and I spent three years with the Cherokee. How many warriors do you think they had?"

"No more than five thousand total."

"And the Creek?"

"We only met them periodically and saw very few. I don't know their strength."

"Guess."

There was silence and then the blackness rumbled, "Maybe three thousand."

"And the Seminole?" Tecumseh continued without waiting for an answer. "And the Choctaw, and Chickasaw, and Omaha, Sioux, Osage, Missouri? Not to mention the other twenty-plus tribes of our allies and our enemies."

Wasegoboah's face emerged from the darkness. "We all fight against each other, Tecumseh. Not together."

"My point exactly. We need to stop that and fight our common enemy."

"And who is this great leader that will stop us from doing what we have done for generations?"

Tensk spoke for the first time all night. "It is Tecumseh." His face beamed. "Tecumseh is that leader. The one that will make Pontiac's coalition look small."

There was a long silence, and then Tecumapese dipped a mug into the whiskey barrel and handed it to Blue Jacket. "So, let me ask the question again, Brother. What do you think of Catahecassa's pronouncement?"

Blue Jacket stood staring into her eyes, sadness running down his face. "I was not born a Shawnee, but I will die a Shawnee. I will fight with the Shawnee. As the Shawnee decide, as our chief leads us, that is my place, and I will honor it to the grave."

* * * *

In August the following year, Blue Jacket and Catahecassa sat on the lawn before General Anthony Wayne's headquarters at Greenville. The lawn was no more than a vast field. Vast enough to seat eleven hundred attending Indians, all of whom had been at Greenville for almost two months. The Indian representatives included ninety-one chiefs representing twelve Indian nations. Every tribe of the Great Lakes region save the Fox and the Sac had come.

The Fox, the Sac, and Tecumseh.

After two months of discussion and hours and hours of conferences among the delegates it had been agreed. Today the Treaty of Greenville in its final form would be read and then the ninety-one would be paraded up to each make his mark.

As the Indians sat on the lawn, Anthony Wayne, dressed as usual in the opulence of a period now twenty years past, sat in a chair with a table between them. On the table rested a parchment sheet, the final treaty ready for all to sign or mark.

Wayne rose to address the assemblage. "My brothers, we have over the years had certain differences that have caused conflict, pain, and disagreement among us. But now those differences are resolved. With the signing of this document, red men and white men will be able to live in peace. From the mountains on our east to the Mississippi River on the west, from the Ohio River on the south to the Great Lakes on the north, we are peoples ready to live together in peace.

"As is the custom among my people, before we sign the treaty, we will have it read aloud. I have asked Captain Harrison to perform that historic duty."

With that he pointed to the hatchet-faced young man with the very long, thin nose and receding hairline sitting beside him. The officer rose and bowed to General Wayne, his bow displaying the shiny new insignia of captain's bars on his uniform shoulder boards.

Wayne sat and Harrison picked up the parchment sheets. "This day is a day that the histories of all our peoples will hold in highest esteem." Harrison's tone carried with it an insincere quality that was evident to all who heard, whether they spoke his language or not. This was the voice of a condescending conqueror.

Catahecassa leaned to put slight pressure on Blue Jacket's shoulder. When he had his attention, Catahecassa whispered, "It is a voice that kills."

Harrison continued, holding his notes. "Agreed in this treaty are the following items: One. The assembled tribes shall vacate and abandon all land north of the Ohio River and east of the Great Miami River below Indian Lake and then south of a line drawn straight from Indian Lake to the Cuyahoga River and from that point all land east of the Cuyahoga River to Lake Erie."

This time it was Blue Jacket who nudged Catahecassa. "That includes virtually the whole of our Scioto River Valley."

Catahecassa, without turning to face Blue Jacket, responded in a whisper, "But our women and children will live."

Harrison's voice rose over them all. "Two. The assembled tribes have exclusive use of all lands not ceded by this treaty.

"Three. Save that within those Indian lands sixteen identified tracts will become property of the government of the United States for the purpose of constructing forts and other military and trade installations.

"Four. Lands held by Indians cannot be sold or negotiated in any way with any individual. Only the government of the United States shall have any future right to negotiate for those holdings.

"Five. Any white man who unjustly kills an Indian will be turned over to the tribes for administration of their justice.

"Six. All prisoners held by either side shall be returned.

"Will the ninety-one chiefs who are to sign this document please line up to my left to commence signing."

All rose, and all signed.

* * * *

When Blue Jacket arrived back in Kekionga, he went straight to Tecumseh's cabin. His first impression was that Tecumseh looked tired and much older than when he had seen him just two months ago. It took Blue Jacket a long time, without one word of interruption from Tecumseh or anyone else in the cabin, to explain the treaty. When he was done, he sat and watched Tecumseh closely. It always interested him to see how Tecumseh approached a problem, but this time he was nervous because the problem Tecumseh would be approaching was him.

"So, we are to have peace with the Thirteen Fires," Tecumseh intoned flatly.

"Yes, but now they are Fourteen Fires. Kentucky is no longer part of Virginia. It is its own fire now."

Tecumseh arched an eyebrow but did not let the news distract his response. "So, the price of peace with the 'Fourteen Fires' is that the Great Lakes tribes give up almost all the land south of Lake Erie."

"Yes."

"And that the Shawnee give up over three-quarters of the land that has been ours since your and my great-grandfather came north to save this country from the Iroquois."

"Yes."

"And that we allow the Fourteen Fires to plant forts and soldiers beside our principal villages."

"Yes." Blue Jacket waited for Tecumseh to speak more, but he did not. "But we gain things as well, Tecumseh."

The younger man stared out the door at the evening light moving from grey to black. "Yes, I know, the women and children get to live." He spoke as though talking to Moneto rather than responding to his brother.

Blue Jacket let his voice cajole. "We gain other things as well, Tecumseh."

"Tell me."

"We will be able to see justice done to any white who kills our people. That's something."

Tecumseh stopped looking at the growing darkness and turned an overwhelmingly sad gaze on his older brother. "In our father's time, Sir William Johnson, the King's agent to his red children, told us we could, and should, kill all whites who marked trees. And then Lord Dunmore warred on us and killed our father for doing just that. My brother, not one white man—ever—will be turned over to Indian justice."

"Perhaps, Tecumseh, perhaps. But I will tell you what will stop. There will be no more of whites stealing what Indian lands are left. No such commerce is allowed. Only the government of the Fourteen Fires can negotiate to buy any Indian land."

"That troubles me," Tecumseh responded.

"Why?"

"Because I can't figure it out. It is a trick. It is too good to be true. I know it, and Blue Jacket, you know it, too. I just can't figure out how the jaws of this particular trap snap shut."

There was a very long silence. Blue Jacket sipped at his whiskey. Tecumseh stared into the fire. The others sat waiting.

"Tecumseh, we need you. Will you stay?"

"No, Brother, I will not. I am at war with an entire race, and I will not pretend it is not so. The Shawnee are at peace with that race. I am no longer Shawnee."

"There is much sadness in my heart, Brother. Where will you go?"

"You are not the first here from Greenville. Chaubenee arrived earlier. The Potawatomi have offered land on the Tippecanoe River, just where it runs into the Wabash. I will go there. We four have talked"—he made an arc with his hand, taking in his sister and her husband and his last remaining younger brother—"We will all go. And we will invite any Indian who wishes as we wish to join us."

CHAPTER 24

NOVEMBER 5, 1795

*Tippecanoe River at confluence
with Wabash River*

Chaubenee and his party of Potawatomi sat quietly, watching the sixteen Shawnee riding slowly along the north bank of the Tippecanoe River toward them. Each of the sixteen led at least one additional horse, all packed high with the entirety of their worldly possessions.

Chaubenee rose and boomed a hearty greeting, "Hello, my brother, and welcome to your new home."

Tecumseh looked up toward him, almost as though noticing him for the first time. His face carried none of the energy Chaubenee was used to seeing there. He seemed much older than he had less than four months ago, when Chaubenee had seen him last.

Tecumseh slid slowly from his horse and trudged the few steps between them. He turned and used his arm to sweep toward his followers. "My brother, what you see before you are all who would follow me. Offer them your greeting as well."

Chaubenee's eyes took in Tecumapese, Wasegoboah, Tensk, nine warriors, and three women, none with children, who had followed his friend to this new place. "Welcome, all. The Potawatomi are pleased to have you come to us and make your home here, in this tranquil place and far from the discord you leave behind." The attempt at filling his voice with joy and goodwill was forced. He felt the tragedy of his powerful friend reduced to nothing more than an outcast, if a self-pronounced one, of his people.

Chaubenee in turn swept his arm behind him to take in the roaring fire and the five new *wegiwas* standing in an arc around it. "We Potawatomi have constructed places of warmth for you. When we leave you and go back to our own village you will have homes, shelter. Go now and rest yourselves. We have venison roasting and mugs of whiskey waiting. Go put your things into the *wegiwas*. When you have unpacked your horses, my men will take them to the river for water and rub them down. Your dinner will be ready by then."

* * * *

Chaubenee sat nursing a final mug of whiskey with Wasegoboah, Tecumapese, and Tensk. Tecumseh had, uncharacteristically, claimed fatigue from the long ride and gone to his *wegiwa* right after dinner.

"Is he ill?" Chaubenee asked. Wasegoboah sipped at his mug and said nothing despite the steady gaze from his old companion of war.

Tecumapese finally answered, "He has a sickness in his heart. He is defeated."

Chaubenee turned his gaze to Tecumapese, the firelight dancing across her face. His first thought was that though she was closer to forty than thirty, she was still a beautiful woman. "Defeated? Tecumseh?"

"Oh, not the Shemanese. They may kill him one day, but they will never defeat him."

"Then who defeats him, my sister?"

"The Shawnee. They have abandoned him, or so he feels. He has never understood that Catahecassa fears his power over men, his power over the Shawnee who Catahecassa thinks of as his own, as his charges, his responsibility. And he knows Tecumseh has the power to talk them away, to change them, if given the chance. Tecumseh does not see that Catahecassa has intentionally led them from him. He sees only that the Shawnee have forsaken him. He is heartsick."

Chaubenee held his gaze steady and thought, *She is not only beautiful but wise, perhaps the wisest of women, maybe even the wisest of all of us.*

His thoughts were gentle, but when he spoke his words were harsh. "Bah! Tecumseh is the only leader of Indians who had the courage to not kiss the ass of the Shemanese general, Wayne, and his lapdog, Harrison. We all know that. All, perhaps, except Catahecassa. Does Tecumseh not know we do? Does he not know that?"

Tecumapese said, "No, he does not. And if he is defeated, we are all defeated. Tecumseh is the hope of all Indian nations. Our only hope.

"Chaubenee, do you not think I see this, that I am not heartsick as well? My own son agrees with Catahecassa and fights for Wayne. Spemica Lawba guided them, advised them to starve our warriors another day before battling at Fallen Timbers. Even now he scouts for them. He is my only child and I love him as all mothers love their sons. My brother, Blue Jacket, led the fight in which my son's warriors killed two of my brothers. Not just men's hearts, their families' as well are broken and torn. Tecumseh is the only savior of the Shawnee nation and the price of that salvation, to me, will be my son. But I am here. I, too, am heartsick."

All sat silent for some time, taking in the power of Tecumapese's words. It was Chaubenee who finally spoke.

"Heartsickness is like other sicknesses. It can kill. But like other sicknesses it can also be cured. It is for us to cure him, and you. How do we do it?" Chaubenee asked.

Again, there was a long silence and this time broken by Tecumapese. "Our brother has many skills. We need to find some way to show him that we need those skills. His sense of duty is strong. If we can appeal to that, he will rise and be cured."

This time it was Tensk who spoke, his words slurred with drink as he did so. "We will have a hunting contest."

Now all heads turned to the half-drunk young man with the eye patch. "Ours is a new village . . ." He paused to burp and then continued. "Winter is here. We have only the crops we carried. We will need much meat . . ." He dropped his head between his knees and spat. "Perhaps Tecumseh can supply us . . ."

Again, Tensk let his vision and mind wander adrift with drink. Then he forced himself back to them. "But we will need more than the meat he can supply. We need him to lead again."

* * * *

Over fifty hunters gathered in the village at Tippecanoe for the contest. Chaubenee's Potawatomi had spent weeks building two large *miskahmiqui* to house the hunters and were using all the winter stores of food and drink they had to host them for the week. Chaubenee sent out runners with invitations, and they had come. They had come from every tribe that had signed the Treaty of Greenville. There were a few Shawnee, but most were from other tribes. Alexander McKee arrived as well.

Because there were so many hunters, it had been decided that the contest rules should be expanded to a three-day hunt to give each contestant time to find a hunting ground not cluttered by others.

While Tecumseh had originally agreed to allow Chaubenee to send runners to the nations with an invitation to the contest, he had shown no enthusiasm for the task. He'd spent little of the energy needed for the building of the guest houses and none whatever on thought of board for his guests. But as the first of the hunters arrived, his spirits seemed to rise. Chaubenee watched as Tecumseh greeted each to his village and, the day before the hunt, busied himself sharpening metal arrowheads and straightening the fletching on his arrows.

At the feast the night before the hunt, one that seriously depleted their winter supplies, Tecumseh spent the evening making certain every plate and mug was full. And when all were content, Tecumseh rose from his seat next to Chaubenee and, using the flat of his tomahawk to bang on a metal pot, gained the attention of all.

"Hunters, I welcome you and your help to our new village. We did not arrive here in time to plant corn or squash or beans. We carried some from Kekionga, but I fear this will be a winter of all meat and great grunting over the latrine pits in the mornings."

They all broke into howls of laughter.

"But with your help we will get through the winter and will all survive to plant our seed in the Crow Moon. And when we do, I invite you all to join us. Not just for the labor of planting, though I admit women's work will be done by men until more women join us."

Tecumapese shouted over the crowd, "I can't wait until all you warriors learn what hard work really is."

Again, the assembly roared with laughter.

When the silence was enough that the only sound was the crackling of the burning wood, he spoke again. "I mean that any who would prefer a life with us should know they and their families are welcome here."

A voice from the back shouted, "This is a Shawnee village."

Tecumseh snapped his eyes around to face the speaker. "Brother, I am glad you spoke. It gives me a chance to say what I wanted. This village on the Tippecanoe is not a Shawnee village."

"Will you all then become Potawatomi?" the same voice asked.

"No, Brother. This is not a Shawnee village; this is not a Potawatomi village." Tecumseh let silence in. "This is a new kind of village. It will be the first of its kind. This, Brothers, is an Indian village. There is no tribe here. Here, we are all one. Now drink your fill. During the next three days, we will pack the drying racks with meat. And I will invite you to drink your fill then as well. I want you to drink every drop of whiskey we brought with us."

Again, there were howls of agreement.

When the noise died Tecumseh turned slowly until he stood looking directly at Tensk. "When you are gone, there will be no more whiskey here. If there is any left, the last of you will pack it out. This will be a village where no man freezes on the January ground, or drowns in the midnight stream, or trades drunkenly with the Shemanese. There will be no whiskey in this village."

* * * *

There were almost seventy of them lying languidly or sleeping around the glowing remains of the huge fire that had warmed them and cooked their meat for the last three hours. As usual, Chaubenee and Tecumseh were together. Tecumseh lay, his head propped on a section of log, eyes fixed on the beauty of the night's moon. Looking at him, Chaubenee sensed he was content. By now Tecumseh had come to understand that this hunt had been staged to rouse him. And it had worked even better than expected. Hunters from every tribe had made it clear they went to Greenville only out of fear. And they knew and said that Tecumseh was the only one who had not given in to his fear. It was a good start. They would listen to Tecumseh. And his little village was secure for the winter.

Winter would give Tecumseh time to think and plan. And Chaubenee knew, given time, his friend would figure out how to do it. How to push the Shemanese back, back to where they came from.

And Tecumseh had won the contest. The closest hunter had fewer than twenty beasts. Tecumseh had more than thirty.

Wasegoboah had told him the hunt was Tensk's doing. Chaubenee knew that Tensk was lazy, vain, and drunken. Tecumseh knew it, too. Everyone knew it. Those things and that he was a coward, certainly not a warrior or a hunter. But he was cunning if not smart. What could he do? What value could be made of that? Not just value to his own work but to give Tensk purpose. Perhaps Tecumseh would figure that out as well.

"May I join you, Tecumseh?"

Chaubenee spun his head up to the speaker, thinking the Shawnee tongue sounded lyrical with the lilt of a Scot's accent, odd but not unpleasant.

Chaubenee had known this was coming from the moment McKee had appeared for the hunt. He smiled, knowing the British Indian agent had picked his time with the artfulness of a seasoned diplomat. Tecumseh sat up, crossed his legs under him, and pointed to the ground beside him.

McKee dropped between Tecumseh and Chaubenee and into a cross-legged sitting posture with the grace of the athletic man he was. He sat quietly, not speaking, looking up at the moon and watching the clouds drift across her face. When he spoke, it was while still looking up. "We would like to help." Only then did his eyes take and hold Tecumseh's. Chaubenee watched with fascination this diplomatic dance going on beside him.

"You have helped, McKee. You have brought us food. And more than most other hunters with that fine English musket of yours."

McKee smiled. "Well, it is slower, much slower to load, having to push the ball down that spiraled groove on the inside of the barrel. Rifling, we call it. The gun is named for it. It's called a rifle. The rifling makes the ball sail straighter.

"But we would like to do more for you and your band than provide a little food."

And here it was. They both knew it. The British wanted Tecumseh as their ally in some way. The perfidious British. Not his enemy, but reliably interested in their own needs, not his or those of other Indians.

"And what do your British want in return, McKee?" Tecumseh's response was brutally direct. But the British behavior at Fallen Timbers had been even more so. Chaubenee knew Tecumseh had no interest in pretending it wasn't true.

The Indian agent seemed not upset at all. "We want your friendship, Tecumseh."

Tecumseh looked up at the moon for a moment. When he pulled his eyes down to McKee's he spoke not just directly but bluntly. "McKee, I like you. You have always been good to me and to the Indians. You married a Shawnee, so in many ways you are one of us. But you are not truly so. You are white. And you always will be. So, when it is time to pick between the Great Father and his Indian children, we both know which way you will pick. I will accept powder, weapons, blankets, iron of all sorts. If that is useful to you, then it is useful to me. And I will fight the Fourteen Fires, the Americans. But I will do it alone and in my own way. I will not be an ally to any European power. It is only for you to decide if that is useful to you or not."

McKee sat silent for a long while. "Yes, we abandoned you at Fallen Timbers. Perhaps you are right. Perhaps we will do it again if it is in our interest. There is a people far to the east of Britain and Europe. A desert people who live in an expanse of sand as big as all this." He motioned with his hand in a wide circle around him. "They have a saying. 'My enemy's enemy is my friend.' For now, let that guide us both."

McKee sat silently looking into Tecumseh's dark eyes.

Then Tecumseh smiled a small smile and almost whispered, "For now."

McKee started to rise and then sat back down. "One other thing you should know. You are aware that for over ten years we British have been in Detroit and other forts south of the Lakes. Ten years after the land was taken by the Americans and given up by us in the treaty ending their rebellious war. But we have never moved out. That is about to end. This summer we abandon Detroit and the others south of the Lakes. If you come to me again, you will find me across the river at Amherstburg. We will build a new fort there—Fort Malden."

As McKee walked away, Chaubenee looked at his friend beside him. Neither spoke for a moment and then Chaubenee's wide face broke into an even wider grin. "That will be interesting."

Tecumseh said nothing but a let a wry grin of his own show in response.

"Tecumseh, tomorrow I leave you and go back to my own village. You know where I am when you want me."

CHAPTER 25

JANUARY 10, 1796

Tippecanoe Indian Village

"Brother, we must talk." Tecumseh rose from his squatting position before the hearth, scraped the remains of his breakfast scraps into the basket by the hearth, and laid the tin plate on the ground. He looked at the sky over his head and the frost on the few remaining leaves on the trees. *Odd feeling to being neither indoors nor out. But now that the fireplace and chimney are complete, we'll be able to get the log walls up and the roof on before snow. I hope.* The thought brought a chuckle to his lips.

"What makes you laugh, Tecumseh?" Tensk looked warily at the one person in life he both revered and feared.

"Nothing, Brother. Now come with me." And he turned and walked through the space where a wall would soon be and headed toward the woods.

Tensk scurried to catch up and when he had, walked a half pace behind. Tecumseh continued for most of a mile along the river and did not look back. Tensk became ever more nervous about what he'd done, or left undone, that would move his leader and elder brother to walk him away from everyone else. Was he to be lectured? Perhaps Tecumseh had discovered some of the whiskey he'd hidden before the hunters left. *He always seems to know everything.*

Finally, Tecumseh slowed his pace, looked behind him at the worried and deformed face of his younger brother, and held an arm out. "Walk beside me, Tensk. Not behind me." Tecumseh kept the arm extended, and as Tensk stepped toward him, he put the arm around him and continued to walk but slowly now. "What will you do with your life, Tensk? Have you thought of it?"

The question dumbfounded the younger man. He stopped walking and turned to look out over at the Tippecanoe. Ice formed on the edges, but the middle still ran slow and smooth, as though it were being reduced by the cold but not yet converted by it.

Tecumseh pulled the arm tighter. "Tensk, each of us must find a purpose in this life. Moneto gives each of us tools and talents, but leaves it for us to find out how to use them. So, what is it that you have a talent for? Something you can give to others, to this village, to the Indians, that will fill you?"

"I don't know, Tecumseh. I'm not good at much. I have a loud voice; I have a taste for whiskey. What of those are gifts I can give?"

Tecumseh gave a small laugh. "Well, first you can give up whiskey. You know it almost ruined me and is doing the same to you. As for your loud voice, it is true. If you could make people listen to it, if you had something to say. Moneto gave you the tools to be heard. You wander in the woods often and alone. What do you find there, Tensk?"

Tensk looked around for a moment until his eyes fell on a small, greenish, leafy plant lying wilted in the frost beside a pool along the river. "Do you see that, Tecumseh?" Tensk asked while pointing.

Tecumseh merely nodded.

"Do you know what it is?"

"No, I don't."

"We have no name for it, but Little Sun calls it watercress. The whites eat it. But it can be dangerous. Do you know why?"

Tecumseh, peering attentively into Tensk's now smiling eyes, shook his head.

"Because it is easily mistaken for an almost identical plant that is poison enough to kill. I have seen deer lying dead near swampy places with that other plant on their lips."

They were both silent for a moment.

"I have learned that while walking in the woods."

Tecumseh threw his head back and roared joy into the morning air. "Tensk, my brother, it is time for you to leave our little village and travel to Tawa on the Auglaize River."

Tensk looked stunned and confused at both the response and the statement. "Why?"

"That is the home of Penegashega," Tecumseh said.

Tensk stood mute.

"Penegashega is a very old man. Perhaps eighty-five now. He was second chief of the Thawegila. When they accepted the Spanish offer and moved to Missouri he chose to stay in the village of Tawa. He is the wisest healer among the Shawnee. Our village will need a healer. He will teach you."

CHAPTER 26

JANUARY 1, 1801

Grouseland Mansion
Vincennes, Indiana Territory

Johnny Logan walked up the long wooden steps leading to the veranda, where he was greeted by the thin smile of William Henry Harrison.

"Welcome to Grouseland, Johnny." Harrison put a hand on Johnny's shoulder and turned him so he was facing back down the quarter mile of snow-covered lawn, gently lowering to the Wabash River. "From here we will bring civilization to the land all the way up that river and to the Great Lakes." Then he turned toward the massive front doors. "Come into my office, Johnny. It is too cold out here. Being out in weather can kill a man."

Johnny had never seen a house like this. Even General Logan's home was small and plain compared to the opulence of Grouseland. It was a two-story wooden structure with finely polished floors and banisters. Intricately milled moldings adorned both the bottom and top of each wall panel. Woolen rugs woven in ornate patterns with vivid colors covered most of the floors. Abundant windows allowed light to flood each room and added just a tinge of color from the stained glass panels at the top of many of them. Harrison's desk was a massive wooden structure with surface enough to allow room for books and papers as well as room to unroll area maps. The fireplace directly behind it blazed with a fire full enough to warm the entire room.

Harrison's thin nasal voice matched his face. "Johnny, today is a very special day. Let us celebrate." Harrison reached for a cut glass decanter filled with amber liquid and poured two fingers of it into two lead crystal glasses. He handed one to Johnny and raised the other in a toast. "Do you know what day this is, Johnny?" And then without waiting for an answer, he said, "To the 19th century!" and drained his glass in one swallow.

Johnny took a sip and set his glass back down. Harrison dropped into his high-backed and ornately carved armchair with seat and back quilted in red velvet. Johnny stepped before the plainer wooden chair before him and sat.

"Johnny, remember today. January 1, 1801. Not only will you and I see massive change, we will effect it. That is why I've asked you here."

Johnny Logan focused his unblinking grey eyes on Harrison, but he said nothing. By now he knew Harrison well enough to know he needed no help unfolding his direction. Harrison needed him to merely listen and then do as directed.

"Johnny, the US Congress, at my suggestion, has divided the Northwest Territory into two parts. The eastern half, Ohio, named after our word for the Spaylaywitheepi, will soon become 'a Fire,' a state. This half, Indiana, will remain a territory and I will remain its governor as President Adams named me when it was formed. As such I will have complete power over everyone in the territory—white or red. But even more

important, I have been given power on behalf of the US government to treat with Indians in any manner I see fit.

"Johnny, you will remember that the Greenville Treaty
specified that no white man had the right to negotiate for the
purchase of any lands the Indians retained after the treaty.
That right rested exclusively with the US government. That
will be me. I will be the government. And the US government,
me, wants to buy land.

"Johnny, I want you to find a chief who will sell me land
along the Wabash north of here."

* * * *

Johnny Logan sat cross-legged on a blanket thrown on the
green, manicured lawn between Grouseland and the Wabash.
He was not alone. Chief Winnemac, with a half dozen of his
warriors, sat beside him. Harrison was with them as well but
sitting in a chair with a small desk between him and the seated
Indians. Behind Harrison stood a half dozen uniformed and
armed regular soldiers. Behind the soldiers was a small wagon
harnessed to two horses, the contents of the wagon piled high
and covered with a brown tarpaulin.

"Chief Winnemac, since Johnny Logan introduced us in
the spring, it has been my desire to purchase land along the
Wabash. You and your people have suggested you might part
with tracts on both sides of the river running from the place
where the Vermilion River enters the Wabash as a western
boundary and then east to the White River with the entire
parcel running fifty miles south from those markers. While
the land was acceptable to my need, you asked far more than
it was worth. But I think we are now agreed. Please feel free to
examine the contents of the wagon and see that it contains the
goods we agreed upon."

Harrison rose, and as he did two of his soldiers removed the covering from the wagon. Winnemac and his warriors all rose and moved forward. Johnny Logan followed behind. It took Winnemac and his men fifteen minutes to count all the goods—metal traps and pots, knives and arrowheads, blankets, kegs of powder, and cases of balls, as well as muskets and a large number of blankets and woolen shirts and trousers, bolts of bright cloth, and beads.

Winnemac had to raise his eyes to look into Harrison's. He spoke in his native tongue. Johnny had stepped beside Harrison to translate.

"It is as agreed, Governor Harrison," Winnemac said in a singularly nasal tone. "But we agreed to more than goods. We agreed to $1,700 in silver as well."

Harrison smiled and pointed back to the desk. "You will see the agreement on the tabletop. We will both sign, and then the wagon and the money are yours."

The men turned back to the desk. Harrison straightened the paper with his palm and pointed to the place where Winnemac was to mark his X. Winnemac took the quill Harrison offered and made his mark. Harrison signed. Then he slid open a deep drawer of the side of the desk and pulled out a pouch of finely tanned leather. "You will find eighty-five pieces of silver in the rather large bag. Each of them a $20 piece."

Winnemac poured the contents of the bag slowly onto the treaty still on top of the desk. A broad smile filled his plump face.

As Winnemac scooped the coins back into the bag, Harrison nodded to one of the soldiers, who produced a tray with a decanter and eight glasses. Harrison nodded again, and the soldier set the tray on the desk and poured whiskey into each of the glasses.

"Chief Winnemac, before you take your goods and return to your people triumphant, let us drink to eternal friendship between the Potawatomi and the United States of America."

The toast was drunk, and Harrison handed the decanter to Chief Winnemac. "Please take this. It was not part of the bargain, but I wish you to remember this moment with pleasure each time you pour from this bottle."

Harrison and Johnny Logan watched as the Potawatomi rode away, a warrior driving the wagon and Winnemac sitting beside him, the others on horses spread out before and after the wagon full of treasure.

"You did very well, Johnny. I have learned I can rely on you." Harrison was beaming.

"Governor, I am glad you are pleased, but what do you think will happen when the Miami and the Shawnee find out the US owns that land?"

Harrison's smile grew even broader. "Johnny, if there are title disputes between the Potawatomi and the Miami and the Shawnee, I will leave it to them to work out. But Greenville gives the US the right to buy land. I am the US, and I have done so." His smile grew even larger.

"Now, Johnny, I want to do something really big and I'll need your help again."

Johnny Logan looked up into the hatchet face and the receding hairline that were Harrison and waited.

"I want to buy Illinois."

A perplexed look came over Johnny's face. "Do you think Winnemac will speak for all the Potawatomi? He may dare defy the distant Miami, but his own tribe—all of it?"

"Oh, I don't want to buy it from the Potawatomi."

"Then who? Illinois is mostly theirs."

"Illinois?" Harrison's voice raised even higher as he said it. "Why, I want to buy it from the Illini, of course."

Johnny's perplexed look folded into a full scowl. "There are no Illini. The Potawatomi and Ottawa and a few others killed them all—mostly in their villages and the last survivors on Starved Rock."

"Oh, Johnny, there must be a few left, and they must have a leader."

"I know of none. I wouldn't know where to even begin to seek them if there were." His scowl had now become befuddlement.

"Johnny, think for a minute. If you were one of a handful of surviving Illini, where would you have sought protection?"

Johnny's face suddenly smiled in understanding. "From the French. In St. Louis."

Harrison drained the last of the whiskey, leaned back deeply into his chair, put his hands behind his head, and looked with pleasure at the beauty of the world he was creating.

* * * *

He sat in the middle of the large canoe, a paddler both in front and behind him. He could watch beads of sweat roll across the glistening muscles of the paddler in front of him. He could not see the paddler at the rear of the canoe. A fading black tarpaulin, covering the supplies they would need to get to St. Louis and back stacked immediately behind him, would have impeded his view even if he had fully turned to the rear. But it did give him a place to rest his back while he thought.

I like having paddlers, retainers to do the work for me. I admit it. In many ways my new life is far better than the labors of my old. All Harrison wants is just what Wayne wanted. My knowledge. What's in my brain.

Johnny laid his forearm on the gunnel of the canoe and dipped his hand in the water, feeling the cool and simple pleasure of the river running through his fingers. Sun danced through the leaves of the trees, alternating flashing of green as it moved over the leaves and yellow when it dodged between them. A school of sunfish made concentric circles in the water as they swam upward to capture the hatch of mayflies rising to the surface.

The rear paddler's joyous scream, "Aiee," broke Johnny's trance just in time to alert him to the rushing shadow of an osprey as it stooped before them and, with grace and timing few of Moneto's creatures could match, hit one of the sunfish as it reached the surface, plucked the wiggling fish from the water, and rose back skyward on the powerful beat of her wings. The three men all watched, the light underbelly feathers of the osprey making her rising flight easy to follow even as she rose well above the trees heading back to her nest.

"The bird brings food to the little ones. She's done her work for the day." The paddler in front gave praise.

Johnny, watching the bird rise high, said without looking down, "I don't think so."

"He's right!" the rear paddler exclaimed. "Look!"

They all saw it now and watched in fascination. High in the sky above the osprey, a bird so large it could only be an eagle was descending upon her. The osprey beat her wings faster, but within moments it was clear she could not escape. She dropped the fish and let it fall. The eagle, paying no further attention to the osprey, stooped down and snatched the fish out of the sky not one hundred feet before it fell back into the river.

"The big bully is a thief!" exclaimed the younger paddler in front.

The older paddler in the rear put his paddle back in the water and pulled, but head still up, he gave an old man's wisdom to his younger companion. "Moneto made them all—the mayfly, the sunfish, the osprey, and the eagle."

As the canoe shot forward, Johnny drifted back into his mind. *Yes, Moneto makes all beasts and they all act out the nature they have been given. So with men, with the Seneca and the Shawnee and the Shemanese. This land is the sunfish. The Shawnee the osprey that wants the sunfish and the Shemanese the eagle that wants it as well. And they will take it. Two years in Kentucky was more than enough time for me to see it is inevitable. There is no reason for the osprey to fight the eagle, and there is no reason for the Shawnee to fight the Shemanese. Catahecassa is right. But I am no longer Catahecassa's to lead. I have left the osprey nest. I have made Logan my family. I fly with the eagles.*

CHAPTER 27

MAY 2, 1802

Tippecanoe Indian Village

"We have been here six years. Our village is successful. We now have five hundred souls from no fewer than seven tribes living here together in peace and goodwill with a new set of rules. And it pleases me that many of them are Shawnee. But it is time to move my thoughts out to all the tribes. I am ready to do that, but before I do, I want you four, my most trusted advisors, to hear me out. I need to make certain of what I say. So, sit and listen. When I am done tell me what I have missed."

Tecumseh stood with his back to the fireplace in their cabin. Chaubenee, Tecumapese, Wasegoboah, and Tensk sat across the table, watching with intense concentration.

"During our lifetime, the lifetime of every Indian who will hear me, the whites have come down the Spaylaywitheepi or across the Lakes into the Indian lands. First a trickle, but after the Americans threw out their king it became a rush. And ever they have signed treaties to which they have agreed but not honored. Ever they took more. Our brother Chiksika said it best, 'The whole race is a monster who is always hungry. What he eats is land.' We Indians have fought him and killed him many times. Killed him easily. But on he comes. There are always more of 'the monster' than of any tribe. But there are far more of us if, only if, all the tribes join together. That is our only hope. We must stop fighting him one at a time and all rise at once. Only then can we push him back behind the mountains and keep the land Moneto gave to us.

"So, we must all agree to fight him together. We must accept one leader and move when that leader directs. All together. All at once. It will take ten years to form an alliance of the whole. Between now and then we must not fight him or each other. We must resist all the Shemanese insults and injuries. We must, for those ten years, do as the white messiah instructed, 'Turn the other cheek.'

"Between now and then our village here on the Tippecanoe must be a place of refuge and teaching. All will be welcome here. And by example we will live in peace and with just three rules. First, there will be no drink. We must not accept the weakness we, and the Shemanese, know is ours. Second, none of us will make any alliance with any white man—American, British, Spanish, or French. We can trade for what they have that we need—powder and weapons and other machined items we have not yet learned to make for ourselves. But no alliance by any tribe or any individual. Our own family member, Spemica Lawba, has shown the damage one Indian can do when he shares his knowledge of Indian ways with the whites. And lastly, and this follows from the second, no Indian may marry, or consort with, any white.

"That is all. That is the message I will deliver from the Seminole to the Sioux, every tribe between the mountains and the Mississippi and from Canada to the sea in the south."

There was a very long silence.

It was Tensk who spoke first. "How will you deliver the message?"

"I will dance it. I will talk it. If need be, I will send other messengers. For instance, I will not be well received by the Shawnee as long as Catahecassa lives, but you, Tensk, now the disciple of the greatest healer of the nation, may find your voice delivers the message to them better than mine."

"Let me suggest another way."

Tecumseh nodded assent.

"Penegashega has taught me much of how the mind works. Very often he leads patients visually—his hands make gestures that make the mind believe what the eyes see. Observe." Tensk reached behind him and from the darkness pulled a quiver full of arrows. He placed it on the table before him and took one out of the quiver and held it between his two hands and snapped it. Then he took four arrows from the quiver and again held them between his hands and again snapped them, but this time with more effort. Finally, he reached back into the quiver and this time came out with all ten arrows left. He struggled with all his might, but they would not break.

Tecumseh understood his brother's point, and his smile showed broadly in the firelight.

"Tecumseh, if I were a Cherokee many days travel south of here or a Fox, days to the north, I may not ask it but what I would wonder is how to know when it was time." It was Tecumapese's soft voice that asked. "The Shemanese can defeat us one at a time. It will only work if we all rise at once. How will we know when the moment comes?"

Tecumseh was very slow in answering. "Tecumapese, I have had a dream. In my dream I was standing right here." He pointed outside the cabin. "Beside that river. I was very big. Huge, really. So big I would see to the north woods and the beach on the sea to the south. I raised my leg and stomped my foot, and the ground trembled from the forest to the sea.

"The answer to your question is, I will stomp my foot!"

* * * *

There were seventy warriors gathered in the open meadow where trails leading to several Indian villages crossed. Most of the seventy were Wyandot and Ottawa. They had been invited to hear Tecumseh speak. They knew of the fearsome reputation as a warrior he'd created in his youth; they knew of his gift for sight shown to all in predicting the exact location where they would meet and slaughter St. Clair's army; and they knew that of all the Shawnee only he had resisted the command of Wayne to come to Greenville and sign the treaty that cost them their independence. And they knew that the force of his conviction had caused him to leave the Shawnee and form an all-Indian village. They did not know his vision for the future. They had been invited there to hear it. It was a message about which they were curious enough to spend days getting there.

"Brothers, think when you were boys. Did your people wander and hunt east of the Cuyahoga and the Great Miami River? Did you as a boy follow your fathers and grandfathers into Kentucky to hunt? Who keeps you out of those lands now? How many treaties has it taken for the white man to gain control of that ground? Have they offered solemn treaties before? Has each of those treaties been broken or renegotiated? In any one of those renegotiations has the red man been given more land? Then whatever is it that makes you think the Greenville Treaty will be honored?

"More white men come now than ever before. They have two sailing vessels on the Great Lakes. Do you think they are there for the white man to cruise about and admire the beauty of the land the Indians still hold? No. They push us even more.

Even now the earliest of them to take our lands have used it up, depleted it. So they move on to find more land to take. The mighty Daniel Boone has moved his family from Kentucky across the Mississippi to Missouri. Ever the white man progresses west and ever more come from the east to fill in the places he has vacated.

"My older brother, who died fighting the white man, said it best about his killers. 'The whole white race is a monster who is always hungry and what he eats is land.' Our land.

"And there is only one way to stop him. But none of us can do it alone. I know. I was born a Shawnee. It was our fate to live along the north side of the Spaylaywitheepi. We were the first to face the Shemanese. Face them we did. They killed my father; they killed my older brother; they killed my sister's husband; they killed my two younger brothers. No matter what we sacrificed we were not enough. Not enough to stop them. And our inability to stop them, to fight the Shemanese, has frightened the Shawnee. Not only has their principal chief, Catahecassa, given up fighting the Shemanese but he has insisted all Shawnee give up. He sees the problem correctly, the Shawnee alone cannot defeat the white man, but he has the wrong solution."

Tecumseh pulled an arrow from his quiver. "This is the Shawnee." He looked around the crowd until his eye fell on a warrior who had brought along his prepubescent son. He pointed at the boy. "Come to me."

The boy looked at his father, who nodded approval, and the child made his way through the crowd until he stood before Tecumseh.

"For just a moment, my brave young man, I want you to do a very unpleasant thing. Would you do it for me?"

The boy hesitated a moment and then nodded yes.

Tecumseh held the arrow out toward him. "You remember I said this arrow was the Shawnee?"

The boy nodded again.

Tecumseh handed him the arrow. "For just a moment pretend you are the Shemanese." The boy hesitated but accepted with another nod. "Now take this arrow in your hands and break it. Break the Shawnee."

The startled boy looked back to his father, who grunted approval. The youth held the arrow in his hands and snapped it. He stood holding the two halves.

"None of us can fight the Shemanese alone or even in small groups. But from Canada to the southern sea there are fifty thousand warriors who, at one time or another, fight against the Shemanese. Only if we all rise and fight at one time can we win and move the white monster back east of the mountains." Then he used both hands to reach into the quiver and pull out the remaining fifteen arrows. He held them up for the assembly to see. "These arrows are not just the Shawnee. These are the fifty tribes between the mountains and the Mississippi all together." He handed the bundle to the boy. "Now pretend you are the Shemanese. Break the strength of the combined tribes."

The boy wrapped his hands around the bundle of arrows and flexed with all his might. They bent no more than half an inch. He then raised his knee and pushed both ends of the bundle down against it. Still they did not bend any farther. Shaking his head, the boy handed them back to Tecumseh.

Tecumseh raised them over his head. "Is there any man here strong enough to break the combined power of all the tribes united?"

The crowd was silent.

"When I call, will you rise with me?"

There was a roar of assent. When it died, a voice in the crowd rose above them. "How will we know the time to rise?"

"I will stomp my foot!"

* * * *

Tecumseh watched the Wabash flow. He was ever fascinated by the yellow-green catkins when storms knocked them loose and sent them shimmering along the river's surface. His consciousness was instantly brought from musing to attentiveness, by what, he did not know. Then he felt something. He knelt and held his ear to the ground, the vibration of trotting hooves clear there. He stepped silently behind a large oak along the path and waited.

When the solo rider came around the bend in the path, he instantly recognized the bearlike figure of Chaubenee and stepped into the path, a large smile on his face reflecting this unexpected surprise. "Hello, my friend, and welcome to my small world."

Chaubenee slowed his roan mare and slid to the ground. The two embraced and in the end Chaubenee held the lighter man at arm's length. "It is always a joy to see my friend, even when I bring ill tidings."

"Are they so ill they will not keep until we get you off your feet and enjoy perhaps a little food?"

Chaubenee released a small laugh. "You know me well. Nothing is so ill that it will not wait for me to eat."

"Then walk back to the village with me and spare that poor mare of yours the burden of your girth."

The two men chatted as they walked to the village and through it to Tecumseh's cabin. *Whatever is bothering him is serious enough to send him on the journey of a week to see me but not so urgent that he must tell it immediately.*

The closed door to the cabin did not hold back the angry and loud tone of his sister's normally controlled voice. They could hear her shouts as they tied Chaubenee's horse and slid the pack off the beast and onto the ground. Tecumseh's surprise and embarrassment showed on his face, and he bellowed at the closed door, "Tecumapese, look who I've brought to dinner."

The shouts stopped in midsentence, and the door opened slowly to reveal Tecumapese's flushed face. She smoothed back her hair as she took control of herself. Upon seeing Chaubenee, her expression immediately changed into one of joy. "Chaubenee, my dear brother, what brings you on a week-long journey? Surely not my cooking?"

The big man picked Tecumapese up off the ground and twirled her fully around. Tecumseh took the moment to look into the cabin and see what the upset had been about. Wasegoboah sat in his dark corner, placid as ever, his low forehead dropped into complete composure.

As the three stepped in, Tecumapese was saying, "Well, you got here in time for dinner and to have a bed before the fire instead of in the woods."

"That very thought drove me and the mare hard all day."

Chaubenee spoke of nothing but his marriage and children, a little friendly gossip throughout dinner. Only after Tecumapese had cleared the table and Tecumseh, Wasegoboah, and the late arriving Tensk had filled themselves and sat quietly did he tell them what had brought him.

"You all know, or know of, Winnemac? Short man, chubby, who is chief of a small Potawatomi village. The southernmost of our villages really. Right up next to the Kickapoo. It is perhaps one hundred miles south of here. A bit west of Harrison's Vincennes."

All four listeners nodded and Chaubenee continued.

"He has sold land to Harrison." Chaubenee spoke no more, letting the impact of the phrase soak in.

Tecumseh jumped to his feet. "He what?"

"Sold land to Harrison. A piece along both sides of the Wabash south of here from the Vermilion to the White."

Tecumseh stood glaring. Then suddenly his face became a smile. "The trap has been sprung."

Tecumapese looked at him in astonishment. "What?"

"For the last eight years I've known the second condition of the Treaty of Greenville, 'no white man may buy any Indian land. Only the US government can buy land from any Indian' was a trap. But I could not figure out how it would be used. Now I do. Harrison is the government. He can."

"It's worse, Tecumseh." The tone of Chaubenee's mellow bass voice filled the room with warmth even as his words brought dread.

"How?"

"Think about it, my friend. The land I described is not Potawatomi. It belongs to the Miami and to the Shawnee."

Tecumseh sat back down. "But now Harrison has his land sale and he will use his soldiers to enforce it. He can buy land from anyone who claims to own it. And we can't stop him."

The room was silent.

Tensk was the one who said it. "If we can't stop him from buying, then perhaps we can stop Indians from selling."

* * * *

Tecumapese had cleaned up after dinner and left fifteen minutes earlier to carry the trash basket out to the community pit several hundred yards into the woods. Tecumseh knew the light of the half-moon would make her walk easy, but he wanted to talk to her—alone—so he left the cabin and followed the moonlit path himself. When he'd reached the edge of the village he saw her walking back, the empty basket waving from her left hand. Tecumseh didn't move, he just stood waiting. They knew each other too well. He knew she had known all evening this conversation would be coming, and that she dreaded it. She slowed her pace to a stop before him.

"May I walk with you?"

She stepped around him and continued on without responding. He said nothing but stepped beside her and walked shoulder to shoulder.

As the path opened into the village, she didn't stop but finally spoke. "Tecumseh, have you ever tried to speak with a man who wouldn't speak, perhaps couldn't speak? Have you ever tried to open your heart to such a man? To share the anguish of death all around? To share the fear that your only son had become a traitor to your tribe and positioned himself to kill or be killed by someone in his family? Sometimes, Tecumseh, it is very difficult to live with a man who does not speak."

CHAPTER 28

NOVEMBER 2, 1804

*Portage des Sioux, American
Louisiana Territory*

Harrison had not enjoyed the trip to St. Louis. Winter had
come early this year, and what he'd expected to be a pleasant
fall float down the Wabash to the Ohio and up the Mississippi,
watching the leaves change along the banks, had been nothing
but cold. There had been no ice to impede their progress, but
the temperatures were freezing and the wind even worse. Still
he was pleased to be here. Until last October, and ratification of
the purchase of the Louisiana Territory from France, his presence here as an official of the US government would have had
to be either very public or very secretive. And there had never
really been an occasion or cause for either, so he'd never come.
But after spending almost ten years in places where a muddy
village of no more than a thousand people and five thousand
hogs counted for a city, it was a pleasure to be in a place with
raised sidewalks, multistory buildings, a theater that also

served as a banquet hall, and thousands of acres around under cultivation. It was still frontier, but it was a city—or almost so.

As governor of the neighboring Territory of Indiana, Harrison would have to attend receptions, banquets, and perhaps a ball. And while Harrison's frequent visits to Washington had kept him familiar with current trends in the niceties of society, his attendance at these events would be his first such on the frontier.

But none of that was why he was here. Harrison had come to St. Louis to capitalize on Johnny Logan's great find. Johnny had found Paskepaho. Paskepaho, the only Illini to get off Starved Rock alive, was now the leader of a small group of surviving Illini living in three cabins at Portage des Sioux just north of St. Louis. His father, Quaqui, had been chief of the small Illini village at Mascouten Bay on the Illinois. But even more than that, he'd been the only village chief to survive the initial attack on his village by the Ottawa. He and his son had made their way to Starved Rock. Quaqui had led the defense there, and as such had become the last principal chief of the Illini. That gave his son, Paskepaho, legitimate claim to be the principal chief of the Illini nation and the legitimate negotiator for its land claims. At least, that was the story Harrison would send with the Treaty of St. Louis to the US Congress. That they would accept it, he had no doubt.

* * * *

It had been cold but not wet during their morning ride to Portage des Sioux. There was smoke coming out of the chimney of one of the cabins, which made Harrison smile. It would be miserable in there, he was certain, but at least not cold.

Harrison and Johnny Logan and the ten soldiers who accompanied him were greeted at the door of the cabin by three old men wrapped in blankets and staring sternly toward them.

"Greetings, Paskepaho," Johnny said as their party came to a stop.

Paskepaho nodded solemnly and raised a hand palm up in a sign of friendship. "Greetings, Johnny Logan. We are pleased to have you join us again. Please get down and come into the warmth."

As the entire party dismounted, Harrison spoke to the captain leading his escort. "Bring one other man into the cabin with you. The rest will have to stay out here with the horses."

The captain gave the necessary commands, nodded to a grizzled old sergeant to join them, and followed Harrison and Johnny into the cabin.

Harrison had been correct. The cabin was mean but warm. The floor was dirt. There was no furniture, simply blankets rolled against the wall and some clothing hung on pegs. A large iron pot hung from a fireplace crane with a swivel arm. A section of butchered deer hung from the rafter nearest the fire.

In addition to the three Indian men and four whites, two Indian women stood beside the fireplace. Paskepaho motioned to his guest to sit. Harrison, who strongly preferred a chair, did so awkwardly and slowly. The other men eased down with practiced grace. Harrison studied Paskepaho. His was the face of an old man. It was thin, not from a natural character but from the deprivation of too many days with too little to eat. The skin had the texture of leather wrinkled and split by long days in the sun. It was hard to believe this man was fifty and not eighty.

As Harrison studied him, Paskepaho produced a ceremonial pipe that had already been filled. He lit it with a twig from the fire. Once it was going, Paskepaho passed the pipe to Harrison, who took a single puff and passed it back. Paskepaho then offered the pipe to Johnny. Then the pipe went around among all the men, but none spoke. When the tobacco was smoked, Paskepaho motioned to one of the women, who produced a bottle of whiskey and tin cups. Paskepaho poured into each cup. Harrison indulged a small smile when he saw that Paskepaho filled his own almost to the brim with the last of the bottle.

"We have smoked to peace and mutual understanding. Let us drink to long friendship," Paskepaho said and took a long drink.

After the ritual Harrison set his cup down and spoke as Johnny Logan translated. "Chief Paskepaho, it is good of you to invite us here to join you. While I, and the government I represent, are pleased to be here, it saddens me that we must meet on this side of the river when all on the other side belongs to you."

"Perhaps it did," Paskepaho responded, "but it was taken from us long ago."

"But you believe it was wrongly taken and is still yours, do you not?" Harrison asked.

"Kitchesmanetoa gave the land between the rivers to the Illini. It is ours, though I do not know how we are ever to recover it. It was my vow to my father that I would see the Potawatomi removed from what was ours."

Harrison let silence fill the cabin before he spoke. "Paskepaho, we both want the same thing. Perhaps together we can make it happen."

"How is that, Governor Harrison? How can we make that happen?"

"Chief Paskepaho, the Potawatomi are strong and many. The Illini have been reduced to a handful of warriors who will never be able to take back what is theirs. But we whites are stronger, and far more numerous, than the Potawatomi. Let us be your strong right arm; let us avenge the wrong done to you so long ago. We will remove them. We will either force them back to the lands from which they emerged or kill them. It is a thing our soldiers can do and will do with the permission of the Illini."

"And all you wish is our agreement?" Paskepaho seemed confused.

"It is not quite that simple," Harrison continued. "We Americans are a just people. We are not like the Shawnee, mercenaries who fight for a fee. We only fight for what is ours. So, we would have to call the land ours before we would send our soldiers. But that does not mean that we could not give our friends, the Illini, something in return for the land."

Paskepaho sat motionless and expressionless for long moments.

Harrison began to feel his knees ache. He wanted to get this over. But he waited because he knew he must.

"Governor Harrison, if we the Illini give up our claim to the land, what will we have?"

Harrison had to struggle not to smile. It was over. He would have the Illinois land. Now they were just talking price.

"Paskepaho, how many are you? How many people are in your charge, how many must you care for?"

The aging Indian looked squarely into Harrison's eyes, and even to Harrison's avaricious soul the pain there was almost overwhelming. "The native speakers of our language? The five you see here and only six others. There are only eleven Illini left in this world."

Harrison was taken aback by the impact of Paskepaho's words. A nation reduced to eleven, and this man had been forced to watch it and live with it. Harrison chose gentle words. "And you, Paskepaho, are responsible for the care of them. So, from us you will receive two things. First, you will get wealth enough that these"—Harrison pointed to each Indian in the room one at a time—"who were kings of this land, will live the rest of their lives like the kings they are. Their end, your end, will no longer contain the pain of reduction."

Paskepaho stared at Harrison but said nothing.

"And also this. Probably most important of all. You will die with the promise to your father fulfilled. You promised him you would see the Potawatomi removed from Illini lands. Your promise has just been fulfilled."

* * * *

The ballroom was brilliant, the cut glass of the large chandelier twinkling with candlelight. Harrison, in a full dress military uniform, sat at an ornate white table with gold-painted trim in the middle of the room, all of his soldiers in formation behind him. The eleven Illini, the entire nation, standing before him.

"Chief Paskepaho, the paper before you on this table is a document that will be known as the Treaty of St. Louis. It gives you, the principal chief of the Illini nation, the sum of $1,000 today and every year hereafter, on the anniversary of this date, the same sum. You and your descendants will receive it so long as there is an Illini nation and a United States of America. It gives to the United States of America all claim of the Illini nation to all of the land between the Illinois River and the Mississippi River.

"If you and the other principal men of your nation will take this quill and mark your *X* there, at the bottom of the page, I will sign also."

Harrison dipped the quill into the inkwell before him, handed it to Paskepaho, and pointed to the spot on the bottom of the page where he and the others should make their marks. They did and then Harrison turned the treaty around to face him and signed his name beside their marks.

And then with great ceremony Harrison picked up the fine kidskin purse on the edge of the desk and handed it to Paskepaho. Harrison stepped around the desk, stood in front of the chief, and took the old man's hand in his. "The pledge of your lifetime is fulfilled. Rest in peace, Paskepaho."

CHAPTER 29

AUGUST 20, 1805

Tawa Village on the Auglaize
River, State of Ohio

The bleak sun was full in the smoke hole at the top of the *wegiwa* and flooding past the flap turned up from the entry. And it was cold. During the night, Penegashega had been too weak to rise to tend the fire, but when he'd been unable to stand the smell of his own vomit, he'd crawled to the tent flap and raised it to let air in.

Penegashega had been without real sleep for two days and nights, tending the sick of his village of Tawa. At ninety he was too old to work so hard, but this was not mere weariness. He had contracted another of the white man's diseases. Its victims all threw up and couldn't keep water down, but at least they didn't shit their lives away as with cholera. So far none had died but they would.

The old woman stooped into the entry and immediately held her nose. She departed without a word and was back in two minutes with a basket and a shovel. She came to Penegashega's side and without comment shoveled the pool of vomit in the dirt by his bedside into the basket, which she then carried outside the *wegiwa*. When she came back, she had a bundle of twigs and larger limbs in her arms. She rekindled the fire first, then picked up the water bucket and left again. This time returning with fresh water and a cloth. Only after she had wiped Penegashega's face and neck clean and held the frail old man in a sitting position to get water into him did he speak.

"Woman, go get two strong warriors who have not been stricken and send them to me."

In less than five minutes they appeared, first their bodies blocking the sunlight from the entry flap and then squatting down by his mat.

Penegashega did not raise his head but did turn so his face was toward the two. "Tawa needs the help of a healer. I may live but I can no longer do my work. You must go immediately to the Indian village on the Tippecanoe and bring Tensk. I've trained him; he must come to us."

Penegashega closed his eyes and exhaled. His face no longer turned to them. No more need be said. As the shadow of the last to leave fell over him, Penegashega thought, *If he's not drunk, he will come. He's not very good, but he is our best hope.*

* * * *

Tensk was very worried. He and Tecumseh had arrived at Tawa the afternoon Penegashega died. Much of the remainder of the village had become sick with the same disease.

"Brother, I have no knowledge that will help here. I will look the fool and my reputation will be ruined if I try."

They were the only two in the *miskahmiqui* that afternoon. Others who may have been traveling this way had heard and circled around Tawa rather than risk being there even one night. The two sat closely huddled against the cold around the small fire in the middle of the floor.

Tecumseh's face became joyous. "Listen to me, Tensk. This is the opportunity for which we have waited."

"How is there opportunity here?"

"Because you will save this village and become the most powerful healer of the Shawnee nation."

Tensk understood his brother well enough to know he meant what he said. Tensk already believed but did not understand how it would become so. But his belief was strong so he asked and listened. His next question displayed his complete faith in his older brother.

"How will I do this?"

"You will spend this afternoon going to every cabin and *wegiwa* in Tawa. You will not ask, you will demand, that everyone in the village—even the sick, no, especially the sick—come listen to your announcement this evening.

"And what you will tell them tonight is this. You will say the illness is the work of three witches doing the bidding of Matchemenetoo, the devil. You will say that your power is stronger than hers and that you will turn her illness back on those three. That within five days her three minions will be dead and all others in the village will be recovered or well on their way to recovery. And the last thing you will say is that after five days, on the night of the full moon, all will come back together and know that what you have said would happen will have happened."

After going to each dwelling with his summons, Tensk demanded that a large fire be laid in the center of the village. He had it lit after dinner, and in the cold of the night, all in the village came to the warmth.

None were happy to be there. A few had to be supported each step of the way, and one old woman had to be carried in a blanket to the assembly. When the last of them staggered to the fire, Tensk started.

"Brothers, I summon you to tell you that all this will pass." His voice was loud and clear. Tensk knew that small, ugly, and one eyed as he was, the look of him did not inspire confidence. But his commanding voice did. "I will make it so!" Tensk boomed.

All were suddenly attentive and silent before him.

Tensk noticed that before he continued, and he worked to suppress a small smile of self-satisfaction. "That is, it will pass for all but three. They will die. They will die because I will make them die."

There was a sharp and collective inhale of breath.

Tensk let it pass before he continued. "This new illness is the work of Matchemenetoo." Again, Tensk paused to let that soak in. "Matchemenetoo has three of her witches here among you. I know them and I will turn the sickness on them."

The villagers seemed too stunned to speak.

"All the rest of you I will save. This will take five days. In five days the three witches will be dead and all the rest of you will be recovered or be on your way to recovery.

"Five nights from tonight is the full moon. Come back here then and we will talk again. Now go home and be warm and recover."

* * * *

The moon was full overhead and beamed down so brightly as to compete with the huge fire before which Tensk stood.

"Brothers, has everything I predicted come true?"

The crowd shouted agreement.

"Have all but the three witches recovered?"

Again, they shouted agreement.

"Have I saved all but the WITCHES?"

This time the voices rose to a high crescendo and rang for long moments.

"There is one more thing I require of you. One month from now, when the moon is again full, I will make a very powerful announcement. It will be made at the Indian village on the Tippecanoe. I want you there. And I want you to send the message to all the Shawnee of what I have done here, of the power I displayed in saving you. And I want you to tell all the important men among the Shawnee to be at Tippecanoe the night of the next full moon."

* * * *

More than one thousand Shawnee stood in the middle of the village at Tippecanoe. A few curious Wyandot, Delaware, Potawatomi, and Kickapoo also arrived to hear the news. Two white traders, who had been in the village with a canoe full of salt that day, also stayed, but the number and excitement of the Indians caused them to linger toward the back of the crowd and appear somewhat fearful.

Tecumseh, Wasegoboah, and Tecumapese stood at one end of a wagon pulled before a fire made of logs that had been stacked as tall as a man. Tensk stood on the tailgate of the wagon, facing the crowd, his normally sloppy mien replaced with an erect posture and commanding countenance. He was scrubbed clean, his hair pulled back and wrapped with the bright headband typical of the Shawnee and with one crow feather set in front and sloping back over his forehead. Even the black eye patch had been brushed clean. The solid red blanket in which he had wrapped himself added to the command his composure suggested. To get here Tensk had been forced to have Tecumseh's constant watch for the entire day. Despite his efforts he'd not been able to swallow any whiskey all day long.

Over the crowd Tensk heard his sister ask Tecumseh, "Is that really our brother?" He looked over in time to see Tecumseh smile knowingly.

Tensk decided he had as much attention as his mere presence could draw. "Brothers," he called out in a clear, unstrained voice that could be heard over the heads of all. A voice filled with authority. "You are here because I invited you. I invited you because what I have to say is important to the entire Shawnee nation."

The one thousand were entirely hushed now, and the only sound his voice had to rise over was the crackle of the large logs.

"You all know of what I have done at Tawa. You know of Matchemenetoo's witches in that village and how they brought a new sickness that killed our revered Penegashega, our prophet. Not only did I overcome the sickness, I turned it on the witches and used their own weapon to kill them. But it was too late to save Penegashega when I arrived. He is now gone. Our old prophet has left us.

"I am Tensk. I am now your prophet. The Shawnee Prophet."

He stopped momentarily and panned the entire crowd. "Only I am able to do this. You know I come from a family with a long tradition of sight. You know I was trained by Penegashega. You know that I have more power than any other healer. Only I, Tensk, am qualified to be your prophet."

The crowd roared approval with sustained shouts. He gave his audience all the time they wanted to cheer. Only when the volume declined did he hold up his hands, calling for silence. And only when he received it did he continue.

"But to be the prophet of a nation requires more than a healer saying he is such. It requires the affirmation of the nation. Penegashega is dead, our leaders are here, my skill has been shown and is known. There is no reason to wait. A prophet is needed now. So, I will ask each leader if he will declare to me that I, Tensk, am now the Shawnee Prophet. If any leader says it is not so, let him speak now."

And with that he looked around his audience, selected the village chief from Tawa, held his arm extended full length, his index finger pointing directly at the man's chest, and waited for agreement. He got it with a smile and an approving nod. He then turned slowly until his extended finger was pointed to another village chief. This man said nothing for a moment and then merely nodded affirmation. One at a time, under his firm stare and pointed finger, each leader of the Shawnee agreed.

He turned momentarily toward his family and watched as Wasegoboah stared in open and abject admiration not at him but at Tecumseh. He watched the three for a moment, seeing Tecumapese's lips and reading the words they formed as she looked directly up into Tecumseh's eyes. "You staged every bit of this, didn't you? Your opposition wouldn't dare oppose the will of the crowd." Her eyes twinkled admiration. She extended onto her tiptoes and kissed him on the cheek.

Anger rose inside him that his family, as usual, gave all their admiration to his older brother. He whirled back around to the one thousand gathered before him and focused his rage there. He roared, "Then it is agreed among the leaders and the people of the Shawnee. I, Tensk, am the Shawnee Prophet."

The crowd roared approval. This time Tensk did not call for silence but waited for the shouts of approval to die away before he spoke again.

"There are things I now want you to know. You already know the rules for this village. All Indians are welcome here. But they must follow our three rules—no drinking, no marriage or cohabitation between Indians and whites, and no alliances between Indians and whites."

He had seen the two traders at the back from the beginning. He used them now. Again, pointing his finger, but this time over the top of the crowd, calling attention to the white men. Upon realizing one thousand pairs of eyes were turning to them, the two men froze.

"You may trade with those men or other whites. But that is all. There will be no mixing with them in any way other than trade. Those have been the rules at this village since it started.

"But now, I, Tensk, your prophet, add one more. There will be no selling of land to any whites. The Treaty of Greenville said no whites could buy Indian land except the US government. Harrison, the governor of the area from here to the Mississippi, has been using that authority to buy land. But he does not bother to buy it from the tribe to whom it truly belongs. Harrison buys from any chief who says the land is his to sell. He bought a piece of Miami and Shawnee land from the Potawatomi chief Winnemac."

Tensk was silent for a moment.

"Did you hear me, Brothers? He bought Miami and Shawnee land from a Potawatomi."

The crowd screeched disapproval.

"But that is not all. There is a leader of the handful of surviving Illinois named Paskepaho. None of us have ever heard of him. He lives with a dozen others. That is all that is left. Harrison bought from Paskepaho all of the land from the Illinois River to the Mississippi. It is Potawatomi land. Do you understand? He bought Miami and Shawnee land from a Potawatomi and bought Potawatomi land from an Illini."

Again, the crowd screeched and hissed disapproval.

"These are not the acts of Indians. These are the acts of men doing the will of Matchemenetoo. They are witches. I declare them such. They are to be killed. Winnemac, the Potawatomi, and Paskepaho, the Illini, are to be executed by any who find them."

One thousand Indians screamed in a voice that was both rage and approval.

He watched the two whites slip quietly out the back of the crowd and to the Tippecanoe River, where they untied their canoe and paddled in the moonlight down to the Wabash and continued south.

*　*　*

The moon was setting and sliding slowly into the Tippecanoe as the first rosy fingers of the dawn appeared across the Wabash. Tensk sat cross-legged with the almost empty jug between his knees, looking from one to the other. His entire night had been spent receiving awed congratulations from what seemed like every one of the one thousand villagers and guests. His family had added their praise as well, Tecumseh congratulating him on his "performance." His brother had stayed close to him at first. *Making certain, no doubt, that some of that praise would bounce off me and reflect on him. Trying to show, prophet or not, I'm still his "little brother," perhaps even his tool. Or is it fool?*

It had taken hours before Tensk could get away from him, but in the darkest hours of the night he'd managed to get away, dig a jug from under the bottom log of the cabin's rear wall, and work his way to this quiet place where he could enjoy the whiskey and clear his thoughts. *The men in our family have ever been powerful. For as many generations as any can remember. My father was war chief, my brother is war chief, my other brother started this village to attract to himself all who are willing to fight for our ways. And I am no different than any of them. I am a man of my own powers. I am not just my brother's useful tool. And someday they will all see it is so.*

CHAPTER 30

APRIL 7, 1806

Grouseland Mansion, Indiana Territory

The two traders, still fearful after a winter of seclusion, sat in Harrison's office babbling out their story. Both trying to talk at once and stepping on one another's telling. Harrison sat unusually quiet, taking it in. Johnny Logan sat behind him on a stool by the fire. When they were finally done, Harrison spoke calmly.

"So, this self-appointed Shawnee Prophet has, by his simple declaration, constrained all chiefs of all tribes from selling me land upon penalty of death?"

One of the traders sat forward as though to speak.

"Yes or no?" Harrison barked. "Which is it?"

The two traders glanced at one another, and turning back to Harrison, spoke simultaneously. "Yes."

Harrison shifted his chair around until he was able to make eye contact with Johnny. "Will they obey?"

"Yes."

"So, some self-appointed savage who claims to speak for God thinks he will stop the civilizing of an entire territory? No, he will not."

Johnny spoke from behind him. "Let me tell you about this prophet."

Harrison bolted straight up from his chair and shouted, "No. I need to know nothing more about this man. He is a liar. And I will make them see him for the fool he is.

"Johnny, you get a message to this Shawnee Prophet and let every village in the Indiana Territory know I've sent it: 'You are a false prophet who claims to speak for Moneto and against Matchemenetoo. You speak for no one but yourself. If you speak for Moneto, you must prove it. Tell Moneto to make the sun stop in its tracks. Then all, even the whites, will know you are indeed the Shawnee Prophet.'"

* * * *

Harrison read the reply sent to him by the Shawnee Prophet. It had been written in English and delivered by a small party of Shawnee warriors from the Indian village. They also told him runners had been sent to every village in the Indiana Territory with the same message.

"You, Governor Harrison, wish me to prove that I am the Shawnee Prophet by stopping the sun. That is not in my power to do, but it is in the power of Moneto and in a dream he tells me he will do so to prove to you, and any other skeptic, that I, Tensk, am his prophet.

"Fifty days from now, when the sun is at its highest, it will stop in its path.

"Know that, Harrison, and beware. The power is mine."

The letter was dated three days earlier and signed "Tensk, the Shawnee Prophet."

* * * *

At noon on June 17, 1806—the day awaited for the last seven weeks along the entire frontier—Johnny Logan stood on the lawn at Grouseland, where he had an unimpeded view of the sky above. He held his hands high above his head to shelter his eyes from the blazing directness of the sun.

The light on one side seemed less bright for a moment and he blinked to correct it. But it wasn't to be corrected. The light was dimmer there, and then a small black curve appeared along the dim edge. And the blackness grew—and grew and grew—until the face of the sun was black with only a golden halo encircling it. Confused birds stopped flying and set to roost.

"There will be hell to pay now," Johnny Logan said to no one and everyone.

CHAPTER 31

JUNE 1, 1808

Tippecanoe Indian Village

Tecumseh sat with his four loyal confidants to summa-
rize his plans. "This entire trip will take three years or better." He pointed to his friend Chaubenee. "I will travel first
with Chaubenee to the Potawatomi and then north to the
Winnebago and the Fox and Sac and then across the river to the
Sioux and Osage. I will stop back here after that, but then I will
travel south all the way to the Seminole. And in each village of
each tribe I will deliver the same message, that together, and
only together, we will move all the Shemanese and the white
settlers they protect back across the Appalachian Mountains
and restore Indian lands to Indian peoples.

"While I am gone there are things you must do as well." He
looked first at Tensk. "There are things you must do. You are to
travel among the Shawnee and the Miami and the Ottawa and
the other tribes along the south of the Great Lakes and give
them the same message. You now have power. You must use it

for our cause. But remember: do not confront Harrison. Avoid him, placate him if you cannot avoid him, but no matter what he does you must not fight him. If Harrison brings a force up the Wabash, you must not fight. If you have to move the village, then do so but do not fight Harrison in my absence."

He looked at Tecumapese next. "You, beloved sister, understand the plan best of all. Counsel your brother to wisdom and help him avoid pride." He smiled back at Tensk and said in a tone of great love, "Pride is your weakness, Brother. You must resist it."

With that he stood up, slung his musket over his shoulder, and walked to the cabin door. As he stepped outside, six mounted warriors, his traveling companions, waited for him. He pulled Wasegoboah to him as he stepped to his horse and slid the musket into its scabbard.

"Wasegoboah, yours is the hardest job of all."

Wasegoboah said nothing but looked at him with expectation on his face. "You, Wasegoboah, must find a way to talk to her." He nodded to his sister. "She is wise, wiser than all of us, but she needs someone to discuss all with. You process thought with your brain. She processes thought with her tongue. She needs you, Wasegoboah. She will not be able to control herself if you do not offer her that—conversation."

Wasegoboah did nothing but nod and fold his hands into a cup to give Tecumseh a boost up.

Tecumseh, Chaubenee, and the six others turned from the cabin and the village on the Tippecanoe and rode to the west.

* * * *

Tecumseh and his small band rode into the Nadoues Sioux village of Chief Red Wing. They were surrounded by a rambunctious escort of more than a dozen young Sioux warriors. The Nadoues Sioux were a powerful and bellicose people. If

Tecumseh was concerned about his reception, he did not let it show in any way. He sat calm, erect, and by all outward signs completely at ease. But he had warned his own young warriors that they must show no sign of fear or antagonism toward these people, for they were as proud as the Shawnee, and young warriors might seek opportunity to prove their courage and skill before their own people. Tecumseh's party would not give it to them. He would not allow it. Besides, they had just left the Wahpeton Sioux, who had assured him that both his fame and the fame of his message preceded him, and that no Shawnee had ever visited this far north and the Nadoues Sioux were awaiting his arrival with eager anticipation.

They were led to the middle of a large village constructed entirely of tepees. Unlike a Shawnee village, these were thrown up in random order without straight lanes between them. But their shouting escort led them with certainty through the meandering way now being crowded by what appeared to be every person in the village stepping out to see them. That they had reached the middle of the village was clear, as the center was an oval some twenty yards across. On the far side a group of older men, standing erect with great dignity, awaited their arrival.

Red Wing was a beautiful man—tall, powerful, erect, and with a face that, while lined with the creases of middle age, showed not even the slightest hint of declining prowess or intellect. His solid black hair was parted in the middle and hung down to his shoulders in two separate streams held in place by leather straps. He stepped forward to meet Tecumseh as he drew his horse to a halt. Tecumseh quickly dismounted. Standing, he had to look up slightly to maintain eye contact with the chief.

The chief welcomed them and had them taken to a guest quarters and shown to a riverbank where they could wash off the dust of their travels. They were given two warriors as escorts. The warriors were selected for this task by the simple expedient of being familiar with the language of the tribes of the Great Lakes. After caring for their horses and washing, they were led to a tepee with the message that they would be escorted to dinner later and that the entire village of some eight hundred souls looked forward to hearing Tecumseh's message.

Dinner was pleasant and filling, and much drink was offered. But under Tecumseh's strict orders, his party accepted none. He would not have his message here destroyed because of some whiskey-impaired decision. When it was time and he was introduced, Tecumseh rose.

"Brothers of the Nadoues Sioux—and I call you brothers because you are. We are all Indian brothers. And I am not here to speak as a Shawnee to a Sioux, I am here to speak as one Indian to another. You are a powerful people whose reputation for skill in war is known by all the peoples of the Lakes."

Tecumseh let the murmur of pride and approval pass.

"You are the masters of the land where you ride, and your neighbors ever offer respect because they fear not to. And this is true not only of your Indian neighbors but of the whites as well. Those that come to you come in humility and peace. They offer you only things you want and take only things you would give them in exchange. You are in command of all around you.

"This is as it was with the Shawnee in my father's youth. One hundred years ago we were invited to the Scioto Valley, our home, by the Miami to keep the peace for them and to keep them safe. And ever we did. Oh, there were battles and much opportunity for young warriors to learn the art of war and earn honor but all stayed in balance among the tribes. And then came the whites. They came first to the Shawnee because our land is on a river that is much like your Mississippi. Ours is the main water that feeds the Mississippi from the east. And it is the way the whites come west from the mountains. And like the whites who come to you, they first came in peace and respect, offering only things we wanted and asking only things we could and would freely give.

"But that has changed for us as it will change for you. Whites are like ants. Once they start coming, they never stop and their numbers ever increase. And like ants they are easy to kill. But also like ants, they multiply even as you do so. Let me tell my Sioux brothers what will happen. Not what may happen, but what will happen. After the traders will come the settlers—peaceful men with families but who want not just to pass through your land but to stay on it. To have it. To possess it and to rip it open. Many of them appear to be honorable men who come in peace. But I tell you, Brother Sioux, they want what you have, and they will take it.

"And what will you do? You will defend what is yours. You will kill them and burn their cabins and tear down their fences and take their scalps. And then do you know what will happen? More Shemanese will come with their long knives and their guns, and they will kill you."

A wave of defiance roared at him. Tecumseh let the wave sweep over.

"Oh, you will kill them also. I have told you that. The whites are easy to kill. But I have also told you they will never stop. They grow. They become more and more and they never stop. They keep coming. And eventually, the Sioux, like the Shawnee, will be pushed into an ever smaller area. Pushed until none of us exist anymore. Our nations gone.

"You doubt me, Brothers. I see it in your eyes. You think you are stronger than we Shawnee. You think you will not be pushed. Well, let me tell you what has happened in your own land. The French have sold to the Americans all the land that drains into the Mississippi River from the west."

Again, there were sounds of protest.

"Do they own it? Of course, they do not own it. You own it. But I tell you the French have sold it to them. And even now the Americans come. Two army officers. A Captain Lewis and a Captain Clark led a party of American soldiers up the Missouri River to scout and to map all the land to the river's source—land that is yours. And, Brothers, this Captain Clark, William Clark, is the younger brother of George Rogers Clark, who led an army out of Kentucky to take from the British the lands of the Illinois just ten years ago."

There was now shouting among the young warriors around him.

"Brothers, there is a way, only one way to stop them. We could not do it alone. You cannot do it alone. There are too many ants for any one tribe to stop. But if we all rise at once, we will push the Shemanese and all the other whites they protect back across the river. I ask you to join me when it is time."

There was wild screaming. The young warriors rose and danced in place.

Tecumseh waited for the crescendo and a decline after. Only then did he hold up his hands, calling for quiet.

"Brothers, this is not a decision for me. This is a decision for the leaders of your tribe"—Tecumseh made a slight bow toward Red Wing—"to make. But I will say this. If you do not join. If you wait, thinking you can handle the whites as they come to you, you will end up as many of the eastern tribes, even the vaunted Iroquois. You will be hemmed in a small place; your buffalo will be gone; you will have no way to support yourselves or your families. What you will have is the white man's liquor, and you will drink it in despair. All you have but your life will be gone. Death would be better for any of us."

A voice of a young warrior rose above the noise. "How will we know when it is time?"

"My name, Tecumseh, means 'a panther crosses over.' The comet we all know. It passed over the night of my birth. When next it arrives, it will be time to prepare. Shortly after that we will all rise together. All the Indian nations will do that at my signal. I will signal you to come by stomping my foot."

* * * *

Tecumseh and his party crossed back over the Mississippi River while it was warm. The easy passage made him smile. He touched his *opawaka*, remembering standing cold and naked before a fire on the western bank with Chiksika, the first time he'd made this crossing. This time it was crossing the other way.

"Brother, I see you touch your *opawaka*. Are you remembering when you had it to keep you warm and I almost froze when we crossed the Spaylaywitheepi so long ago?" Chaubenee beamed at him.

"It was a bit chilly that morning, I admit."

Chaubenee roared laughter. "It was freezing that morning. Admit it."

"I admit. It was. But what I remember more clearly was watching you leave us and turn north to go back to the Mascouten Bay to marry, to become a Potawatomi and chief of your village."

"And it is where I must go again."

"I wish you could stay with me, Brother."

"As do I, Tecumseh. As do I. But you know my people need me now. After that Illini bastard Paskepaho stole my birthright or tried to by selling what wasn't his to sell to the Shemanese, all my people north of the Illinois River have felt Harrison's oppressive hand. I have told you the Shemanese are building forts on the land. Last year they built what they named Fort Dearborn on the Chicago River. We will fight them over it and I must be there. My people are the only obligation I have that comes before you."

Tecumseh nodded. "I will go on without you. I must. I'll stop at home before continuing on south to the Cherokee and Choctaw and Creek and Alabama and eventually the Seminole and the dozen lesser tribes. I will speak to each of them before returning home next fall. And if I have the success we had in the north with the Ojibwe, the Chippewa, the Winnebago, Fox, Sac, Sioux—not one of whom has said 'no' to us, not always a direct pledge to join but never a 'no'—we will be well on our way to the fifty thousand warriors."

Chaubenee's wide smile showed the joy he always seemed to beam into the world. "And each time you will finish by saying, 'My name, Tecumseh, means "a panther crosses over." That is the comet that crossed over the night I was born. When it comes next, prepare. Very shortly after, I will stomp my foot. Then we will all rise together and reclaim the land that is ours.'

"And Brother, when you stomp your foot, I will be there."

CHAPTER 32

JULY 5, 1810

Grouseland Mansion, Indiana Territory

"So, the Shawnee Prophet says I buy land from those who don't own it and have no right to sell it. That is his claim, is it not, Johnny? That has been his claim for five years now."

Johnny Logan sat in a chair before the fire, sipping whiskey in one of the fine leaded crystal glasses Harrison kept on his desk.

"Yes, Governor, that is his claim."

"And he uses his self-proclaimed authority as prophet to label all those who do as witches and orders their death? And that has stopped legitimate land purchases by the US government, by me?"

"Yes, Governor."

"Then, Johnny, it is time. It is time to confront the problem head-on. I will invite him here to prove his claim publicly. If he cannot, and he won't be able to, I will have disclaimed him. It will either debunk his authority with the tribes or give me license to remove him by force as a false prophet and an assassin." A look of smug satisfaction flickered on Harrison's face.

Johnny Logan set his drink down on the leather coaster on Harrison's desk and steeled himself. He had to say this now. "Governor, when you challenged the prophet to stop the sun . . ."

Harrison's head snapped toward him, anger now showing.

Johnny Logan held up his hand palm out to stop him. "I know you won't like this, Governor, but you need to hear it."

The expression remained but Harrison sat back deeply into his chair to signify he was listening.

"When you first challenged the prophet, I tried to tell you about him, but you did not want to hear."

Harrison stayed deep in his chair but gave a slow, single nod of his head.

"He is my uncle."

Harrison did not move, but his left eyebrow shot up in astonishment.

Only when he was certain Harrison would not speak did Johnny continue. "I tell you this so you may believe that I understand what I am about to say. You have a phrase in English to describe him. He is 'a puppet.'"

Now Harrison sat up. His motion was slow but enough to indicate he would again engage in conversation. "Of whom?"

"My other uncle."

"I'm afraid you'll have to explain all this to me, Johnny."

And for the next fifteen minutes Johnny Logan gave William Henry Harrison a brief history of his mother's family. Harrison sat quietly attentive the entire time and, aside from the soft noise made when his glass was set onto the coaster, didn't make a sound the entire time. When Johnny stopped talking, a satisfied smile spread slowly across Harrison's face.

"Johnny, the first book ever written regarding warfare was penned five hundred years before Christ by a Chinese general named Sun Tzu. His first two rules were know thyself and know thy enemy. Only then may you begin to prepare to vanquish him. I am now ready to begin."

CHAPTER 33

JULY 7, 1810

Tippecanoe Indian Village

Tecumseh was in the lead of his party of six as they crossed the stream, rode out of the woods, and started up the hill that obscured Tippecanoe Indian village. From the top of the hill Wasegoboah appeared, walking his horse slowly toward them. Old warrior that he was, Tecumseh realized Wasegoboah had stood hidden in the copse at the top of the half-mile-long hill trail until he was certain it was them before letting himself be seen. Upon seeing him, Tecumseh elevated their pace to a trot coming up the hill.

He pulled up beside Wasegoboah and put his arm out and onto the old warrior's shoulder. "How are you, my dearest and longest companion?"

"Glad to see you at home, Tecumseh."

The two rode side by side, their horses at a walk. Resisting any temptation to tell of his yearslong journey, Tecumseh insisted Wasegoboah give him the local news and said not a word as he did. By the time they reached the village, he knew it had grown to almost two thousand in his absence, but that Tensk had enjoyed no success in any conversions outside the village and was drunk most of the time. What he didn't hear was one word about his sister, and that was enough for him to know there was much to learn. He also learned of Harrison's summons.

Over dinner, Tecumseh related the story of his journey to them all and told of the open ears his message had fallen upon almost everywhere he spoke. He admitted that the message would need to be reinforced before he called the fifty thousand to rise, but he had made excellent progress.

They all sat listening intently, even after Tecumapese rose to clear the table. Only when she was back and seated did Tecumseh commence the difficult part of his evening's work.

"Tensk, my younger brother"—his face showed affection even darkened as it was with the fire at his back—"you among us carry the most difficult load."

Tensk had dropped his head in expectation of the scolding he knew was coming.

"Of the men I love most, you alone cannot find the courage to go through your life without the shelter of alcohol. That I understand, Brother, because it was the crutch of my youth as well. But unlike you, I was struck sober. Struck sober by a buffalo hoof." Tecumseh let a small smile come to his lips as he pointed to his shortened leg. "I traded a crippled life for a crippled leg. It was the best trade I ever made. But that good fortune has not been yours. So, Brother, I—no, not I but we, all of us sitting here and the two thousand Indians in this village—will protect you."

Tensk's expression changed to one of complete astonishment. He had expected many things when Tecumseh came home, but not this understanding and even love.

"Here we can, and will, scrub every jug of whiskey from existence. We've not done well enough at that but will do better. I will have the pack and canoe of every trader who comes to this village inspected, and I shall let it be known that anyone who brings alcohol into Tippecanoe will be banished. And you, Brother Tensk, will stay here, in the village. Here where those who love you can protect you. There will be no more traveling for you. You are needed here. You are needed sober."

All sat silent. Tecumapese inhaled as though to speak, but Tecumseh raised his hand to stop her. The silence lasted until the crackling of the fire became clear, distinct notes as sap, heated to the point of expansion, snapped the wood holding it in place.

"Now, Brother"—Tecumseh peered into the single eye—"I would like to see the summons sent by Harrison."

Tecumapese rose but not to speak. She merely picked up the trash basket and walked out the cabin door.

Tensk rose and turned to the shelf behind him and pulled down a letter folded and closed with Harrison's wax seal. He handed it to his older brother and sat back down.

Tecumseh studied the envelope. It was addressed in bold strokes to "The Shawnee Prophet." The seal had been broken. "Did you have it read to you?"

Tensk merely grunted.

Tecumseh spread his finger under the seal and unfolded the paper. He read aloud, "News has come to me that since the US government purchase of land along the Wabash River from the Potawatomi Chief Winnemac, you have complained I purchased land from those who do not own it. If you have a complaint that I purchased land from those who do not own it, just come to me and prove it and I will restore the land. William Henry Harrison, Governor of the Indiana Territory."

"Well, it is short and direct," Tecumseh said. "And it leaves no choice. If I do not go and prove our case, Harrison will say we have none. He will say it to all the tribes and they will hear him. At least some of them will hear him."

As Tecumseh said, "if I do not go . . ." Tensk raised his head, his expression perplexed.

"It will be I who goes," Tecumseh said, staring purposefully in response to his brother's expression.

Tensk's face disappeared back into the darkness.

His comments complete, Tecumseh rose, walked to the cabin door, opened it, and stepped out into the night air. He walked toward the village dump, his pace very slow. Slow enough to intercept Tecumapese upon her return.

When he saw her coming toward him, she was slumping, head low. But when she raised her eyes and saw him, her shoulders immediately became erect, her posture challenging. "Wasegoboah informed me of all the news of the village as we rode in together. But he did not mention you. Not once. Since he will not speak of you, it is you I must ask. How is it with you and your husband?"

She continued past him just a few paces, stopped abruptly, and turned back toward him. "We've not shared a bed the entire time you have been away." She said it slowly and firmly. After a long silence while peering up at him in the darkness, she added, "That should tell you all you need to know."

Tecumseh put an arm around her shoulders and continued walking but took a fork in the path that led away from the village and toward the river.

"Sister, I believe you married Wasegoboah because he was already a member of the family in all but name. You were familiar with him and knew him to be a good man. But you know now, if you did not then, that you are the sun and he is the moon. You are brilliant and full of the things that make the world change. He is steady, reliable, and quiet. You are a poor match. But you have picked him. Can you not see him for what he is and stop trying to make him be different?"

The two stood staring up, the older sister who was virtually a mother to him and the leader of an entire race who had become teacher to them all.

"Tecumseh, I am glad you are home. You have been away far too long. Not only do your people need you, but your sister needs you as well. But so much has happened since Wasegoboah and I married." She pointed in the moonlight to the river before them. "Do you think this river is the same as it was twenty years ago?" Then she changed the direction of her arm and pointed downstream to the much larger Wabash. "Do you think that river is the same as it was twenty years ago?" And then she dropped her hand, turned to face him, and put both hands on his shoulders. "Do you think these two rivers can possibly be together the way they once were? If I am the sun and he the moon, I am also this little river before us and he is the larger one just downstream. I merging with him does not, did not, change him in any way. And I no longer exist for myself. So now my life is just a small part of a strong, silent body. There is little left of me."

He spoke not at all and left a very long silence.

"I will try, Tecumseh. For your sake, I will try."

CHAPTER 34

AUGUST 14, 1810

Grouseland Mansion, Indiana Territory

"My God, Johnny, how many is he bringing?" Johnny followed Harrison's glance as he looked down from his porch at Grouseland to the bank of the Wabash, where canoe after canoe was pulling up on the beach.

As what appeared to be the last canoe slid in from the river, Johnny took another moment and responded. "It appears something over one hundred. And from the markings I see, there are at least six other tribes in addition to Shawnee. Do you understand why they are here?"

"What I want to understand is should I be concerned? Should I get armed troops up here now?"

"No, Governor, that is just what you should not do. They come with their leader to show he does indeed speak for them. Since he speaks for so many tribes, a few of each have come along to validate his leadership. And from what I see before me, Governor, that leader is not Tensk. See there, in the middle of the warriors gathering on the beach"—Johnny Logan pointed—"the Shawnee of middle height? That is Tecumseh."

Harrison looked severe but no longer concerned. After he studied the gathering for several minutes, his only response was, "Johnny, make certain they are all put up along the bank to the north."

Johnny nodded understanding and started down the steps leading off the veranda.

"Johnny," the voice behind him said sharply, "for tomorrow, tell them to bring a dozen only to council. The remainder should watch from the riverbank below."

Johnny walked with a steady pace toward Tecumseh. As he approached, his uncle saw it was him coming and stood staring directly at his approaching figure, his face offering nothing.

"Hello, Uncle," Johnny said.

"I am sorry to see you here, Spemica Lawba."

"I am to be Harrison's interpreter. I will speak your words honestly."

"I know you will, Nephew. I merely wish not to find you doing service for the white governor." And before he could respond Tecumseh added, "Your mother sends her love and greeting."

"Please send my love back to her. And to everyone else. Governor Harrison requests that your party tomorrow be no more than a dozen and that the remaining warriors stay here. We will meet on the lawn above. You will always be within sight of them."

"How large will Harrison's party be?"

"His will be no larger than yours. And like your party, there may be several hundred curious people from Vincennes standing around Grouseland. The governor requests you not come armed."

"Will his party be armed?"

"Harrison and the officers may have ceremonial swords, but there will be no long guns."

"Then we will do the same. We will carry nothing but hand weapons." Then he added, "Your old friend Chaubenee is with the Potawatomi"—Tecumseh inclined his head upriver to the campground—"if you want to greet him."

* * * *

When the dew had burned off the grass, Johnny Logan watched as Tecumseh and his party started up the hill. Moments later, he and the rest of Harrison's party started down it. When they met, Harrison spoke first. "Greetings, Tecumseh, from your Great Father in Washington, President James Madison." Johnny translated into Shawnee even as Harrison spoke.

Tecumseh pointed to the sun and responded in Shawnee. "My father is the sun and my mother the earth. I will sit here while we talk and take comfort in her bosom." And so saying, he and his party all folded gracefully to the ground.

If Harrison was annoyed, he masked it quickly and, adjusting his sword, sat down. The remainder of his party followed suit. When all were seated and settled, Harrison spoke. "Tecumseh, welcome to my home. This, our first meeting, is important to both of us. My invitation was to allow you the opportunity to make your case that lands purchased north of us along both sides of the Wabash from the Potawatomi Chief Winnemac were not his to sell. As I promised, if you can prove the Shawnee claim, I will restore the lands. So please, the opportunity is yours. Use it well."

Johnny's translation, almost simultaneous, ended just seconds after Harrison stopped speaking.

Tecumseh, speaking in Shawnee, spoke for two hours. His was a long history of the perfidy of the whites since the coming of the English and then the Americans. It was a history of broken promises and treaties. After finishing the history, Tecumseh changed his comments to a description of Indian tradition and the custom that land was held not by individuals but merely occupied and used by tribes—the idea being that land was a common thing and that Moneto had given this land to the Indians. He gave the land across the sea and beyond the rising sun to whites. Now the whites had greedily decided that they should take Moneto's gift to the Indians for themselves. And while, by force of arms, they could take it, there was no format for an individual Indian, be he chief or warrior, to sell. The only way for a tribe to give up land was for all of them to give it up collectively. And finally, he concluded that the lands east of the Wabash were not possessed at all by the Potawatomi. That all east of that river was owned and used by the Miami and Shawnee. If any Indian said differently, that Indian would have to answer to all the Indians. So, unless Harrison restored the land to the Miami and Shawnee, the tribes of the Great Lakes would meet in a grand council and agree to punish all who sold land without the consent of the tribe. And that would cause great trouble to the whole land and make Harrison's task of governing almost impossible.

His final statement was, "Governor Harrison, I have made the point you said was a condition of restoring the land. Now do as you promised and restore it to its rightful owners—the Miami and Shawnee."

Harrison rose slowly and somewhat awkwardly, his sword, though small and ceremonial, still cumbersome in the motion. It took a cough for his English to come out smoothly after much of a morning of listening. When he did speak, his speech was a rebuttal. "Tecumseh, you complain that the land was Shawnee and no one had the right to sell it without Shawnee permission. But the land cannot be yours. You and your people are not even from here, much less landholders here. You are from the south. Far south by the southern sea. There is a river that flows into that sea that we in English call the Suwannee River. It is named for your people.

"You and your people are merely mercenary soldiers. You are here by hire from the Miami and not even permanent. If the Miami have a dispute to the Potawatomi title, let them come to me. You and the Shawnee have no standing of any kind in the Ohio River drainage."

Tecumseh leaped to his feet and screamed in English, "YOU ARE A LIAR!" and throwing off his blanket and putting a hand on his war club, he stood not two steps from Harrison, face red and distorted with rage.

Harrison put his hand on his small sword, the sound of metal against metal filling the air as he pulled it from its scabbard. The armed troops standing next to Grouseland started to race down the one hundred yards of hill between them and their governor. Immediately, the Indian warriors below grabbed muskets and raced up the hill.

Chaubenee and the other ten with Tecumseh jumped to their feet, throwing off their blankets, pulling tomahawks and knives from their belts. Chaubenee's great bulk leaped forward, putting himself between Tecumseh and the onrushing soldiers.

Logan forced himself between Harrison and Tecumseh. Unarmed, he put a hand forward onto each of their chests. He said very calmly, first in English, "Gentlemen, neither of you wants this fight. Stop now. Put your weapons away." His head moved back and forth between the two men, maintaining eye contact with one or the other until the animal gleam was gone from both.

Harrison slammed the sword back into the scabbard so that the sound was abrupt. He straightened to his full height and looking past Johnny Logan and Chaubenee to Tecumseh, said, "This council is over. There is nothing more to be said." And then he turned on the balls of his feet and walked up the hill.

* * * *

The fifteen canoes pulled with steady strokes up the river. Chaubenee sat in front of Tecumseh in the middle of one of the larger and swifter ones. The motion of the boat breaking through the placid flow of the Wabash was enough to create a small wake as it broke off the bow.

Tecumseh took his paddle out of the water and laid it across the gunnels. He reached forward and tapped Chaubenee's shoulder. "Turn your ear toward me, my friend. We must talk."

Chaubenee turned around as far as his great bulk would allow without tipping the canoe.

"I've made a mistake, Chaubenee. A bad mistake."

As was his manner, Chaubenee chuckled at the remark. "Well, now I can say I've seen you lose control of yourself. It's a first, even in battle."

Tecumseh's tone remained sober. "He now knows how implacable an enemy I am. There will be no fooling him. He is a good enough soldier to seek a fight on his terms, not mine. And with Johnny Logan by his side he will know soon, if he does not now, that I am assembling a force that will be overwhelming to any troops he can muster. He will decide to carry the battle to us before we are ready to bring it to him."

"When will we be ready?" asked Chaubenee.

"Not soon enough. Tensk has failed entirely with the Indians of the Lakes. They need to be enrolled in our cause before we can make any moves. And our allies in the south need one more visit to solidify their commitment. I had hoped to do both over the next two years. But we no longer have two years. It will take Harrison a year, maybe less, to prepare for all-out war. As soon as he is ready, he will come. That means I only have time to make one journey. Only I can solidify our allies in the south, but you can win the Lakes tribes. Will you do that?"

Again, Chaubenee twisted as far to the rear as he could without unsettling the boat. "Brother, I told you long ago I am committed to you, but my tribe comes first. I will help if I can, but soon, the Potawatomi will assault Fort Dearborn. I will be, must be, part of that. How will I do this if my own fight with the Shemanese takes me away?"

For the first time all day, Chaubenee heard humor in Tecumseh's voice. "My beloved brother. You are not without fame. All know that you were the youngest Potawatomi chief ever. That you are respected in battle and council. You will be heard. It may not take you as long as you think. But to use your time to best advantage, I suggest you start with the largest group of warriors, the Shawnee. Specifically, the Shawnee war chief. Start with Blue Jacket."

Even with Chaubenee twisting to look back over his shoulder, Tecumseh could see the startle on his friend's face.

"Sixteen years ago, after the signing of the Greenville Treaty, Blue Jacket insisted he would die a Shawnee. But for all those years he has watched Catahecassa give up more and more land to Harrison and his Shemanese. Blue Jacket has watched Catahecassa support petty chieftains who sold land to Harrison. He has had to watch as Catahecassa has condemned Tensk's authority as prophet and insisted, had he been at Tippecanoe village the night the assembled chiefs confirmed Tensk's status as prophet, that he would have stood against it. Blue Jacket has even had to watch Catahecassa condemn the rules of Tippecanoe village against intermarriage and alliances with whites and continues to allow his people to be cheated by white traders with cheap whiskey.

"I think our brother, Blue Jacket, may be ready to come and bring his authority and his warriors with him."

* * * *

As the large canoe carrying Tecumseh and Chaubenee turned out of the main stream of the Wabash and into its smaller tributary, Tecumseh could see the unmoving silhouette of Wasegoboah standing alone on the landing beach of Tippecanoe village. As their canoe slid onto the gently sloping mudbank, the two men lifted themselves up and out of the canoe almost in unison, the bull's and the panther's bodies in odd harmony, given their difference in size. Both smiled up at Wasegoboah, standing higher up. He walked toward them with a gait that was slow and rigid, even by his standard.

Tecumseh was the first to reach him, throwing his arms around the old warrior. In return he received a look that was at once sad but affectionate. Tecumseh, recognizing the emotion that must have created the odd expression, held the older man back at arm's length, staring into his brown eyes, appearing oddly high against the low forehead. "What is it, Older Brother?"

"I wait here for you because this is news you must hear from your family." The voice rolled out in its usually slow wave but this time with extreme sadness. "Your brother is dead."

"Tensk?"

"No, Tecumseh. Your older brother, Blue Jacket."

Startle showed all over Tecumseh's face. In a world of constant change this was one he had never imagined. "How?"

"I'm not certain. Alexander McKee arrived this morning with the news. It was not war or violence or even disease. It seems he just died. McKee is in your cabin. I left him there. Perhaps he knows more."

Tecumseh turned and gave a knowing look to Chaubenee, whose slightest of nods said that he had heard and he shared both Tecumseh's sorrow and his knowledge that his task had just gotten harder, much harder.

Without another word Tecumseh trudged up the bank and to his cabin.

McKee was seated at the table, sipping tea. Other than him, the house was empty. Tecumseh, followed by Wasegoboah, walked through the cabin door and stood but had no words to say. Tecumseh's face confirmed what McKee had assumed, that Wasegoboah left him here so that he could tell Tecumseh himself.

It was Tecumseh who spoke first. "You have come a long way, old friend, to deliver very sad news. It is an obligation others could have borne more easily. I thank you for having accepted the task."

McKee watched the deep sadness engraved in Tecumseh's face and wondered at the ability of the man to be ever gracious, even when taking such a blow. "Tecumseh, it is a burden I was more than willing to carry, but not one I chose. I left three weeks ago to come see you. It was only along the way that I heard of Blue Jacket's death. I did not know I would be the first to your village with the news."

Tecumseh accepted the information without change of expression and then said, "Please, McKee, sit down and we'll join you. Is there any more you have learned of his death?"

"Almost nothing. From what I heard he had finished his dinner and was smoking by his front door and just fell over. I am told he was dead when he reached the ground."

"Perhaps," Tecumseh opined, "Moneto wanted him." After a moment of silence, he added, "Tell me then what brings you on this long journey."

"It is to renew my offer of long ago. The British would like to ally with you, Tecumseh."

"And tell me, McKee, what has changed that would change me?"

"England and America will again fight. We want you with us when it happens."

"And when will it happen?" Tecumseh asked.

"Soon, Tecumseh. Our ship, *Leopard*, fired on an American merchant ship and took some American sailors off. The tension is long brewing. America is an adolescent developing strength faster than wisdom. She does not know when it is in her own best interest to accept an insult. Perhaps a year. Perhaps more; perhaps less."

The three sat quietly. Wasegoboah had no need or intention of talking. McKee knew now was a moment to be still until Tecumseh responded. Which he did.

"McKee, ever you have been honorable in your treatment of the Indians. But when I say 'you' I do not mean your master, the British. I mean Alexander McKee. I must have allies I can trust. Not allies that I can only trust when using me is in their best interest.

"I suspect it may be that we will be useful to you in that we too may fight with the Americans. If that happens, this adolescent with the new strength will not be able to use all of it against either of us. But after Fallen Timbers I will never again trust my back to the care of the British.

"Now, McKee, let us have no more of business unless you have more to say. Let us indulge in something more important: friendship. It is time for dinner. Feast with us."

Wasegoboah, rising from his corner, said, "Let me prepare what we have." He walked around the table to the fire, put beans and water into the kettle, and swung the crane into the flame. He pulled a side of smoked venison down from the rafter, sliced up the loin, and laid the strips into the skillet and slid it from the hearth into the heat.

When dinner was over and pipes had been smoked, Tecumseh escorted McKee to the *miskahmiqui* and again thanked him for his long journey to ask for his alliance and to deliver the tragic news. After fond good nights, Tecumseh walked back to the cabin. When he walked in, Wasegoboah had just finished cleaning up. The kettle was hissing in the fire.

Tecumseh put tea leaves into a mug and poured hot water from the kettle over the leaves.

"May I make you a cup as well, Wasegoboah?"

"Yes. Thank you."

Tecumseh poured the second cup, handed it to Wasegoboah, and sat down with his own. He blew over the top of the mug to cool it a bit, took a sip, and looked up. "Where is Tecumapese?" He stared softly into Wasegoboah's eyes and waited.

"I do not know. Probably with friends."

"And when will she be back?"

"I do not know that either. Perhaps never."

Tecumseh blew once more over his tea, took another sip, and looked back up, a small smile on his lips. "You were never a man of many words, but I think I deserve to know more than you are telling."

"I threw her out. We are divorced."

It was the response Tecumseh expected, so he had no surprise to show. "I know why, so you needn't say more about that, but what now. Do you really want her gone?"

"No. It was a mistake of anger. After two days I asked her back."

"And?"

"She said, 'No.'" Then it was Wasegoboah's turn to smile. It was a soft, self-deprecating smile. "Nothing more than that. Just 'no.'"

Tecumseh stared into the dark corner and saw nothing but pain in the eyes there. "I will talk to her tomorrow."

* * * *

Again, they stood beside the river but this time in the warm summer sun. "He needs you, you know."

She did not look at him but simply kept her gaze focused on the small fish rising to the late afternoon hatch. "Many people need me, Tecumseh. They always have. And I have enjoyed being needed. I admit it. It was my place. But I am weary, Tecumseh." And now she looked up at him. "Very weary." And she cast her gaze again to the river. Speaking as though to the river, Tecumapese continued. "I have needs, too. I have lost a father, a mother, a husband, three brothers, and for all intents and purposes, a son. That is perhaps the most painful of all, because unlike the others, my son chose to leave. I cared for them all and they have left me. Wasegoboah is right. He should leave me, too. Of all them, he is the one who has given me the least. It is time, Little Brother. It is time I take care of myself."

They stood saying nothing for a long while. Tecumseh finally spoke.

"Perhaps a good place to do that is on the other side of the river. Back with the Kispoko."

Her face beamed more joy than he'd seen there in many years. "Yes. I would like that." And then a sudden moment of sobriety overtook her joy. "But you still need me here."

"I will find a party of young warriors to take you there. It is warm and summer. Now is a very good time for a journey. I will come and collect you when you are needed here."

CHAPTER 35

NOVEMBER 9, 1810

Shawnee Village, Louisiana Territory

Tecumapese walked through the front door of Francis Maisonville's store at the large Shawnee village west of Cape Girardeau. She came here every week now. As the small bell over the door announced her entry, Maisonville looked up from the counter, brushing a mane of rich black hair out of his eyes as he did. Upon seeing her, his sensuous lips broke into a huge smile. "Mademoiselle. What can I do for the prettiest customer to ever grace my humble shop this chill fall morning?"

Tecumapese, who was always in control of herself, found she was oddly uncertain in the presence of this charming Frenchman.

"Good morning, Francis." She smiled back and could feel a slight blush coming to her cheeks as it always seemed to with him. She still felt a little uncomfortable calling him Francis, but he insisted. If she called him "Monsieur Maisonville," he would always correct with a smile: "Francis, *ma chérie*."

She knew no French, but his English was good, if lyrically accented. The more she spoke the language Little Sun had taught her, the better she became at it.

She looked at him without an answer. She knew there was nothing she needed. She had just found herself walking here for no reason. Well, there was a reason and she had to admit it to herself. She just felt good in his presence. All that went through her head when she realized she stood looking at him rather than answering his question.

He did nothing but smile and wait.

"Uh. Well . . ." And finally she was in command again. "You know I only came from Indiana Territory in the late summer. It will be cold soon and I didn't bring my winter furs. Perhaps some heavy woolen cloth to make a cape. Do you have any bolts of heavy cloth?"

"But of course, *ma chérie*. Just walk around the counter and let me pull some things off the shelf." He turned and with one hand swept the curtain to the back room open. "Mic, come out for a while to watch the counter while I show the lovely Tecumapese some woolens."

A young man with unruly hair scurried out, nodded to Tecumapese as she came around the counter, and offered, "Morning, ma'am," with the sharp twang of a hill country accent.

Tecumapese nodded to the young man and offered a simple smile in return as she walked to the wall behind the counter where Maisonville waited. He had pulled a bolt of red serge cloth, which he was holding for her inspection. He raised it against her cheek.

"If you cut it so the collar is high around your neck and so it hangs low to your ankles, it will keep you warm even in our coldest weather." His eyes gleamed with mirth as he added, "And it will look beautiful against your skin. The color suits you."

"Francis, I fear you will make my color match the cloth if you insist on flattering me." She felt in control of herself again.

"*Ma bijou*, it is no flattery to tell a beautiful woman the truth."

She smiled and wondered if all Frenchmen were like this or if this was the only man who was so comfortable with words.

"How many yards would I need to cut such a coat, Francis?"

"Here, step on the bottom of this roll with your heels and let me pull it up and over your shoulder."

She did and he slowly unrolled the bolt to extend it up to her shoulder. "Now put a hand onto the bolt and hold it in place while I pull it back down."

Tecumapese held the cloth in place as he unrolled it down her front. He smoothed it across her thigh with his hand. It wasn't necessary and they both knew it, but the stroke felt good. They both knew that as well.

He smiled up from her feet, where he was now kneeling. He marked the bottom of the cloth with chalk and stood back up. He turned and laid the bolt across the counter, where he measured it. "It's a little over three yards of cloth, *chérie*."

"How much will that be?"

"Will you pay me in dollars or furs?"

She let a smile cross her lips as she looked up at him. "I will pay with silver."

"The serge, *mon ange*, will be a dollar a yard so three dollars. But may I ask a question?"

She merely nodded.

"Are you good with scissors? Are you good with a needle?"

"I've never cut a coat before, just dresses and trousers. I'll have to figure out how to cut a collar and sleeves, but I suppose I can do it. And sewing is easy for me. I've done it all my life. Why do you ask?"

Again his face broke into a full, sensuous smile. "Because, *ma chérie*, you will be beautiful in this and it would be a shame if you cut it wrong. And also because you will look even more lovely in it if you cut a full hood instead of a collar."

She stood next to him behind the counter, the cloth spread out before them. She knew she was standing too close, but she liked it. "What should I do?"

"The hood will take an extra half yard. I have a woman who comes in. She is a good seamstress. If you will buy the three yards, I will throw in the extra cloth for the hood and have it cut and sewn for you." Her hand was lying on top of the cloth. He put his on top of hers. "You will look so pretty. I want to see you that way."

And it was agreed. The seamstress was in on Tuesday and Friday. Tecumapese would come in on Friday and model for the cutting. They would select buttons then. She paid and walked to the door.

"Tecumapese." He spoke her name and she turned. "If I could dress you in silks and coif your hair, I could present you in any salon in Paris."

* * * *

The little bell tinkled, announcing her arrival as she walked into Maisonville's store. Her hooded red coat was to be finished today, and she'd be here to collect it. But today she was not wearing her usual deer hide dress, but instead a long riding skirt with a white cotton blouse buttoned down the front. She knew the skirt emphasized the flair of her hips, and the blouse fell over the fullness of her breasts. She'd worn her long hair down, as usual, but swept back and tied with a leather thong, giving full vent to the beauty of her face. For a moment Maisonville was speechless.

Tecumapese stood still in the doorway, a coquettish smile brightening her face.

"You are ravishing, *ma bijou.*" He finally spoke.

"Ravishing? I do not know that word," she said as she strolled toward him.

"Ravish means to eat with abandon. You look good enough to eat, *ma chérie*," he said with a smile.

She mocked a startled expression.

He gave a hearty and full-throated laugh. "Just an expression, *ma douce*. It means you are so beautiful a man has to fight his desire to consume all of you."

Again, her face returned to coquettish. "Why thank you, monsieur."

They stood separated by only the counter, neither speaking. Finally, Maisonville spoke. "It is here. Let me get it for you." He turned to walk into the back room. Looking over his shoulder, he added, "Wait by the mirror."

As he walked up behind her she was watching his reflection in the mirror. He unfolded the coat draped over his arm and held it out to her spread at the shoulders. Without turning, she offered an arm, which he slipped into the sleeve. After they repeated the process on the other side he dropped the coat and let it fall onto her shoulders. Then he picked up the hood and placed it over the top of her head. Finally, he stepped within inches of her and, putting his arms around her waist, found a button and led it through the buttonhole. Only then did he step back from her. She could see him admiring her in the mirror. She continued to maintain eye contact with his reflection. He put his hands on her shoulders and spun her all the way around, the hem of the coat floating around her calves.

"You look lovely, *ma chérie*. Just lovely," he said. It was no flattery.

When the magic of the moment was broken by time, he spoke again. "Did you do as I asked today?"

"Yes, that's why I dressed in the riding skirt and boots, so I could ride astride. Where are we going?"

"I thought we'd try your new winter coat and ride down to one of the Lakes. I've had Mic prepare a small lunch for us. Willing to try, *mon ange*?"

She pirouetted one more time in her coat. "My afternoon is yours, Francis."

They trotted across the prairie, a winter breeze cool on her face. She had her hood pulled up against it. The grasses, golden now but still high as their horses' bellies, swayed in the mild wind. A mile in the distance trees signaled the water of a lake.

"In France, we have a story of a woman like you. Do you want to hear?"

"If you want to tell."

"She was a beautiful young woman whose most prized possession was a red-hooded winter cape. We call her 'Little Red Riding Hood.' She was taking a lunch"—Maisonville turned and patted his saddlebag carrying their lunches—"to her grandmother, who lived by the river." He now pointed ahead. "A wolf wanted to ravish the beautiful girl . . ."

She looked sharply but with a smile and interrupted. "Ravish? Did you not use that word about me, Francis?"

Maisonville smiled at her and continued. "So, the wolf raced ahead of her to her grandmother's and ate her grandmother. Then he put on granny's clothes and waited in bed for Little Red Riding Hood to come so he could eat her as well."

Again, she interrupted. "Then, monsieur, this time I think Little Red Riding Hood must beat the wolf to grandma's house."

And with that and a full-throated laugh she kicked her horse hard. It leaped and was at a full run in one stride. She stretched low across its neck, turned, and blew a kiss into the wind behind her.

Maisonville seemed to take a moment to realize a race was on. Looking back, she saw she was twenty yards ahead of him before he reacted. He'd told her he rode well, and she guessed he thought he'd catch her.

If he did, he was wrong. He never came close. She was off her horse and standing placidly, not even out of breath, when he arrived.

She smiled up. "Francis, I arrived early just to pick this spot for our lunch. I hope the view meets your approval."

It was stunning. The riverbank grew grass all the way to the water, with birch trees spaced far enough apart to allow a blanket to be spread. The stream was wide enough to flow at a pace that created ripples where rocks projected from the surface. On the other side of the stream, the terrain sloped slowly upward to the horizon.

He bowed slightly after dismounting. "Mademoiselle, I apologize for my tardy arrival to your luncheon. I'd not realized you'd arrive so quickly." And without another word he emptied the saddlebag of a tablecloth and wrapped lunches.

While he was working, she said, "Francis, it is cool. Shall I prepare a small fire to warm us?"

"*Ma bijou*, your beauty is enough to warm my heart, but perhaps my hands could use a little fire."

She laid it quickly and lit it efficiently. By the time he had plates and chicken out on the tablecloth, she had a warm fire beside them.

For the first time there seemed an awkwardness now that they both managed in the same way, with silence. When they'd finished the chicken Maisonville rose, walked to his horse, and took a small box out of the saddlebag. When he walked back, she was no longer sitting but lying, looking up at the afternoon sun. Seemingly at complete peace. He sat and opened the box and took out one dark chocolate.

"*Mon ange*, have you ever had a chocolate-covered cherry?"

She smiled up at him and shook her head. He kneeled beside her and, holding the chocolate between his thumb and forefinger, extended it toward her mouth. She didn't rise to receive it but merely opened her mouth and invited him to insert it. He did. Slowly.

As the treat melted in her mouth, he licked the chocolate from his fingers, staring down at her.

"Monsieur Wolf?" She opened her twinkling eyes. "Do you still wish to ravish your Little Red Riding Hood?"

He put his hands on either side of her face and bent slowly to her. When he was so close she could see nothing but his blue eyes, he mouthed softly, *"Mon coeur."* Their lips met slowly and ever so gently. For just a moment. And then she put both her arms around him and pulled him down onto her.

CHAPTER 36

OCTOBER 2, 1811

Tippecanoe Indian Village

The seven young warriors standing before Tensk were on fire with energy and anticipation. He was almost amused at the effort they used to appear cool and in control of themselves. *But this protracted peace Tecumseh has enforced has given them no opportunities to test their skills in war. They are not used to the anticipation.*

The leader spoke with more fervor than he would have liked, but the young warrior could not help himself. "They are just a few horses, Tensk. We do not seek permission to kill any whites or burn their cabins. It is just a small opportunity to replenish our herd a bit. So many have joined the village and sometimes with so few horses. We need them.

"And they are available!" the young warrior added for emphasis.

Tensk sat quietly in his chair behind the table. He knew what his answer would be, but he enjoyed the sense it gave him to make them wait and remind all it was his permission that was required.

Wasegoboah's deep voice rumbled out of the darkness in the corner, "Tecumseh's edict was that we not annoy Harrison, or his people, in any way."

Tensk did not even turn to face the speaker. "I lead here, not Tecumseh," he said forcefully. "Take no scalps, burn no property, harm no white, and come to me to report your successes when you return."

It was all the young men could do not to bump into one another rushing out the door.

* * * *

The moon was just a sliver giving barely enough light to see. None of the seven had done this before, but they had listened for years to the stories told by their elders. Each was stripped naked and recently washed to reduce the scent they carried. The horses would know there were strangers among them, but hopefully their caution would keep the dogs from finding out. Six held a rawhide halter in one hand. They walked slowly, very slowly, taking only one step, then halting momentarily. It took thirty minutes to reach the log corral. One at a time they rolled under the lowest log. None of the horses woke, or if they did, they did not startle. Each young warrior walked with slow but certain steps to one of the horses. They whispered soothing words into the ears of each and then gently stroked their foreheads. Then one small lump of sugar was offered on the same palm that held the halter. With the gentleness of changing a baby, a halter was slipped over the head of each horse. So far not even a nicker.

As the six warriors led their horses to the gate, the seventh slowly lifted logs from the gate and placed them gently onto the ground. All six walked through, leading their horses, the corral picked clean.

* * * *

Tensk was awakened by the whoops and hollers as the seven rode into Tippecanoe village leading six new horses. They raced the horses through town to Tensk's cabin. He wrapped himself in a blanket and stepped outside to greet them. They came running hard to the last second and then pulled their horses sliding to a full halt, dust flying up to the ridge beam of the structure before them.

"Well done, young warriors. Your skills make your people proud. Now go release your new horses into the herd and feast on a well-deserved meal."

Tensk heard Wasegoboah's footfalls as he walked out the cabin door and stood behind. "No good will come of this," he grumbled.

Tensk just looked up at the greying warrior with a smile of triumph on his face.

* * * *

The fifteen white men he looked at were armed to the teeth. Each held a musket and had a tomahawk at his belt. They looked fierce and angry. Even surrounded by a mob of five hundred milling Indians, they had the look of men who did not fear death. Tensk had to struggle to keep his face calm. *Why do I feel fear when only fifteen of them are surrounded by five hundred of mine?*

"The tracks of the entire herd led straight up the trail to your town. They're ours, and we aim to have them back." The tall man wearing buckskin and a raccoon skin cap finished his speech with a demonstration of that awful habit many white men had. He spat a stream of brown, viscous tobacco juice at Tensk's feet, the last dribble running down his chin.

Tensk almost shuddered at the sight. *Why do they do that? What a vile habit.*

Wasegoboah leaned forward and rumbled softly into Tensk's ear. "If you harm these men, it will be over for all of us."

Tensk regained control of himself and managed an insincere smile as he looked up at the man. "If your horses are in our village, of course we will give them back. But how will we know if they are yours?"

The big man visibly relaxed and set the butt of his musket on the ground. "Well, Chief, I reckon they'll be the only six horses with shoes in the herd over there." He picked up his musket and with one hand used it as a pointer toward a herd of over a thousand horses gathered at the edge of the woods. "Or you might just ask the young warriors who took 'em which ones they are."

Tensk looked up at Wasegoboah and barked, "Get those young warriors to halter those six horses and get them over here—now!"

Wasegoboah turned and, pushing his way through the crowd, headed toward the horses.

Tensk looked back at the party of whites. "We have no whiskey in the village. Let me get a pipe and we'll smoke while they are collected." Tensk nodded toward the maiden who cared for the house. "Bring my pipe."

Once he'd loaded the pipe and it was lit, he drew deeply and passed it to the big man who appeared to lead. *After he gets that slime all over it, I will smoke that pipe no more.*

Tensk again forced a smile as he looked at the man. "It must be so with your young men as well. They are sometimes hard to control. Youth wants adventure, but here in Tippecanoe village life is quiet. They sometimes do pranks I don't know about or approve."

The big man cleared his throat and spat but said nothing.

He watched six young men make their way through the crowd, leading six shod horses. When they were all in front of Tensk, he motioned them toward the party of whites. Without words they led the horses to the whites and handed the halter lead of each to one of them.

"Here are your horses. Please forgive the youthful prank of each of these." Tensk pointed to the rather contrite-looking young men standing before him. "Go in peace and with my apology for your inconvenience, Brothers."

Tensk and Wasegoboah stood shoulder to shoulder watching until the whites disappeared down the trail. Then Tensk turned and walked into the cabin, slamming the door behind him. When Wasegoboah entered, Tensk was lying facedown on a sleeping mat and beating it with his fists. "What humiliation. That I, the Shawnee Prophet, had to kiss the ass of that barbarian in front of half the village. I'll kill the bastard."

Wasegoboah sat slowly into his chair in the corner, a look of utter contempt on his face. He spoke even more slowly than usual. "You will do no such thing."

Tensk rolled over onto his back and looked harshly toward Wasegoboah. "I will do whatever I want. I'm not only the Shawnee Prophet, I'm in charge of the largest village in Indiana Territory. You don't tell me what to do."

Wasegoboah rose slowly, strolled the three steps to the mat, kneeled down, put his hands on both of Tensk's shoulders, and pulled him slowly up until their faces were fingers apart. "Outside this cabin, I do you the honor of your position, not because you deserve it but because to do otherwise would cause chaos. But here, I do not tolerate your shit. We do Tecumseh's work together. You are the mouth, but the work comes from him. I am here to ensure that the mouth with which you speak only speaks Tecumseh's message. Do you understand?" And he hurled him back to the mat.

* * * *

Tensk stood on a chair before his door overlooking the crowd he'd called. "I, your prophet, had a dream last night—a vision. It was a vision that calls for action. It is a command from Moneto. I saw these seven"—he pointed at the young warriors who had stolen the horses—"on horseback, each with a rifle in his hand, surrounding a group of whites, some of the same whites who were here yesterday. In the other hand each held the halter of a horse to lead them home, to our home. Not a shot was fired, no Indian was hurt. It is Moneto's message. Those horses are ours."

He looked down at the seven and screamed, "Go now and get them. They are ours."

And five hundred voices echoed, "Go now. They are ours."

* * * *

The seven had been standing in the woods but spread out around the cabin and newly built barn. Each stood quietly by his horse. It had been agreed that only when the two men and the young boy were all in the open would they rush—even if it took all day. Early in the morning, the boy had come out to bring the cows from the barn and into the pasture. He'd then gone back into the cabin. It emitted an aroma that told of breakfast for all. Shortly after, one of the men had come out and pulled a pail of water. But it was midmorning before all three were outside and visible at the same time. The leader jumped on his horse and screamed, rushing forward. The other six instantly followed from all directions. Before the whites could react in any way, they found themselves staring into the muzzles of seven muskets.

Four on horseback stood holding the three men in place. The other three haltered the horses in the corral and led them all out. When each of the horses was led by one of the Indians, they turned, kicked their mounts to a gallop, and ran them, dirt flying from under their mounts' heels, away.

Tensk's vision had been correct. Not a shot was fired. Not one Indian hurt.

CHAPTER 37

NOVEMBER 6, 1811

Territory of Mississippi

It was a cold night even this far south, cold but very clear. Tecumseh and his escort were camped alone and heading back home. Their work here done. All the southern tribes had agreed to rise. He was content. *Not so very many will die. There will be so many of us and we will be everywhere, the whites will see they must leave or die. We will be too many.*

The fire had burned to mere embers. All were wrapped tightly in their blankets. Tecumseh, who had never needed much sleep, was using the time to clear his mind and focus on the immediate challenge of facing Harrison. And then in the west he saw it, coming toward him from the west and high in the sky. It was large and growing larger and green, an almost vivid green. He watched it come to him and then pass over, turning south as it did.

The panther has crossed over. Time is very short now. They will all have seen it and know. Now is the time to prepare. And my first preparation is to get Tecumapese and bring her home. I will need her counsel, wisdom, and steadiness now. And she will need to be seen with me, part of my family surrounding me. In the morning I will send them all home with news to Tensk and Wasegoboah that I will be less than ten days behind them and I will be bringing Tecumapese with me.

   It has begun.

CHAPTER 38

NOVEMBER 6, 1811

Tippecanoe Indian Village

Tensk lay on his mat, looking up at the stern countenance that was Wasegoboah.

"He, like his mentor, Anthony Wayne, has come slowly, always scouts, always flankers, always a rear guard, and every night a defensive fortification. Now he and his Kentucky volunteers plus eighteen hundred regulars are within half a mile of our village. Tomorrow he will strike, and he will destroy us. Tensk, it is time to leave." Wasegoboah's voice didn't plead, it lectured.

"Wasegoboah, I run from no man. We stand and fight." The one-eyed prophet spoke with the assurance of the seer he claimed to be.

"No. Tecumseh said we were not to face Harrison until he returned. His companions have returned. He will be only days behind. No, we must abandon the village and retreat."

"Tecumseh is a mere man. I am the prophet. It is I who see"—Tensk's voice, a screech now, rose to a crescendo—"and I see victory."

Wasegoboah's look was now hopeless. He hung his head as Tensk rose, stormed past him and out to meet the gathered village. Twenty-five hundred stood outside the door waiting for him.

Facing the crowd, he was elated. He looked at the two warriors closest to him. "Boost me up onto the roof," he commanded.

He stood on the eave and raised his voice to its loudest. "Warriors! Our enemy comes. The one who has tormented us for fifteen years. The one we need to kill." He stared at them until there was silence and then shouted, "The one we will kill tomorrow."

Twenty-five hundred voices roared agreement.

Wasegoboah stepped out the door and with the effort of an old warrior pulled himself onto the roof. The crowd fell silent, watching him. "My brothers, this we must not do. Tecumseh will be back soon, and only then will we be led to victory."

It is the longest speech I have ever heard from him, Tensk thought. Tensk pointed to the warriors below and commanded, "Drag him down from here and tie him firmly in the *miskahmiqui*."

Hands reached up to Wasegoboah's ankles and pulled him down from the roof.

Tensk added, "If he tries to escape, kill him!"

There was a hushed silence over the crowd as Tensk again looked down at them. "My brothers, listen to me. Moneto speaks through me. Am I not the one who stopped the disease?"

He waited, got a rumbling of agreement, and continued. "Am I not the one who stopped the witches from selling Indian lands to that Shemanese?"

There were shouts of agreement.

"Am I not the one who stopped the sun?"

This time it was a roar of approval.

"And I will be the one to stop Harrison. Let me tell you what Moneto has shown me. Tomorrow we will not only win, but the white man's muskets will do us no harm. Oh, a ball may strike, but it will pass through as though harmless. There will be no wound; there will be no damage; there will be no death."

Now there was stunned silence.

"When you leave here, you will go surround Harrison's army. You will not allow yourselves to be seen or heard, and you will not fire. I will have a hollow log set on the high rock between here and Harrison." Tensk pointed to the rock rising thirty feet above the ground at the base of a hillside next to the village. "When the sun rises, I will drum the log loudly. And as I do you will rush straight at the Shemanese and fire and strike and cut. And you will not be hurt. But you will kill. You will kill as long as I drum that log, and I will not stop drumming until Harrison and every one of his soldiers are dead.

"I drum; you kill. Do you hear me?"

Twenty-five hundred, including some fifteen hundred warriors, roared approval until overtaken by ecstasy.

* * * *

Harrison, in full uniform, stood outside his tent warming over the fire, a cup of coffee in his hand, waiting for the dawn to break in the east. The sky was beautiful and clear with stars still visible in the west, the grey ambassador of the dawn covering the east. He was ready. His men were ready. Ready for this moment of his greatest triumph.

As the first golden ray of aurora rose above the eastern horizon, a deep note as from a bass drum sounded. And then another. And then the screams of war rose on all sides. And as the screams rose so did the warriors who made them. They were not hiding behind trees but grey shapes running full speed toward him and his army, directly at the redoubt. And as the murderous shapes ran forward, his men dropped—felled by the full assault of fifteen hundred almost maniacal savages.

Harrison was stunned at the ferocity, but not panicked by it. Cool as ever in battle, he told an aide, "Have that bugler sound battle stations." And then immediately he told another, "Have Colonel Ingram swing all the cannons to the perimeters. I want them all loaded with grapeshot and firing now." And he told another, "There is no time to pull in regimental commanders. We need to stop the hand-to-hand immediately. I want squares formed and orderly firing commencing in less than two minutes. The way the enemy are standing in the open any steady fire will be withering. Now get my white mare, I need to be up."

The first cannon roar drowned the sound of the drum. It also dropped four charging Indians in one blast. Within moments thereafter came the clear command from Harrison: "Front line, kneel. Front line, fire." And then the sound of sheet fire as twenty muskets discharged at the same instant.

"Sir, another officer grabbed your white mare. I've brought you this gelding."

"Damn," Harrison cursed as he pulled himself up and into the saddle.

As the second line began to fire, a thing happened that stunned Harrison as much as the maniacal charge. The attack stopped just as abruptly as it had begun. The Indians disappeared, now running in the opposite direction as though all the fury had turned to fear after the first round of return fire. In less than five minutes, there was virtual silence.

Harrison stood against an eerie silence punctuated only by periodic moans from the wounded or dying as his commanders came trotting to his side.

"Gentlemen," Harrison said, "if that assault was just to trick us into a broken chase, it was far more expensive to the Shawnee than they could have imagined. But I've never seen or heard of anything like it, so we will proceed with caution. I want all the cannons pulled together where they can be protected by a single regiment. Then three regiments—Lucas, yours to the middle, and Dyson and Chambers on the flanks—move forward toward the village in regular order. No matter what device the enemy employs, we will not break and charge. We fight this a single step at a time, as though the enemy were still before us, whether they are or not. All others set up a secure perimeter save Johansen's regiment. You will stand in reserve.

"It is hard to believe the day is ours that easily, but I believe it may be. The Battle of Tippecanoe may turn out to be the shortest battle in the history of Indian warfare."

CHAPTER 39

DECEMBER 10, 1811

Shawnee Village, Louisiana Territory

Tecumseh, his blanket wrapped tight around him, sat on his horse, both of them blowing clouds of crystalizing water vapor into the freezing air. He'd driven the beast hard for most of the night, but they were here—in the pass between the low hills overlooking the hundreds of cabins, *wegiwas*, and tepees that made up the Shawnee village west of the Mississippi. The last time he'd looked onto this view was twenty-two years before, when he and Chiksika, Chaubenee, and the others had arrived on their youthful adventure. How different those times had been; how different he had been then. This time there was no reception party. The stars were still visible, with the barest hint of grey daylight coming up behind him. The village would be awake soon, but for now all was peaceful and still.

When he was one hundred yards from the village the first dog awoke, startled by his presence, and began to warn all others. Soon a small pack of the yellow curs ran barking toward him, forming a flanking, and noisy, escort. The first warrior was out of his cabin within moments, naked save for a blanket over his shoulder, musket leveled and ready to expand the alarm if necessary. When the young warrior saw only a solo Shawnee approaching, he lowered his weapon, pulled his blanket tighter around his shoulders, and waited patiently for the arrival of the half-frozen stranger.

Tecumseh spoke more directly than mannerly conversation would have called for. "I am Tecumseh. Where is Tecumapese?"

The young warrior's expression took on a more serious tone. "You are welcome to our town, Tecumseh. Let me lead you to the lodging of our chief. It is he to whom you should direct your question."

And with that he turned and started down the lane to the center of town. By the time they arrived, the sun was cresting the hill down which Tecumseh had just come. There was no warmth in it yet, but the light was enough to give anticipation of its coming. When they reached the largest cabin in the center of town, the young warrior stepped to the door and pounded with his open fist. Tecumseh slid slowly off his horse and wrapped the beast's reins around the crossbar on the hitching post. He stood waiting, trying to draw as much warmth as possible from the rising sun, until an old man with disheveled hair came to the door and exchanged a few words with the young warrior. He stepped into the light and toward Tecumseh.

"I am told you seek your sister?"

Tecumseh nodded his head slightly in assent.

"She is not here," the old man intoned very slowly, his voice weary in the saying. He said no more and waited for Tecumseh to respond.

"Where is she?"

The old man stretched his arms over his head and arched his back straight. When his arms were again at his sides he spoke. "Come in. You are cold and hungry. There is warmth and food inside. Let your young escort take care of your horse." Instead of awaiting an answer, the old man turned and walked the few steps back to the cabin door. He opened it but rather than stepping in, held it for Tecumseh.

Once inside, Tecumseh shook off his blanket. An old woman took the frozen blanket from his hand and hung it on a peg near the fire. Then she pointed to a chair next to the hearth and the fire that was starting to build. Tecumseh extended his hands to warm them. The old man sat next to him but said nothing. Momentarily, the teakettle hanging over the fire began to hiss. The old lady took the kettle and returned with two steaming mugs of tea. Only after Tecumseh had taken a small sip and then a long one did the old chief speak.

"It is true your sister graced us with her presence. She had stayed with my woman and me and was a source of help to her and delight as well as wisdom to me and many others. Two weeks ago, she rolled her possessions into her sleeping mat, put her few others in a valise, dressed herself in boots, a riding skirt, and a hooded winter coat, and announced she was leaving."

Tecumseh turned his head from his tea to look directly at the speaker but said nothing and looked back into his teacup, waiting.

"She did not say where she was going, but it was clear why. She was leaving with Francis Maisonville, the French trader who ran a small store at the western edge of the village."

This time Tecumseh's head snapped up with such force that he dropped his tin cup, which rattled across the hearth. "She what?"

The old chief said nothing for a moment. His wife scurried over, cloth in hand, to collect the cup from the hearth and wipe up the spilled liquid. Only when she was done and had stepped away, the teacup in one hand and the wet rag in the other, did he continue.

"She had been seeing Maisonville. Oh, they were quiet and discreet about it, but those who were paying attention knew. And now they have gone. None of us knows where."

"Where is his store?" Tecumseh said.

Upon receiving directions, Tecumseh rose and departed without a word. He strode purposefully across the western half of the village to Maisonville's Trading Post. A freshly painted sign hanging from the porch eave read, "McNess Trading Post."

The small bell rang as Tecumseh opened the door. He stood silhouetted by the morning light behind him, not moving.

"Close the door, stranger. It's hard enough to keep it warm even when it's closed." This came in with a twang from a young, tall, thin man with a head of unruly blond hair.

Tecumseh left the door open and walked with slow, deliberate steps toward the counter. "I come for my sister. Where is Maisonville?"

There was a momentary flicker of fear on the young man's face before he controlled his expression, making it as placid as he could manage. "He's no longer here. He's gone."

Tecumseh said nothing but stared hard and unblinking into the young man's blue eyes.

The white man swallowed and then said, "I'm McNess. I worked for Maisonville. He sold the place to me and left. Two weeks ago."

"Where did he go?"

McNess swallowed again and then with a small stammer said, "He . . . he didn't say. He just left."

Tecumseh, with the ease and speed of a compressed spring unleashed, vaulted over the counter, grabbed McNess's neck with one hand, and twisted him backward across the countertop.

With his other hand he drew the scalping knife from his belt and held the point of it against McNess's Adam's apple.

Tecumseh put his face within a foot of McNess's. "Where?"

McNess's breath came fast, terror spread across his face. "They said they were going toward New Madrid and would start a store somewhere along the river. Probably south of there."

Tecumseh removed his hand from McNess's throat, stood back up straight, and sheathed his knife. He walked around the counter and toward the door.

As he reached it the twang called out behind him, "You're Tecumseh, aren't you?"

Tecumseh stopped and turned to him. "Yes."

"She said you wouldn't understand. That's why they left."

* * * *

New Madrid, on the Mississippi River, lay due south of Cape Girardeau. It was quicker for Tecumseh to travel due south overland than to follow the river around the Kentucky bend.

Once Tecumseh got there, it wasn't hard to get directions to the new Maisonville store some miles south of town along the river road. Even in midafternoon, it was cold and he could see smoke rising from the chimney before the trees revealed the little house. If Maisonville planned to build a store, it wasn't up yet. Perhaps he was just working off the porch of the house. Tecumseh rode straight to the front door and tied his horse. He did not knock, nor did he kick the door open. He merely pulled the latch string and walked in.

Tecumapese looked up from her work as he entered. Her face registered momentary surprise and then she turned toward him, feet planted at hip width, face turned expressionless. Maisonville was nowhere to be seen.

"You found us quickly. The comet went over a month ago today. I thought you'd go back to Tippecanoe where you'd be needed to fight the war." She spoke in an expressionless tone.

"I thought you'd be at the Shawnee village and there would be time to collect you first." He responded in the same flat tone.

"And when you had to make a choice, you came after me instead? That makes no sense, Brother. You are needed elsewhere, not here."

"Tell me, Tecumapese, what Indian would follow a man whose own family will not live by his code?"

The corners of her mouth held the hint of a sad smile. "Families can be difficult."

"Pack!"

"No!"

"Sister, I need you now. More than just personally, my cause needs the symbol you provide. You are held in extraordinary esteem by all the tribes. For you to betray my trust may cost us all. I need you to be seen standing beside me. Now pack."

"No. I told you I need to take care of myself. And I have. I will stay right here."

Tecumseh walked to the fire, squatted before it, and extended his arms to its warmth. When the cold left his hands, it was still in his heart. He rose and faced her.

"Sister, you may stay, but not with that man. As long as there is hope for my cause, you cannot betray the fundamental rule. If you stay, I will kill him. It is up to you."

The two stood staring at one another, neither speaking. Finally, she walked toward her mat, threw her clothes upon it, and started to roll it. "You will find my horse and tack behind the cabin. By the time you get him saddled and back to the front, I will be ready to go."

* * * *

They traveled toward New Madrid, where they would find transportation for themselves and their horses across an inhospitably cold Mississippi River. Neither had spoken in two hours. Tecumseh's gelding started to prance and move almost sideways. He tightened up the bridle to settle it. But it didn't settle. Instead the horse reared straight up, and when it came down, tried to race. Tecumapese's stallion began to do the same thing. While they struggled for control, there was a sharp cracking sound above and a foot-thick limb of oak snapped and fell, narrowly missing both. And then the ground began to rumble.

Tecumseh looked up at the road and saw it coming toward him in undulating sheets like a blanket tossing on a line. A sharp wind suddenly shot at them. Trees rose and snapped. The ground sounded of thunder. The earth opened and Tecumapese's stallion stepped in a foot-deep crack and then was thrown forward as the earth came back together. The horse screamed in agony as its leg twisted at an unnatural angle. As Tecumapese fell, Tecumseh's horse danced toward her body. It took all his strength to keep it from trampling her. He jumped off the beast, letting it run as he rolled along the ground. He tried to rise but was knocked down by a falling limb, so he got on his hands and knees and crawled to her. He pulled himself on top of her and stayed.

The rumbling continued for what seemed like fifteen minutes. When it finally stopped, everything became silent and still, the noise, the wind, the undulation of the ground. All of it just stopped.

Tecumseh and Tecumapese rose together. The forest and the road looked like the site of the Battle of Fallen Timbers times ten. Never had either seen anything like it. The only noise remaining was the periodic and softening scream of the horse, with its grotesquely distorted leg still entrapped in the earth. Tecumseh stepped over the fallen limbs and made his way to the horse's head. He pulled the large pistol from his belt, stroked the beast's nose with one hand, and pulled the trigger with the other. The pathetic screams stopped. He pulled Tecumapese's bedroll from the horse's haunch and threw it over his shoulder, untied the valise from the saddle, picked it up, and walked back to her. Tecumapese was brushing the dirt and bits of trees off her coat.

"Let's go," he said. "Hopefully, we'll find my horse. If not, it will be dark and very cold by the time we get to New Madrid."

* * *

They found Tecumseh's horse unhurt and nibbling grass a short distance away, but by late afternoon they were still miles from New Madrid. The going had been slow due to all the debris.

"A rider is coming," Tecumapese announced as she peered into the gloom.

It quickly became apparent it was one rider with two horses, the trailing mount carrying supplies. When the rider was two hundred yards away, he stopped to take them in and then started toward them again. As he came closer, Tecumseh recognized the rider and looked up at Tecumapese. She was frowning. He knew she would be.

The horses came to a stop directly before them, and Tecumseh addressed his aging friend. "Hello, Wasegoboah. It is very good to see you, but a surprise. What brings you?"

"I came looking for you." He looked straight toward Tecumseh as he spoke, never acknowledging his ex-wife. He stepped down from his horse, pulled a water bag from behind the saddle, and offered it to Tecumseh. "I come with news."

Tecumseh sipped from the bottle and handed it to his sister. "You have supplies, I see. It is too late to reach New Madrid tonight. Let us stop here for the night, and you can tell us the news over a fire and dinner."

Tecumapese stepped down to the ground and started the work of creating a fire and clearing places for their bedrolls. Wasegoboah began to unpack both utensils and supplies to prepare dinner. It was all done wordlessly.

The night sky was crystal clear and belied nature's fierce destruction of the day. The fire gave both warmth and some small sense of protection from the devastation that surrounded them. Tecumapese lay with her back to a tree.

The two men sat on the ground beside the fire. Tecumseh produced a pipe that he lit with a glowing splinter. He puffed until the tobacco was burning smoothly and then handed the pipe across the fire to Wasegoboah. "Now is the time for you to tell, Brother, and begin by telling how you found us."

Wasegoboah took a long and slow inhale from the pipe. As he began to speak the smoke came out of his mouth in small puffs. "Your escort came home without you but with the information that you'd gone to the Shawnee village west of Cape Girardeau. So, I went there. And there I found out you were here. It was not complicated. The news I have, however, is very difficult to tell. But the burden is mine."

Tecumseh stared intently at Wasegoboah's anguished face as he continued.

"Tensk allowed Harrison to come and meet him with our warriors, in defiance of your direct orders. He not only had our warriors meet Harrison, but he told them the Shemanese bullets would not harm them. So, they rushed forward madly. The first charge was so forceful that we killed or wounded perhaps two hundred and fifty of the Shemanese. But quickly Harrison gathered his men's courage and they fought back. As soon as they did, it became apparent that the prophet had no powers. Our men, in the open, started to fall. We lost no more than forty, but all our warriors lost faith and ran. All this I hear; I was not there."

Tecumseh sat as though in a trance, showing no emotion. "Why were you not there, Brother?"

"I was tied in the *miskahmiqui*. The night before the battle I'd tried to stop Tensk. He threatened to have me killed but had me tied instead."

"Where has the village gone?"

"I moved the few hundred that chose to remain to Wildcat Creek. Then I came after you."

"Does Tensk live?"

"Yes. He ran from the battle. We survivors took him. He is prisoner at Wildcat Creek."

Tecumseh reached his hand across the embers of the fire to receive the pipe. "Tomorrow we head toward Wildcat Creek."

* * *

Tecumseh had Wasegoboah redistribute the supplies so the packhorse could be ridden. He loaded his gelding only with Tecumapese's tack, bedroll, and valise. They kicked out the fire and stepped to the horses.

Tecumseh put his hand on Tecumapese's shoulder and turned her to him. "Sister, you are free to do as you please."

She let a look of startle cross her face but said nothing.

"I still need you, but the cause does not. There is no cause anymore. So, you are free to make your own choice. Come with me or go back to New Madrid and Maisonville. Your life is your own."

She said nothing but turned and walked to the gelding, which she mounted and then turned toward Tecumseh. When she came beside him, Tecumapese bent down low from her saddle and kissed him on the cheek. She straightened up, looked at him momentarily, kneed her horse gently, and started back down the road to New Madrid.

* * * *

Tecumseh and Wasegoboah rode into the sad little village at Wildcat Creek. Two hundred survivors stood waiting. There were no cheers or friendly greetings. There was only the silence of failure and fear.

Tecumseh dismounted and said, "Take me to Tensk."

He was led to a mean *wegiwa* and upon entering found Tensk tied by his wrists to a pole buried in the earth. When he saw Tecumseh enter, he awkwardly rose to his knees and whimpered in fear. Tecumseh strode into the room, followed by all who could squeeze in behind him. His face reflected nothing but cold rage. Tensk looked up as Tecumseh pulled his knife from his belt. His terror reduced him to crying with mewling begs for his life. Tecumseh said not a word, walked to him, reached down, and entwining his fingers into the filthy hair, yanked the one-eyed man to his feet, his arms jerking as his bound wrists bounced up the pole. When he had Tensk extended to his full height, Tecumseh pulled even more until the prisoner was on his toes. Tecumseh then tugged the hair back until the pleading eyes looked into his and laid the blade of his knife against the naked neck before him. He slowly drew the blade across the skin until blood oozed out.

"You miserable creature. In one day—*one day*," his voice boomed, "you have ruined ten years of work. You have destroyed the aspirations of hundreds of thousands who placed all their hopes in our cause—the cause you have now destroyed. It was not William Henry Harrison who destroyed it. It was Tensk, the drunken, incompetent coward."

Tensk's one eye stared wildly at Tecumseh. His whole body shook with fear.

"Would that I let my hand have its way right now," Tecumseh whispered in his ear. "But that would be far too easy a death for you."

Tecumseh extended his knife to the back of the pole and sliced the leather bonds that held Tensk's wrists. Then he let go the hair and watched him collapse to the dirt floor.

"You, pretend prophet, are no more. You are no longer Shawnee, no longer Indian, and no longer my brother. You are an outcast. You will live, wither, and die on your own. Be gone."

Tecumseh reached down and again wrapped the fingers of one hand in the greasy hair and with the other grabbed the back of Tensk's pants. Holding him so, he looked at the crowd and said, "This is my command. Let no man hurt this wretch in any way. But let no man give him comfort or aid."

Then he threw Tensk into the watching crowd, all of whom stepped back, leaving a clear, sunlit path to the door. The half-blind half man scrambled to his hands and knees and scurried out of the village into the forest.

Tecumseh righted himself, regained his composure, and strode out into the daylight.

As the crowd pressed around, now to greet him, Wasegoboah came beside him and whispered into his ear, "Alexander McKee is here and wishes to see you."

"Bring him to me by the creek. I need some clean air."

Tecumseh stood, his hands folded into the small of his back, watching the small stream, frozen solid, before him. The trees were completely denuded of leaves and stood with dark, twisting limbs rising into the bleak winter sky. He heard the sounds of both horse and man crushing the brown leaves on the ground as they came to him. When they were just feet away, they stopped. Tecumseh neither moved nor spoke nor even looked toward him as Alexander McKee dismounted.

"I would, my old friend, that this were any other day." McKee spoke very softly.

Tecumseh said and did nothing, his whole demeanor suggesting his mind was far away.

After a decent interval McKee spoke again. "Tecumseh, perhaps I am a small ray of good news on this most miserable of days for you."

Tecumseh turned slowly until he was looking directly into McKee's eyes and held his gaze unblinking but did not speak.

"When last I visited you, it was also a sad time. But even in your sadness you were able to be clear with me. You would not accept my offer to join the British in any future fight against the Americans. Britain asks again for your help. You will no longer be strong enough on your own, but together there is still hope for your cause."

The two men faced one another, not speaking, just looking.

Tecumseh finally broke the silence. "You are wrong about one thing, McKee, and I think you know you are wrong. The British forces on the Lakes, even combined with the Indian strength, is not enough. When the war is over, the Americans will still be here."

McKee's face showed disappointment as he dropped his eyes.

"Nevertheless, my followers and I will be there when you call. I will fight this to the end. The end approaches but is not yet here."

McKee looked up with a small smile, but he did not speak. He turned to his horse, reached behind the saddle, and untied a long, thin bundle extending across the flanks of his horse. He held it outstretched in two hands as he stepped back to Tecumseh. "This is for you."

Tecumseh took the awkwardly shaped bundle and unrolled it from the cloth protecting it. As the cloth unrolled it revealed a brightly polished brass sheath from which extended a sword handle with a heavily ornate guard. Tecumseh held the sheath in one hand, held the handle in the other, and pulled the blade free. The steel gleamed even in the soft light of overcast. He held the blade to his face for inspection and tried to read the inscription down the length of it but could not. "What does it say?" he asked.

"It is Latin. It translates to 'Bend to my will.' It is a gift, Tecumseh. I was directed to give it to you whether you agreed or not. It is from Major General Isaac Brock, commander of His Majesty's forces in Upper Canada. But General Brock, knowing your reputation of disdain for any gift designed to get an Indian to accept a white man's offer, specifically instructed I was not to give it to you until the conversation ended and you had made your position known. It is, or was, Brock's own. He wanted you to have it as a token of his personal esteem for the work you have done and the battles you have won."

For the first time in over a week, Tecumseh's face broke into a full-toothed smile. "It appears I now have a long knife. I am a Shemanese."

CHAPTER 40

OCTOBER 4, 1813

McGregor Creek at Thames River, Upper Canada

Tecumseh was running at full speed, his feet deftly landing on the eight-by-eight support members, all that was not yet consumed by the flames burning the bridge that crossed McGregor Creek. Bullets flew through the flames, splintering the bridge rails and splashing in the creek below. It was as though all one thousand of Harrison's dismounted cavalry on one side of the creek were aiming at one man while one thousand Indians on the other side watched their leader dance unharmed through the fire and the flames. He was the last to cross.

Once across, he dove into the waiting arms of his comrades. He smiled up at Chaubenee. "That will hold them until tomorrow."

Chaubenee could not help but share the joy at not just the success but the theater of the whole thing. "I haven't seen a fire that big since last August when we Potawatomi burned Fort

Dearborn to the ground and did it without your help," he said with a proud smile.

He received a large smile from Tecumseh in return. "This little fire will hold them long enough for Procter to get those two small field pieces of his off the field. Harrison won't pursue until he gets it rebuilt so he can bring his own along.

"We'll leave a few snipers to ensure Harrison's engineers can't work tonight. Tomorrow morning he'll bring up those guns to chase off our snipers to let his engineers do their work. My guess is that will take them most of the day. At least all morning." And then Tecumseh's look turned serious. "That gives me this evening to try to get Procter to hold and him all morning tomorrow to dig in."

Chaubenee looked skeptical. General Henry Procter, who took over command after General Brock had been killed near York, had done nothing but run ever since Harrison crossed the river.

"Why do you think he'll stop now?" Chaubenee asked.

Tecumseh looked all around them. "Because this is as good ground as Procter will find to defend. The Thames River will cover his left flank, and that swamp"—he pointed away from the river—"will cover his right. The only way Harrison can get to him is either leave his field pieces and trudge all the way through the swamp or rebuild this bridge and cross here. It's now or never."

"The coward may opt for never, turn his six hundred red-coats," Chaubenee said with a sarcastic tone, "and run."

"Harrison will run us if Procter doesn't stand. And the only way Procter can run before them will be to abandon his artillery. I've never known a British general who would do that.

"Get fifty sharpshooters in covered positions before the bridge. I'll go talk to Procter." Tecumseh turned to walk away but stopped suddenly. "Wasegoboah will expect to stay and command the snipers. Don't let him. I want to talk to both of you tonight."

By the time Tecumseh returned from Procter's headquarters, most of his warriors had settled in. Very few had eaten, as they were preparing themselves and their weapons for tomorrow's expected battle. Fires and conversations were going all around the small area where Chaubenee and Wasegoboah had laid out their bedrolls and built their own fire. They had also peeled Tecumseh's bedroll from his horse and placed it between theirs. Neither rose but both looked up in anticipation as Tecumseh approached.

"He will stand. Tomorrow we meet him who has been, and remains, our greatest enemy. If Moneto smiles, perhaps it will be I who kill William Henry Harrison."

Both men smiled and moved slightly apart to make room for their friend and leader. As he sat down, Chaubenee said, "Would you enjoy a pipe, my friend?"

Tecumseh settled next to the warmth and nodded agreement. Chaubenee rolled slightly to one side and picked a pipe and tobacco from his kit. Once he'd loaded and lit the pipe, he puffed and then passed it to Tecumseh. After taking a long pull of the satisfying smoke, Tecumseh passed the pipe to Wasegoboah, took a moment of silence to collect himself, and then began.

"We have won many victories." He turned to gaze on Chaubenee with great affection. "You and your Potawatomi have taken and destroyed Fort Dearborn in Chicago." Then he turned to Wasegoboah. "And you and I, my longest companion, have done what even the great Pontiac did not accomplish. We took Detroit."

Even the stoic and grizzled old warrior could not help but smile, basking in the praise.

"But even as we win, the ants multiply. Every time we kill one, three more appear. No matter our victories, they swarm to us. It has taken me long to understand. I always knew this was about survival for the Shawnee. Only recently have I come to see that it is about survival for the whites as well. Our cultures cannot exist together, and they know it. Tomorrow it will be decided which shall continue to exist between the mountains and the father of rivers and which shall not."

Chaubenee and Wasegoboah exchanged a brief look, sensing what came next.

"You both know the men in the family of Pucksinwah have sight. Pucksinwah himself predicted the day of his death. And you were both there when his son, Chiksika, also predicted the date and hour of his own. Now, Brothers, that vision has come to me. Tomorrow I will die."

The two listeners looked sharply at Tecumseh, but neither objected. They both knew better. It was Chaubenee who first spoke. "Is there no other way?"

Tecumseh looked directly into the massive face and answered, "Perhaps." And then he turned to face Wasegoboah. "I will die of a gunshot to the heart in the middle of the battle, and I will fall dead as my brother did. But you, Wasegoboah, may restore me."

Even the taciturn old warrior was moved to speech. "How may I do that?"

"Keep an eye on me so you see me fall. When I have fallen, rush to me, the ramrod from your musket extended. If you reach me and can tap me with that rod, I will rise. When I do, we will sweep Harrison, his two thousand foot soldiers, and one thousand mounted Kentucky horse soldiers before us. But more than that, the fifty thousand will hear of my resurrection and they will rise. We will sweep all the Shemanese and the white settlers before us. But if you do not tap me with your ramrod, I will remain dead. And with me our cause will die."

Now he turned to Chaubenee again. "This I say to you especially, Brother, for you are young. If I die tomorrow, fight no more. Ever. Our cause will be lost and with it any possibility of stopping the white man. Do not fight it; do not fight him. Do whatever you must for you and your people to live in peace. There is no other choice save meaningless death and suffering for you and all you hold dear."

Tecumseh stopped talking and took the pipe back from Wasegoboah. After he took several pulls he again looked at Wasegoboah. "Hand me my bedroll, please. All of it. Everything there."

Wasegoboah stood and stepped away from the fire, returning momentarily with Tecumseh's possessions wrapped in his bedroll, the entirety of it lying across his arms. He laid it into Tecumseh's lap.

Tecumseh dug into the gear and pulled out the sword and scabbard, the gift given by McKee from General Brock the year before. This he took in both hands and extended to Chaubenee. "This is yours, my friend, to keep in war and peace, a memory and a trophy of all we have done together."

Chaubenee accepted the gift and said nothing, the small tears forming in his eyes robbing his tongue of speech but saying more than it ever could.

Tecumseh again dug into the gear and came back up with a brass medal some six fingers in diameter and suspended on a purple silk ribbon. On one side was a bas-relief of King George III and on the other a Latin inscription of appreciation. "This was the other gift Isaac Brock gave to me. It was in grateful appreciation of the power of the Shawnee and the desire of the Crown that we be ever friends and allies to it. Oddly, he called it 'The Peace Medal.'

"Do with it as you like, Wasegoboah, but I ask one thing: wear it tomorrow."

* * * *

Tecumseh watched as Harrison's cavalry came over the restored bridge crossing McGregor Creek. The Kentuckians seemed unable to keep any sort of order, but they did all manage to break left after crossing the creek to become Harrison's left flank. It would be for them to confront the Indians they had fought so often, Tecumseh's Indians making up Procter's right flank. Harrison would use his regulars to take on Procter's regulars in the center. The cannons would be there, and expecting volunteer horse to take on that and the redcoats was not in his plan.

The horse charged the covered Indians, but Tecumseh was ready. He had his fifty best marksmen in the swamp on his far right. The loose ground would protect them from the mounted troops and enable them to fire continually into the flank of the Kentuckians. The body of his warriors lay on the ground awaiting the main assault. They were used to this by now. He knew they would shoot calmly and for the horses. They would not turn and run. The Kentuckians, half-drunk this late in the day, charged erratically as he expected. Much of their first wave had been brought down, either unhorsed or themselves shot. But the unhorsed Kentuckians did not retreat. Dismounted, they lay on the ground and made very small targets of themselves, moving forward using whatever cover was available.

Tecumseh lay belly low in the grass—waiting. He was naked save for a breechcloth and armed with only his rifle and war club. He would wait for the Kentuckians to spend themselves getting ever closer. Only when they were close enough would he run into battle as he liked—quickly, hand-to-hand, and never standing still. Until then, he would content himself with the periodic shot at any Kentuckian fool enough or drunk enough to make a standing target of himself.

As the sun started to move low before him, the Kentuckians got closer. One, sensing the distance, stood to fire. Tecumseh's shot hit him squarely in the chest, and he dropped like a bird taken on the wing. One of the younger Indians, with an over-eager sense of timing, judged the distance short enough and rose, running the less than twenty yards now separating the forces. Every opposing musket seemed to fire at once, and the riddled warrior tumbled backward. A cloud of black powder smoke rose over him and blocked the visibility of all near.

This was the moment for which Tecumseh had waited. The cloud would cover his charge while he ran across the ground. He was running full speed before he was erect and screaming a defiant war cry as he came.

* * * *

Wasegoboah, trying to stay close, saw only the shadow of the man, pistol in hand, who fired from behind the cloud. Tecumseh had dropped without even his momentum carrying him forward. The moment arrived just as he'd predicted, and Wasegoboah pulled the ramrod from the guides below the barrel of his musket and raced as fast as his beating heart would let him. The brass medallion bounced off his chest as he ran. When he was only a few paces away from Tecumseh's fallen body, Wasegoboah heard a shout from the enemy.

"He's mine!"

Like Tecumseh, Wasegoboah never heard the roar of the shot that killed him.

ACKNOWLEDGMENTS

Writing may be a solitary task but publishing, I have discovered, is not. There are a whole lot of people that have stood between me and my "final draft" of *A Panther Crosses Over* and you, the reader of this, the actual final product. And each of them has had to display literary and professional wisdom and talent in order to offer you a story you may enjoy. They have provided creative editing, line editing, marketing, website creation, book design, including page layout and cover design, and so much more. In fact I have a Gantt chart of details that had to be created, cared for, and approved. That chart is three pages long and single spaced. And every line was the responsibility of some competent professional. I can't thank them all, but I do want to offer my acknowledgement and gratitude to a few.

Dan Crissman offered a creative edit that gave the current structure to the book you have just read as well as an arc of character for the major players in the story. *A Panther Crosses Over* is a much better work thanks to his efforts on my, and your, behalf.

I also want to offer my most sincere thanks to Leslie, Karen, Georgie, Sara, Rachel, Bethany, and Devon. They are the women who created and ran that three-page Gantt chart. They are accomplished, professional, and so considerate of an author who was frequently wrong and seldom willing to come easily to that conclusion.

CHARACTERS IN
A PANTHER CROSSES OVER

Listed in order in which their names first appear

Pini—Young Illini warrior; assassin of Pontiac and catalyst
for the invasion of Illinois and the destruction of the Illini
nation by Pontiac's Ottawa and other Indian enemies of
the Illini.

Chatonis*—Member of the party hunting Pini.

Spotka—Potawatomi ally of Ottawa; first leader of Potawatomi
village at Mascouten Bay; father of Canoko.

Opawana—Nephew of Pontiac; second in command of invad-
ing force seeking revenge for Pontiac's assassination;
becomes member of Spotka's Potawatomi village; father of
Chaubenee.

Quaqui—Leader of the Illini village at Mascouten Bay; last living chief of Illini nation; leader of the Illini last stand at
Starved Rock; father of Paskepaho.

Paskepaho—Son of Quaqui; only Illini to escape Starved Rock
alive; tasked by dying father with removing Illini land

from Potawatomi control; signatory of Treaty of St. Louis selling all of Illinois north and west of Illinois River to US government.

Singing Bird*—Medicine woman killed at massacre of Illini village at Mascouten Bay.

Howls at the Moon*—Illini warrior killed at massacre of Illini village at Mascouten Bay.

Buffalo Fish*—Illini warrior killed at massacre of Illini village at Mascouten Bay.

Hukuwia*—Quaqui's wife; Paskepaho's mother; killed at massacre of Illini village at Mascouten Bay.

Makatachinga—Leader of Illini village at Peoria; principal chief of Illini nation; tortured by Ottawa to find Pini's motivation for the assassination of Pontiac.

Otussa—Eldest son of Pontiac; leader of search for Pini and subsequent annihilation of Illini.

Raven's Cry*—Ottawa roasted by Illini on top of Le Rocher.

Chaubenee—Son of Opawana; raised in Potawatomi village at Mascouten Bay; became its leader after marrying Spotka's daughter, Canoko, and thereby becoming a Potawatomi; follower of Tecumseh since he was seventeen; only one of Tecumseh's closest followers to survive the Battle of the Thames.

Chiksika—Eldest natural son of Pucksinwah, the war chief of Shawnee until his death at the Battle of Point Pleasant;

older brother of Tecumseh; predicted the day and hour of his own death, as had his father and as did Tecumseh.

Tecumseh—The panther who crossed over.

Chiungalla*—Second civil chief of Shawnee; guardian of all Pucksinwah's children after his death, save Blue Jacket who was married and living with his wife's sept.

Blue Jacket—A Virginian captured at age seventeen by a Pucksinwah-led Shawnee raiding party. He was subsequently adopted by Pucksinwah, making Blue Jacket his eldest son (Chiksika was two years younger). He followed closely in his adopted father's footsteps, becoming war chief. In that capacity he won two major battles against the US Army, defeating General Josiah Harmar's First American Regiment (approximately fourteen hundred regulars and volunteers) in October 1790 at the Battle of Pumpkin Field and General Arthur St. Clair in 1791 at the Battle of the Wabash, where St. Clair was routed and lost over eight hundred killed. Blue Jacket died of natural causes in 1810.

Spemica Lawba (also known as Johnny Logan)—Son of Tecumapese and Chaqui and nephew of Tecumseh. He was captured and adopted by Kentuckian General Benjamin Logan at age eleven. He was returned to the Shawnee in a peace negotiated by Blue Jacket. Before he was returned, Johnny Logan swore an oath never to fight against his "father," Benjamin Logan, and ever after lived with one foot in each of the two worlds that was the Northwest Territory. He worked as a scout, interpreter, guide, messenger, and advisor, first to Anthony Wayne and then William Henry Harrison.

Moluntha*—Leader of Shawnee village of Mackachack; most ancient and revered of Shawnee leaders; killed, after he had surrendered, during General Benjamin Logan's attack on his village. Eleven-year-old Spemica Lawba stood over the body, defending it from mutilation.

Wasegoboah—Companion of Chiksika; early mentor of Tecumseh; late ex-husband to Tecumapese. After Chiksika's death Wasegoboah followed Tecumseh the remainder of his life and died trying to resurrect Tecumseh at the Battle of the Thames.

Morgan*—Partner at Baynton, Wharton & Morgan trading post near Cahokia.

Methotasa—Wife of Pucksinwah; mother of Chiksika, Tecumapese, Tecumseh, and the only set of triplets born in the Shawnee Nation for four generations. The triplets were all boys: Tensk, Sauwaseekau, and Kumskaka. Methotasa was a Cherokee captured by Pucksinwah on a raid when she was fifteen. His name was said to be the last word on her lips.

Tensk (also known as "The Shawnee Prophet")—His actual name was Tenskwatawa. I have shortened it for ease of reading. He was Tecumseh's brother. He was also a drunk, a liar, a coward, and a ne'er-do-well, but Tecumseh found him useful in controlling some Indian chiefs' impulse to "sell" land they did not own to Harrison. Tecumseh also found him useful in hiding his own identity as the power behind the rising consolidation sentiment among the Indians west of the Appalachians. In the end, it was Tensk's attempt to use Tecumseh that brought down their entire plan and created the history of America.

Sauwaseekau and Kumskaka*—Neither of these two of Methotasa's triplets seems to have had any significant talents. History suggests they paled in the shadows of their powerful and charismatic siblings.

Chaqui*—Tecumapese's first husband and the father of Spemica Lawba. He died at the Battle of Point Pleasant with his father-in-law.

Tecumapese—Second child and only daughter of Pucksinwah and Methotasa; mother of Spemica Lawba; elder sister of Tecumseh by ten years and his most long-term and trusted advisor—until shortly before the end.

Mukonse—Cherokee who led war parties with Chiksika and later Tecumseh.

Sequoyah*—Cherokee scholar who developed the written Cherokee language.

Osceola*—Seminole chief.

Catahecassa—Principal chief of the Shawnee and implacable foe of Tecumseh with great political, personal, and philosophical differences.

General Arthur St. Clair—Commander of the US Army. In 1791 he led an army of fourteen hundred plus eight cannons out of Fort Washington (adjacent to Cincinnati) to bring the consolidated tribes of the Northwest Territory to heel. St. Clair was met "at the place where the Wabash can be jumped by a horse" by a force of some three thousand Shawnee and Miami, as well as warriors from almost every other tribe in the Northwest Territory. St. Clair survived but more than eight hundred of his forces did not.

Colonel Richard England—English commander of Fort Detroit from 1792 until July 1795, when the Jay Treaty required Britain to surrender the fort to the United States. He was not, however, the last British commander at Fort Detroit, as a combined British and Indian force (Tecumseh commanding the Indian troops) recaptured it briefly during the War of 1812.

Alexander McKee—A turncoat American who joined the British in revulsion over the US Indian policy. He became Britain's Indian agent for Upper Canada.

General "Mad Anthony" Wayne—American general during the American Revolution brought out of retirement to combat Indians of the Northwest Territory. He successfully broke the power of the allied tribes at the Battle of Fallen Timbers in August 1794.

William Henry Harrison—Patrician Virginian whose father signed the Declaration of Independence. George Washington appointed him a lieutenant in the US Army. He served as an aide to Anthony Wayne at the Battle of Fallen Timbers. He rose in the army and politics, eventually being named by President John Adams as governor of Indiana Territory. In that position he was the only man authorized to obtain land titles from Indians. He used that power to "buy" most of Indiana and Illinois from them.

Major William Campbell*—British commander of Fort Miami, who refused to open the gates to Shawnee retreating after the Battle of Fallen Timbers.

Sir William Johnson*—Named in 1756 as British superinten-
dent of Indian affairs. In that capacity Johnson managed to
affirm that all land between the Ohio River and the Great
Lakes and between the Appalachian Mountains and the
Mississippi River belonged to the Iroquois. And then he
bought it from them.

Little Sun and Little Moon*—McKinzie sisters, ages eleven
and eight when captured by the Shawnee in 1778. When
given the opportunity to go back, they elected to remain
Shawnee. Little Sun taught Tecumseh to speak, read, and
write English.

Penegashega—Ancient and best healer among the Shawnee.
He taught Tensk what healing skills he had and positioned
him to become the Shawnee Prophet.

Winnemac—Minor Potawatomi chief who sold Harrison
a large tract of land on both sides of the Wabash River,
a piece of land not owned by the Potawatomi but by the
Miami and Shawnee.

Red Wing*—Chief of the Nadoues Sioux.

Francis Maisonville—A French trader and lover of Tecumapese.

Chambers*—Regimental   commander   at   the   Battle   of
Tippecanoe.

Dyson*—Regimental commander at the Battle of Tippecanoe.

Johansen—Regimental commander at the Battle of Tippecanoe.

Lucas*—Regimental commander at the Battle of Tippecanoe.

Mic McNess*—Maisonville's clerk and subsequent owner of his trading post.

Major General Isaac Brock—British governor and commander of His Majesty's forces in Upper Canada. After his death at Niagara in the Battle of Queenstown Heights in October 1812, command of the British forces devolved to General Henry Procter.

General Henry Procter—Commander of British troops retreating from Fort Malden on the Canadian side of the Detroit River during the War of 1812. Procter was court-martialed for his handling of that campaign and the Battle of the Thames. While he was acquitted, loss of stature and dignity hung upon him the remainder of his life.

*Characters present but of insignificance in this story

HISTORICAL FOOTNOTES

1. The New Madrid Earthquake of December 16, 1811, is presumed to be the largest ever in the contiguous forty-eight states, estimated between 7.9 and 8.1 on the Richter scale. The quake was so large it moved the course of the Mississippi River in several places. One was Kaskaskia, Illinois (the first British fort taken by George Rogers Clark) where the Mississippi moved its channel to the east of the city, making it still the only town in Illinois west of the Mississippi River. It is connected to the rest of Illinois by a bridge across the Mississippi.

2. Paskepaho, Tecumapese, and Tenskwatawa (Tensk's complete name) walked into the gloom of history with no further recording of their lives or deaths.

3. In July 1812 the British put a bounty of $150 on the head of Spemica Lawba/Johnny Logan. He was killed in a battle with the Potawatomi in November 1812.

4. Alexander McKee had a pet deer he had raised from an orphaned fawn. In his cabin outside Fort Malden, the deer playfully butted him as he bent to add a log to the fire. One of the deer's antler tines punctured McKee's femoral artery. He bled to death.

5. Catahecassa outlived Tecumseh. After leading the Shawnee through their decline as a martial power, he also led them to Kansas, where he hoped they would become farmers. He moved back to Ohio, where he died in 1831.

6. Harrison's Kentucky volunteers, believing
    Wasegoboah to be Tecumseh because of the medal
    he wore, mutilated and skinned his body, cutting his
    hide into trophies. One Kentucky politician made
    himself famous with the self-promotion that it was
    he who had killed Tecumseh. He wore a belt made of
    Wasegoboah's hide.

7. The night after the Battle of the Thames, Tecumseh's
    followers removed his body from the battlefield. It has
    never been found. A quote attributed to Chaubenee
    says, "No white man knows, or will ever know, where
    we took the body of our beloved Tecumseh and bur-
    ied him. Tecumseh will come again."

8. By way of repayment for breaking the Shawnee and
    making Indiana and Illinois available for settlement,
    the citizens of the United States elected William
    Henry Harrison, running on the Whig ticket, president
    in 1840. His running mate was US Senator John Tyler,
    a fellow Virginian. Harrison was so well known for
    his destruction of the Shawnee that his nickname was
    "Old Tippecanoe." His campaign slogan didn't bother
    to include his given name. The slogan was "Tippecanoe
    and Tyler too." Harrison's was the shortest presidency
    in US history. On the day he was sworn in, March 4,
    1841, he stood bareheaded in the rain for two hours
    while he delivered his inaugural address. He developed
    a fever and died one month later, April 4, 1841.

SNEAK PEEK FROM
BEARDSTOWN

~ *The* ~
AMERICAN
TRILOGY
BOOK 2

"The test of a first-rate intelligence is the ability to hold two opposed ideas in the mind at the same time, and still retain the ability to function."

F. Scott Fitzgerald

CHAPTER 1

OCTOBER 1818

Edwardsville, Illinois Territory

Enos Marsh stood behind his bar, wiping a shot glass. Even at midday the room was dim, the only light in the log building coming from one unshuttered window and the flicker of a low fire in the hearth. He'd debated lighting the fire at all. The weather this mild October day didn't yet require it, but he'd had fifteen cords of wood chopped and put away so he had plenty to last through the winter. But he liked the smell and the light, as well as the warmth, of this first fall fire so he'd lit it.

Marsh saw the explosion of light before he heard the door burst open. He turned to it, looking at a figure that almost filled the space. Backlit as the man was, Marsh could not make out much more than that he was tall, more than six feet, wearing a wide-brimmed felt hat with a low crown, had shoulders broad enough to cut off most of the light and waist and hips thin enough to suggest youth. As he stepped into the room and closed the door behind him, the stranger removed his hat.

That and the ambient light gave Marsh a better vision of the man's face. He was in his early twenties. His hair was light brown, thick, and grown oddly inward from his temples, giving the sense of a low, narrow forehead. He wore long side whiskers that showed a reddish tint, but he had no mustache or beard. His lips seemed thin and his nose long and robust. His buckskin jacket was festooned with foot-long cords of fringe across the chest and down the length of the sleeves, many of them missing, obviously cut off for some use. His pants were rough-finish homespun wool brushed smooth in the wearing. His collarless shirt was of unbleached linen. In the dim light Marsh could not make out his eye color, but his whole face and being gave a sense of great vitality and warmth. He was a complete stranger, in a new place, and nonetheless his face beamed joy and goodwill. His broad smile was not one of a man who is uncertain and wears it to announce he presents no danger. It was the smile of a man who genuinely enjoyed his life and felt very much in command of it.

He strode straight to Marsh and extended his hand across the bar. "Name's Beard, Thomas Beard. Call me Tom. I'd like a beer, a warm meal, and a room in that order. But before I do any of that, even the beer, I need a place to stable my horses and unload the pack animal. I've got a surveyor's transit tied on there. I don't want to take my eyes off it for more than a moment."

Beard was tall enough that Marsh was forced to move his hand up to accept the offered one. And his smile was infectious. Marsh could finally make out the stranger's eye color. They were a light, almost ice, blue, and they twinkled delight with the world. Marsh could not help but be infected by the young man's mood. "We can do all of that, Tom. Edwardsville is an orderly town, but on the frontier you never know. Unhitch your horses and lead them around back. We've a stable there where they can get rubbed down and fed. I'll bring one of my men to help with the gear, and we'll get that precious transit of yours to a safe place."

By the time Beard got his mount and packhorse around back, Marsh and a middle-aged black man were there to greet him. Beard presumed the black man was free, here north of the Ohio, but you never knew.

Marsh pointed the helper to the horses and said, "Jim, lead them on in and get the saddle off Mr. . . ." And then he said quizzically, "Beard? It was Beard, wasn't it?"

"That's right, but make it Tom." And there was that smile again.

"Take Mr. Beard's horses, Jim, and get the trap off his mount once you get it in the stall. It doesn't look overworked on this cool day, but rub it down anyhow." And then moving his glance to Beard, he said, "Tom, would you like us to store those things on the packhorse?"—he pointed to the beast, whose burden was covered in white canvas, the three legs to a transit sticking out the back—"aside from the transit, of course. Or would you like to have it all taken to your room? Room's small but it will fit."

"I'll take the transit, and the musket but"—and now looking at Jim—"would you be so good as to bring those trade goods up to my room. I'm going to need them soon."

Marsh nodded to Jim, confirming he was to do as requested, turned to Beard, and said, "I believe a beer was the next thing on your list. Soon as you pull that transit out, come on in the back door and to the bar. There will be a cool one on the counter." And with that he turned and walked away.

Beard ran his hand over the flank of his mount as he stepped by, took the lead of the packhorse from Jim's hand, and walked it into a stall. As he untied the canvas wrap, Beard looked over the rail separating the stalls at the black man pulling the saddle off his roan and throwing it up and over the rail on the other side of the stall. His most noticeable feature was his beard. It was short, curly, and starting to grey. He was muscular and lean. "Jim, you slave or free?"

The black man turned to face Beard and looked directly at him, his face opening to a smile that showed pride. "Free. Complicated, though."

As Beard untied the transit from the horse's back, he said, without looking back, "Complicated? How's that?"

Jim picked up a large piece of burlap and began to rub the roan. "I was born a slave. In Tennessee. When I was 'bout ten years old, the Cherokee raided the little settlement my master started. Killed the men but took women and children captive. Me, too. So I was a slave to the Cherokee for a while. I was traded around a few times and ended up with the Shawnee. None of them treated me any worse than my white masters so it didn't much matter to me.

"Maybe five years ago, Mr. Marsh was trading with the Shawnee along the Wabash. He stopped to talk to me. It was tough remembering my English, but as we talked it came back. He told me that in the end the Shawnee were going to get whipped and had I thought what would happen to me then? I hadn't.

"Mr. Marsh said if I wanted to come back to a white world, he'd buy me from the Shawnee and not leave me as a spoil of war when it was over. I told him I had no world. I was neither Indian nor white. In both worlds, I was a slave. Then Mr. Marsh made me the damnedest offer. Said he'd buy me and free me, give me papers, and I could work for him if I wanted or not. That'd be up to me. No one ever did anything like that for me.

"So, I took him up on it and he made good. I got my papers right here." Jim touched his hip pocket. "I can leave anytime. But why? Got no place to go. Here I have a room of my own to sleep"—Jim pointed toward the rear stable wall and a small door leading through it—"and he pays me enough wages to keep myself and set a little aside. Who knows? Maybe one day

I'll meet a nice black woman. I may have enough to buy her free if she ain't already."

Even the garrulous Beard seemed to have nothing to say, but he was smiling. "Jim, hand me the musket that was in the saddle scabbard if you please."

Jim did as directed. Beard, with his transit thrown over one shoulder and the musket dangling from his other hand, turned to walk toward the stable entrance, the smile still on his face.

"Mr. Beard!" The call came from over his shoulder. He stopped and turned to look at Jim. "Mr. Marsh's a good man. You can trust him."

Beard whistled as he walked away.

When he walked into Marsh's public house he was met by the little man's oddly deep voice.

"As promised." Marsh pointed to the cold beer sitting on the bar, foam running down the sides of the mug.

Beard took a moment to study Marsh for the first time. He was a small man, but one sensed that his character was far larger than his stature. His jet-black hair was not parted but combed straight back. His eyes were oddly large and, in this light, as dark as his hair. His thin nose was perfectly coupled with his thin face. His ears were just a touch large. Those and his large, almost sensuous, lips converted the suggestion of his face from that of a man with a weasel's cunning to that of a man with an owl's wisdom. Marsh's clothing was out of place for one with his role. The entire costume was refined; wool pants of store-bought quality fabric tucked into well-polished high leather boots and a brocade waistcoat suggested his station was above that of mere innkeeper. Beard decided Jim was right, Marsh was a man to be trusted until proved otherwise.

"Drink that now and then go on up to your room. Jim may have your goods up there by then. He's quick," Marsh said. "By the time you come back down, there will be some warm venison and bread waiting for you. I'd like to hear what you're up to. If you're interested in telling me, that is."

Beard took that beer down in one long pull. As he set the empty mug on the bar, Marsh handed him a brass key.

"First room on the right at the top of the stairs."

By the time Beard returned, the dining room and bar were half-full of men. *Not a woman in the place,* he noted with no surprise. The men were boisterous and full of vigor and life. He could hear it before he even walked into the room.

Marsh saw him the moment he did and pointed to a small table by the fireplace. Beard walked to it. As Beard pulled the chair out to sit down, Marsh delivered another beer and said, "Dinner will be in ten minutes."

And within ten minutes the multitalented Jim placed it before him.

"You cook as well, Jim?"

The lean man smiled down at him. "I do pretty much everything except bank the money. Let me know if you need more." And then he turned and walked away.

Beard sat quietly taking in the place and the crowd as he ate the venison. It was no different than any public house on the frontier. Full of boisterous men. Good souls, by and large, but men who were used to taking care of themselves and doing as they pleased. There was seldom malice in such a group, but most innkeepers kept a double-barreled musket packed with small pellets behind the bar.

As he sopped the last of the venison gravy with his corn bread, he saw Marsh coming across the room, a shot glass in either hand. He set them both down on the table and said, "I thought a corn whiskey might top off that meal better than a beer. May I join you?"

Beard smiled one of his white-toothed smiles and said, "I'd enjoy the company. Haven't had much the last couple of weeks."

Marsh pushed one shot glass across the table toward Beard, sipped from his own, looked directly into Beard's twinkling blue eyes, and said, "So if I'm not prying, want to tell me what you and that transit are up to?"

Beard killed his whiskey in one quick swallow, sat the empty glass down gently, looked intently into Marsh's eyes. "Me and my transit are here to build a town, maybe a city." He said nothing more, leaving time for the audacity of his statement to soak in.

"And just where do you plan for this vision to bloom?"

"That, Mr. Marsh, I do not know but I'll know the place—"

"No. No Mr. Marsh. Call me Enos. Most folks do."

"Fair enough. Enos it is. Enos, I like your metaphor of blooming a city. It's apt."

"How so, apt?" Marsh asked.

"It may be fall but it's the season for planting here. The St. Louis Treaty gave America rights over everything in Illinois north and west of the river. Yeah, it was contentious but the Potawatomi, even though they haven't signed on, haven't made a peep since Thames River. I think they will sign soon, maybe even this year. And since the Treaty of Ghent ended the second war with the Brits, most of the natives have taken the same attitude. Certainly, the Shawnee have and the Miami. If there is lingering trouble, it's been the Kickapoo. But since Governor Edwards had Howard march up the Illinois River and rough up a couple of their villages, they may still grumble, but they haven't taken any scalps. And Monroe has made it clear to William Clark he wants them to sign over control and move west of the Mississippi. That will happen soon, Mr. Mar—Enos."

"You do keep up on politics, Tom."

Again, Beard broke into that broad open smile that was the trademark of his face. "It's my business to, Enos. I've been wandering the frontier for going on two years now, doing nothing but a little trading to live and learning all I need to know to make this biggest decision of my life the right one.

"And I'll tell you something else we all know that fits here. All those soldiers who fought in the second war are going to accept their mustering-out bonus of one hundred sixty or three hundred twenty acres in the Illinois land north of the river as soon as the survey is complete. And then they will be coming in the thousands, maybe tens of thousands."

Marsh interrupted with a sardonic chuckle. "Don't you pity those fellows who signed up early when the bonus was only one hundred sixty acres? They served longer and got less than those who came later when Madison really needed troops."

"True," responded Beard. "But they'll be coming to collect their share. Maybe they'll come grumbling but they'll come nonetheless. And I'll be there to greet them."

Marsh took another sip of his whiskey. "So, if now is the season to plant, where is the place to plant?"

Beard composed his thoughts for a moment before answering. "Let me tell you what I do know. It has to be a place with a few Indians left because I've got to make enough to live on until these settlers come. Trading is the only way I know to do it. Second, and most important, it must be on the Illinois River. If my town is to be a center of commerce, it will have to fulfill two requirements. First, the land must be rich so farmers will be prosperous enough to have surpluses to sell. Second, it must be near transportation so those surpluses can get to markets—St. Louis, New Orleans, or on to the east coast. And that means river transportation. It's the only way. So, on the river and with good anchorage for a port and surrounded by rich land."

Beard laughed, a deep rumbling laugh. "Bold enough plan for a young man, Enos?"

Before Marsh could respond Beard added, "Two more things, Enos. It's going to have to be on the south side of the river because everything north is reserved for all the bounties that are mustering-out bonuses for those veterans. But they'll all be coming from the south, from this direction. And because they will all want to get to the north side, I'll have to provide ferry service. I need to be able to get them to their land, as they come looking to plant. And they'll need to get to me, as they come looking to sell their surpluses. For that I'll need a ferry. If I can create a ferry, that will create the town. And if my little transit and I can lay out a town, in a spot like that, we'll have lots to sell and places for merchants and city dwellers to build.

"That's the plan, Enos. You know a place where I can plant my garden?"

Marsh finished the last of his whiskey and smiled a slow, easy smile. "No, Tom, I don't. But I know a man who does."

* * * *

Enos Marsh stood in the street before the horses of the two young men he'd introduced less than a week ago. As he looked up at them, his face carried the pensive gaze of a man pondering whether he had done a truly significant thing or merely a foolish one. Young as Beard was, Murray McConnel was even younger, just twenty-one. But he was an experienced woodsman and trader who had wandered the continent's frontiers since he was fourteen years old and was one of the few men who knew the Illinois River Valley for more than a few miles north of the river's confluence with the Mississippi at Alton. Alton was the spot where a retired army colonel had opened a trading post and built a ferry across the Mississippi earlier in the year and had pretentiously named it all after his infant son, Alton. Marsh had introduced the two young adventurers over dinner, thinking McConnel might be able to serve as Beard's guide. When Beard told his story to McConnel, he'd added that he planned to pole his ferry across the river, so it would have to be a place where the bottom was shallow. Marsh remembered clearly what had happened then.

Murray's long, red, bushy eyebrows immediately shot up into a knowing arch, and his high-pitched tenor voice filled the room. He shouted, "I know just the place!"

Every head at the bar turned toward them and McConnel looked down, embarrassed to have brought attention to their conversation. By the time he looked back, others in the tavern had realized nothing of interest was happening and had gone back to their own talk. McConnel, now in control of himself but with blue eyes still twinkling, said, "There's a small Potawatomi village at mile eighty-eight. Us boys with Howard in '13 marched there to revenge the Fort Dearborn massacre. But the Potawatomi had all gone. Every last one of 'em went and hid. They eventually came back, but that was after Thames River and they have been quiet as a church mouse since their defeat there. The place is just below Mascouten Bay. That's the entrance to the swamp formed where the Sangamon runs into the Illinois. Water is deep enough for easy navigation to that point, but right in front of the village the alluvial flow from the Sangamon forms a bar clear across the Illinois."

He'd looked at Beard then, all mirth gone, his face now reflecting his more usual stoic coolness. "I can take you there."

That had been just six days ago and now here they were, final supplies of grub and trading goods purchased, horses well fed and rested, last kitchen-cooked breakfast either would have for a long while in their bellies, morning sun on their faces, the eagerness of youth in their hearts, and ready for whatever the world had to hurl at them.

Marsh patted Beard's roan on the neck, stepped back, and smiled up at both men, his gaze holding on to Thomas Beard's eyes. "Tom, you'll succeed at this. That I know. But the one thing you'll need to build this town of yours is money. When the time comes to buy the land, you'll need a moneyman. Come to me then."

And with that he turned on his heels and stepped up onto the wooden sidewalk and through the front door of his public house.

* * * *

The two men, each mounted and with one packhorse behind, rode straight and steady across prairie through grass tall enough to brush across their stirrups and boots and along the horses' bellies. To Beard its expanse and undulation in the breeze made it appear as a sea of grass, unlike anything he'd ever seen. McConnel, taciturn man that he was, led without conversation in a straight line headed due north.

"Murray, I've never seen anything like this," Beard said to the back of McConnel's head. "Does this grass never end?"

"Not used to this, are ya? Where you from, Tom?"

"From a world of forests, Mo. May I call you that?"

The back brim of Murray's hat tipped up in a small nod.

"Born in Upstate New York but my folks moved to the Connecticut Western Reserve when I was five," Tom continued. "I may have been just five but I remember it like yesterday. Storm in January. Why would a man move his family into the wilderness in January? Was the coldest I've ever been. My kid sister was just three and almost froze to death. There were five of us on two horses. That's it, just two horses. Ma held the baby with me behind. My kid sister rode in front of Pa. We'd have all frozen to death, had my uncle—he'd gone there first—not come back and found us.

"Uncle had convinced my dad that the Reserve would explode with army vets from the Revolution coming for their mustering-out land bounty. And he was right. It will be no different here. Just different vets from a different war but same signing bonus paid at mustering out. Paid in land.

"Anyhow, my uncle had found a stream what would push a grinding mill. Figured all the incoming farmers would need one. He was right. Dad was big on education. Us kids labored all day but every night after dinner he became the teacher. Eventually, the mill got enough work that he had to hire men. They got included in night class. Dad insisted. Finally, the mill made enough money to send my sister and me to school for a couple of years. Kid brother stayed home to help on the farm. I got a little education." Beard jerked his thumb toward the transit legs sticking out from under the canvas covering his goods on the packhorse. "Learned to do that. That's what I got. Surveying skills and a transit. Kid brother will get the family farm and half the mill one day."

"That why you started wandering?" McConnel asked.

"Sorta but not quite. Men in my family have always been soldiers. Grandpa fought in the Revolution. When the Brits wanted a second shot at us, my dad, Jedediah, thought it was his turn. So, I came back from school to run the farm and help with the mill. He came home in '14. I stayed around for a few years but left home two years ago and wandered down through Ohio and Indiana before I got here."

Beard gave a laugh. "That's all trees, Mo. All trees. Never seen nothing like this. A man wouldn't even have to clear it. Just put a plow in the ground and start farming."

For the first time in Beard's recitation, McConnel turned his head back toward him. His thin, pale, freckled face showed no more expression. Beard had learned that was its norm. But the blue eyes twinkled excitement. "Some Frenchman, guy named Jolliet who was about the second white man to see this territory, said somethin' very much like that. Don't remember it exactly but it was somethin' like, Illinois River Valley is most beautiful and suitable for settlement. A settler would not have to spend ten years cutting down and burning trees. On the very day of his arrival, he could put a plow into the ground."

They rode silently for a few moments before Tom spoke again. "America is going to get rich here, Mo. Very rich."

McConnel stopped his horse and waited for Beard to come up beside him, looked over at him, and cracked his face into the first smile Beard had seen there since he'd shouted, "I know just the place."

"And you and me with it, Tom. You and me with it. Rich, very rich. That's what we'll get."

* * * *

The two men had camped in a grove of hardwood trees along a stream that seemed to feed them. The wood was mainly oak and elm, but there was one large black walnut. McConnel allowed as how he had enough of a taste for walnuts to get the black stain on his hands. Stains that would come from removing the soft outer husk. So, after they'd pulled into the trees and unloaded the horses and hobbled and released them to eat to their contentment of the tall grass, McConnel went collecting walnuts and Beard took his musket to provide a turkey for dinner. It took neither of them long to collect what they wanted.

McConnel used his hands to rub the outer husk off the walnuts and two rocks to split the hard inner shell. He had two full cups of rich walnut meat before Tom got the feathers off the bird.

"Do wish I had a pot of boiling water to dip this beast into and make pluckin' these feathers easier."

"Just keep plucking, Tom, you'll get there." McConnel handed Beard a cup of walnut meat. "Nibble these. They'll give you strength for the task. Meantime I'll get a fire going and set up something to roast that bird on. When you finally get it ready."

That had been two hours ago. They now both sat with their backs against trees and close enough to the glowing coals to collect some warmth as the cool of a fall evening fell upon them. They'd consumed most of the turkey and McConnel pulled a bottle from the gear and poured three fingers of whiskey into each of their cups. Theirs was the silence of shared contentment. But silence was something Beard could only tolerate for just so long.

"Mo, you asked me earlier about my story and I told it. Your turn now. How'd you get here? How'd you come to know this valley?"

McConnel looked into the glowing coals as though for inspiration, sipped at his whiskey, and in his pitchy tenor voice, still full of an Irish lilt, if not an accent, started. "Like you I'm from Upstate New York originally. Like your father, mine's a farmer though no other trade. And like you I had a couple of years of schoolin'. Mine was subscription school not boarding. But I learned to read and write easily and do figures. Maybe it's that my ancestors are Irish but I have a great love of words."

Beard interrupted from across the fire. "Well, for a man who loves words you don't bother to use many of them."

McConnel barked back, but with twinkling eyes illuminated by the firelight, "Well, maybe it's because you talk enough for both of us. Hush and I'll see if I can't spin a few together.

"I left home at only fourteen and afoot. Walked to Fort Pitt, doing day labor here and there along the way for room and board. When I got to Fort Pitt, I found work on a barge and floated to Lexington. I labored there for a year. As you know Governor Edwards of Illinois Territory called for volunteers to join Colonel Howard in a march up the Illinois to punish the Potawatomi and Kickapoo for the Fort Dearborn massacre. I'd started out to see the country but found myself stuck laboring in Lexington. Signing up seemed a good way to change my circumstances. I'm frugal, and disciplined, as you'll find out. I'd saved enough to buy a musket. So, I got one and a shot bag and powder horn to go with it and joined the volunteers. Some fourteen hundred of us from Kentucky were going to go. For reasons I still don't understand, the regiment fell apart. In the end we weren't going to go. Well, maybe not 1,399 others but I was. I found a job poling a flatboat downriver, and when it got to the Mississippi I hopped off and walked north to Edwardsville. I arrived just before Howard left. They welcomed me, and our little force of no more than seven hundred now walked on up the Mississippi to Alton and then started up the Illinois River Valley.

"Mascouten Bay was the first place we thought we'd fight. But the Potawatomi village was entirely deserted. They knew we were coming. Almost all their warriors were with the Brits in Canada. Those who stayed behind, mostly women and children I'd guess, decided the best thing to do was vamoose—that's from a Spanish word I learned later. Means 'be gone'—and it was a good idea. I'd have done the same thing were I them. But the Kickapoo were not so smart. They had a village just a few miles away back from the river, near the bluff. We killed a bunch of them and burned their village. Then we walked a bit farther up the river, found another Kickapoo village, and did it again.

"That was enough punishment for us. We were pretty much all militia. When we thought it was time to go home, we did. That's how I learned this territory."

McConnel took another sip of his corn whiskey and stared back into the flames.

"Mo, that was four or five years ago. What you been doing since?" Beard asked.

"Oh, Jefferson bought all that land from Little Boney when I was about five. I've always wanted to see it. Still do. But I've managed to see some of it. I worked on a boat down to New Orleans and then wandered to Tejas. Not many white people there. A few Mexicans and a very few Americans. They do have some of the biggest Indians you've ever seen. All of them big as you. Name is Karankawa. Americans just call them Kroncs. Also got the meanest Indians you've ever seen. Called Comanches. They live by stealing other Indians' stuff. Only business they practice is slavin'.

"I wandered a bit with groups of traders I could find. Not a place for a man to wander alone."

McConnel was silent again. Beard decided he was through talking and going to go to sleep. So, Beard moved away from the tree, threw his saddle close to the fire, laid his head on it, and pulled a blanket over himself as a little protection from the frost he knew would come tonight. McConnel did the same.

Just as Beard's eyes were blinking closed, McConnel added, "I'm home now. Not as certain as you what my future is but it will be in this part of the country."

* * * *

After three days of nothing but tall grass with periodic copses of hardwood, they reached it. Below, the river ran in a straight line across the land. Straight save that it seemed to flow out of a slough that covered the valley floor as far north as they could see. The river was some three or four miles in front of them. For two miles the trail ran down a hill sloping toward the water. The third and fourth miles seemed almost at grade with the riverbank. On the other side the valley extended for what they guessed to be five miles before a bluff shot up sharply. Both men sat just taking in the majesty of it all. Without comment Murray nudged his mount and started slowly along an old trail that wound downward. As they moved down the grade, the soil, which had been rich loam for three days, became ever sandier. The plants were lower, with few patches of real green.

"Mo, you ever been on the other side of this river?"

"Yep," was the taciturn response.

"We're riding through the poorest soil I've seen in this state. Loam has given way to sand."

"Seems so."

"But on the other side of the river what soil I see, that isn't covered with tall grass, seems so rich it looks black."

McConnel answered the question before it was asked. "Don't know where all this sand came from. But I know about the soil on the other side. You're right. It's rich. Take a handful, hold it up to the light, let it crumble through your fingers and it still looks black. Richest soil I've ever seen. Most springs this river overflows its banks. On the north side there is almost no bank. That land is damn near at water level all the way to the bluff, on the far horizon. So it floods. Every year. Been doing it for all of time, I suppose. Maybe thousands of years. When the flood recedes it leaves all that topsoil the river's been carrying and deposits it here. That's nothing but topsoil maybe ten feet deep."

He was silent for a moment before he added, "Try to farm it now, you'll just get flooded out. That's why the Indians put their villages on this side. But get some Dutchman here who knows how to build dikes, and that will be the richest farmland in America."

At the bottom of the hill the soil was still mostly sand but seemed to have enough loam to support a richer plant life and even a few trees. They rode the last mile to the river in silence. Theirs was the silence of men pondering; pondering whether Indians would be here, and if so, would they bring trade or would they bring trouble; pondering the wonder of this entire river valley; pondering the future of the life they were choosing.

They knew they were close because they could see the black richness of the north side very clearly now. The terrain was flat but high enough above the river to cut off any vision of water. And then there it was. Their horses stood on a low bluff, a tall riverbank really, no more than twenty feet above water level.

McConnel nodded to it. "The French loved this place. Called it Beautiful Mound Village."

"Mound Village? Why?"

"You'll see 'em," McConnel explained. "Don't know what they are but they're manmade for certain. Though by what men, no one seems to know. Biggest one is maybe eighty feet tall and five hundred feet in diameter. Down there a mile or so." McConnel pointed downriver.

Then he turned to look upriver at a crumbling log structure some fifty yards upstream. It was nearly covered by the brush and small trees thriving along the riverbank. "That was the last French trader's place. They had to give all this up after the Brits took over Canada. So that building's just been decaying for more than fifty years now."

The two men just sat on their horses taking in the valley—upriver a great meandering swamp of a wetland, from which the river seemed to flow, almost as though it were the source. The wide river flowing gently along, separating them from the richest soil either of them had ever seen, covering the valley beyond the north shore.

McConnel turned and looked at Beard. When the bigger man's focus came back toward him, he spoke. "Tom, you're going to stay, aren't you?"

This time the loquacious Beard was laconic. "Yep."

"Winter's coming. The first thing we'll have to do is keep you from freezing to death. Let's spend what's left of the day looking for a place to build a cabin. Got to be high enough not to flood."

"How about here?"

McConnel pointed downriver five hundred yards to a copse of hardwood. "You, and your horses, may want to drag fifty to sixty trees a quarter mile, but me and my horse would kinda like to find a place where we can drag them just a few feet. Let's wander down that way."

McConnel turned his horse downriver, riding along the top of the bluff. It didn't take long to find what they sought, a wooded knoll that stood on the riverbank but high above it. The knoll was flat on top and treeless, offering a clear view upriver, downriver, and across the river as well as behind them to the south. At the foot of the knoll a copse of straight timbers grew. They would be just the right diameter for the cabin wall and close enough to drag up the knoll without a great deal of effort. This would be Thomas Beard's new home.

* * * *

Dinner was fresh venison and bread they'd packed for the trip. Afterward, McConnel broke the bottle of corn liquor out of his pack, poured three fingers into a mug, and handed it to Beard.

"Mo, the stain from those walnut hulls ever going to wash off? Your fingers look like they belong to a black field hand."

"Nope. Won't wash off. Have to wear off. Be a week or so. Man wants to eat walnuts, that's the price." He froze as he said it.

Beard saw him motionless, save his eyes darting about with a franticness that Beard knew meant he was locating his musket. Beard whirled to look at whatever had frozen McConnel. An Indian, motionless save for the fluttering of his long hair in the evening breeze, stood at the top of the knoll. He was no more than twenty yards away.

The Indian was a big man, or at least wide. Beard guessed maybe five feet eight inches and well over two hundred and twenty pounds. He wasn't holding a musket and had no other visible weapon, but the blanket that covered his upper torso from his huge shoulders to his broad hips could have concealed almost any weapon, a tomahawk, war club, or knife. His legs were covered in fringed buckskin trousers and his feet in moccasins. His hair, heavily streaked with grey, was unadorned, hanging long to his shoulders. He appeared to be alone.

Without moving the Indian said, in very clear English, "My name is Chaubenee. I've been expecting you."

AUTHOR'S NOTE

A Panther Crosses Over is a work of historical fiction. The characters and events within it are based on actual researched history of the Northwest Territory. As a novelist, I feel my obligation is to the storytelling narrative rather than precision of facts. In this spirit I have taken some liberties with the story. These include: units of measurement, the timing of events, dialogues, and reasons behind character actions. One example is Tecumapese's relationship with the French trader. It is factually true that after her divorce she left his Indian village and went to the Kispoko village in Louisiana and from there ran away with a French trader. It is also true that Tecumseh's trip to retrieve her disrupted the timing of his planned assault, but the details of her departure with the man and her abandonment of Tecumseh and his cause are unknown to me. Therefore I used this opportunity to add a fictional dramatic turn of events into the story.

ABOUT THE AUTHOR

Foster lives and writes overlooking R.A.T. Beach in Torrance, California. He is the author of the five-star reviewed *Alpha Male* and the Pushcart Prize–nominated *Non-Semper Fidelis*.

Made in the USA
Las Vegas, NV
09 November 2023

80540118R00219